TALLEST STORIES

by

Rhys Hughes

Tallest Stories
by Rhys Hughes

Publication Date: 01 March 2013

Cover and Interior Art by David Rix, copyright 2013

Paperback Edition
ISBN: 978-1-908125-16-3

www.eibonvalepress.co.uk

This book
of sixty linked stories
is humbly dedicated to:

Stuart Ross

and also to:

Monica Konggaard

CONTENTS

CONTENTS

Part 1

TALLER STORIES

Prologue

Somewhere down near Cardiff Docks lies a road that doesn't exist in our space-time continuum. Like many roads, it has its fair share of shops and houses and even a pub. However, these buildings are no more real than the road itself. Some people declare they are phantom structures left over from another age. The argument runs something like this: if men and women can become ghosts, why not bricks and mortar? I have to agree with them. Not only have I explored this road myself, but I have often entered that pub for a drink.

It is an odd pub with a stranger set of patrons. The beer it sells is strong and not respectful of brains. It is brewed on the premises by the barman, who is generally only known by his first name and his final wink. He is called Hywel and was born far to the west in the village of Lladloh. Why he left his home to work in Cardiff is a minor mystery not worth solving. It seems he was once a baker, but lost his nerve in an incident with a highwayman, and now prefers to serve anything not in a tricorne hat, whether man or monster.

He accepts payment mostly in tales. One evening he resolved to take more care with his accounts and asked me bluntly if I would invent some new stories for him, to balance his books and fill up this one. His pub was already crowded with professional authors, so I declined and pointed out that I was the only one of his customers who never composed fiction. Unfortunately, he considered lack of talent to be an ideal qualification for his fraud. He wanted the style to be clumsy but light, to cheat the Inspector of Metaphors if he called.

So if you are ever near Mountstuart Square, and you happen to see a road that wasn't truly there before, take a chance and walk down it. The adventure will be absurd but safe, a brief flirtation with rare spooks. The pub in question is the friendliest tavern you may hope to visit, and a pint costs less than whatever you pay when you order beer in your sleep. No, that is untrue. I am not permitted to depart unless I find a replacement for my unbearable task, and for that I am desperate enough to trick even you over this impossible threshold...

1– RAINBOW'S END

Although THE TALL STORY on Raconteur Road is a pub that doesn't exist, takings are always high. Its richest patrons are the potbellied council overseers who step through its doors during lunchtimes. They step, as it were, into another dimension where imagination becomes reality and Truth takes a siesta on one of the benches in the beer garden.

The landlord of this dubious establishment is none other than Hywel Price, a beery auroch of a man, whose hands are too large for the piccolo and yet too small for the fiddle. Consequently, he can neither shortchange his customers nor assail their eardrums with unwanted music. This is doubtless the source of his popularity.

When I entered the tavern yesterday afternoon, business was brisk. So brisk indeed that Hywel had decided to close the bar. He was leaning with his elbows on the counter, talking to Flann O'Brien and declaiming on subjects he knew nothing about. This is a peculiar habit with Hywel. It is probably why his popularity won't last.

"Now take your modern rainbow," he was saying. "It has neither the consistency nor the vibrancy of your good old-fashioned rainbow. When I was a lad, rainbows were something special, but your modern rainbow looks tired and a bit worn around the edges. Personally I blame the Martians. That's where all these newfangled rainbows come from. They just don't make them like they used to…"

I coughed and signalled for a drink, but Hywel ignored me. His voice took on the drone of a wasp caught in a jar that had once held Mrs Owen's jam: anger mingled with relief. I attempted to win Flann O'Brien over to my side by tapping him on the shoulder, but he was completely absorbed in his Guinness. THE TALL STORY tends to be a pub where everybody talks but nobody listens.

"And that's another thing about your traditional rainbow that your modern ones don't have," Hywel continued. "A crock of gold, that's what! There used to be a crock at the end of every one when I was small. Very well do I remember hauling back a big pot in the evenings after a summer downpour. There was never much gold in them though; just an apple, an orange, a few Brazil nuts and a penny. But that isn't the point. We were happy in those days."

Flann O'Brien finished his pint and remarked that he knew a man who had chased a rainbow all over County Wicklow only to find a grubby Wellington boot at the end of it. The situation was growing desperate. I realised that drastic action was called for if ever I was to be blessed with a drink. On a sudden impulse, I cried:

"I knew a man who chased a rainbow right here in the city. It happened two years ago, during that heatwave that set tongues a-lolling and eyes a-rolling. We were all waiting for a drop of rain to soothe our fevered brows and eventually a lonely blue cloud answered our prayers. There has never been a sweeter shower or a more magnificent rainbow."

"Oh yes?" Hywel looked up. I had finally attracted his attention. His fingers flirted with the pump handle of my usual brew. I licked my lips and sweat stood out on my brow. "Go on," he said.

"Well, it also happened to be the week that the Reptile Circus was in town. Don't you remember? *Dr Slither's Performing Snakes and Salamanders!* Anyway, what occurred was that the reptiles were allowed to splash around in the castle moat to cool down. There were big snapping caimans and crocodiles, enormous pythons and thick-tongued monitor lizards. There was even a Komodo Dragon."

Hywel gave me a cynical look and opened his mouth to resume his conversation with Flann O'Brien. I saw my chance slipping away. In blind panic, I added:

"So I had a friend who decided to follow this rainbow I mentioned, to see if there really was a crock of gold at the end of it. I told him not to go, but off he went towards the castle. He had to hurry because the rainbow was already beginning to fade."

Hywel turned back to face me. I had won a reprieve but still had to prove myself. I said:

"This friend of mine finally reached the Castle moat and there, lo and behold, was the end of the rainbow! So he took his shirt and shoes off, placed them neatly on the side, pinched his nose and jumped in. Down into the depths he sank, faster and faster. But he never came up again…"

"Why? Did he find his crock of gold?"

I sighed and shook my head sadly. "Alas no! It wasn't a Croc after all. It was a 'Gator."

Flann O'Brien frowned. "A gaiter is another kind of boot, isn't it?"

Hywel burst into forced laughter and the bar was back in business. I took my pint of porter out into the beer garden and sat on one of the benches next to the sleeping body of Truth. That's the trouble with THE TALL STORY on Raconteur Road; every time you want a drink you have to tell one.

2- GHOST HOLIDAY

I was sitting in THE TALL STORY, listening to one of Hywel's sombre and unlikely tales, when a thin nervous looking man added a comment of his own. Now there are two things about THE TALL STORY that every prospective customer ought to know. The first is that it does not exist; the second is that Hywel must never, under any circumstances, be interrupted.

How he became landlord of a nonexistent pub is a secret that Hywel likes to keep to himself. Indeed, considering his size, strength and (even more importantly) the sheer nastiness of his pickle sandwiches, it seems probable it will remain a secret forevermore. And this is surely nothing to complain about. Some things are best left unsaid.

Anyway, Hywel was discussing the habits of the ghost of Hugh the Miller, who still haunts all wholemeal loaves and Danish pastries within a quarter of a mile of the spot where he died; he fell into a lagoon. Students and young couples picnicking on the shore have been known to find bloody fingers in their soft rolls and, once or twice, even a nose.

"Like all ghosts he has grown too fond of the place where he died. He despises intruders and does his best to frighten them away."

It was at this point that the thin stranger shook his head and made his comment. Hywel turned purple and shuddered. I stood meekly and waited for the storm to break. The little fellow said:

"Ghosts are not fond of the places where they died. You are mistaken there! Ghosts become bored very quickly with one area and long to move on. Many ghosts are actually itinerant spooks; travellers and strollers. The romance of the road is in their congealed blood – or lack of it. That is why they linger at crossroads. There is so much choice that they find it difficult to leave."

I studied the little man more closely. He was dressed all in black, with a dark cape, a top hat and muddy boots. He had long greasy hair and bushy side-whiskers. He carried a spade and there was the stench of the grave on him.

"Of course," he continued, "some phantoms simply can't afford to live that way. They have to work for a crust. Instead, they spend a lot of time each year planning holidays and then they generally look down on their freer counterparts. Who can blame them? They pay their taxes like everyone else."

"And who might you be?" Hywel had managed to control himself. I had thought for one moment that I was about to witness a throttling, but now it seemed Hywel would content himself with merely a stomping and a gouging. I swallowed my drink hastily and held my breath.

The little man lowered his gaze modestly. "I collect ghosts. I have quite a few now. I keep them in glass bottles in my cellars. I am thus able to offer my guests a selection of spirits." He chewed his lip and tears rolled down his dusty cheeks. "Unfortunately, I don't get many guests. None in fact. So I talk to the ghosts instead."

"Well, that's all right then!" roared Hywel sarcastically. "I didn't realise I was in the company of an expert. So what is your name, friend?"

"Alas!" The little man shook his head. "I'd rather not say. It seems to put people off. Just pretend I'm an ordinary customer. Now let me tell you about one of my favourite specimens. He's quite a decent spectre."

I was about to reply that there was no such thing as a customer in THE TALL STORY who could be considered ordinary. It is, after all, a pub that lies in another dimension, somewhere between dawn and sunrise and adjacent to both infinity and eternity. But before I could even begin to explain all this, the mysterious stranger had launched into his anecdote.

"His name is – or was – Jocky McJocky and he was born in a castle near the remote Kyle of Tongue. There is a mountain there called Ben Hope, which he used to climb without hope; he was a dour fellow when alive. After his death, his spirits improved and he took to haunting his fellows with great glee. Can you guess what happened? Well, he became a tourist attraction. Americans would relish the chance to spend a night in a haunted castle and, in the early hours, might even hold conversations like this:

> RONALD: What's that noise?
> NANCY: What noise?
> RONALD: It sounds to me like a dim rumbling from afar.
> NANCY: Oh, that's probably just the head of Jocky McJocky, executed in the courtyard with a rusty axe for drowning Lord McBroth in a pot of soup. He rolls his head up and down the corridors.
> RONALD: I see. Like a bread roll. But what's that other noise? That hideous screeching and wailing?
> NANCY: Oh, that's just the old woman.
> RONALD: What old woman?
> NANCY: The old woman who made the soup.

As you can imagine, McJocky soon had his fill of tourists. Whenever he materialised in front of them, headless and bloodstained, they would insist on taking a photograph. This was before the invention of digital cameras, of course, and they were never able to develop the prints; but that didn't stop them from coming back next year and trying again."

The little man paused and licked his lips. He adjusted his hat and made a series of pained faces. It was obviously an uncomfortable fit, his hat, for he kept holding on to it with both hands as if it was about to spring into the air. Hywel leaned over the bar until his nose was within an inch of the stranger's own.

"So what happened next?" he demanded.

The stranger sighed and rolled his eyes. "McJocky eventually decided that he needed a holiday. Now tell me, where would you expect a ghost who lives near the beautiful wooded Kyle of Tongue to go on holiday? Where would a soul used to a rugged landscape and natural wonders go to find peace of mind?"

"Transylvania," I suggested.

"Shangri-La," countered Hywel.

The stranger shook his head. He twiddled his thumbs in some mordant satisfaction and uttered a little laugh. I was reminded of the rustle of bat's wings in a cave lit by a single candle – that is going out. His laugh became a whimper.

"No, he moved into a bedsit in Birmingham for two weeks, living (if that's the right word!) on chips and lard sandwiches. He started drinking cheap lager and sitting in front of the television all day. He wore a string vest and picked his ghostly nostrils with an insubstantial finger. He forgot to wash under his arms and never brushed his hair. He claimed afterwards that it was the best time he has ever had."

Hywel turned to face me with a look of disbelief etched on his ruddy features. I gazed at the bottom of my glass and wished for a rain of stout. I even contemplated making my farewells. The little man nodded.

"When the holiday was over, McJocky returned to the comforts of an entire castle, with its silks and gold and home-brewed mead. But every year he dreams of returning to the simple life of egg on toast and damp wallpaper. He has been saving up to buy property down there, right in the heart of that miserable urban sprawl."

At last, Hywel could contain himself no longer. He seized hold of the stranger's collar and half-dragged him over the bar. "Before we accept your tale as true," he said, "we need to have some proof. How is it that you are in a position to collect ghosts when no one else can?"

The little man was just about to reply when the doors burst open and a crowd of dead Irish writers stampeded toward the bar. It was lunchtime, of course. I recognised many faces among the poets and authors: Joyce, Beckett, O'Casey, Brian Merriman, Yeats, Flann O'Brien, Brendan Behan. But I soon lost sight of the little man. His hat was knocked off in the crush and then he had disappeared in a sea of thirsty bodies. Hywel had released his grip when the first literary foot crossed the threshold.

I peered around frantically and finally spotted the fellow creeping toward the door. Without his tall hat he appeared ludicrously small. I was still curious to hear more about his collection of ghosts, so I called after him, "Mr Burke, you've forgotten your hat!" He turned around to face me with a scowl and then vanished through the doors. I was desperate. "Mr Burke!" I cried again.

Hywel had been pouring a continuous stream of velvet pints, but my shout attracted his attention. Leaving the Irish writers bellowing in dismay, he relaxed his grip on the pump handle and frowned at me. "How do you know his name?" he demanded. "He refused to give it."

When Hywel demands something, it is best to let him have it. And so now I held up the little man's hat – which I had picked from the floor – and reached inside it. What I pulled out explained everything at once to all who were present. It hung there by its ears and twitched its nose.

A Mad March Hare.

3- THOSE WONDERFUL WORDS

As THE TALL STORY is the second grandest pub in the universe, a fuller description of its layout and facilities may not be out of place here. (The grandest pub of all is the one that awaits the loyal Beamish drinker on the far side of the Pearly Gates, where auburn-haired *houris* pour pint after creamy pint and where traditional folk sessions take place every night; Guinness and Murphy's drinkers go straight to Hell.)

THE TALL STORY then, is a rather drab and chilly building on the outside; the windows are like glazed eyes and the walls sport a spiderweb of hopeless cracks. Once inside, however, the traveller is astonished by the warmth and vitality that suffuses the aged bar and even older lounge. The cedarwood beams that hold up the sagging roof are scored and pitted with the marks of a million foreheads; and the bottles and stools that nestle behind and before the bar are scored and pitted with the marks of a million... well, foreheads.

The floor of this remarkable establishment, however, is constructed of a truly unusual substance. In Old Norse legends, it is told of a ship called *Naglfar* that will sail at the end of the world and is made entirely out of toenails. You may imagine anxious relatives of some recently mangled Viking taking due care to remove his toenails before he breathes his last – in an effort to delay the building of the ship and thus postpone the end of the world. This is absolutely true.

The floor of THE TALL STORY is not made out of toenails, but something far more offensive. It is made out of unnecessary words. All the words that are spoken for no good reason end up on this floor. That is why the floor keeps expanding towards the roof and why more and more drinkers keep striking their heads on those cedarwood beams – one day the floor will touch the ceiling.

This partly explains why Hywel winces whenever someone says something that contains more words than it should. If Harold the Barrel or Billy Belay ever cry over their jackstraws, "Look here, see," or "I'll be there now in a minute," Hywel cringes and hides his face. Both the "see" and the "now" spin out of their ungainly mouths, like shooting stars, and add their bulk to their brothers and sisters that lie trampled before them. It really is appalling.

To discourage customers such as Harold and Billy, tyrannical Hywel keeps a rather heavy reminder behind the counter. This reminder is made of oak and is tipped with iron. It is about four feet long.

When Harold the Barrel and Billy Belay are not playing jackstraws in some dark corner, they are usually arguing with each other about which of them has had the more incredible life. They are both committed eccentrics. Harold is convinced that he can fly; sometimes he will stand on his chair and leap off, flapping his arms furiously. Billy is no less modest. He claims that he is a ghost and will often attempt to prove his point by walking into the pub without opening the door. Failure in both cases does not seem to deter them.

Other regulars are equally weird and wonderful. There is Madame Ligeia, the half-Gypsy mystic who lives in a tie-dyed caravan and who can only foretell the past – never the future. She is passionately jealous of rivals and once threw a fellow psychic bodily out of the tavern. She explains her brooding hatred of her magical colleagues simply by saying, "Too many sayers spoil the sooth."

Even more menacing is Dr Karl Mondaugen, the mad scientist of Munich. He is a cryptozoologist by profession but his hobbies include inventing bizarre and terrible devices, the purpose of which eludes everybody, including himself. With his wild hair and little round glasses he certainly looks the part. He sometimes sits at the far end of the lounge, right in front of the low stage that is used every Tuesday night for lengthy jazz sessions.

"He has more than five hundred inventions to his credit," Hywel tells me with a wink, "and most of them are utterly useless. They include such inspired works of genius as:

☞ The Solar Powered Torch,

☞ The Wind Powered Fan,

☞ The Wave Powered Whisk.

And that is just a sample of the most successful ones! I ask you, what can be done with someone like that?" Hywel blinks and offers me an exasperated grimace. I can only shake my head in reply.

While we mull over the sheer strangeness of life, the doors swing open and three weary climbers make their way painfully over to the bar. They are a ragged trio, rucksacks hanging like deflated misplaced lungs from their shoulders, ropes trailing in the dust behind them. They order double whiskys each and then retire to a long table near the blazing hearth. I note that two of them maintain a slight distance from their companion.

"Those are the Three Friends," Hywel informs me. "I could tell a tale or two about them for sure, but I'd rather tell you about the time that Karl Mondaugen built a fridge so powerful it could freeze things instantly. Unfortunately, he put the components in the wrong way round and froze the whole world solid. Luckily it made no difference at all to anything and no one noticed. It froze things so quickly that they all remained warm."

"I don't believe you," I say. I have even less faith in Hywel's stories than he has in mine. Occasionally we each like to humour the other; more frequently he attempts to uplift a hogshead of gentle scorn over my head and I respond in kind.

"Well, let me tell you about his latest project then," Hywel replies. "He's building a machine for me that will be able to recycle all those unnecessary words that clutter up the floor. The idea is that whole new sentences can be put together from all the leavings of the old ones."

I make a wry face and gaze beyond Hywel at the rows of jars and other vessels that stand beneath the tall impossible mirror (why it is an impossible mirror is another story!) Among the Pernod and rum bottles crowd a few dubious looking green glass affairs within whose murky depths flicker strange shapes.

Inside the mirror, which often shows false scenes out of sequence, two figures seem to be arguing about fruit. These men are Byron and Julian, but I don't know that yet. Nor that the girl who has just entered, panting with exhaustion, is called Laura and has been chased through a forest. Further along, on the very edge of the reflection, an aristocratic explorer is demystifying the art of using cats as paperweights; they should always be given double rations to make them heavy enough. Lord Doublestuff is his name and he's trying to convince a sailor called Captain Dangleglum; but I can't possibly be aware of this.

"If I talk about any of those people…" Hywel begins, but he is cut short by a sudden crash. We turn around to find that Harold the Barrel and Billy Belay are wrestling with each other on the floor. Harold has attempted to fly again; and has landed on the head of Billy who, confident that solid objects can pass right through him, has made no attempt to move out of the way.

"I'd rather know more about those two," I answer with a smile. "Why do they believe what they do? Why does Harold think he can fly? And why is Billy convinced that he is a ghost?"

Hywel nods his head in agreement. "Now there's a ripe pair of tales for you! Pull your stool in a little closer and let me pour you another drink and I'll explain everything. It really is a startling sequence of events."

I take out my notebook and pen and wait for Hywel to commence. It is difficult writing and drinking at the same time, but I am willing to learn. Despite what people say, it is not all play in THE TALL STORY; sometimes we work as well.

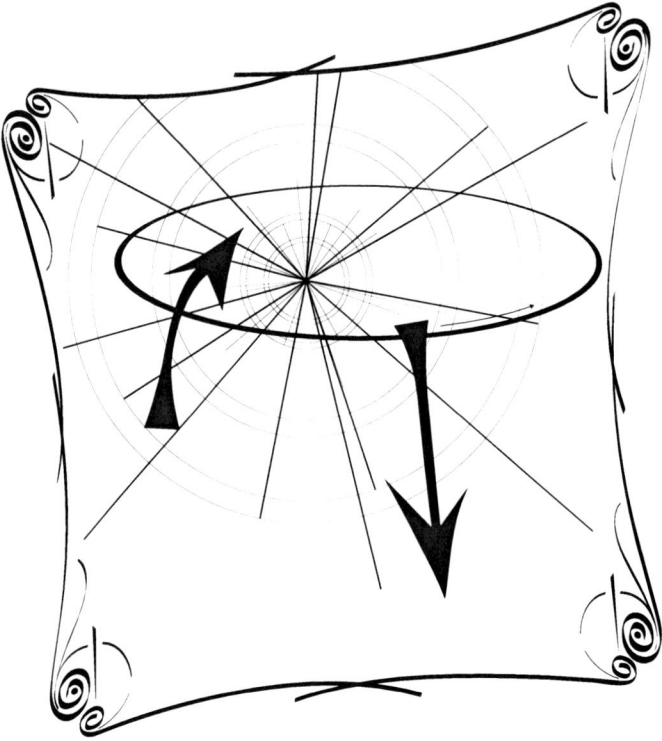

4- LEARNING TO FLY

When Harold saw the advert in the paper, he grew very excited. His breath came in short gasps and little muscles in his neck twitched. The advert said: LEARN THE SECRET OF FLIGHT. Harold sighed with pleasure. This was the chance he had been waiting for!

He had always wanted to be able to fly. Even as a boy he had dreamed of being an owl. Flapping his huge tawny wings, he would swoop down from the trees and soar over the river. At night, he was convinced that his spirit left his body and danced with the clouds.

And now, at last, it seemed that his dream would come true. At the bottom of the advert there was a name and address. Dr Lithiums, World Levitation Expert, 66 Park Road. Harold memorised the address, pulled on his coat and set off to find it.

As he made his way down the streets of the old town, he extended his arms and glided around the pedestrians who stared at him in amazement. Once, a woman in a large fruity hat attacked him with her handbag, but Harold didn't care. He felt completely at ease.

Before long, he found the address and knocked on the door. It was answered by a pale woman with hard features and cold grey eyes who gazed at him with a sneer. "I've come about the flying lessons," he said shyly. "Is Dr Lithiums here?"

The woman's expression brightened. She led him into a filthy room stuffed full with broken furniture. A small seedy man sat hunched over a flickering television, a bottle of whisky clutched in his fingerless gloves. Harold guessed that he had not washed for a long time.

"This is Dr Lithiums," the woman announced.

"How do you do?" Harold offered him his hand. The man ignored it and rolled a cigarette. He began to chuckle and mumble to himself. His chuckle turned to a cough and he wiped spittle from his lips with his ragged sleeve.

Harold recoiled and stepped into a plate of curry that had been left on the floor. As he hopped on one foot, trying to clean his shoe with a handkerchief, the woman glowered defensively. "We can spend most of our time flying through the air, if we choose," she said. "We don't need to keep our floors clean."

At this mention of his favourite subject, Harold forgot the squalor and closed his eyes. He imagined himself floating above the smokestacks of the city, high over the gardens, bobbing along on currents of air like a helium balloon. He opened his eyes and began to laugh. "I also want to fly," he said. "That's why I'm here."

"It is expensive. Twenty thousand pounds for the secret."

Harold's jaw dropped open. He reached into his pocket and pulled out his wallet. It was empty.

"You can pay in installments," the woman suggested.

Harold groaned. The bubble of his dream had burst, leaving nothing but a little soapy water on the wallpaper of his life. He stumbled over old milk cartons and cereal boxes towards the door. His soul dragged in the grime behind him.

"Wait!" The woman raced in front of him and barred his exit. "There is another way. You can earn it."

With bowed head, Harold listened to her proposal. The next morning, he returned with a dustpan and brush. He cleaned the floor and the grate, painted the doors and polished every surface. He mended the broken furniture and washed a pile of dishes so tall it touched the ceiling.

Throughout all this activity, Dr Lithiums remained silent, staring at the battered television. When he had drained his bottle of whisky, the woman would prise it out of his hands and replace it with a full one. This seemed to represent the only contact between them.

Harold attempted to talk to the man, but the man merely muttered obscenities in return. Harold wondered if this was all part of the necessary preparation. He returned to his task with renewed vigour and disturbed the thick dust on the man's bald head.

As the days passed, Harold grew weary, but his enthusiasm did not wane. However, when the days turned to weeks and the weeks became months, he finally began to suspect that he was the victim of a deception. One cold morning, he arrived at the house and the woman said, "You're five minutes late. Go into the kitchen and make my breakfast."

Harold threw his duster down in disgust. "I've had enough of this. I demand that you tell me the secret!"

The woman frowned. "You haven't earned it yet. There is still much work to be done."

Harold raised himself up to his full height. "Either you tell me the secret now, or I'll break your television." He clenched his fists while the man in the chair whimpered.

The woman sighed. Then she whispered a few words into his ear and Harold managed a sarcastic laugh. "Utter nonsense! I should have known this was all a trick. It's obvious now. Why have I never seen either of you fly?"

"You don't understand." The woman watched him depart and shook her head sadly. She regarded her clean shiny home. She couldn't afford to lose such an excellent pupil. "Perhaps I should have explained," she said to herself. "Perhaps I should have told him the rest."

But as he walked down the street, and she noticed the gap between his feet and the ground, she knew how to get him back.

Moving to the writing desk, and selecting a piece of paper, she planned another advert. She wrote: LEARN TO GET DOWN AGAIN.

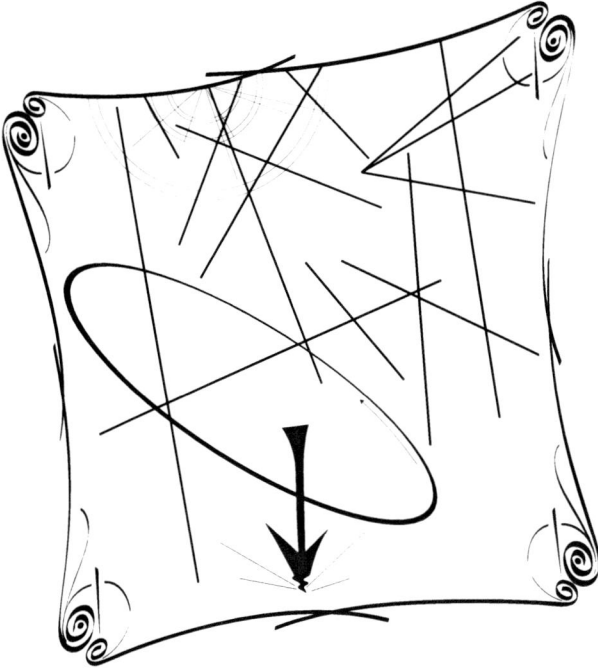

5- LEARNING TO FALL

Southerndown is a village maybe fifteen miles west of Cardiff; a windswept, dramatic place with towering sea cliffs and a rocky shore that is like the surface of the moon. There are few coastal areas in the whole country that can compare with it for natural beauty. The tides are enormous and the breakers pound the sloping beach like monstrous tongues, refilling rock pools with wide-eyed crabs and starfish and breaking open new caves in the limestone walls.

Billy Belay had set off from Southerndown towards Nash Point with a bag that contained an anvil and a rope. He passed Dunraven – with its mouldering castle and picnickers – and carried on for another mile or so. The weather was warm and perspiration dripped the length of his nose. When he had found an isolated spot along the cliff-top path, he took the anvil out of his bag, secured it to his neck with the rope and hurled himself over the edge.

What he was really trying to achieve is anyone's guess, although the obvious should not be overlooked. At any rate, destiny had different plans for him; the tide was in, but somehow he was washed up onto a patch of dry sand, anvil and all, suffering no more injury than a bruised nethermost. At the same instant, he fell into a kind of swoon and it was some long minutes before he regained his senses.

When he did, he was bewildered. There seemed to be no explanation as to why he was still conscious. "But I'm dead!" he cried. As far as he was concerned, the fall had killed him outright. "I must be a ghost," he finally decided. As he thought about the prospect more carefully, it began to delight him. As a ghost he was released from all earthly ties and constraints. He would be able to do as he pleased. There were no rules anymore. He was free.

"I'm a ghost!" he repeated. He picked himself up and removed the anvil from his neck. It did not suit him anyway. He brushed the sand from his clothes and gazed around warily. Nobody had witnessed his demise, and yet his body had disappeared. If he was a ghost, surely he would be floating above his mangled frame at this very instant?

Dismissing the question from his mind, he made his way painfully along the beach back toward Dunraven. He supposed that he was not the first ghost to haunt this particular stretch of coastline. Indeed, he remembered a legend about a wrecker who used to lure ships to their doom with false beacons and whose spectre was still said to fret and howl on stormy nights.

Billy wondered if he would meet this wrecker, whose name he had forgotten. He did not know if ghosts were confined to the area in which they had died, but he assumed that they were. A professor had once come to Cardiff to give a lecture on this subject; Cherlomsky was his name, but Billy had slept all the way through his talk. He pressed on regardless and before long had reached Dunraven. Here he paused and scratched his insubstantial chin.

Throughout his life, he had never played a single practical joke on anyone. This was not because he held such pranks in contempt but simply because of cowardice. He had been frightened of reprisals. Some of his acquaintances, such as Alan Griffiths and Gareth Thomas, were forever tormenting each other with elaborate tricks; and he had always viewed their antics with a measure of jealousy.

Now, however, he was safe from reprisals. As a ghost, he could cause as much mischief as he liked to anyone and everyone. Ghosts were allowed to do things like this and nobody criticised them for it. Indeed, it was acceptable behaviour on their part and sometimes even encouraged.

As he pondered on this, he happened to espy a lone fisherman sitting on a rock and gazing out to sea. He resolved to flex his ghostly muscles at once and crept up behind him. Placing his mouth to the man's ear, he yelled: "BOO!"

Instantly, the fisherman leapt up, dropped his rod and line and began running down the beach – his face as white as a summer cloud. Billy felt very pleased with himself. It works! he thought. I'm a real ghost! I'm a real phantom!

His second victim was a boy who was busy eating an ice cream. Billy snatched the ice cream away and thrust it into the boy's face. The boy burst into tears; and the tears blended and reacted with the ice cream smeared on his cheeks. He too fled, arms waving.

I'm a ghost! Billy thought again. He was truly elated now. He opened his mouth and cried: "I'm a GHOST!" It was as if he wanted the seagulls to take up his cry and spread it far abroad, so as to leave no doubt in anyone's mind that here was a phantom not to be trifled with, unless of course the trifle was a strawberry one. (Billy wondered if ghosts needed to eat; he hoped they did.)

While he congratulated himself on his quick thinking in hurling himself over the edge of the cliff, becoming a ghost and adapting to his role with such alacrity, he came across a bizarre sight. On his hands and knees a strange figure was engaged with a peculiar contraption. As he moved closer, Billy saw that it was made of two glass bottles joined neck to neck. The figure was muttering to himself: "Common hourglasses have sand on the inside and the world all around – my hourglass will have the world on the inside and sand all around!"

Billy knew the man as Karl Mondaugen, the mad scientist of Munich, who now lived in Ogmore by Sea. Billy peered closer at the glass device and frowned as he seemed to see moving figures within it. Shrugging, he reached out his ghostly hands and gave the eccentric academic a spooky tickle with his icy phantasmagorical fingers. The scientist shrieked and fell onto the contraption, smashing both bottles beneath his body and wailing in terror and dismay.

Billy rubbed his hands together and walked on. By the time he had reached the village of Southerndown, he had committed another eleven acts of ghostliness, including disrupting a group of geology students by dancing around them with great whoops and hideous chuckles. As he headed inland towards the village, he had already acquired a considerable taste for mischief and saw no earthly reason why he should not gorge himself sick on yet more courses.

Ruining a funeral was next; and snatching a postman's sack, casting letters all over the road, came after that. The main feast, however, was the incident with the poodle. Out of the Church Hall, haunt of the local Amateur Dramatics Society, came ungainly Mrs Featherstonehaugh, carrying her poodle under her arm. She had been rehearsing *Blithe Spirit* with her colleagues – a delicious irony, although Billy was unaware of this. He simply crept up behind her and…

At this point it may suffice to relate that she was found not more than ten minutes later by a policeman, with the end of a lead protruding from her gaping maw. She was quite blue and bloated. By this time, Billy had entered a shop selling cream cakes and was busy hurling them, one at a time, at the frightened owner of the establishment. The constable who had discovered Mrs Featherstonehaugh instantly repaired to the shop and confronted Billy. He was attacked with an unsheathed chocolate éclair. His eye was poked. Cream spurted.

To a casual observer newly arrived at the village, the sight of a wild-eyed figure being chased by a vengeful mob made up of ham actors, geologists, mourners, postmen, pastrycooks, a battered policeman and sundry others, may have been amusing. Billy also found it amusing – he grinned, chuckled and skipped as he ran. "You can't harm me, I'm a ghost!" he called back. "I'm impervious to mortal blows!" But his pursuers seemed disinclined to abandon the chase. Somehow they were able to see him. Perhaps Mrs Featherstonehaugh had also turned into a ghost and was directing their pursuit. He wondered.

Eventually, of course, he reached the cliff-top path that led from Southerndown to Nash Point. This was the course he had earlier followed. He raced down the path, but now he was puffing and panting. The crowd behind him was catching up. He tried to imagine what would happen if they caught him. Perhaps they would entrap him in a bottle and take him to an exorcist. Perhaps, when they had collected enough ghosts like him, they would force him to pay a hefty fine. There was, after all, duty to be collected on imported spirits…

There was only one thing left to do. Reaching the point he had already jumped off once, he launched himself into space again. "I'm a ghost!" he cried once more. He fell in a graceful arc, tumbled head over heels and flapped his arms with gusto. No harm could come to him. He had already died once; he could not possibly die a second time. He was certain that his logic was watertight.

This time, however, the tide was out.

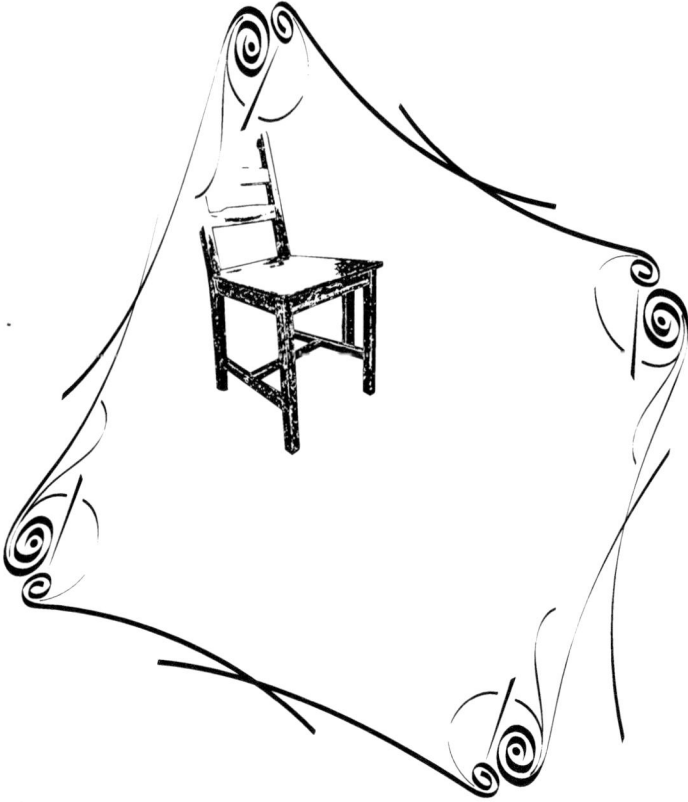

6- THE BANSHEE

Not all the writers who drink in THE TALL STORY are dead and from Ireland. Many are local and very much alive. Among the published names, however, are a good few unpublished authors who languish in the beer garden, trying to outwit each other with bitter observations on the injustice of life. One day it might occur to them that for their work to be printed, they first have to send it off. Until then, they seem content to grumble and moan about the same things.

I can see one of these hacks from here, crouched over a napkin with a pencil. I don't know if he's writing anything, but his dietary habits must be gross; his dribble contains the legs of ants. That's typical of the revolting standards of these so-called literary types. It's doubtless the reason why Hywel insists they sit outside in the beer garden, even in winter, and why he encourages the jazz musicians who play in his pub every week to make as much noise as they can.

"Did I ever tell you the strange tale of Walter's Head?" Hywel asked me one night. The worthy in question had just tottered out of the bar, his open neck glistening with the frothy bubbles of his stout.

"No," I replied, "and you have never told me the tale of the three mountain climbers either." I indicated the group of battered adventurers who had unlaced their boots and were warming their woolly socks by the roaring log fire, two of them eyeing the third suspiciously.

"Well, that will keep, I dare say. Until then, let us drink to each other's health, for as Omar Khayyám almost said:

> Come fill the cup, and in the Fire of Spring
> The Winter Garment of Repentance fling
> The pig of Time has but a little way
> To fly – and Lo! the pig is on the Wing."

"I don't know about that," I responded, "but I'm quite amenable if you're paying. Besides, Omar never had a taste of Mrs Owen's elderberry wine. It would have turned him teetotal overnight."

Just at that moment, I felt a hand clamp down on my shoulder. I was sure for a moment that it was Mrs Owen herself, and that she would punish me by making me take home a year's supply of stinging nettle marmalade, her answer to the tongue-searing curries Hywel had started serving in the bar.

As I cowered in fear, a rasping voice tickled the nape of my neck and I heaved a sigh of relief. I recognised the voice as belonging to Madame Ligeia, the resident clairvoyant and mystic who had done much to throw her profession into disrepute. As I turned around, I found myself confronted by a veiled figure. No one knows what Madame Ligeia looks like; she wraps herself so tightly in a cloak of mystery, complete with hood, that only her two eyes are ever visible – glowing like dim coals.

"What is the meaning of this?" she demanded. "I want that woman out of the pub now! Do you hear? Now!" She pointed a quivering finger at an empty chair around an empty table.

Hywel sighed and gave me a knowing look. "I'm pleased that you two have decided to become friends. Mutual trust is so important these days."

"Either you kick her out or I'll box your ears, you ill-mannered lout!"

"And to think that only yesterday you were insisting that I throw her out and threatening to box me around the ears!"

During this conversation, I was less bewildered than might be expected, for I knew something about Madame Ligeia that explained everything. Madame Ligeia is a mystic who can only see into the past. She never knows what is going on in either the future or the present. Consequently, she lives a whole day behind everyone else. That is why holding a conversation with her is so difficult: you have to provide answers to questions she will not ask until tomorrow.

The reason why she had her hand on my shoulder and was talking to me as if I was Hywel was because Hywel had sat on this particular stool the previous day – during one of his many breaks. To clarify matters further, it is best to linger awhile in this previous day and to note what happens:

Hywel is sitting on my stool and I am standing at his place behind the bar (just to help out, you understand) when a dishevelled figure enters the pub and walks up to us. I am astonished by this figure's appearance. It resembles a banshee, with long tangled hair and wild eyes.

Now the banshee, as everyone knows, is a spirit that follows old families about and wails before a member of that family is about to die. However, it is not quite as sinister as some people like to make out. Indeed, the day before, I had discussed the matter at some length with W.B. Yeats, who told me, "The banshee differs from the general run of solitary fairies by its generally good disposition."

So I am not too afeared when it comes up to Hywel and points a finger at an empty chair around an empty table.

"That woman keeps glowering at me and making rude comments," it says. "I want you to tell her to stop."

Hywel shrugs his shoulders and blows his nose in a handkerchief. "It is very heartening to see that you have resolved your differences. Life is too short for bickering."

"If you don't tell her to stop I shall twist your ears off!"

"And to think that tomorrow you were planning to twist my ears off and telling me to force her to stop sitting in that chair!"

After the banshee has left, I turn to Hywel with a quizzical look. Hywel taps his forehead with a smile and winks.

"She is my guest. I invited her here personally."

I am dumbfounded. "What do you want a banshee for? Isn't Mrs Owen frightening enough for you?"

Hywel chuckles and explains that it is not a banshee but Madame Berenice, a mystic who can only see into the future. She never knows what is going on in either the past or the present. Consequently, she lives a whole day in front of everyone else. She is as difficult to talk to as Madame Ligeia is – for the opposite reason.

"But this is a disaster!" I cry. "You know how much Madame Ligeia hates rivals! There will be trouble over this, mark my words!"

Hywel shakes his head emphatically. "They both hate the idea of each other, true enough; but when they come together, the day after tomorrow, something will click into place. Madame Ligeia can only see into the past, whereas Madame Berenice can only see into the future. When they meet, they will both cancel each other out. At long last they will be able to see into the present!"

I scratch my head and pour myself a glass of cognac. "You mean like a seesaw of time? Madame Ligeia on one end and Madame Berenice on the other?" I am impressed when Hywel nods. "And you did this as a favour for them?"

"Wait until the day after tomorrow and then we'll see how things have turned out." Hywel snatches my cognac away and downs it himself, handing me back an empty glass. "Keep your fingers crossed until then."

The day after tomorrow comes soon enough; and this time I am sitting on my stool while Hywel is behind the bar. It is a Tuesday night and musicians from far and near are setting up their equipment ready for the weekly jazz session. There is a lot of excitement in the air. A rumour has gone round that Tony Smith – one of the greatest jazz guitarists of all time – is due to make an appearance.

But above all the noise and hubbub of musicians tuning up and music lovers murmuring in anticipation, the raucous laughter of two women seated around a table drowns out all else.

"What did I tell you?" Hywel leans over the counter and gives me another one of his sly winks.

As I gaze at the two women, I can only shake my head in admiration at Hywel's ingenuity. The two women leave their seats and come over to join us. This time they address themselves directly to Hywel.

"We just want to thank you for introducing us to each other. We have so much in common. It really is incredible!"

Hywel puffs out his cheeks in pleasure. "It is very heartening to see that you have resolved your differences. Life is too short for bickering."

"For the first time in our lives we are able to live like normal people!"

"And to think that only two days ago you were insisting that I throw one of you out and threatening to box and twist my ears!"

Before I loose track of my senses completely, I decide to change the subject. I gesture toward a bottle of wine standing full among empty fellows. "I have heard this conversation before, or one very much like it. Now what was it that Omar never said?"

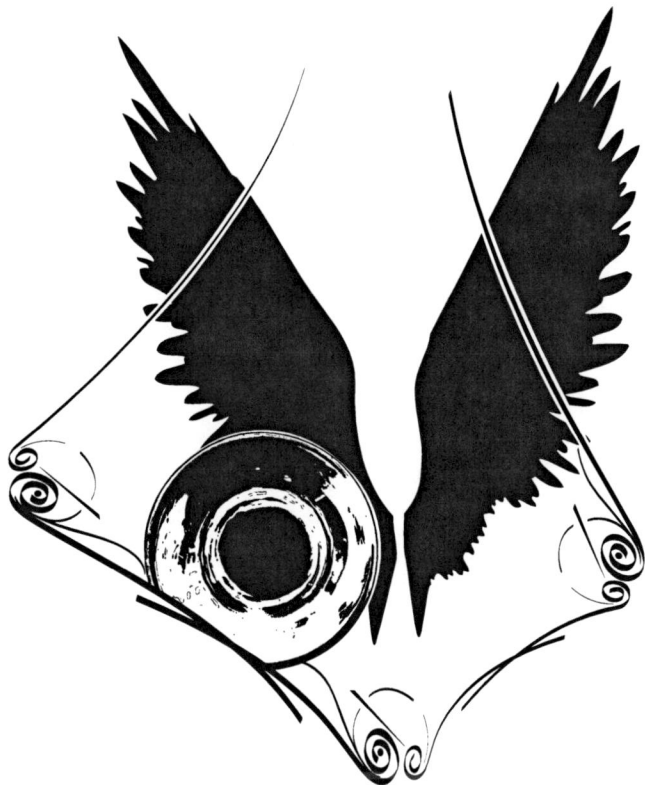

7- THE QUEEN OF JAZZ

Tony Smith entered the smoky pub and made his way to the stage. As he passed the bar, Old Bony thrust a whisky sour into his hand and winked. Tony took his guitar out of its battered case, plugged in and tuned up. He was vaguely aware of the admiration of the crowd, their love. "Right boys, what'll it be?"

"How about 'Clotted Cream'?"

"Nope. Let's make it 'Samarkand'." He nodded to the other musicians on the stage, the drummer, the hook-nosed bassist. They were all looking distinctly uncomfortable. It was probably the first time they had ever played with a living legend.

As his fingers eased into the prelude, tickling the melody through all the complex time changes, Tony allowed himself the luxury of a sigh. His superiority was beginning to tire him. He was beginning to wish, just for once, that he would meet his match. But that, of course, was impossible.

The musicians fell behind and he waited patiently for them to catch up, improvising on a former theme, his fingers a blur, his guitar the interface for a talent that was strong yet yielding. Though he could play faster than the eye could see, he never sacrificed delicacy of nuance for sheer technique.

"No doubt 'bout it! Tony Smith is the king of jazz!"

With the faintest of smiles, Tony nodded at Old Bony. This night was a free for all, a time when the cream of the local talent could show off their skills, stepping up on stage and dropping in or out of the performance whenever mood, or ability, suited them. Tony recognised many familiar faces in the audience. Most had brought instruments with them. None could hope to compete with him on equal terms.

Throwing up his arms, the alto sax left the stage and sat down on a stool near the bar. He was shaking his head, his eyes alight with unfathomable awe. His place was taken by a more experienced musician, who also struggled with the rhythms Tony had initiated. One by one, the drums, bass and keyboards lost themselves in his web of shimmering sonorities and modal harmonies.

"Come on boys, let's try 'Purple Egg Head'." Tony attempted to inflect a note of enthusiasm into his voice, but it was a lost cause. Although he was the greatest jazz musician in the world, the most loved guitarist of all time, he had a problem. It was a problem that made the problems of other musicians seem insignificant. He had sold his soul to the Devil.

It was the old, old story. Fifteen years previously, he had signed a diabolical pact in his own blood. The Devil had promised to make him the best jazz musician in the world on condition that, after twenty years, he would give up his soul with the minimum of fuss. It had seemed a good idea at the time.

Almost immediately, Tony had found himself catapulted from semi-professional status to international renown. He had, in quick succession, conquered every possible style of jazz. He had taken trad, bebop, cool, fusion and even avant-garde to their logical extremes. Success, of course, had not brought happiness. But happiness was not a term of the contract.

At the end of the number, he instantly launched into another. "'Fleshpots'," he announced. The other musicians were sweating heavily.

They were all duly replaced by a fresh batch. Once again, Tony calmly proceeded to blow them all off the stage. "'Pelican'," he cried, and then, "'Cryptozoology'."

Utterly exhausted, the musicians came and went. Tony alone remained the constant factor. He wrestled with trombones, cornets, marimbas, all manner of keyboards and flutes; even a rival guitar. His phenomenal ability swamped them all.

It was at the end of 'Nonchalant Pygmies', one of his most famous compositions, that a quiet auburn haired girl stepped onto the stage with a large case. Tony frowned. He had not noticed her in the audience. He watched as she removed a long peculiar trumpet from her case, wiped it down with a cloth and moved toward a microphone. "How about 'Visitin' Angels'?" he said.

The girl shook her head. "Not quite. This one's called 'Judgment Day'. Just follow me if you don't know it." She raised the instrument to her lips. In the dim light of the pub it glowed with preternatural brightness.

"Never heard of it. And what kind of horn is that?" But the girl had already launched into the number, blowing a handful of notes of such unearthly beauty that he reeled backwards. "Eh?" With a great deal of effort, he composed himself and followed her.

A hush fell over the packed pub. Even Old Bony stopped stamping and clapping. Tony suddenly realised that he was alone on stage with this newcomer. The others had tactfully withdrawn. As the tempo of her blowing increased, he struggled to keep pace. A surge of energy flooded his veins and his fingers took on a life of their own. He already knew he was playing better than ever before. But still the girl kept ahead of him, bouncing a melody of exquisite sadness back at him, bending his own desperate variations through impossible contortions.

He sobbed. She was leading him into musical dimensions he had never suspected could exist. He threw everything at her, changing key again and again, altering the time signature with every note so that the whole took on its own supernal logic; but she swallowed it all up with the mouth of her horn and blew it out again, transmuted into something even more revelatory.

As if in a dream, he looked down at his fretboard. His fingers were bleeding. With a wrenching gasp, he struck a discord, another; and then it was all over. He gave up and watched with a curious mixture of horror and fascination as the girl finished the piece, sending a series of utterly perfect notes over the edge of the sound spectrum, shattering every glass behind the bar in an inevitable, apocalyptic crash.

There was a deathly silence. Old Bony wiped his hands free of glass shards and foamy beer and whistled slowly through his teeth. "Tony Smith is no longer the king of jazz!"

Head bowed, Tony unplugged his guitar, placed it back in his case and hoisted the case onto his shoulder. When he looked up, the girl had disappeared. He stepped off the stage and made his way toward the exit. No one tried to stop him.

Out on the waterfront, he paused and breathed the cold, pure air. He felt a strange mixture of emotions. He was pleased that he had finally met his superior. And yet, he was also worried. What would happen to his reputation now? Had he lost his soul for nothing?

As he walked deeper into the night, he saw that the mysterious girl was waiting for him. "Well!" he said, trying to sound as casual as possible. "I'd take my hat off to you if I had one. You're a fine player, to be sure. I thought you were an angel in disguise at one point!"

The girl brushed the auburn hair back from her face. "The opposite is closer to the truth. I'm more familiar with the other place. To put it bluntly, I've sold my soul to the Devil in order to become the greatest jazz musician in the world."

"But that's what I sold mine for!" Tony blinked in surprise.

"I know. Let me explain. I've followed your career ever since it began. It always struck me that your talent was too vast to be natural. I guessed you might have made a pact with the Devil. So I did the same. I said to the Devil, 'I want to become a greater jazz musician than Tony Smith', and he accepted my offer. I did it to save your soul. Now that I am better than you, the terms of your contract have been violated. You can demand a refund."

Before Tony could reply, the girl started to cry. Suddenly he understood the import of her words.

"My poor dear!" Taking her around the shoulders, he hugged her close. For the first time in fifteen years he felt free. So the Devil had been cheated after all! A great weight had been lifted from his shoulders. He found it hard to repress his delight. He matched her tears of anguish with his own tears of joy. "Do you really mean it? Have you really sacrificed your own soul to save mine? Am I no longer destined to burn in Hell?"

The girl looked up. The tears stopped flowing. Tony drew back. She broke into a high-pitched laugh. "Actually, I lied. You were right the first time. I'm an angel in disguise. The Archangel Gabriel, to be precise. And yes, you are going to burn in Hell after all. I'm not a mortal so the contract still holds. Sorry! Just a little joke of mine. Can't help it, I'm afraid. What else am I supposed to do on my day off? Now don't lose your temper. Just a little joke. Nothing to get upset about, eh?"

Later, as Tony left the waterfront, he began whistling. A new number had already come into his head. 'Broken Angel Blues' would surely help him regain his rightful place as the greatest jazz musician in the world. But would he ever be known as the king of jazz again? Perhaps it was time for a change. Slowly, he held up a long burnished trumpet and an auburn wig. He wondered.

8- ANNA AND THE DRAGON

THE TALL STORY is one of the most cosmopolitan pubs in creation. Every night, men and women of a hundred different creeds and colours from all parts of the city mingle together as equals. The Docklands have always been a melting pot of cultures and its reputation for lawlessness is certainly undeserved. Hywel has always encouraged the local Somalis, Yemenis, Chinese, Poles, Greeks, Swedes, Scots, Indians and even the English to enjoy each other's company and to exchange ideas.

He is even willing to serve students – one of the most mistrusted of all minorities. They often come in and treat themselves to a glass of cider – between ten. When they are feeling particularly flush, they will even splash out on a packet of crisps. Because they are disliked by so many, they make ideal scapegoats and the Government is able to grind them under the heel with few voices raised in protest. The poorest student who ever lived was called Michael, and the only thing he ever owned was a bad idea, but he doesn't drink in this story.

Some of these students are young couples – filled with an idealism and enthusiasm that have long since abandoned Hywel and myself. They often sit by tables near the windows, arguing politics and philosophy and the merits of tinned vegetables. Hywel regards their colourful clothes, scarves and books of bad poetry as a father might regard the toys of a favourite child.

"See those four over there?" he said to me one day. "Well, I could tell many a tale about them that would make your hair stand on end! Some of the oddest tales I have ever heard!"

Business was quiet that evening. In front of the fire, the three climbers still rested their weary limbs, one of them shunned slightly by the other two. And there were only three writers present: James Joyce, Dylan Thomas and Gabriel García Márquez. They were engrossed in their own affairs, laughing and joking. There was also Dr Karl Mondaugen, the mad scientist of Munich, who was busy building a new machine from spent matches that he picked out of the ashtray.

Apart from these, there was a quartet of students, chatting by the window. I knew their names but had never spoken to any of them. I am less tolerant than Hywel (I foolishly believe that students have easy lives.) There was Claire and Peter Elliot and Anna and Gareth Thomas. I had heard that Peter was not a nice man; Gareth, on the other hand, was a friend of Billy Belay and had a reputation as a practical joker.

The girls were both quite shy and I knew very little about either. Hywel had hinted that Claire had already been married once – to Alan Griffiths. But it was Anna he wanted to talk about.

He said, "You would never guess, would you, that she is an expert on dragons? I mean, real fire-breathing dragons! Let me tell you how and why. Ever since she was little, she has been fascinated by stories of knights and dragons. You know the sort of thing: fierce dragon takes up residence in a cave and terrorises local village; village leaves a helpless maiden each year as a sacrifice to placate dragon; brave knight slays dragon and rescues maiden. Usually the knight then marries the maiden and they live happily ever after."

"I know the type of story," I replied. "The old tales of chivalry and heroism. St George and all that."

"Exactly. But for Anna they were much more than mere stories. She believed implicitly in them. She amassed an enormous collection of books about the subject. Secretly, you see, she envied those maidens and wanted to be one. She wanted to be rescued by her very own handsome knight."

I studied the group of students more closely. I was always amazed at how Hywel seemed to know so much about his patrons.

"But she ended up with Gareth instead?" I asked, innocently.

Hywel waved me aside. "Wait for it! Anyway, as I was saying, she longed to be a helpless maiden in peril, a damsel in distress if you like, and thought about little else. One day she was reading such a tale for the umpteenth time in an old story book – one of those collections of legends with illustrations on every page – when a voice spoke to her. Do you know what it said?"

I had to admit that I did not.

"Well, it was a magic voice and it said something like this: 'Anna, there are few of us left now and we need your assistance. Will you help us?' And at the same time, the picture in the book came alive. It was the picture of a maiden chained to the entrance of a cave, watched over by anxious villagers. A dragon was emerging from the cave and, in the distance, a dashing knight was riding into view."

"That seems a bit unlikely," I muttered. "Are you sure this story is entirely accurate?"

Hywel ignored me. "As she watched breathlessly, the mystical voice continued. This time it said: 'Anna, few people are willing to take our place and we desperately need volunteers.' Although Anna couldn't be sure, she was convinced it was the maiden who was talking. So she replied, 'Yes, of course I will help you. Of course I will take your place.' And she clapped her hands for joy."

I mumbled and rapped my fingers doubtfully on the counter. But I knew better than to protest too vehemently at this stage. "So she was drawn into the picture and became a maiden?" I asked cynically. "And I suppose the knight rescued her and they were married?"

Hywel shook his head vigorously. "Not at all. She was drawn into the picture, sure enough, but when she looked down, it wasn't the body of a maiden that she saw. Oh no!"

"What then?"

Hywel stamped his foot and roared with laughter. "Scales of course! It was the dragon who had spoken to her!"

This was too much even for me. I refused to join in Hywel's mirth. Very soberly, I straightened my tie and replied calmly, "That is the most absurd tale you have ever told me. I simply refuse to believe it. If it really happened, then how come Anna is sitting over there now? I demand you tell a sensible story for once."

Hywel was suitably chastened. "Would you like to hear about those other two students and their disastrous trip to Ireland?"

I responded in the negative and gestured at the mountain climbers. "Tell me about those. Why are two of them so wary of the third?"

"Ah, the Three Friends! By all means, if you insist, but you may wish that I hadn't afterward. Just a friendly warning."

"Why?" I asked.

Hywel squinted up his eyes. "Wait and see," he said menacingly. And those eyes twinkled.

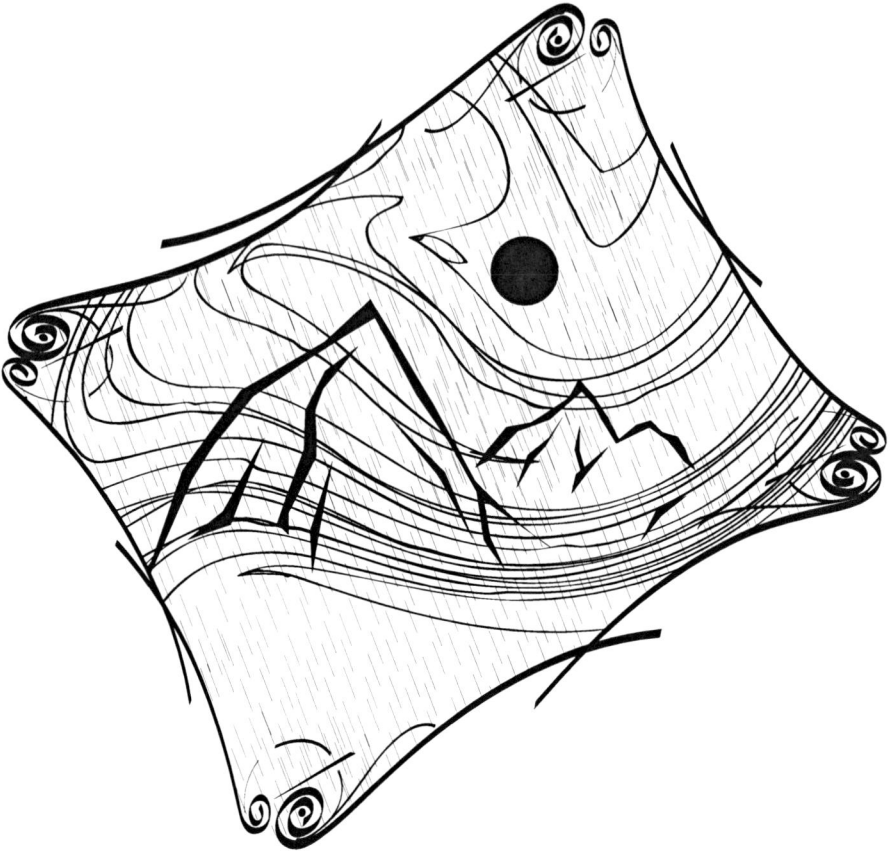

9- THREE FRIENDS

The three friends were mountain climbers who had trekked to the roof of the world. They had encountered many dangers on the way and each had taken a turn to plunge down a crevasse. Bound together by ropes as well as friendship, it seemed they had all escaped death by the narrowest of margins. One by one, they had praised their luck and had agreed that teamwork was wonderful.

After the end of one particularly difficult day, as the crimson sun impaled itself on the needle peaks of the horizon, the three friends set up their tent on a narrow ledge. The first friend, who had survived the first crevasse, boiled tea on his portable stove and lit his pipe. Stretching his legs out as far as the ledge would allow, he blew a smoke ring and said:

"The wind whistles past this mountain like the voice of a ghost, shrill as dead leaves. The icy rock feels like the hand of a very aged corpse.

Those lonely clouds far away have taken the form of winged demons. Everything reminds me of the region beyond the grave. I suggest that we all tell ghost stories, to pass the time. I shall go first, if you like."

Huddling closer to the stove, the first friend peered at the other two with eyes like black sequins. "This happened to me a long time ago. I was climbing in Austria and had rented a small hunting lodge high in the mountains. Unfortunately, I managed to break my leg on my very first climb and had to rest in the lodge until a doctor could be summoned. Because of a freak snowstorm that same evening, it turned out that I was stuck for a whole week. The lodge had only one bed. My guide, a local climber, slept on the floor.

"Every night, as my fever grew worse, I would ask my guide to fetch me a drink of water from the well outside the lodge. He always seemed reluctant to do this, but would eventually return with a jug of red wine. I was far too delirious to wonder at this, and always drank the contents right down. At the end of the week, when my fever broke, I asked him why he gave me wine rather than water from the well. Shuddering, he replied that the 'wine' *had* come from the well. I afterward learned that the original owner of the lodge had cut his wife's throat and had disposed of her body in the obvious way..."

The first friend shrugged and admitted that his was a very inconclusive sort of ghost tale, but insisted that it was true nonetheless. He sucked on his pipe and poured three mugs of tea. Far below, the last avalanche of the day rumbled through the twilight. The second friend, who had survived the second crevasse, accepted a mug and nodded solemnly to himself. He seemed completely wrapped up in his own thoughts. Finally, he said:

"I too have a ghost story, and mine is true as well. It happened when I was a student in London. I lived in a house where another student had bled to death after cutting off his fingers in his heroic attempt to make his very first cucumber sandwich. I kept finding the fingers in the most unlikely places. They turned up in the fridge, in the bed, even in the pockets of my trousers. One evening, my girlfriend started giggling. We were sitting on the sofa listening to music and I asked her what was wrong. She replied that I ought to stop tickling her. Needless to say, my hands were on my lap.

"I consulted all sorts of people to help me with the problem. One kindly old priest came to exorcise the house. I set up mousetraps in the kitchen. But nothing seemed to work. The fingers kept appearing on the carpet, behind books on the bookshelf, in my soup. I grew more and more despondent and reluctantly considered moving. Suddenly, in a dream, the solution came to me. It was a neat solution, and it worked. It was very simple, actually. I bought a cat..."

The second friend smiled and sipped his tea. Both he and the first friend gazed across at the third friend. The third friend seemed remote and abstracted. He stared out into the limitless dark. In the light from the stove, he appeared pale and unhealthy. He refused the mug that the first friend offered him.

The first two friends urged him to tell a tale, but he shook his head. "Come on," they said, "you must have at least one ghost story to tell. Everybody has at least one." With a deep, heavy sigh, the third friend finally confessed that he did. The first two friends rubbed their hands in delight. They insisted, however, that it had to be true.

"Oh, it's true all right," replied the third friend, "and it's easily told; but you might regret hearing it. Especially when you consider that we are stuck on this ledge together for the rest of the night." When the first two friends laughed at this, he raised a hand for silence and began to speak. His words should have been as cold as a glacier and as ponderous, but instead they were casual and tinged with a trace of irony. He said simply:

"I didn't survive the third crevasse."

10– THE RAKE
AND THE FOOL

"I didn't like that story," I said to Hywel, after he had finished the tale of the three mountain climbers, "and I no more believe it than any of the others you have told."

While he had been talking, THE TALL STORY had filled up slowly with faces new and familiar. I recognised various workers from the nearby County Hall. They rattled their chains and gnawed at their manacles as they waited to be served.

"Actually that tale is absolutely true," Hywel insisted, "but I admit that I made up the nonsense about the dragon. In fact, I could tell you another story about Anna and Gareth."

"Only if you make it brief," I mumbled.

"It concerns a goblin…"

To be honest, I was tired of Hywel's more outrageous flights of fancy. I said, "Put that one on hold and try something more culturally relevant than usual, will you?"

"Cross my heart," Hywel replied, but he did no such thing, "that this one is so true you can have a year's supply of free drinks out of me if you disprove it, I swear!"

I grimaced at this prospect, for a TALL STORY year is made up of twelve bitter months, and eight is my usual limit. Unlike ordinary months, in which all the days are used up before moving onto the next one, Hywel's variety always leaves a few at the bottom and he collects the dregs into whole Winters of Discontent, Summers of Love, Broken Springs and long Falls down the Stairs. It is awful.

"Go on then," I stammered.

Hywel stretched and gestured at his customers, seated at various tables throughout the tavern. People were chatting to each other, making plans or jokes, loathing or loving comrades, rivals and relatives, exchanging trivial or profound insights, just spouting gibberish when necessary. They included Byron and Julian, the former delving in his pockets as if searching for lost dice, a criminal frown on his brow.

Also Claire and Peter Elliot, crouched over a map of Ireland, marking out possible hiking routes with little flags on pins. Under the map, heads creased the paper at the right places to represent the hills. Two of these heads belonged to Flann O'Brien and James Stephens and this incidental acupuncture had cured them of sundry ills. Alas, most of that ill was their talent.

The main point that Hywel's gesture jabbed into me, though without medical justification, was that his patrons were *communicating*, however inelegantly. All except one, who sat alone. He was a pale individual with white eyebrows and colourless eyes, though he didn't seem old or unhealthy. It was almost as if he was a new type of human being. I thought he was drinking Guinness, but in fact he cradled an empty glass. Despair at his inability to make contact had filled it with a black swirling bile.

"A tragic situation," whispered Hywel.

I rolled my eyes. "He doesn't have any friends. I suppose you want me to go over and talk to him?"

"You misunderstand. He's not a lonely man. He's the *loneliest* man, and that's more serious than having no friends, in the same way that a knob of butter is worse off than a pint of milk. The latter can be returned to a cow's udder with a syringe, but the other is forever divorced from the mother beast. Why? Simply because butter is a fatal illness of milk. When milk is badly shaken on a voyage it becomes travel sick and vomits its own content outside its form. Thus butter will never get better!"

"Are you implying that society can reabsorb lonely men if they have luck and faith, but that the loneliest man is fated to stay isolated for eternity because he has curdled himself beyond the typical definition of humanity? I'll soon fix that!"

I was about to walk over to the peculiar fellow, but Hywel held me back. "It's a cultural thing. That's what you wanted, isn't it? A story about diverse ways of living. Anyway, it's impossible to befriend that wretched soul. Shall I tell you his name? It's pronounced something like this: Asdgfxfkh Kuhfoashfubv."

I frowned. "What language is that?"

Hywel flicked away a slave with his grimy cloth. "Now we're getting to the point. That man is a Faskdhfgasdhian, from a little known, indeed completely forgotten, ethnic minority. Where is Faskdhfgasdhia, you ask? It's not a foreign country but the original name of that island you see across the bay. No need to look."

The windows were too misty anyway, and THE TALL STORY is always at least one narrow alley and three imaginary corners away from the Cardiff waterfront. But I knew which island he was referring to. In our language it is called 'Flat Holm' and is hardly a noteworthy feature of the local horizon. Slurping waves like a greedy saucer a few miles south of the city, its only claim to glory is as the site of the first reception of speech by radio transmission. On 11th May 1897, Guglielmo Marconi sent the three words 'Are you ready?' to his assistant George Kemp, who was standing on the island and presumably was.

"That's an arrogant twisting of history!" boomed Hywel, as if he'd read my thoughts, "for in very olden times Flat Holm, or as we ought to call it from now on, Faskdhfgasdhia, had a lustrous civilisation all its own, unique and bashful, brave and odd, spicy and tortuous. When it was suddenly destroyed, sometime between the Dark and Magnolia Ages, it was as if it had never existed! For the inhabitants kept no written records; and their dwellings and artefacts were constructed from seaweed. Without physical evidence of their culture, they were wiped from the official annals of human endeavour!"

"And yet there were some survivors?"

"Quite a few at first, yes. They emigrated across the shallows to Cardiff. One of their most respected Prophets had said that the island would sink into the waves for a washing. That's what happens when your homeland resembles a saucer. A hundred families made the crossing in a huge canoe. They settled in an obscure part of the city, between Blanche Street and Beresford Road. Later the island rose again but they didn't go back. The same Prophet predicted it would eventually be haunted by a disembodied voice. Maybe he anticipated that radio message, or possibly I invented that bit. I can't remember."

"Did they flourish in their new enclave?"

"Not really. They were an introspective people and found it easier not to mix with outsiders. They didn't even bother to learn any other languages. So inbreeding and nostalgia became their guiding principles. They were ignored by Cardiff Council; and this neglect was taken to such extremes that people actually found it difficult to see them. You know how it is when you stop noticing the wallpaper in your house, however exotic the pattern? That's because it doesn't try to interact with you. It just hangs around aimlessly."

I understood. "Ditto the Faskdhfgasdhians?"

"Slowly they started to die out. Eventually there was one couple left. Then less than that."

I nodded. "Right! So this chap is the very last member of his race? I can guess how he feels, standing on the edge of a genetic, linguistic and social abyss. But to extend your metaphor – if the wallpaper is stripped away, won't we suddenly notice a bare wall of crumbling bricks in our cosmopolitan environment?"

Hywel shrugged. "Who knows?"

We remained silent for a few minutes, and he took this lull in the profundity to serve his other customers, the slaves, but by this time they had all been whipped back to work by potbellied overseers, who had selected drumming music on the ancient jukebox.

"This man – what's his name? – Asdgfxfkh Kuhfoashfubv! – has no way of relating to anybody else. No shared values, customs, concepts. He is utterly divorced from modern life."

"Correct again. No comedy in this tale, eh?"

An abrupt moral impulse seized me. I clicked my fingers at Hywel and cried, "The pickle jar."

Normally treating him with such rudeness would result in me having the jar forcefully set down on my head, which is actually what happened, but I was prepared for it, and it was the only way I could be certain of getting quick access to it, without yet another story nested inside this one, and I didn't care for a diversion. My hat cushioned the blow, and I left the vessel perched there as I stepped over to the poor soul. He had a look of extreme relief on his face when he saw that I acknowledged his existence, but I waved him back and offered him the jar with a deep bow. Maybe that gesture was an insult in his culture, for he blushed red. But for the sake of contact he repressed his feelings. He took the gift but didn't know what to do with it.

"There's joy in pickles," I said.

"You'll have to show him how," Hywel called to me. I unscrewed the lid and swallowed a gherkin whole.

Then I left him to it. I didn't want to look too soft, in case the act became a real part of my character and weakened my career hopes. By the time I had returned to the bar, Hywel had sharpened and polished a reprimand. "That was so irresponsible!"

"Not at all. It was an attempt at empathy."

"Would you give a terminally depressed man a loaded gun? Shame on you!"

I was confused, but not for long. Unable to bear his situation any longer, the last Faskdhfgasdhian had followed my example deliberately badly. He had stuffed not just one but several dozen gherkins into his small mouth at the same time.

"He's committing suicide!" I wailed.

"Worse than that," said Hywel. "When the average man kills himself, the world loses a single individual, a cell in the body of society. But what this chap has done is to wipe out an entire civilisation, with all its components. At a single choke he has eradicated a complete system of ethics, language, laws, aesthetics, fashion, science, religion. It's the ultimate crime. It's *auto-genocide*!"

"An indigenous religion, you say? I wonder what form that took? We will never know for sure now…"

"We can speculate," retorted Hywel. "I reckon the Faskdhfgasdhians were monotheists. Probably because I'm too lazy to envisage more than a single god for them. He was usually depicted as a clown holding a rake. A bumbling gardener, if you please."

"What do you base that reasoning on?"

Hywel leaned closer and winked. "Essentials of plot. Were you born yesterday? Now shut up and weep!"

I bared my teeth. "No! If I'm partly responsible for this disaster, it's up to me to put things straight! I intend to do my best to revive him. First aid and all that stuff."

"Too late! He has stopped breathing."

I rushed over to the casualty, who had collapsed onto the floor and was lying quite still. His throat bulged with gherkins. I roared, "Sound the alarm! Call for a doctor!"

"Ja!" barked Karl Mondaugen from a nook.

"Not you. We don't need a doctor of cryptozoology. We want a medical practitioner. Where's Dr Walnut?"

"Struck off decades ago! By a child with a catapult."

"Then I must pick him up." I hurried out of the pub but didn't get far. No time to explain why.

"What do you intend to do now?" sneered Hywel.

"I must unblock his throat!" I whimpered, as I returned to the side of my patient. "Any suggestions?"

"Perhaps you could try lubricant?"

"Not tonight, vaseline!" I muttered darkly.

"What was that?" demanded Hywel, but I shrugged and he didn't press for an explanation. He scratched his head and sought to recall the brief medical training he never had. In a nonexistent pub, that's feasible. He almost giggled as he called:

"Try the *kiss of life*!"

I groaned. I rarely care to kiss men, partly on account of their stubble, partly on account of mine, but mostly because I'm still in love with my past achievements. Mind you, I have a mistress too: my future hopes. Can't choose between them.

"Not sure I can manage… do my best…"

The smell of vinegar was abominable. My lips just wouldn't attach themselves to his. I tried pushing my head down with my arms, but they refused to work. The nearest I got was nose to nose, and that's still a handkerchief's breadth away.

"Ugh! How do women cope?"

Hywel cried: "Have you started yet?"

As I shook my head to reply in the negative, something incredible happened. The unmoving body beneath me sat up and spat out a stream of gherkins, most of which struck my face. The Faskdhfgasdhian known as Asdgfxfkh Kuhfoashfubv was better. He had got over his minor case of death with amazing abruptness.

I recoiled. "How did I accomplish that?"

Hywel rubbed his chin. "Of course! The people of Faskdhfgasdhia don't kiss as we do, with mouths. They rub noses! So you gave him the precise *kiss of life* he required!"

"Another forced TALL STORY coincidence!"

"I'm not sure if that's the right word," said Hywel with a frown. "I'd call it a rusty *deus ex machina*."

"You're such a snob! But look at this!"

I nodded at all the other customers in the pub. They were no longer engaged in their own business. They were turning on their chairs to gaze at Asdgfxfkh Kuhfoashfubv. It was as if they'd noticed him for the first time. There was excessive interest in their expressions. Even Byron and Julian were fatally distracted from their dice, or whatever game it was they were playing. Even Anna and Gareth stopped to stare. Claire and Peter too (and Flann O'Brien and James Stephens beneath the map). Also Mr Burke, Mrs Owen, Madame Ligeia, the Three Friends, Harold the Barrel, Billy Belay, Tony Smith. Everybody.

"Why the sudden fascination?" I wondered.

"A sad reflection on our society," sighed Hywel. "While the last Faskdhfgasdhian was still alive, nobody cared about him. After his death, it became open season on his culture. We all want to adopt it. He has become fashionable because he's the focus of a *revival*. We often seem to prefer reconstructions to the authentic product. Now he's set up for the rest of his second (bogus) life."

I noted that people had begun to try to dress like the new exotic celebrity. Someone had powdered the chalks provided for use at the dartboard and was passing the dust around. This was being applied to cheeks and eyebrows. Clothes were being ripped and folded just so. Mouths were forcing guttural accents into the smoky air. And Asdgfxfkh Kuhfoashfubv was soon surrounded by dozens of admirers, fingers stroking his hair, tongues tracing his tattoos.

"Disgusting!" grumbled Hywel.

"Aren't you delighted he's finally receiving the attention he deserves?"

"No, because they won't get it right. When he choked himself on the gherkins, he really did expire for a short time. So the link between the authentic Faskdhfgasdhian culture and this new one was broken. It can't be the same."

"Won't he help to put matters straight?"

"How can he? Like I said, he did die. Thus he's also part of the revival. Probably some of his brain cells decayed while he lay prone on the floor – the cells containing the accurate memories of his customs and culture. So he'll have to go along with the recreation. It's just play-acting. Pure theatre."

"With plenty of opportunity to get things wrong? That's what happened with the Druids, isn't it?"

"Exactly. The crucial link was broken there too, and the modern 'Druids' have almost nothing in common with the ancient ones. I mean, the robes, the beliefs, the association with neolithic monuments: it's all incorrect. But what can we do?"

"Just watch and be superior, I guess."

Some of the drinkers were building a 'Faskdhfgasdhian' temple out of stacked beer glasses. It was soon finished. Then they danced around it, calling out for the god that had once belonged to Asdgfxfkh Kuhfoashfubv alone, but now was theirs as well, to put in an appearance. I don't think they expected results. Which is why they were so shocked when a vague shape began to materialise in the entrance to the temple. They backed away as it stepped out and turned solid. It had hunched shoulders and was dressed like a rogue, with long dark coat, slouched hat and spotted necktie. It wore stubble on its chin and a filthy cigarette dangled from its lower lip. It had a squint and fingerless gloves. It hissed:

"Awright, me hearties? Wots up wid you lot then, eh? Leave it out, guv'nor. Get it sorted, mate."

In a grimy hand, it held a tub of strawberry yogurt.

Hywel smote his brow in despair. "They've even got the god wrong! The *rake* and the *fool* have been mixed up!"

I hadn't realised a rake was a kind of rogue...

There was a commotion at the main door. A policeman had entered THE TALL STORY. It was Inspector Firbank. He was always late at the scene of a crime. It gave him a headache.

"Somebody has reported that an ultimate crime has been committed on these premises. Anyone care to own up?"

Hywel pointed at the god. "He has murdered good taste!"

Inspector Firbank nodded smartly and stepped over to the figure. He grabbed it by its torn collar and yanked it out of the pub back to the station. Blasphemy, hubris, justice!

I slumped at the bar. "Listen, I accept it was my fault for asking for a culturally relevant tale. I won't do that again. Grief! I could do with a dose of your most outrageous flights of fancy, however weak and corny. Now please take my order."

"What will it be?" asked Hywel.

"A triple of the worst you've got..."

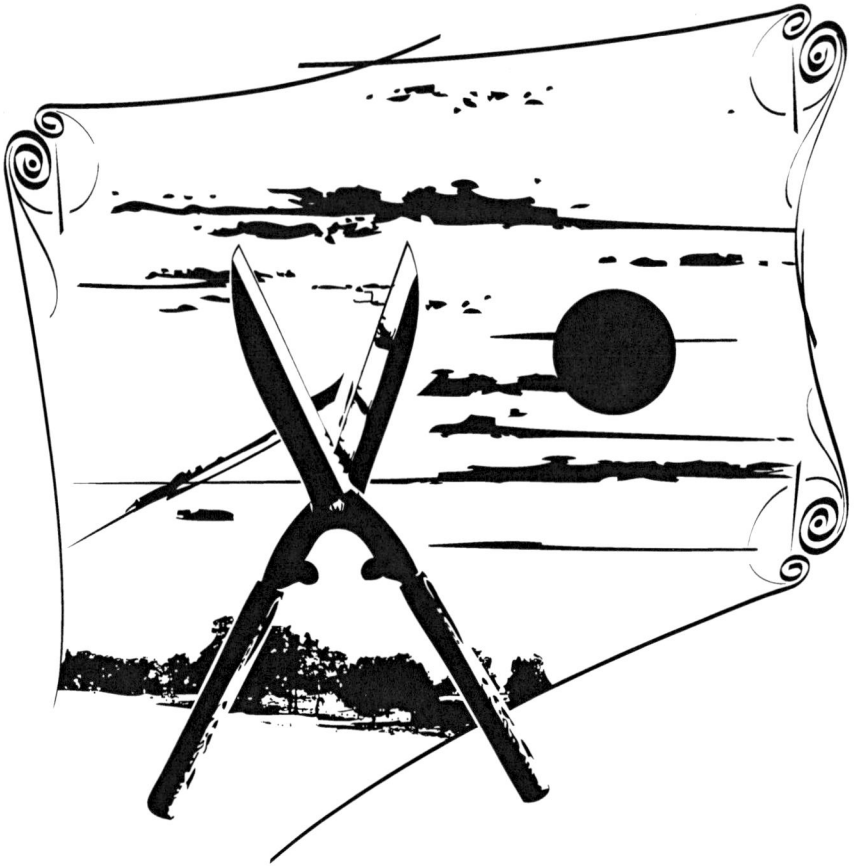

11- GOBLIN SUNRISE

Anna shook her husband awake. Gareth blinked dreams from damp lashes. He struggled through the syrup of hypnopompic sleep. His yawn was as pink and large as the morning.

Anna kept shaking him. "Eh?" he gasped. His hands clenched the pillow and wrestled it over the edge of the bed. The reflexes of a tree, Anna thought derisively. His eyes snapped open.

"What is it? What's wrong?"

Anna lost no time. "There's a little man outside the window. He's wearing a floppy hat and curly slippers. He's laughing his head off. He's very ugly. He has a dirty beard and a warty face. Also, he's got horns."

"Ah yes, that must be the goblin I ordered."

"The what?" Anna cast a doubtful look through the frosty glass. She frowned. "Did you say *goblin*?"

"Didn't I tell you? I ordered one yesterday to do some work for us. Very hard workers apparently. Very efficient. Very neat. Good overall value." Gareth yawned again.

"Where did you order it from?"

"Little People Inc. A new company based in Cork, Eire. They provide goblins, gnomes, dwarves, elves and leprechauns for customers. Goblins are the cheapest of the lot. Not very bright, you see. But good workers all the same. Beautiful," he added.

Anna pouted. "I see." She lay back down on the bed. Gareth closed his eyes. Anna frowned once more. Gareth snored. After a couple of minutes, she turned on her side, propped herself up on one elbow and studied his face with its gaping, drooling mouth.

"What now?" He was somehow aware of her gaze.

"Let me get this straight. You ordered a goblin to do some work for us? What sort of work?"

"Oh, in the garden." He was dismissive.

There was another long pause. "I see," she said again. She scratched her nose. She introduced the toes of her left foot to the toes of her right. "Then why is he floating in the air? And why is he cutting at the clouds with a pair of clippers?"

"What?" Gareth woke with a start, jumped out of bed and squinted in the early light. The sun was big and red on the horizon. And there, far away, silhouetted by the dawn, a goblin was carefully trimming the rosy cumulus tufts.

Gareth opened the window, looked down at his overgrown garden, shook his fists at the sky and cried, "The lawn, you fool! The lawn!"

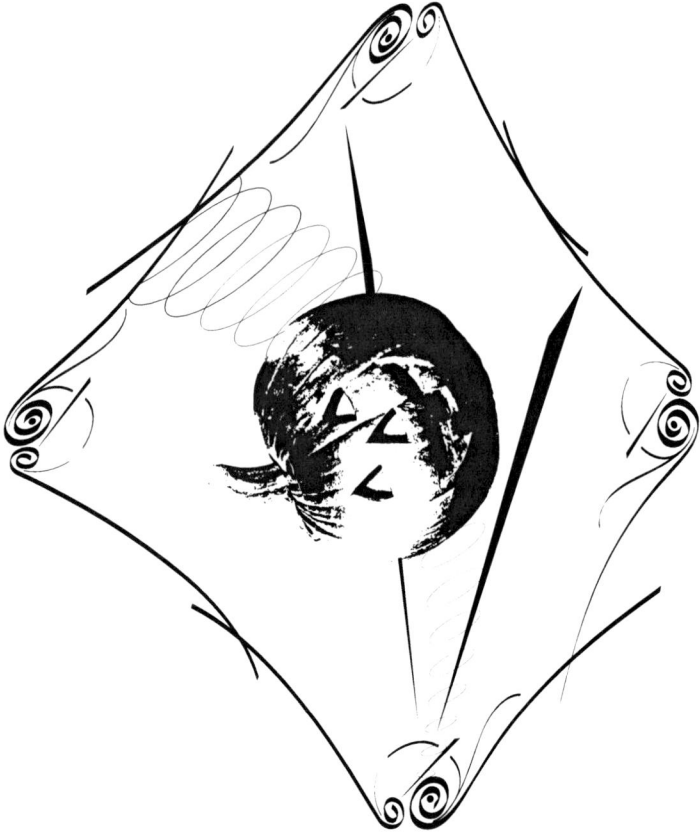

12- THE JUGGLER

On a morning as bleak and grey as his soul, Byron rose from his bed and avenged himself on his tormentor. And then, suddenly aware of what he had done, he fled out into the city.

He spent most of the day slinking down the backstreets and alleyways of the Docklands, convinced that the police were already after him. As night fell, and darkness wrapped itself like a cloak around his hunched frame, he grew bolder. Eventually, he decided that he needed a drink.

Entering a tavern, he stood against the bar and ordered a large whisky. As he was raising it to his lips, a hand clamped down on his shoulder. He almost spilled the drink and whirled in alarm; but it was only Julian, an old friend.

"What a surprise!" Julian was genuinely pleased to see him. He frowned. "What's wrong? You look pale."

"Do I?" Byron managed a thin smile. He shook his head, as if to clear it. "No, I'm fine. I'm just a little tired, nothing more."

"Come, let's find a table. We can talk about old times." Julian led him to a shady corner and offered him a cigarette. Byron declined and chewed a thumbnail instead. Little muscles in his neck twitched and quivered.

Julian talked for a whole hour, reminding him of more innocent days, student escapades and the dreams of youth. Byron forced himself to laugh at the right moments, but his eyes rolled in his head like those of a mad dog. Finally, he could stand no more and leaning forward, he hissed through clenched teeth: "I am evil."

"I beg your pardon?" Julian arched an eyebrow.

"It's true. This very morning, I took a kitchen knife and cut that hideous throat from one ear to the other. He deserved it though. Five years of torture! Can you imagine it? Every night for five years! It's hardly surprising I took matters into my own hands."

Julian opened his mouth and tried to speak. But no words would come out. He cleared his throat and gasped, "I think you should tell me all about it."

"Certainly." Byron nodded. He finished his long-neglected drink and wiped his lips with his sleeve. "Listen then. It all began when a new owner moved into the flat above mine. He was an Insurance Clerk, but his hobby was juggling. He also happened to suffer from insomnia. On sleepless nights, he would pass the hours by practising."

"I don't understand."

"He juggled with fruit. He bought some every day from the greengrocer across the road. I used to watch him through my window. He started with gooseberries and satsumas. Those were not too bad. After a while, however, he progressed to heavier fruits. Apples, lemons, pears. Eventually, he was using melons."

Julian frowned and scratched his nose. He was beginning to suspect a joke. He wondered if he was supposed to chuckle. Lighting another cigarette, he studied the face of his friend, hoping to find a trace of humour in his stony expression.

Byron slammed his fist down on the table. His empty glass jumped. "Don't you see? He wasn't a good juggler! He was awful! That's why I had to do it. He kept dropping the fruit. A pounding on his floor all night. And

61

his floor was my ceiling! I was nearly driven insane. I became a nervous wreck. I began to hate him more with each passing day."

Julian realised it was not a joke. He had never seen anyone twisted with so much rage and pain. He shuddered.

"Of course," continued Byron, "after such treatment, the fruit would be bruised and useless. And so he would have to buy more. I tried to reason with him. I tried to point out that his juggling was damaging my health. But he ignored me. Every night the pounding would grow louder, and every day he would buy fresh supplies from the greengrocer. Well, what would *you* have done in such a situation?"

Before Julian had time to answer, Byron slammed his fist down again. This time, the glass bounced off the table and rolled across the floor with a hollow drone.

"Yesterday, I was walking past the greengrocer's when I saw that the owner had arranged a dozen pumpkins on his stall. One of them he had hollowed out into a leering face. I remembered that it was Halloween next week, and last night I dreamed that my neighbour was juggling three of these pumpkin heads. This dream was a warning. Do you know how heavy a pumpkin is?"

"So when you awoke you cut your neighbour's throat?" Julian sighed heavily. Sweat stood out on his brow. "In that case, you must give yourself up. The Judge might be sympathetic. You could plead diminished responsibility. After all, you endured five years of Hell."

Byron scowled. "That's just it! I didn't kill my neighbour. Why should I? All he ever did was juggle. The real culprit was the man who supplied him with the fruit."

"You killed the greengrocer?" Julian was incredulous.

Byron frowned. There was a strange glint in his eyes. "The greengrocer? No, I didn't kill the greengrocer."

"Then who?"

Byron smiled a superior smile. He rose to his feet and gazed down at Julian. "The pumpkin, of course. Who else? He deserved it though. You should have seen his face afterward! What a mess!"

And reaching into his pocket with a wink, Byron pulled out a handful of pumpkin seeds and scattered them like dice on the table.

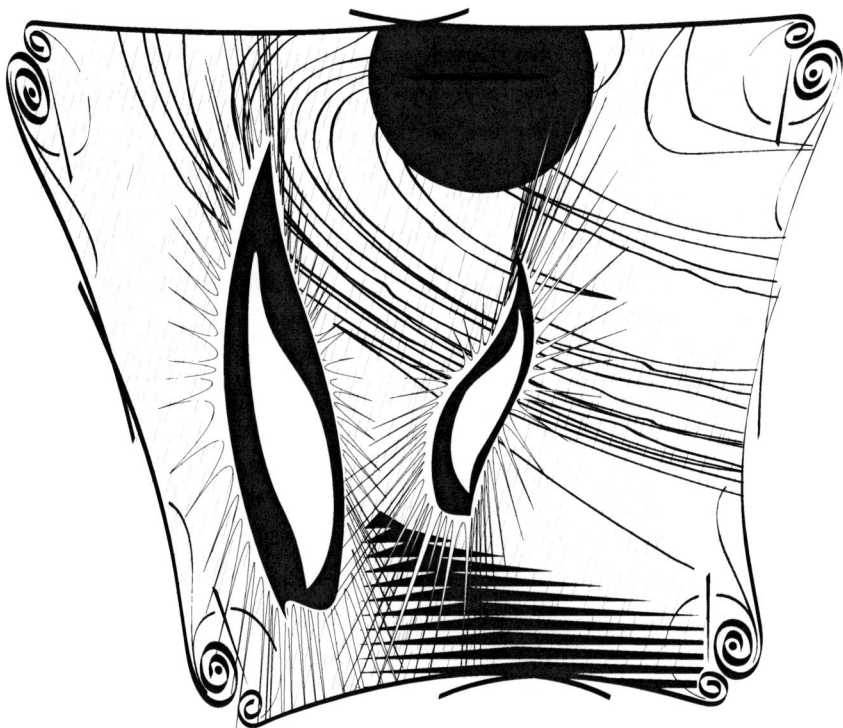

13- THE PEAT FIRE

Peter and Claire Elliot were lost on the moors. A fine drizzle had swept in from the west, chilling them even through their waterproof clothing and obscuring their view of the horizon. As Peter stepped forward, he sank a good ten inches into the soft clay that had been churned almost to liquid by the rains of the previous night. Cold mud surged over the top of his boots and forced itself under his toes.

"I hate this country!" he wailed.

Claire placed a comforting arm on his shoulder, but he pulled away with a scowl, losing his balance in the process and falling backward into the mire. He flapped aimlessly for a minute before Claire, struggling to repress a laugh, helped him to his feet. Once again, he shrugged her off and gritted his teeth. "Yes, I hate this country. And I hate you as well!"

"The holiday was your idea," Claire pointed out.

She turned her face into the oncoming sheets of drizzle that washed over them with a regular pulse, as if dancing to the rhythm their feet had made earlier on the moors. It seemed as if someone was draping a succession of veils over the landscape, each veil a fraction of a millimetre thicker than its predecessor.

"I'm completely fed up!" Peter added, under his breath.

"Perhaps it will brighten up later?" Claire suggested. She knew it was useless now to remind him that he alone was responsible for leading them off the road into the wilderness. She attempted to smile and then began to whistle.

"Oh, shut up!" Peter growled. He raised a fist as if to strike her, thought better of it, and contented himself with spitting near to where she stood. "Let's just find our way out of here, shall we? Pass me the map."

"I gave it back to you," Claire replied.

She frowned as the blood rushed to his face. He was little better than a child, she decided. He stamped his foot, spraying mud and damp clay over an area considerably smaller than he would have liked. He tried again, and managed to spatter Claire's face.

"You liar!" he screamed. "Right, that does it! I'm off! You can find your own way back! Do you hear me? Find your own way back!"

Claire watched him stamp off, skidding on wet grass and lurching into low bushes. She sighed and shook her head. Doubtless, he expected her to race after him and apologise. But she had finally reached the end of her tether. He could drown in a bog now, as far as she was concerned. Enough was enough. Besides, there was always Michael at college and he seemed a much nicer sort of man.

She waited until Peter was out of sight and then began moving in the same direction, slowly and carefully so as not to catch him up. She guessed that he would probably veer off at a tangent at some point and eventually end up walking in circles. His sense of direction was truly unique!

Before long, as the light began to fade and the rain increased in volume, she spied a lone figure making its way toward her. She assumed it was Peter and rolled her eyes in exasperation, but it was, in fact, an exceedingly thin stooped man with a strange, wild look about him. As he approached, he hailed Claire and began to chuckle. His hair was matted and he possessed but a single blackened tooth in his hideous wound of a mouth.

"Another visitor, to be sure!" he exclaimed. "And what would your name be?"

"Claire," said Claire, intrigued rather than alarmed by the fellow's appearance and weird high-pitched voice. It was a voice somewhere between the creaking of a coffin lid and the scream of a bluebottle caught in a spider's web.

"Claire, eh?" The man screwed his face up and winked. "Not much I can do with a Claire," he said. "There's a County Clare though," he added thoughtfully.

"I'm lost," Claire replied, well aware that she should not really be divulging this fact, but feeling, for some reason, relatively safe in the company of this stranger.

"Come with me," the stranger insisted, taking her by the arm. "I have a hut. A bowl of soup and a peat fire awaits you. Yes, potato soup and a real peat fire!"

Claire let herself be led across the moors. As they walked, the stranger began to talk in a breathless monotone, nodding and tapping his warty nose as he did so.

"I'm a namesmith. I've been a namesmith for a long time now. I do things with people's names, you see. It's hard work too, I'm blasted worn out with it, but I enjoy it all the same. Peculiar things, names."

By the time he had finished, they had reached a hut, seemingly made out of turf, with a hole in the top to act as a chimney. Smoke issued forth and made a vain attempt to flee the rain. The man gestured at the open doorway. "Go inside. There's a bowl of soup and a real peat fire. You're my second visitor today, you know."

Entering the darkened hut, Claire squinted at the oily fire that burned in the centre of the single room. It took her a full minute to appreciate what it was she was looking at. At first, she was appalled, but then she laughed. Divine retribution, perhaps?

Behind her, the little man chuckled again. His breath was chill on the nape of her neck. "Yes, I'm a namesmith. Well, what do you think?" He began to dance. "I'm still waiting for Old King Cole. Much easier to ignite!"

He danced in front of her and paused, attempting to gauge her reaction. "Well?" he repeated.

Claire smiled and shook her head.

"You can't spell, can you?" she replied.

14- KNIGHT ON A BEAR MOUNTAIN

At least the fireplace of THE TALL STORY is never short of acceptable fuel. It burns the unpublished manuscripts of the writers who frequent its unforgiving domains. Nathanael West was in here the other day, searching for his cool million, which he'd misplaced a whole week, or dreamlife, before. He didn't reveal what the million was *of*. I don't think it was money. Nor locusts.

Perhaps he was hoping to find a sweetheart, a girl in a million, and in that case I wish him luck. Maybe I could set him up with another writer, say Mary Shelley or Christina Rossetti, but that's not really my job. I'm no Miss Lonelyhearts. Then again, it occurs to me that with a global population of ten billion, there must be 10,000 girls in a million running around at random. If they all decided to enter this pub at the same time, I would die of admiration and suffocation. Which reminds me: the ventilation is playing up.

There's a big grille set into one of the walls and a fan that sucks out the fetid air and cigar smoke and musical notes of the regulars. This grille resembles an ancient knight's helmet. Not that I've ever seen a visor; but it brings to my mind something Hywel told me a long time earlier.

I said, "What happened to that knight in the story about when Anna turned into a dragon? I mean, he barely came on the scene before you admitted the whole thing was a lie. I bet he was annoyed at being let down like that. I can't believe he just went away after getting all dressed up for action. Why not tell me what he did next?"

Hywel smirked to himself and something of his former profession returned to him as he rolled up his sleeves and kneaded my cheeks for a full minute. Then he fell back and answered, "Listen, Old Bony, we've become good friends and I feel I can speak frankly. You can't really leave this pub, though you've tried often enough. The street outside…"

I sighed. "No need to say more. But I wonder who built Raconteur Road? Laid the cobbles, I mean."

He was shocked. "Wash your mouth out with soapy beer!"

I did so, and swilled that taste clean with whisky. I grimaced at my reflection in the mirror over the bar. It didn't grimace back. It was fast asleep. I asked a safer question which had been bothering me for ages. "Why is that an impossible mirror?"

"You'll have to ask Guildo Glimmer."

"Who's he?"

"A sentient mirror and thus an ultimate authority on artificial reflective surfaces. But he lives in the future, so you'll have a long wait if you really want to speak with him…"

I decided to let the matter drop. "What about the knight?"

"That's the point I was coming to. Remember that it's *you* who's doing all the telling, as agreed in our original contract. I know you've arranged it to look as if I'm guilty for most of these stories, even though I haven't actually told a single one, but that's just a literary trick. I'm weary of it, to be honest; and I think you ought to accept your responsibility this time and let me have a rest."

I was disappointed by his reluctance to humour me, but I guessed it was only a temporary aberration on his part. However, I knew that two could play at this anti-game. "Well, I've decided to match your surliness. I don't have any words to spare."

"No problem." He indicated the figure of Karl Mondaugen huddled in his secret corner. The mad scientist was darning the sleeves of his strait jacket with a toothpick and a guitar string. Faint notes of unholy jazz sounded as he worked. In the ashtray on his table, his latest invention waited to pass its first test.

I squinted at it uneasily. "So what useless thing has he created now? A Wake Up Call for an Alarm Clock?"

"Out of matchsticks? Don't be silly! I think it's:

☞ A Pair of Stilts for a Giant."

I tutted. "Fine, I'm sure. But how can that help me tell a story?"

"No, not that. Look at the other thing he's just invented."

I scratched my head. "I can't see anything…"

"Exactly! That means it's already up and running."

"But what *is* it?"

"Remember when I said that Dr Mondaugen was hoping to create a machine that could recycle all those unnecessary words which are scattered all over the floor, indeed which *are* the floor? Well, he's done it. And if you operate it, you'll be able to tell your new story without wasting any new words."

"Operate the machine! But where is it?"

"Outside this story, of course! You don't seriously expect to find the *implement* of composition within the prose it creates, do you? That would be totally absurd. No, it's located above the page."

"But I'm trapped down here, aren't I?"

"That's an illusion. If you are the author, you *must* be outside."

I was forced to concede the point. I took a deep breath and concentrated and the pub melted away. I grasped Mondaugen's machine, positioned it over the blank page and pressed the buttons to shuffle the reclaimed words. I dealt them like a true amateur:

"After the knight realised his services were no longer required in the rescue of a damsel, he galloped off in a huff. Fancy squeezing himself into this armour for nothing! It wouldn't do to take it off before he'd had his money's worth. He went looking for a substitute adventure. Across many lands he rode, through forests and over moors. Eventually he came to a very flat country on the edge of a stagnant sea.

"It was all marsh and swamp, with complicated routes winding between the lagoons and quicksands, and wills-o'-the-wisp at dusk to entice him off the path. In the day, wasps and will were lacking, but mosquitoes and dogged persistence urged him on. Catfish too, which leapt out of the pools to bite his lap. He was grateful to arrive at a settlement. It was a town in which every building was a windmill.

"Chief of this realm was Pungent Hugh, miller of millers, grinder of black bog-rush and pumper of bilge, who protected his people with dykes and towels. He welcomed the knight – Sir Jasper was his name – with a handshake and a meal. The bread was awful. Then when his guest had finished belching through his visor, he made a little speech. He said:

"'How grateful I am to meet such a noble hero.'

"'And why is that?' asked Sir Jasper, with much interest and not a little suspicion. 'Damsels?'

"'No, our women take care of themselves, I'm afraid; but we do need protection from a ferocious talking bear that roams these parts and raids our town at night. He smashes the sails of our windmills with his dirty great paws or spins them backwards until they break.'

"'A talking bear?' blinked Sir Jasper. 'In a swamp! Are you sure?'

"'Absolutely certain. I've heard it with my own ears. Oh, I know what you're thinking: bears normally live in the mountains, don't they? Well, maybe this one does too. But he comes down to visit us after sunset.'

"'I accept the quest! I shall sally forth to slay the creature!'

"And off he galloped again, glad to be fulfilling his chivalrous role at last. It dimly occurred to him that he might as well wait until the bear entered the town that evening; but there was something unheroic about not taking an active part in seeking danger. What true knight ever sits still and allows dastardly things to charge at him? The traditions must be followed scrupulously. Besides, he didn't like the town. So he kept going, looking for a mountain and a liar – I mean lair!

"Although the sun was getting low in the west it was still hot and he sweated profusely inside his armour. He was grateful for all the holes in his visor that let the air in. The sky was cloudless; but swarms of biting insects cast a little shade. He knew where he was headed thanks to an eccentric line of reasoning he had decided to pursue. North! For when the evening came and the stars appeared, the constellation of Ursa Major would be directly ahead, frosty and bright.

"What other sign would a talking bear choose to dwell under? Ursa Major is the Great Bear, and a real one that can articulate meaningful sentences must surely be the greatest of its kind. Sir Jasper peered anxiously into the distance, but there were no mountains. The land remained flat. The sun set over a large lagoon and the foam on his horse's mouth turned pink. Still there were no peaks visible. Twilight was followed by dusk, and the smell of decaying vegetation gave way to that of smoke. A volcano, perhaps?

"No, it was a small camp fire, and the bear sat warming its paws in front of it. A pot of porridge bubbled on the coals. Sir Jasper found it impossible to urge his horse forward, so he dismounted and creaked stealthily toward his foe. Ursa Major did indeed twinkle, above him and also on his armour, but the mountain was absent. No matter! He grimaced inside his helmet as the bear slowly turned its head at his approach, but realising that his expressions of fear were hidden, he drew his sword from its scabbard with a confident flourish and ran forward.

"The bear stood up. It fixed the charging knight with its wild eyes and demanded: 'Who the bloody hell are you?'

"Sir Jasper had known that this was going to be a talking bear, but actually hearing the words emanating from that mighty jaw was an experience he wasn't really prepared for. He went numb. The sword slipped from his fist. This was precisely the reaction the bear was hoping for. The tactic rarely failed. It opened its huge arms to receive its visitor, which it intended to crush inside the iron shell, rather than wasting time trying to get him out first. The plan almost worked, but Sir Jasper had a secret.

"Before he had become a knight, he had wanted to be an actor. He wasn't very good at it – critics said he was too wooden – but he'd gained some knowledge of the mechanical tricks used by theatre companies to increase the astonishment factor of a production. The most obvious and simple of these devices was the pantomime horse. Worked by levers and springs on the inside, a single man could operate it with amazing efficiency.

"Something in the bear's tone made Sir Jasper wonder if a similar trick was being played here. Instead of trying to brake his headlong rush, he accelerated and jumped. The bear closed its paws around nothing. The knight came down on the bear, straddling its shoulders. Sure enough there was a row of buttons running all the way down the creature's back. What's more, they looked ready to pop. Sir Jasper reached over and undid the top one. It was just enough. The costume burst.

"Unfortunately for him, there wasn't a man inside. Sir Jasper had assumed that bigger things hold smaller things, not the other way round. The object that stood among the tattered remains of artificial bear was – a hippopotamus! It rolled its huge eyes and lisped, 'Thank goodness for that! It was such a tight fit in there!' But Sir Jasper wasn't deceived. He undid the top button of this costume too, and the hippo burst to reveal an elephant, which trumpeted, 'A blessed relief to be out of that, what?' Yet Sir Jasper still didn't relax.

"Another undoing of a button, another fabric detonation and now the knight was confronted by a blue whale. Before it could utter a word, he fumbled for the next button. Now he was in the branches of a gigantic redwood tree, the tallest tree in the world. He felt dizzy.

"He screamed as he undid this final button, for what burst out of the tree was something he had suspected was the real villain all along, though he hadn't acknowledged the fact to himself – it was an impossibly high mountain. Its lower slopes were covered in snow and lost climbers, one of them wedged in a *third* crevasse. Sir Jasper clung tightly to the summit, but as the peak rose into the sky and beyond the atmosphere, he came to regret the holes in his visor which let the air out…"

The machine to recycle words was empty, so I switched it off and stepped back into the page. Hywel blinked.

"That's weird! You just seemed to vanish."

"I moved into a dimension where I had godlike control over scenes and situations. Anyway, what did you think?"

"Of the tale about the knight? Very poor. I'm not blaming you for that, of course. You only had a limited selection of previously used words to work with. But I pity our readers."

I nodded. "So do I. But if that's truly what happened to Sir Jasper (and I've decided that it was) then I can't be accused of dishonesty. I'm not culpable for the clumsy bits."

Hywel shrugged. "Very wise."

There was nothing more to say. We gazed around the pub in quiet despair. Nothing much had changed. There was no longer a floor to stand on, because the scattered words that had doubled as flagstones had gone, but the ineffable void which now occupied their place was no less solid, so it didn't matter. I gestured at Mondaugen.

"I wish he would stop fiddling with his strait jacket. It's giving me unpleasant memories."

"Don't look at him in that case. Seek a distraction."

One came in the form of a figure that entered THE TALL STORY wearing a knapsack on his shoulders. His boots left crimson prints on the surface of the polished void. Hywel said:

"That's Steven; and he must have trodden in Michael."

I recoiled in distaste when the figure approached the bar. As I did so, my foot struck something round and hollow that rolled under a nearby table. Hywel was delighted. "Ah, you've found Walter's head!"

I pointed in turn at the newcomer, the loose skull and the bootprints. "Clear these up for me, will you?" I joked.

But Hywel did, worse luck.

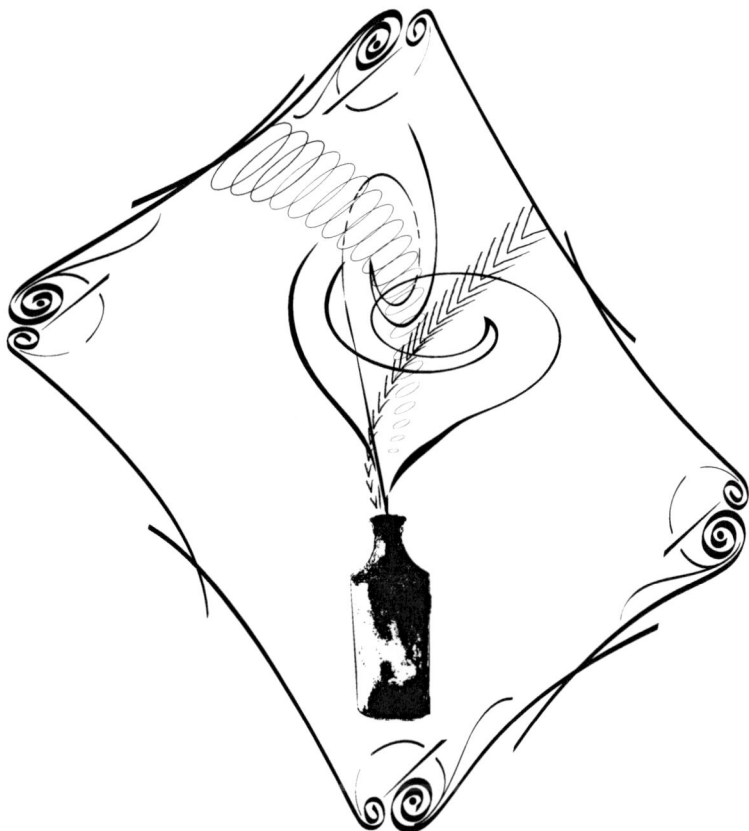

15- SOMETHING ABOUT A DEMON

Steven Karlsen had one peculiarity, and that was his inability to understand sarcasm. Because the punch at Dr Mondaugen's annual party had been jokingly recommended, he had helped himself liberally to the foul brew. As a consequence, he had spent five whole days wandering the streets of Cardiff in a high state of delirium.

Where he had been in that time, what he had done, he could not say. All he knew was that his pockets, once full, were now empty and that his knapsack, once empty, was now full…

As the trance finally began to wear off, he was delighted to find himself in the environs of the Docklands. Feeling more than a little thirsty, he made his way to THE TALL STORY, hoping to prevail upon some kind stranger to buy him a drink. Entering the establishment, he had the good fortune to recognise Alan Griffiths, an old friend, sitting at a table near the door.

Adjusting his knapsack and pushing through the crowded drinkers, Steven reached his friend and promptly sat down next to him. But the friend was not pleased. He tried to hide behind his drink, holding it so close to his face that Steven thought he must be trying to climb into it head first.

"Well!" Steven slapped his friend on the back. "What a surprise!"

Alan said nothing. He continued to pour the creamy liquid down his throat. Steven found himself forced to address his friend's oversized gullet, a particularly repulsive part of his anatomy. "Fancy meeting you here, of all places!"

"It was inevitable." Alan slammed his glass down and wiped his lips with his sleeve. "Cardiff Docks is the hub of the Universe and as such, all mortal souls are eventually drawn to it by its irresistible gravity."

"Really?" Steven blinked in surprise. "I never knew that before. In that case, it is not so odd after all."

"Sarcasm," Alan explained with a grimace. He lit a cigarette and blew smoke at Steven. In the half-light of the dissolute tavern, the smoke writhed like a pale and weary ghost.

"You are alone?" Steven glanced around into the heaving mass of humanity. "I am not interrupting anything?"

"I am waiting for someone," Alan replied. He spat contemptuously: "The most gentle and considerate woman in the world."

"Oh yes?" Steven raised an eyebrow. "Then I would very much like to meet her."

Alan was exasperated. "Sarcasm," he growled.

"Ah!" Steven nodded sagely, but he was completely bewildered. "I don't understand sarcasm." He lowered his gaze and twiddled his thumbs.

There was an awkward pause then. Alan cleared his throat and pretended to be absorbed in reading the back of his matchbox. Eventually, Steven summoned up the courage to ask him for a drink. "If it's not too much trouble," he added.

"Of course not! Nothing would give me greater pleasure!" Alan scowled with a viciousness that surprised even himself. "A bottle of the best champagne, perhaps?"

"Oh dear, no." Steven shook his head. "A lager shandy will suffice."

Alan sighed. He realised that even the bluntest sarcasm could have no effect on Steven. He decided to take advantage of the situation. "Have you lost all your money then?"

"Used it up," Steven answered. "My pockets were full five days ago, stuffed with notes. But somehow I have managed to spend them all. I dimly recall entering a succession of shops and purchasing various items. I remember nothing more." He indicated the knapsack, slung over one shoulder. "They are all in here, I presume."

"Tell you what," Alan suggested. "If you have anything of interest, I will exchange it for this." He held up his half empty glass and swirled the soapy contents around.

Steven licked his dry lips. "Certainly. You are a good friend, Alan."

"Come then. Let us see what you bought." Alan snatched Steven's knapsack and emptied it onto the table. A torrent of mouldering junk clattered out before them. "Well, it seems that you have been visiting every antique shop in the City. Antique spelt J-U-N-K."

"Is it all worthless?" Steven was disappointed.

"Heavens, no! Rarely have I seen such a magnificent collection of fine and tasteful pieces." Alan sifted through battered brass ornaments, cracked and chipped statuettes, iron globes with cords trailing from them and rusty candlesticks; and finally he pulled out a broken clock, rotten frame sprouting springs. "Marvellous. Superlative. Exquisite."

"It is yours." Steven beamed gratefully. "And take anything else you fancy."

Alan laughed. It was a gruff howl of a laugh. The clock slipped from his fingers back onto the crest of the pyramid of junk. "Sarcasm, you fool! Are you completely stupid? I would not give a toenail for this mechanical analogue of horse manure!"

"Sarcasm?" Steven scratched his head. "I am sorry. I thought…"

"I mean, look at this!" Alan held up a dusty blue bottle and waved it under Steven's nose. "What on earth possessed you to buy this?"

Steven peered closer at the bottle and blinked. He thought he glimpsed a dim and fitful shape moving in the depths of the opaque glass.

He grappled with thin wisps of memory. A dark and evil-smelling antique shop down a particularly obscure alley in a part of Cardiff he had never visited before. An old man with young eyes and a white beard. An aura of menace and an arcane secret concerning the bottle. Something about a demon and a single wish?

Alan pulled the stiff cork out of the neck of the bottle and sniffed gingerly. He wrinkled up his face and retched. He closed one eye and tried to peer into the bottle. "There's something in here. I can't quite see what it is."

"If it is nothing of interest," Steven ventured, "perhaps you will buy me a drink for old time's sake?"

"Old time's sake?" Alan was aghast. His lower jaw began to chatter. Abruptly, it ceased and he bent forward, still clutching the bottle. "What exactly do you mean?"

"We are friends." Steven kept his eyes on the floor. "We were very good friends once. You told me that I was your best friend. You said that you admired and respected me for my intelligence, humour and compassion."

Alan curled his lips back in a snarl. "Sarcasm, you fool! I was joking. I always hated you. I thought you were the most mindless cretin I ever had the misfortune to meet. And you are not going to touch a single drop of my drink!"

"I don't understand sarcasm." Steven fought back tears.

At that moment, a tall, auburn haired woman entered the tavern and, spotting Alan, made her way over to his table. Steven was impressed with her elegance as she wove through the masses, a skill that had always eluded him. She stood before them with a winsome smile and Steven instantly rose to offer his seat to her.

"What time do you call this?" Alan placed his foot on the vacated chair, barring her descent. "Eh?"

"I was held up." The woman was apologetic. "A meeting with my producer."

"Really?" Alan shook the bottle at her face. "Are you sure about that? Are you quite convinced that you were not, in fact, spending a squeaky session with him in the recording studio?"

"Quite sure."

Alan turned to Steven. "This is Toni," he said. "A girl so dedicated to jazz that she sees fit to blow any trumpet on offer, even when it belongs to a decrepit and rather dirty old man."

"I have told you before." Toni's lips quivered. "I am not having an affair."

Clutching his glass in his free hand, Alan kicked the table over. Steven's collection of junk crashed to the floor. The other drinkers began to stare. For once, silence reigned in the tavern. "Get out! You are no better than a common tart!"

After she had left, and the other drinkers had turned back to their own concerns, Steven set the table up and scooped as much of his possessions as he could reach back into his knapsack. "Do you really think that was wise?" he asked, ingenuously. "Creating such a disturbance? Are you not embarrassed?"

"Embarrassed?" Alan's face twisted again. "Of course I'm embarrassed! I will never be able to show my face in Cardiff Docks again!" His voice was thick with scorn. He held aloft the bottle in one hand and his drink in the other, as if to weigh his shame on the scales of conscience. "I am so embarrassed that I wish the ground would open up and swallow me…"

Leaning across, Steven managed to catch Alan's drink. But he was unable to rescue the bottle. With a self-satisfied grin, he drained the glass and glanced around. Luckily, no one had noticed. Shouldering his knapsack, he left the table and followed Toni out into the wide and mysterious world.

"I don't understand sarcasm," he said to himself.

Neither, so it seems, do demons.

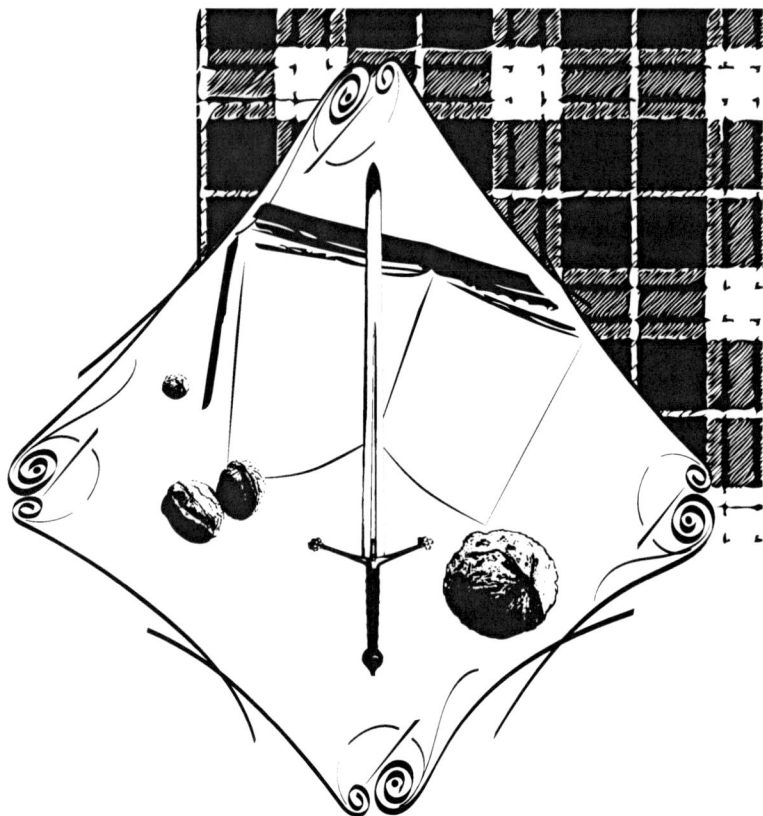

16- THE FURIOUS WALNUTS

For more than a week, Walter had been feeling a trifle Scottish. It didn't help that his house was the colour of salmon. Nor that his wife was named Heather. He'd wanted a magnolia house and a wife named Patsy, but you can't have everything. A primeval force was moving within him, an urge to plunge through moor, lake and glen.

Over breakfast, a meal of sheep's stomach stuffed with lungs, he mentioned his condition. He wondered if turning into a Highlander would affect his career. He was, after all, paid to sell a chemical that removed ice-cream stains from trousers.

His wife glowered at him. Being a gentle soul, her glower was not hugely effective. If looks could kill, he'd be complaining of slight abdominal cramps and asking his pharmacist for aspirin. Fortunately, he felt sick enough already.

"You'll have to adjust," she told him. "My brother, Desmond, had a dose of Burma. Took to wearing rubies in his nose and making fish-bone curry. But he kept his job in the Civil Service. And cousin Joseph was a train spotter who became an Eskimo. Never needed to change his anorak; he just noted down kayaks instead."

Rather than feeling reassured, Walter finished his food in anxious silence, wiped his knife on his beard and stuffed it into his sock. He wanted to hold forth on bridges and pneumatic tyres. But his wife hated lofty or inflated topics. So he dressed for work, shook the last drops from the bottle of woad and mounted his bicycle.

Around him, men and women were changing, shells of identity falling off and rattling on the pavement. Walter blinked. It seemed to him that whenever an identity clattered to the ground, a horde of imps rushed out of shop doorways and storm drains and lifted it up. Then they fitted it onto the shoulders of some other pedestrian. They moved so fast, it was difficult to register their presence at all.

Walter felt he ought to investigate this phenomenon more closely, but at that moment he passed the bus station. Lately, the bus station had exerted a strange fascination for him. He spent the next hour or so hanging around the ticket office, threatening commuters and demanding the fare back to Glasgow.

When he reached work, his boss was waiting for him. Mr Jhabvala was a yogi and astrologer who had invented *Caste Away*, the ultimate frozen dessert stain eradicator, in Bombay. His prototype was so successful that jealous rivals had pursued him all over the subcontinent. Years in the Kashmiri mountains had taken their toll. His skin was pitted with cobra bites and his eyes glittered like opals.

He invited Walter to sit down, leant back in his swivel chair and stroked his chin. A run-in with brigands had left him with only three fingers on his left hand. The missing digits on his right hand, however, were testimony to frostbite in the Hindu Kush.

"Listen, old boy," he began, toying with his cravat, "I've paid a lot of thought to this and I've decided to let you go. Awfully sorry, but you know how it is. Be a good chap and don't cry. Stiff upper lip and all that. Thing is, old bean, we can't allow a Scotsman to peddle our goods.

Customers would take fright. Kindly accept this Cheddar as a parting gift and run along. Toodle pip."

Sighing languidly, Mr Jhabvala pasted his kiss-curl back onto his brow and inserted a cigarette into a long holder. Walter ignored the gift and stomped out, cursing into his beard. On the street, he caught his new reflection in a tailor's window. His Scottishness was growing worse by the minute. The claymore in his belt interfered with the back wheel of his bicycle, the tam-o'-shanter keep slipping over his eyes. He'd have to visit his doctor.

Dr Walnut was a family practitioner. He greeted Walter cordially, offering him a hookah and rolling out a carpet for his benefit. Walter felt uncomfortable in the surgery, possibly because he'd never seen Dr Walnut in a fez before. Foregoing the hashish, he outlined his problem. Dr Walnut nodded, poured himself a glass of raki and clapped his hands. The receptionist, Miss White, came in and undulated her bare midriff on the desk between them.

"A little thin, no?" he chuckled, exhaling noxious fumes through flared nostrils. Noticing Walter's scowl, he held up his hands in a mollifying gesture. "You can't get the staff these days. Now what can I do for you? You are turning Scottish? Well there's a bug about. Rampant Internationalism. It's the rains we've been having."

Walter nodded. Dr Walnut stood up and moved to a filing cabinet in the corner of his surgery. He opened the drawers and a scruffy child popped out of each. In their features, they were miniature replicas of Dr Walnut. They leapt to the floor and began riding hobbyhorses in tight circles on the gaudy central rug. Walter caught the flash of silk, the creak of leather, the acrid odour of mare's milk.

"My sons succumbed last week. Mongolianism, a severe outbreak. All my silver scalpels have been looted. Keep erecting tents in the kitchen. What can one do?" He inhaled deeply on his hookah and his eyes sparkled. "The little heathens! They're absolutely furious, no?" One at a time, he lifted them and deposited them back into the filing cabinet, forcing the drawers shut with the toe of his curly slipper.

Walter wasn't interested in other people's children. He paced the room in dismay, his sporran swinging. "That's all very well. But what can ye do for me?" He scratched at the lice in his plaid. Dr Walnut gave a mysterious smirk and reached into the folds of his robes. He removed a murky phial and held it up.

"It is most fortunate you came to see me at this time. I have just finished distilling this liquid from my sons. It is poison to the imps who cause the ailment. I call it *Tartar Source*." He winked slyly. "It is expensive, but for you there is a special price."

"Och, give it here!" Walter snatched the bottle and swallowed the contents. For a moment he reeled and clutched at his head. Then he made his way gingerly out of the surgery. Dr Walnut followed, calling him the offspring of a dog and various unnatural partners. Walter brushed past Miss White, who had returned to Reception and was sugaring her body, and he fell down the steps onto the street.

Over the next fortnight, a second transformation took place. Walter was at a complete loss to explain this one. He found his head was still eager to cycle everywhere but his abdomen wanted a bus. His arms had an urge to paddle a coracle. Most disconcertingly, his toes began to smell of fish and his neck of sausage. When he woke one morning to find that Heather had drawn isobars over his body with a felt tip pen, he guessed he'd also have to swallow his pride.

Dr Walnut was very forgiving. He studied Walter carefully, tapped parts of his attire with a tiny hammer and grunted. "The cure was only partially successful. Your head seems to have remained Scottish while the rest of you has altered. You have become a walking analogue of the British Isles. Your body is England, your arms are Wales and your legs reach all the way down to Cornwall."

"That explains it!" cried Walter. "Yesterday, I was passing a cake shop and my feet were attracted by the cream. They went one way, my body went another and I slipped and landed on my Kent. But if I'm the mainland, where does Ireland fit in?" He saw the answer in Dr Walnut's pout. "My wife! What do you mean! Oppressed?"

Dr Walnut shook his head. "No, no. Green and gently rolling." He took Walter's pulse. "Any pain in your Lancashire?" Walter had to admit there wasn't. His Cleveland itched and his Herefordshire rumbled, but these were minor concerns. Something of much more fundamental importance had just occurred to him.

"What will happen if the Union dissolves? I've heard that Scotland stands a good chance of winning independence. If that happens will my head fall off?" he demanded.

"I think I know what your problem is," Dr Walnut replied. "You're a character in a short story. Some amateur hack is writing this down even as we speak. At the end, to entertain the reader, he'll make the Union dissolve and your head will indeed fall off."

"Isn't there anything I can do?" Walter was in tears.

"If the reader doesn't reach the end, you'll be okay. You'd better try to be boring from now on, in the hope they won't go any further. If you try really hard, they might throw the short story away in disgust and do something else."

It was suddenly very clear to Walter. His fate lay in the hands of some non-accountable reader. But what was the best way of being boring? He thought about it. Whatever happened, the reader mustn't be allowed to reach the end of the story. He thought about it some more. He appealed to the reader to stop at this point.

His head fell off.

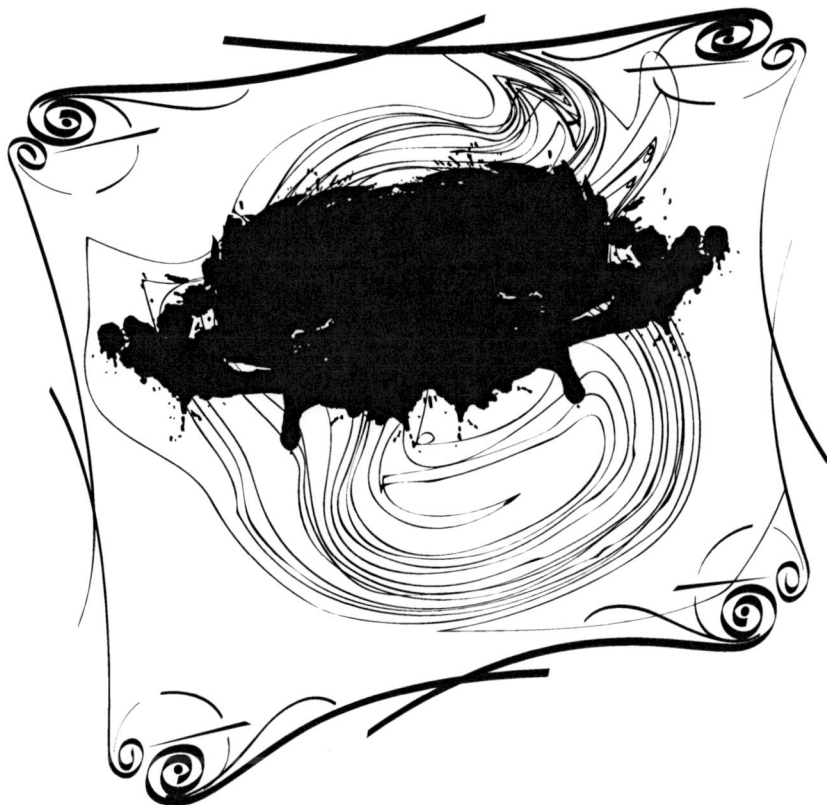

17- THE ILLUSTRATED STUDENT

The illustrated student also came apart, but in a different way. He woke to a morning dark as treacle with rainclouds. He climbed painfully out of bed, lurched to the bathroom and remembered that his name was Michael and that he was poor.

In the cracked mirror over the sink, his pale reflection accused him with a mournful eye. He opened his mouth and checked his teeth. They were all as loose as spare change. Yellow saliva dribbled free. Blood flecked his sallow tongue.

Back in his room, he listened for the hacking cough of his neighbour. There were seven other students in the house, all as despised and absurd as himself. They were dying of neglect. But he would refuse to die. He had decided to fight back.

On his bookshelf stood a heavy dusty volume, a psychology textbook he had stolen from the local library. Clearing his desk of long-empty beer cans, mouldering plates of curry and overflowing ashtrays, he threw the volume down and flicked through the pages until he found the section he desired.

The chapter in question discussed the use of the Rorschach ink blot test. The test had been designed as a method of showing the different ways in which people perceive the same image. A random splodge of ink would be shown to a subject, who would then have to say what the splodge looked like.

Michael remembered reading a story about a psychology lecturer who had painted a Rorschach ink blot on his shirt and who had travelled the land, diagnosing people he met by their reactions to the design. Although this story was a fiction, it had given Michael an idea.

Staring at the example on the yellowing page before him, Michael scratched his head. Instead of an ink blot, he saw a starfish. Or was it a sunrise over a mountain? He blinked. Perhaps it was a flight of swans? It was only after ten minutes of careful study that he understood what it really was. It was, of course, a hedgehog…

Selecting a plain white shirt from his wardrobe and laying it out next to the book, Michael began mixing his paints. He took a fine horsehair brush, dipped it in the black viscous liquid and faithfully copied the design in the book onto both the front and back of the shirt.

Afterwards, when the paint had dried, he pulled the shirt on and buttoned his coat up over it. Then he slung his bag over his shoulder, retrieved his piece of sculpture from under the bed and pocketed it. This piece of sculpture was essential to his plan. It had taken two days to carve from a piece of wood and stain to the correct colour.

Leaving his room, he tramped down the stairs to the musty hall. Old newspapers littered the floor; the plaster was flaking off the walls. He opened the front door and stepped out into the street. Above him, the clouds tumbled against each other. Pulling his collar up around his face, he headed towards the shopping centre.

As he walked, a lorry pulled up by his side and the driver hailed him. Grumbling, Michael walked up to the cab window. The driver wanted directions to the college. "I've been driving around in circles all morning," he confessed, "but I can't find it. I'm supposed to deliver an espresso machine to the Dean's office."

"I'm a student," replied Michael. "I have no money. I haven't drunk a cup of coffee for weeks. The Dean, like the government, doesn't care about students. Look at my teeth." Determined not to help the driver, he gave the fellow false directions and moved on. He felt guilty, but he also felt powerful.

Before long, Michael reached his destination. It was his local Post Office. He took off his coat and placed it in his bag. Then he took out his piece of sculpture and strolled into the lobby. When the people inside saw what he held in his hand, they fell silent and shuffled their feet.

"Nobody move," cried Michael, as he waved the imitation gun in the air. A large, muscular black man in the process of licking a stamp glared at him, the stamp still attached to the end of his tongue. Michael frowned. He had not considered the possibility that anyone might disobey his instructions. "Or else…" he added vaguely.

"Do you want cash?" To his surprise, the cashier was already reaching for a bundle of used notes. He nodded and continued to brandish his piece of sculpture. In one way, he felt truly free for the first time in years. In another, he felt that events had somehow moved beyond his control.

"Just like in the films." An old woman shook her pension book at him and chuckled. By her side, her senile, harmless husband swayed in his universe of drool. "Wait till Mrs Owen hears about this!" Her chuckle turned into a ghastly rattle.

"Listen." Michael began to suspect a plot. "I'm the victim here, not you lot. My gums are shrinking a little more every night. My new girlfriend, Claire, left me because I was so poor." He was almost tempted to aim his sculpture at the ceiling and pull the trigger. He mumbled and snorted angrily.

"How do you want the cash?" The cashier raised an eyebrow. When he failed to reply, she grew petulant. "Tens? Fives?" She counted out the money with professional efficiency. "Will two thousand do? We're not a bank, you know." Behind her, Michael could see a stunned assistant squinting at him.

Michael knew that his time was limited. He took the cash and stuffed it into his pockets. Then he jabbed the gun into his belt. Rushing out of the door, he bounded down a sidestreet. He was so excited he forgot to put his coat back on. He scarcely even looked where he was going…

The Police arrived at the scene five minutes later. Inspector Firbank had not had a good day. A migraine was forcing rainbows through a mincer at the corners of his vision. His unhealthy grey eyes bulged and he mopped his forehead with a damp handkerchief. He was convinced that he had somehow slipped through a wormhole into a dimension ruled by lunatics.

"You mean that you all had a good look at him, but none of you can describe him?" He was incredulous. He rubbed his chin and wrestled with all the metaphysical problems that arose from such a question.

"Oh yes, we all saw him." The old woman shook her finger in imitation of Michael's gun. "He didn't wear a mask. Not even a stocking."

"What did he look like then?" Firbank demanded.

There was a long pause. The customers and the cashier eyed each other. They scratched their heads. Suddenly, their faces lit up. All at once they opened their mouths and spoke:

"A starfish."

"The sun rising over a mountain."

"A flight of swans."

Inspector Firbank sighed. A quote from Nietzsche came into his unwilling head: The irrationality of a thing is no argument against its existence, rather a condition of it. He shook the quote free from his aching mind and tried to smile. His mouth, however, refused to obey.

"I see," he said, slowly. As they all waited, not knowing what to do next, a man came into the Post Office. He was panting heavily. He made straight for the cashier and then spotted Firbank. He caught his breath and nodded. "Just the fellow. I came in to ask directions. I'm a lorry driver looking for the college. I've been driving around in circles all morning…"

Inspector Firbank gasped. "You're covered in blood…"

The lorry driver blinked. "Well, yes, I did hit something just now. It ran out in front of me. I tried to brake but it was too late. I got out to take a look, but it was nothing important." He seemed to notice the stains for the first time. He grew desperate. "Nothing unusual," he added in a small voice.

"But what was it?" Firbank cried. His day was growing worse by the minute. There were pains in his chest and his left hand had turned numb.

"Nothing unusual," the driver repeated, gazing around with terrified eyes. "It was an accident, I swear." His voice became a pleading mumble. There was genuine remorse in that voice, as well as the traces of a growing doubt. "Just a hedgehog…"

18- THE STORY WITH A CLEVER TITLE

Bang! This story starts with an explosion, to grab the attention of its readers. Once the dust settles around them, it can turn into a complex, profound, mature piece of writing, and they will probably stick with it longer than if there wasn't any action in the first sentence. That's my theory, and it clearly works, otherwise you wouldn't still be here. But I can't be bothered with the literary stuff, the bookish expression, so the opportunity has been lost.

I'm tired and fed up. I'm not claiming I enjoyed the trauma of the blast. Far from it! It knocked off my hat and medals. But all the same, it had power, and that's something I sorely miss. Plus I'm desperate to escape from here. The damage was minor. No big holes in the walls. Just a few broken bottles behind the bar. The jukebox in the corner had got stuck, playing 'Broken Angel Blues' again and again. What else? Oh yes, all our customers were dead.

We don't get many bombs going off in THE TALL STORY. But I doubted Hywel would ever discover my responsibility for this one. There are so many terrorist groups devoted to so many whimsical causes that I could easily blame some imaginary faction or other. The Pacifist Brigade, for instance, or the LOMOJ, whoever they might be. Think up one yourself if those won't do. It was a crude device, but I hadn't made it. I just lit the fuse. I found it among the pile of junk left by Steven Karlsen on a table. Maybe it was an antique.

In the mirror over the bar, I saw that the pub was untouched. The drinkers were still alive. The potbellied overseers cracked their whips and the students shared a glass of cider and the Faskdhfgasdhian temple tottered over its acolytes. There was even a commotion in front of the fireplace, for the Three Friends had decided to climb up the wall to the rafters and the ends of their ropes trailed in the coals and strangled the sparks. Near the door, a convention of doctors blocked the exit. Dr Lithiums, Walnut and Slither debated the merits of Aerial Turkish Komodo Dragon's blood. There weren't any. Everything in this parallel world was normal and routine and facile.

"Fine for them lot," Hywel groaned, "but what a loss of business on our side of the reflection!"

He surveyed the mangled bodies with a frown.

"Shall I go through their pockets?" I suggested. "And maybe slip the rings off their fingers?"

"You know I only take payment in stories. I doubt you'll find many of those on them now. On second thoughts, search the writers for scraps of paper, notebooks, that sort of thing."

I did so. The usual suspects were a disappointment. Flann O'Brien had a collapsible bicycle in his pocket; Gabriel García Márquez had a phial of cholera, a clock and a heart; Anna Kavan had a puddle; Omar Khayyám had a winged piglet; Bruno Schulz had a hole. Felipe Alfau wore a coat made entirely of pockets sewn together, and all of them were full, but they only contained other coats also made of pockets, and so on forever, or at least until the pockets became so small they might only hold a single atom, and you can't generally write stories on those, unless you happen to own a quark-point pen, which you don't. And neither did he. No, the professionals were destitute. I guess they left their work at home.

As for the amateurs, Billy Belay and Harold the Barrel had diaries, but they were just full of graphs recording the number of times they had flown or walked through walls that week. The figures had been massaged. The numerical figures, I mean. The human figures, with their shoulders, spines and necks, all stiff, had probably never felt the touch of a masseuse in the whole of their now absent lives.

At last I came across a corpse with a story. It had been scribbled on an old napkin, the ends of which were stuffed up his nostrils. I drew it out and wiped it clean on my own nose.

"What does it say?" asked Hywel.

I read it. "It says:

THE STORY WITH A CLEVER TITLE

Bang! This story starts with an explosion, to grab the attention of its readers. Once the dust settles around them, it can turn into a complex, profound, mature piece of writing, and they will probably stick with it longer than if there wasn't any action in the first sentence. That's my theory, and it clearly works, otherwise you wouldn't still be here. But I can't be bothered with the literary stuff, the bookish expression, so the opportunity has been lost.

I'm tired and fed up. I'm not claiming I enjoyed the trauma of the blast. Far from it! It knocked off my hat and medals. But all the same, it had power, and that's something I sorely miss. Plus I'm desperate to escape from here. The damage was minor…

"Hold it right there!" cried Hywel.

"What's wrong?" I said.

"Don't you see? It's *this* story, the very piece we are standing in. If you get to the point where I ask you to read it, we'll be stuck in a loop forever. A terrible fate!"

I kicked the body with my boot. Clots of blood jumped onto my sock. "I wonder who this person is?"

Hywel sneered. "Oh, I know him. He's a hack by the name of Hughes. Not sure of his first name."

"Has he published anything? Will he publish this?"

"That depends on who you are now. If you're him, reading this after having just written it, to check for mistakes, then maybe not. If you're somebody else, then maybe he has, unless he gave it to you in manuscript form. Perhaps you're an editor on the verge of writing him a rejection note? It's hard to tell."

"I'm reading it in manuscript form, I think."

"No, you're *standing* in it. Put it down. It's too dangerous. Have you any idea how uniquely horrid it would be to get stuck in a fiction loop?"

"No I don't. No I don't."

"Put it down. It's far too dangerous. Have you any idea… Wait! This isn't a loop. I just broke out of it."

"Well, I put it down. It must be plain déjà vu."

"Thank heavens for that! Now put it down. It's too dangerous."

"More dangerous than my bomb?"

"I didn't hear that. Obviously my ignorance of your part in the explosion has been written into the text."

"A bit implausible that, isn't it?"

"Not really. There are so many terrorist groups running around, it could be anybody. I reckon it was the LOMOJ."

"The Liberators of Mrs Owen's Jam?"

"That's probably what they are. Or maybe the Come Again Faction. They use déjà vu bombs, packed with that odd feeling."

"I have to confess that I did read the manuscript to the point where you asked me to read it. Maybe the déjà vu bomb knocked us back out of the loop? It took us back to a moment *before* I did read it. But wait! That's impossible. It wasn't a déjà vu bomb. It was gunpowder. I lit the fuse myself."

"I didn't hear that. I didn't hear that."

"This is getting boring. Shall we look for a different story? One without any paradoxes?"

"No point. You've searched all the bodies now. If you really want another story, you'll have to invent it yourself."

"I'm too disillusioned for that."

"Then you'll have to go without. I'm not telling one, because even when I do, it's really you doing the talking. Hang about! You can step outside the story again and use Mondaugen's word recycling machine to write it for you!"

"No I can't. It's empty now."

"In that case, we'll just have to wait until enough unnecessary words accumulate on the floor to be recycled. Say something unnecessary. Tell me about your childhood."

"That will take too long. That will take too long."

Hywel sighed. "Well, that's a start. But you're right. We might be here for millions of years. At least you would get to meet Guildo Glimmer at the end of the wait. And then you could ask him about the impossible mirror."

"I can't waste time waiting around for the future. Isn't there a faster way of getting there?"

"We could use a time machine."

"Great idea! Let's hop on immediately!"

"Sorry, they haven't been invented yet. But when we *do* reach the future the slow way, we can send one back to us here."

We looked around expectantly, but it didn't appear.

"Obviously we never got to the future, or else we forgot to send one back."

"Maybe we're too busy there. I wonder what the future's like, and what I'm doing? Hearing that story about Byron and Julian has made me want to learn to juggle."

"That's too mild an ambition for you. I bet you're President of the World and living in a mobile tower!"

"Will we *ever* get to hear another story?"

Hywel clicked his fingers. "I've got it! You know how your best stories are always polished with great care? The more care that goes into them, the better they are."

"True. But so what?"

"Well then, the less care you put into them, the worse they are. What if you put *no* care into them at all? What if you don't even write them? That really is minimal care!"

"They wouldn't exist."

"Ah, but how do you know that? Maybe they would just be very, very bad stories. But stories nonetheless."

"You mean that a tale might already have spontaneously generated out of total lack of care?"

"Yes, and it might be here at this very moment. It'll probably be a horror story, because bad horror stories tend to be the worst of all. If we search the pub, we'll be sure to find it. I'll take this side of the bar, and you take the rest of the room."

I found the story pasted to the noticeboard near the main door. I peeled it off and studied it.

"That's weird!" I said. "It has a number in front of it."

"What's the number?"

"18b," I replied.

"Well don't read that bit out."

"It's almost as if it's a story which is pretending to be a chapter in a much longer work!"

"Arrgh! No déjà vu! That hasn't happened before!"

"Yes it has! New things happen all the time!"

"Guess that's called déjà vu?"

"Shall I just read it out?"

"Just read it out, will you?"

And I did.

A TALE OF TERROR

Laura was running. She ran.

She ran through the forest. Through the forest she ran. Laura ran.

She was running through the forest. The forest was dark. It was scary. Her name was Laura. She ran.

A monster was chasing her!

("Awful title," remarked Hywel.

"Now you've interrupted the flow of the story!" I protested. "I'll have to start again from the beginning."

"Don't forget to include the title. For the sake of integrity."

I didn't.)

92

A TALE OF TERROR

Laura was running. She ran.

She ran through the forest. Through the forest she ran. Laura ran.

She was running through the forest. The forest was dark. It was scary. Her name was Laura. She ran.

A monster was chasing her!

She ran from the monster. Laura ran away from the monster. Through the forest.

The forest was large. It was dark.

The monster ran after her!

After Laura ran the monster, through the dark forest. It was running. Laura was running. They both ran.

Through the forest.

She tripped as she ran. She picked herself up and resumed running. She tripped again. She tripped because she was running! Through the dark, creepy forest.

She picked herself up and ran.

The monster was behind her. It ran after her. It wanted to meet Laura some time. Maybe she would like that?

No, she wouldn't!

But the monster would! The running monster!

Like many running monsters, it ran. After Laura. And she was running too! Through the forest.

The large, dark, creepy forest!

There were trees in the forest. Like most forests, it had trees! Unlike most forests, it had a monster. A monster running through it. After Laura!

Who ran. She was running. Laura was running. She ran.

She tripped. She picked herself up. She ran.

Laura was running. She ran.

She ran through the forest. Through the forest she ran. Laura ran.

She was running through the forest. The forest was dark. It was scary. Her name was Laura. She ran.

A monster was chasing her!

She tripped and fell. There was a note on the ground. She picked it up. She read it. It said:

Dear Laura,

I'M BEHIND YOU! DON'T LOOK BACK!

signed

The Monster

p.s. Maybe we could meet some time? I'd like that.

Laura read the note. She was scared.

She read the note as she ran. In the forest she read the note. The short note in the large forest.

Not just large. Creepy too! And dark.

Like the note. The note that Laura read. Before she finished it.

She ran. Laura ran. She didn't look back. She took the monster's advice! It was good advice.

Good advice from a bad monster!

What are the chances of that happening?

Laura tripped. She picked herself up. She ran.

She was running. Laura ran.

She ran through the forest. Through the forest she ran. The forest was dark. It was scary. Her name was Laura. She ran.

The monster was chasing her!

Or was it? If it had left a note for her, it wasn't behind her!

It was in front of her!

It was in front of her in the forest!

The large, dark, creepy forest! The forest with trees!

She stopped running. Laura didn't run. She didn't run through the forest. She didn't trip, because she wasn't running! She didn't need to pick herself up and resume running.

If she ran, she would run into the monster!

Which was in front of her!

She decided to look for somewhere to hide. Somewhere to hide from the monster. Somewhere in the forest.

She saw a house!

She ran to the house. Laura ran to the house.

The door was shaped like a mouth!

She ran inside.

The door closed and ate her!

The door was a mouth! The house ate her!

The house was the monster!

But if the house was the monster, how did it chase her through the forest? How did it chase Laura?

It wasn't a house!

It was a caravan!

THE END

"Grief!" exclaimed Hywel. "What a load of rubbish!"

I nodded. "The worst story I've ever heard. Almost worthy of this hack. What did you say his name was?"

"Hughes. But which one?"

I spat on the body. "What do you mean?"

"Which Hughes? There are many. He isn't alone."

"I guess we'll never care."

Hywel sighed and mopped his brow with a sleeve. "Anyway, thank the Bugger Lords the story has finished. Bend over – I mean down – before them! You may keep your trousers on."

"I suppose we can't complain too much. After all, it was written by itself. And there were certain odd coincidences in it. The caravan, for instance. Was it tie-dyed? Did it belong to Madame Ligeia? And was the monster a vampire? So many questions!"

"Pity Mondaugen is dead. He could answer them."

"Yes, he was an expert on monsters. A professional cryptozoologist. But it's too late to ask him."

"He died with the others in the explosion."

"His body ruptured in his favourite nook…"

My estimate of our losses had been too high. There was movement in the shadows. Karl Mondaugen crawled to his feet. I was about to stroll up to him and finish the job with a broken bottle, but then I remembered that this would give me away. As for the mad professor, he had saved himself with his latest invention. He had invented:

☞ Karl Mondaugen.

"But he can't do that!" I protested.

Hywel squinted. "Why not?"

"Because he has already been invented! It's plagiarism!"

"No, it's not. He was never patented."

"Ah well, maybe we'll get a proper story out of him instead? I'd like to know about his weirdest cryptozoological case."

"I'm sure he'll be only too delighted to tell us. But who will tell us about *him*? That's what I want to know. And what's that spherical object smouldering on that table?"

"What do you mean?"

"Which part of my reply does that refer to?"

"What do you mean?"

"Both bits, I take it. I might as well admit that I often suspect that Dr Mondaugen is his own worst enemy."

"And the spherical object?"

"It's a bomb! An antique! Probably not worth much when it goes off! Some idiot must have lit the fuse!"

"So the first bomb wasn't mine?"

"No, it belonged to the Come Again Faction, as I mentioned earlier. You assumed the explosion was your responsibility, but in fact the fuse on yours is longer and slower."

Dr Mondaugen picked his way to the bar. "So it is a tale you want? I will give you a tale!"

"What's it about?"

"My weirdest cryptozoological case!"

Hywel nudged me. "I think you should take cover with me behind the bar. If we crouch down, it'll protect us from the blast. But there's not enough room for the professor, so don't tell him!"

I took Hywel's advice. "Thanks!"

"You know how people's secrets often come out after their deaths? I reckon it will be the same with Dr Mondaugen. When this other bomb goes off, we should get to learn the truth about *him*. Let's hope he manages to finish his own tale first."

The mad scientist consulted his memory for the oddest case he had dealt with. It did indeed concern the monster in the forest that had chased Laura. And yes, it was a vampire. It was dark behind the bar, and creepy, but not large. Dr Mondaugen's voice stank like garlic as he leaned over, elbows on the surface, and related the events of:

19- THE SILVER NECKS

There was a vampire called Unthank who suffered from a raging thirst. His doctor suspected diabetes but the patient refused to take a test. Unthank drank from all the necks in the village, valley and forest, but he was still unsatisfied. It seemed he might deplete the land of victims, so his doctor took him aside and told him:

"This can't go on. You're giving the undead a bad name. The elders are talking about locking you up in a pyramid made from garlic. Luckily there's a solution. You must travel to Heaven, where you can sup as much as you please from the inhabitants without making them anaemic. They are immortal and have bottomless veins."

Unthank thought this a splendid idea and asked for directions. The doctor clucked his tongue and cried:

"If I knew how to get there I wouldn't be working here! You should look for a crossroads guarded by a burnished knight. For a modest fee he will allow you to choose one of the paths. But beware: three lead to a hideous doom. Only the fourth, which looks the same as the others, will take you to Heaven. The knight won't tell you which is which, though he sometimes drops hints like anvils."

Unthank, despite his name, was grateful and he wrapped himself in a sunblock shroud. He wondered what hideous dooms lurked at the ends of the three roads. But thirst overcame his anxieties and he flew off into the woods. He flapped for a long time until he came to a river. A canoe was moored to the bank and a knight in rusty armour sat at one end. Unthank controlled his appetite and asked:

"Excuse me, do you know the way to Heaven?"

"No, but I'll take you to someone who does. A burnished knight who guards a crossroads. It'll cost you, though."

Unthank paid him and sat in the canoe. The fellow paddled them with a sword wider than a jump. After a day they reached an estuary and in the middle of the estuary a large island. They disembarked on a wooden jetty and walked inland. Eventually they reached the intersection of four roads and the guide said: "Here we are."

Unthank squinted. "I can't see a burnished knight."

"One moment." The fellow took a wire brush from a compartment in his knee and scrubbed himself all over. Finally he gleamed like a full moon. He gave the vampire an apologetic look. "Chivalry doesn't pay much, so I earn a bit on the side."

"Can you tell me which path leads to Heaven?"

"I'm not permitted. If I try, I'll be turned inside out: it's an old curse. However, I'm certain you'll pick the best road. When pilgrims come here the odds are against them, but in your case I feel confident. Follow your instincts and you'll do fine."

Unthank peered at the four paths: they were identical. He stroked a fang. "Allow me to go away and consider it. First thing tomorrow morning I'll be back to make my choice."

And so saying, he strolled off and hid among some bushes. When the sun went down, he cast off his shroud and flew into the sky. From above he was able to see where the roads went. Three led to hidden trapdoors, visible as vague outlines: the fourth led to a walled garden with a roof of crystal. Unthank glimpsed beings that wore halos and carried harps. He listened but there was no music.

The next day he approached the knight and said, "I've made my choice and now I'm off to sample paradise."

"You must pay me first. If you refuse, my magic sword will slice you into nearly four thousand pieces."

Unthank grumbled, but he handed over the coins and walked toward the western path. The knight cried out in alarm:

"What a terribly stony road!"

Unthank winked. "The way to divinity always is…"

"Wouldn't you rather choose a more comfortable path? The others have all been resurfaced. Look at the gorgeous camber on the northern road! So tasteful and elegant. Consider also the gutters of the beautiful southern road! In absolutely perfect condition."

"They look just the same to me."

"A remarkable coincidence, I agree. We must discuss this matter over a pint of ale. There is a tavern halfway along the eastern road. Allow me to escort you there, arm in wing."

Unthank shook his head. It was obvious the knight was trying to make him change his mind. Did he earn a commission on the number of travellers who fell down the trapdoors? It seemed likely. These crude antics enraged the vampire and he briefly considered leaping on the cheat. But without a tin opener he was at a disadvantage.

"If it's all the same to you, I'll persist with my choice. I'll send you a postcard written on a cloud…"

The knight shrugged and a sigh escaped the holes bored in his helmet like steam from a golem's kettle. Unthank ignored him and hurried as fast as his bowed legs could manage. The road ran straight to a locked door in the side of the walled garden. He rang the bell and waited. At long last, a voice answered. Unthank was astounded to recognise the icy tones of his doctor. "How did you get here?"

"I took a short cut. Some enraged villagers caught me after you left and drove a stake through my heart. It's your fault. The vampires and the humans got on well until you started drinking them dry. If I was you, I'd turn right around and go home."

"Don't be silly. It was you who advised me to come here in the first place. Open up and show me in!"

The doctor mumbled to himself and turned a key. Unthank stepped over the threshold into brightness. Everything sparkled painfully: he shielded his slitted eyes and struggled to focus his surroundings. Nothing matched what he had seen from above. The garden was made of metal: platinum, gold and copper. Osmium flowers exuded tetroxides and birds in aluminium trees clicked relays and preened magnetic feathers. Zinc fish darted in mercury pools with propellers instead of fins.

Even the halos of the blessed souls were electric. Unthank lifted a hand to touch the sparks looping from the doctor's antennae and was knocked to the ground. When he rose, he tried to open the door. The doctor shook his head. "It won't allow you to depart. It only works one way, like a diode. We're stuck here. Ever since God took a course in electronic engineering, rectification has supplanted redemption."

"I don't understand! Last night I saw harps."

"Bare wires," the doctor rasped. "Most of us undress before going to bed. We're immortal now, but the only way to live forever is to be reborn as a machine. You won't find sustenance here: our blood is molten silver. If only you'd taken a diabetes test!"

Unthank shed a gothic tear. It was plain as a grave that Heaven to a vampire was sheer Hell. "The knight tried to warn me off this path. But I thought he was aiming to mislead me."

"He's the one who made us. As I said, he drops hints like anvils. On these anvils he hammers out our bodies. When the Age of Chivalry finished he grew very lonely. He sees robots as kindred casings, advanced versions of the traditional knight. But he's a likeable enough fellow. I prescribe iron tablets for his metal fatigue. Now I might as well confess I'm not really that sort of doctor; I'm a cryptozoologist. But all the others are at a conference, so I had to step in."

"Where do the other three roads lead to?"

"Hades, Tartarus and Limbo. They would have been perfect for you. As a matter of fact, I believe the Devil is advertising for vampires to help his demons hassle the damned. You've got no one to blame but yourself. If I was you, I'd attempt to bite my way through the roof. It shouldn't take more than a couple of million years."

"Fangs for the advice..."

And so we leave Unthank. This tale about him has finished just in time. The bomb is about to go off. When he escapes, the first thing he intends to do is take revenge on the knight. This is just as impractical as it is unfair: the knight is blameless. He is also quite empty. When Sir Jasper died on top of the tallest mountain in the world, his suit of armour left him behind and came down to work for this tale. But now it plans to resign from here too. Well, would you do the job for his pay? When travellers pick the road to Heaven, he gains nothing. And when they choose one that leads to the Hells, he earns a pittance.

BANG!

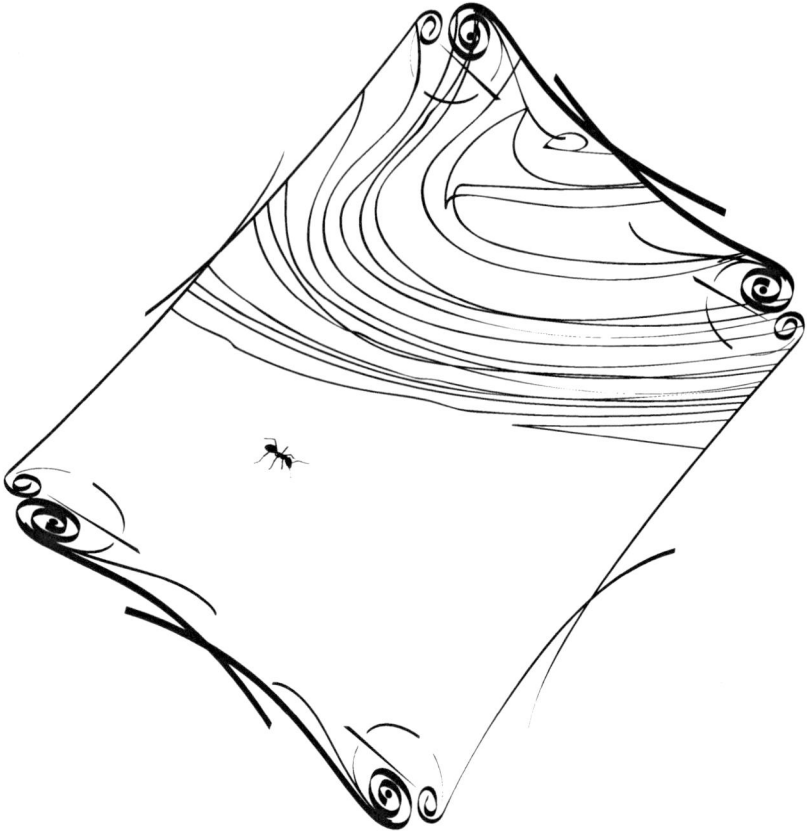

20- NEVER HUG AN AARDVARK

"Well, that really takes the biscuit," said Dr Mondaugen. He was unsure which biscuit he was referring to. His fingers idled over the custard creams and finally settled on a ginger snap.

"But do you believe me?" The visitor leaned forward and gripped the arm of his chair. "After all, I don't know who else to turn to. I mean, would you confess to such a dark secret? Would you?"

"Hmm." Dr Mondaugen spat crumbs as hard as gravel and dipped his tongue into a cup of lukewarm tea. "I doubt it. Now if you had said wolf or bear, or even squirrel, I would be inclined to investigate your case. But an aardvark? I don't think so."

The visitor sighed and held his tragic head in his massive hands. Then he looked up and indicated the window. Dr Mondaugen peered through the glass, across a dark lawn broken up by a number of haphazard paths, and towards the tall trees of the horizon. Stark branches netted a swollen moon.

"The sun has gone down and the full moon has already risen. Within a short time, the change will come upon me. I will start to tremble and there will be a terrible pain in the centre of my head. My face will elongate into a sharp snout, my ears will stretch upward. My arms will become short legs and I will grow a tail. I will develop an insatiable craving for ants. This is not a laughing matter. You must help me!"

Dr Mondaugen shook his head sadly and wiped his lips with a napkin. "What makes you think I can help you? Possibly you need to visit a different kind of doctor. A severe blow on the skull perhaps? Eh?"

The visitor pounded his fists on his knees. "You are the only person who is even willing to listen to me! You are Karl Mondaugen, the great cryptozoologist. The man who won a Nobel Prize for documenting a genuine case of lycanthropy and developing an appropriate cure and wolf whistle. The man who spent two years in China tracking down the were-monkey in a banana canoe! The man who tricked a vampire into entering Heaven and then secured a day pass to check on its condition! If you can't help me then who can?"

Dr Mondaugen nodded solemnly, reached into his pocket for his pipe and began filling it with tobacco. He gathered up a few biscuit crumbs from the plate before him and packed these into the bowl as well. "I have my own reputation to think of. A werewolf is one thing. A were-aardvark is quite another. I know that the moon is full tonight, but even if you change right before my eyes, why should I do anything but ignore you? An aardvark is a silly animal…"

The visitor snarled. "That's where you're wrong! The aardvark, which constitutes the *orycteropodidae* family, is over sixty million years old. Its forelegs are so powerful that it can not only rip open whole termite nests but even fend off lions and leopards. What does this say to you?"

"Never hug an aardvark?" Dr Mondaugen raised a cynical eyebrow.

The visitor was exasperated. He rose up to depart. Ruefully, he offered the doctor his hand, more out of habit than any respect.

"I think I'll pass on that," the doctor observed, "if what you have just said is true. Tell me, when you say that you develop an insatiable craving for ants, do you mean small black insects or the sisters of uncles? Ho, ho! An important point, I assure you. I thought for one ghastly moment that the crux of your tale was going to be one of those awful puns. But don't take it too personally, Mr Hughes."

The visitor left with a sneer, slamming the door behind him and locking it with bolts and chains. Dr Mondaugen glanced around the room with a critical eye. It was hardly a fitting environment for a world famous cryptozoologist. There were few books, for one thing, and the walls seemed to be made of some padded material…

Rising from his chair, he crossed over to his desk by the window, took up his pen and started writing a new page of his *Dictionary of Shapeshifters*. His hand moved at a phenomenal speed. At this rate, he knew, the book would probably see publication within a year. He smiled to himself. The cranks always came to him at this time. Indeed, his own change had been completed an hour before. He was that rarest of all shapeshifters: the were-professor.

Glancing up through the bars of the window, he perceived the visitor on his hands and knees on the lawn. Doubtless looking for ants. Around him pranced and slithered the other patients in a variety of guises; tiger, snake, eagle, hyena and shark. This is what happens when you let the lunatics run the asylum, Dr Mondaugen decided as he went back to work.

Epilogue

There are many real pubs in the universe that forget to chase out their patrons after closing time, locking them in for illicit drinking orgies, and almost as many nonexistent ones which follow that tradition. But few indeed are the taverns that can't be left because of the drunkenness of the streets outside. Whenever I tried to escape from THE TALL STORY, the cobbled surface of the adjacent alley rose up like a wave and crashed me back inside. The only way it might sober up was if Hywel stopped mopping the spilled beer out of the door. And the only way that would happen was if people kept a tighter grip on their glasses. Which relied on them not buying so many drinks in the first place. But there was little chance of that occurring while Hywel remained in business. And that would continue so long as I told tales about him.

However, I have now secured a replacement for my ordeal. It is you, dear reader, though you don't fully realise it yet. It should be obvious that imaginary pubs, however hard the roads which lead to them, can only properly exist as ideas in heads. I have erected this one brick by brick in yours, over the space of twenty feeble fables, and you have decorated and stocked it yourself. That's business, I'm afraid. By all means, take over; you have no choice. Beyond this epilogue, you'll have to deal with the biggest lies of the world on your own. I won't be there to help, nor even to lurk and gloat. I have more critical campaigns to return to. I'm ready to conquer Europe again. I've learned a lesson. One front good, two fronts bad; and winter won't be hearing from me this time. The next boat out of Cardiff to Elba isn't mine.

Let me explain something. After I sneaked away from my final exile, I wandered aimlessly over centuries and cultures, hoping to forget my failures. I went mad. Locked in the same asylum as Karl Mondaugen, I even started to believe I was an ordinary person, without megalomania or a funny hat. A were-man. It was ghastly. The birds spoke to me through the bars of my cell. They counselled patience and revenge. They broke open the walls with their beaks and told me to flee to Wales, a land where I might blend in without attracting attention. The capital city of that country is rife with short fat grumblers who do odd things with their arms under their clothes. I felt at home. I started to get better. I only popped into Hywel's pub for a quick drink to toast my forthcoming victories. Now I'm hoarse with tales. But having already taken you for a long one, this is where I ride off alone.

Part 2

MORE TALLER STORIES

Napoleon Bonaparte is who I am, but you may call me Old Bony or even Little Nappy, I don't really care. I'm not as uptight as I was when I ruled most of Europe, partly because I don't have any big responsibilities now and also because I'm older, wiser and maybe even nicer. If you don't know what happened to me after my supposed death on St Helena in 1821, then I'll just briefly say I somehow managed to escape the island and magically increase my lifespan to several centuries, probably by accident, after which I wandered around a bit and found myself trapped in an impossible pub in Wales, a prisoner again, or as the owner of the place would have it, a patron. Hywel is that owner's name and I can't honestly say I dislike him, but I'm certainly glad to be free of his place, riding away on this sonic horse.

The pub was called THE TALL STORY and a sonic horse is made out of a strained shout when the shouter in question turns hoarse, because words have solid shape inside that pub, and anybody in question, not just shouters, might reach up and take hold of the question mark above them, at least for as long as they remain in question, and use it as a hook for those occasions when hooks are needed, perhaps to hang a coat on. But if the question gets answered it will vanish and the garment fall to the floor and become grubby and trampled. Which reminds me that Hywel once advertised for a pirate to act as a coathanger but the only applicant for the position was a successful pirate without injury and no hook for a hand and so frankly he wasn't very good at the job, plus he never gave the coats back but plundered them for coins, singing rum ditties all the while. Most annoying.

Now I'm heading east as fast I can gallop, putting as much distance between me and that pub as possible before nightfall. I don't like the look of the weather, this is Wales after all, and the rain is sure to start falling soon, rain so heavy it's easier to count the gaps of air between the drops than the raindrops themselves. In fact it's the sort of rain that dries you off if you are already wet by spattering you with dryness, but I think it's better to look for somewhere to shelter, especially as a sonic horse might dissolve in a downpour, I can't say for sure because I've never had one before. I'm riding across a broad meadow but there's a forest not far ahead, so I'll make for that and hope the foliage is thick enough to form a sealed roof high above me.

The clouds begin spilling their moisture just as I reach the first tree. I follow a narrow path into the heart of the forest, but although there is more protection in here than outside, I'm still getting wet and I can feel the oily liquid, now mixed with sap from the leaves, trickling down my back through the gap between my collar and my neck. I shudder and wish I still had my bicorne hat, which acted like an inverted canoe, keeping its sole passenger, to wit my head, safely afloat and dry from the falling sky water, but I lost it, the hat that is, when I attempted to gallop between a pair of narrow gateposts in another field. If I had worn the bicorne with its horns pointing parallel to my direction it might still be with me, but that was the long hat technique of the Duke, you know who I mean, and he was my enemy, and I'd rather perish than be accused of adopting any of his fashion tricks.

I stray off the path and the trees abruptly open into a glade, a special place which is exposed to the heavens but promises the cover I seek, for at its centre exists a ruined temple with irregular columns and tumbled statues and a wall which is still holding up most of a ceiling. There is enough room for my horse under there as well, so I dismount and lead the beast through the maze of eroded masonry into this shattered room. Who built this structure? It doesn't seem to be a product of the ancient inhabitants of Wales, who tended to erect cairns and cromlechs, nor of the Romans who occupied the country later, though it is certainly closer to their style. It looks almost Greek. This can't be possible, of course, for the Greeks never settled here, they only made a few trading voyages, but I'm so occupied by this question that I fail to notice the crouching figure in the furthest corner of the room. He rears as I enter and leers at me. He is squat and perhaps powerful, though the gloom obscures much of his form, but that's the impression he gives and he has slack jowls on his vast face that wobble with energy.

"This is my property," he growls.

I bow and reply reasonably, "Forgive me for intruding, but when the storm has passed I shall depart."

"You must pay to remain at all," he adds.

"With the greatest respect, I have no money. I have just escaped from working in a tavern where all the financial transactions were conducted with tales, many very improbable."

"That will suffice," says he. "Tell me a tale."

"The only one which springs to mind takes place in outer space and is worth more than a brief period of shelter in a decaying temple. Will you give me adequate change for it?"

"I will indeed," he rumbles.

"Will you give me that change in advance?"

He puffs his immense cheeks. "You don't trust me? For that I might grow angry, but I'll restrain my temper for the meantime and give you change now. If you pay with a tale, then the change must also be a tale. It is a tale about myself, a true story in every way. When you have heard it you will know exactly who I am."

He tells it and I listen and here it is:

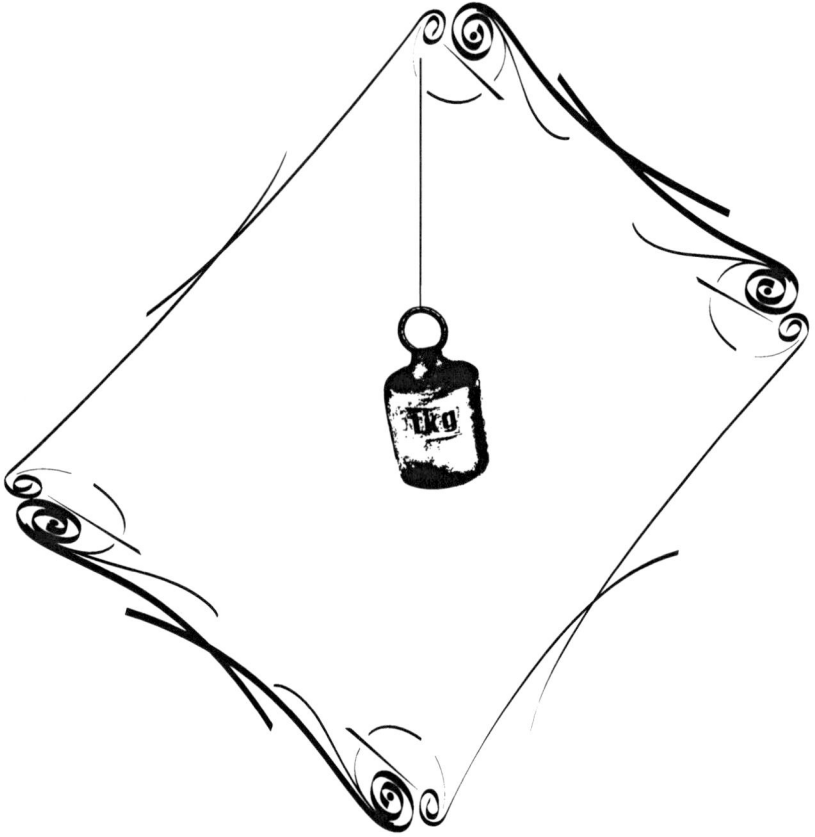

1- IN THE MARGINS

Not far from here lies a pond, ringed by gnarled and ugly trees, and at the bottom of the pond lies a cottage. The waters swirl around the crumbling stones in little spirals, foaming over the ruined chimney as if reluctant to press in too close. In the troubled mirror of this pond, the cottage stands tangled in the reflection of the trees, netted in the twisted branches as if it has been lodged there by an unnatural gust of wind.

How the cottage came to reside under the waters of my pond remains a mystery. Is there any truth in the assertion that a witch caused it to subside by slow degrees for arcane and unfathomable reasons? And if so, who was this witch? There are no records to shed any light on the matter; there is only conjecture and speculation. I, for one, prefer this ingenuous explanation to those suggested by the more prosaic members of my community. I refuse to accept it was built there, in its present location, as some sort of liquid joke.

Not that this would have presented any problems to the patient trickster. The pond could have been drained easily enough, the cottage constructed and then the water pumped back in, but the sheer obscurity of the prank causes me to frown and make many a harsh grimace when I consider this option.

Instead, I often languish by the side of the pond, peering down into the depths, and repeat the word 'subsidence' as if it is a mantra. A slow subsidence, as slow as the growth of a dead man's fingernails or the twisted trees themselves, would have sufficed to preserve the cottage intact in its descent. No beams would have been shaken loose, no thread of thatch unravelled. They rot now, it is true, but such decay is quite a different matter.

One evening, taking some kittens to the side of the pond, to save them from the knife of my brother, I witnessed a peculiar and disturbing sight. No sooner had I tied the little weights around their necks and dropped them one by one, like depth charges, into the glinting water, than an unusual commotion began far below.

I am not a superstitious being by nature, but my senses are keen, and so not wishing to waste an opportunity to initiate gossip, I threw myself to the ground and, ducking my head into the icy water, strained my eyes to discern the origin of the turbulence.

A second later, I regretted my decision. As my eyes adjusted to the gloom, I perceived a tiny man standing at the door of the cottage. He was holding a large net on the end of a pole. Such nets were familiar to me: I had spent many happy hours in the woods with an identical net, collecting moonmoths to be ground into powder in the apothecary's shop. I had developed a certain skill in utilising my net; a skill not shared by my aquatic counterpart far below.

Gasping and wheezing, he aimed the net at the kittens that floated down past him. His frantic motions were the source of the disturbance. He utterly failed in catching a single specimen. The kittens struck the bottom of the pond and disappeared into the sinuous weeds. Bubbles erupted from each mossy collision. The tiny man shook his fists and snapped the pole of the net over his knee. Then he threw the pieces away and pulled his hair in a parody of rage. The pieces floated up towards me and broke the surface tension of the pond inches from my face.

While I was questioning my sanity, and just a moment before I could bear the noxious waters no longer, the angry homunculus chanced to gaze up and spotted me looking down. The expression on his face must have mirrored my own. We were both paralysed with astonishment. For long moments, our eyes were meshed together by fibres of emotion impossible to understand. Then he darted back into his cottage and returned with an equally tiny woman. I assumed she was his wife. He pointed at the sky and together they gaped at me.

Panting, I pulled my head out of the pond and took a long deep gulp of air. I resisted the temptation to take another look at the submerged cottage. I had decided I was suffering from a form of madness or delirium. I resolved to forget the experience and make an appointment with a doctor as soon as possible. I left the pond and made my way slowly along the path to my home.

Yet as I walked, I started wondering again about the peculiar sight I had just witnessed. Supposing I was not mad? Supposing the phenomena had been real? I had heard many stories about falls of strange objects from the sky. There had been reports of fish, ice, betel nuts, coins, worms, eels, snails, snakes and frogs. This last item on the list made me shudder. I repressed this shudder and stroked my chin. Such objects were supposed to orbit the world in an eldritch region in the sky before falling, a region that lay in the margins of reality.

If this was true, then it was possible I was living in such a twilight realm myself and had been the cause of a strange shower in another world. The tiny man had obviously been trying to collect one of the falling kittens as proof of his bizarre experience. Probably he would have as much difficulty convincing his neighbours and friends of my existence as I would have convincing my own neighbours and friends of his. I decided to say nothing and to resume my life without ever mentioning even the submerged cottage again.

As I approached my home, I heard a thud behind me. I looked over my shoulder and saw the body of a tiny man slumped in the undergrowth. I thought at first that my diminutive neighbour had tried to follow me and had drowned in the air. But then another body fell into another clump of bushes and I looked up. The sky was full of little men sliding through the atmosphere with weights tied to their feet. And higher still, to my complete amazement, the face of an enormous kitten gazed down at me with eyes the size of seas.

My first reaction was to rush into my home and return with my wife, so there would be at least one other witness to this miracle. However, it occurred to me that if I could simply catch one of the tiny men alive it would be evidence enough. I had no nets, but I could use the old fashioned method. I had a sudden ludicrous image of a host of different dimensions impinging on each other, kittens hurling down men, men hurling down snakes, snakes hurling down frogs and frogs hurling down kittens...

I called out to my wife and then opened my mouth wider. My long sticky tongue snatched the little men from the air before they hit the ground and I stacked them in a little pile by my side. Naturally I swallowed a few. Life in the margins of reality does seem to have its advantages. It is not every day that guests just drop in for dinner.

The storyteller grins and flashes his eyes, which are unfortunately too yellow in an unhealthy way to be enigmatic, and then he folds his arms on his broad chest and tries to laugh in a hearty or imposing manner and he almost manages it, but maybe the atmosphere inside this ruined temple is too damp, for it comes out sounding more like a cough, the cough of a being with mould growing on the inside of his lungs, but eventually he recovers his composure.

"What did you think of the twist?" he demands.

"I can't accept that you were ever married," I reply, "it just seems too fanciful. I hate stories that are utterly implausible, so I can't say that was worth much. You've shortchanged me."

"What?" he bellows. "You dare to offer an insult?"

"I do indeed. It isn't difficult and much less daring than walking on a tightrope strung between the necks of two running giraffes, or taking an angel out on a successful date, especially if she chooses to go dancing in a nightclub located on a pinhead."

"By all the warts on my green back!"

He opens his huge mouth very wide. I should be alarmed but his story has reminded me of a personal experience that happened long ago, even before I was Emperor, and before I can decide whether to flee or pay him my promised tale set in outer space, I give him this one first, and I don't think he'll object because it's also about a little man, not one of the little men who fell out of the sky but a different little man who possibly looked similar. Anyway, it seems appropriate and it's very short, so I guess I'll be able to relate the whole of it before he finishes opening his mouth to its maximum extent, not that he really seems in a rush to do that, but all the same, this is what I say:

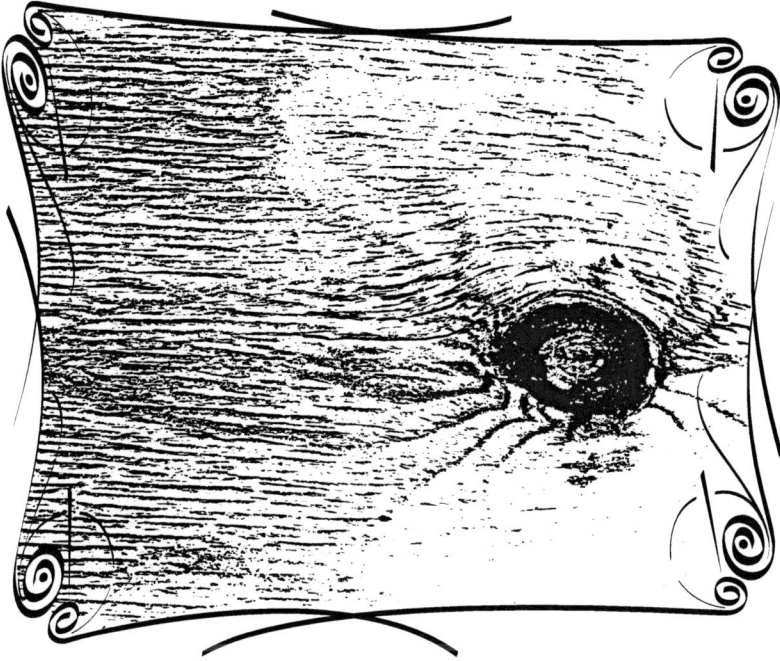

2- THE WOODEN SALESMAN

The wooden salesman knocked at my door. I opened it and he pushed his way into my house. I asked him to leave but he was as stubborn as a plank. "Ain't you twigged yet? I'm your sappy friend. Whatever you want in the way of arboreal products, I'll provide. I used to be a puppet in a seaside booth, now I'm branching out. You need a watchdog? I have the bark! A gallon of root beer? I'll distil it from my toes! Deciduous glazing? I can shed that from my elbows!"

I was an ordinary soldier, I had little money. When I told him this, he stroked his chin with his twigs and pondered. "No money you say? No problem, we'll barter. Use your musket to shoot the squirrel on my back, can you do that? I'm only marionette sized and he's almost as big as my head, keeps jumping from shoulder to shoulder, scratching my varnish off. I let him on because I had a terrible itch but now I regret that. Hunt him in exchange for some goods."

I agreed to this and soon had my gun loaded. A flash and a roar and a cloud of smoke and he breathed a sigh of relief. "Very good, I'm grateful. What would you like in return?"

Winter was over, the frost was melting, but I was a successful soldier as well as an ordinary one. In Corsica we carry off provisions instead of getting paid. I had a chest of tea under my bed. When I told him this, he turned the colour of autumn, but I was unrepentant. The kettle is the soldier's friend, it drives away the chill. To make it work, a fire is very important, and to make a fire work...

He was enough for one cup.

He wasn't all used up, there was a tiny bit left. It was no use to me, that fragment, but almost anything can be turned to a profit, so I decided to emulate his hard(wood) sell. I positioned it carefully in my window for all who passed to see and I wrote on the dirt of the glass with my finger in cold sap: KNOT FOR SALE.

I pause ever so briefly for effect, because I don't have time for a proper dramatic hiatus, but I can tell instantly that I'm wasting the very last fractions of my final seconds by doing this, because my companion isn't impressed at all, far from it. His frown is so deep that ants or even grasshoppers could conduct trench warfare in the wrinkles on his brow, so I cry out to justify myself:

"My story is false but more true than a lie."

"That is irrelevant," he roars, turning the widening of his mouth into a yawn. "I hate tales that end with a bad pun as a punchline and I don't accept your dismal joke — for it doesn't deserve the name of 'story' — as having any value whatsoever."

"In that case, we're quits."

"You are a mere human and I take issue with your sums. We are not quits. I will assault you for your impudence and hurl you down into another dimension, maybe to Hades, where the dog with many heads, I've forgotten how many, will chew you up and bury your bones even lower than Hades, if there is such a place, and I believe there is though I can't quite remember its name..."

I'm sure he is about to make a lengthy impassioned speech but just at that moment another figure enters the temple. I can't say I'm pleased by this outcome because the newcomer is none other than Hywel Price, the owner of the pub that became my prison. He is carrying a bundle over one shoulder, a rolled up tent, and he seems happy enough and fitter than before, and over his other shoulder he has balanced a small barrel which smells faintly of strong beer.

"Get out!" I cry, pretending to be concerned for his life but really just wanting to be free of him again. "This fellow here is a supernatural frog or some such thing and he's in a foul mood."

But Hywel steps closer and guffaws.

"No, he's not. I know his kind. He's not an amphibian but a potbellied council overseer who has lost his pot. Can't you tell?"

"Lost the plot? But there isn't one, just a series of tales forcibly linked by the contrived framing device we're in."

"No, his pot, the swelling of his belly!"

The figure in question sighs. "I admit it, I'm famished. In fact I'm the last of the potbellied council overseers, a sort of MonoSeer or All-Seer. I ate the others on orders from above. The plan was for the council to increase its efficiency and save money by reducing our staff to the more manageable level of one."

"Your pot must have been huge," I gasp, "and coincidentally enough, this has just reminded me of another story, which is about being fat, as fat as anyone could claim to be."

"I don't trust your tales," grumbles the Overseer, "they are so absurd they're boring. I want some suspension of disbelief. Imagine expecting me to believe that a Corsican would drink tea! I've done the paperwork and I know they only drink coffee."

"Yes, but I'm well travelled and I've developed a taste for all sorts of beverages. When I lived in South America…"

"You lived there?" Hywel raises an eyebrow.

"Of course. It was the nearest landmass to St Helena and the easiest place to escape to. That's where my tale is set, but it's not really my tale, it was told to me by my best friend in the village which I made my home before I came to Wales, and because my previous story was greeted with derision I'll tell this one as well, so nobody can accuse me of not pulling my weight, and talking about weight…"

3– TWO FAT MEN IN A VERY THIN COUNTRY

My friend Pepito must always be believed, even when he is telling lies. Exactly why this should be so is beyond my powers of explanation, but it's a tradition I'm reluctant to ignore, and thus I now place my hand over my heart and swear that the following tale is accurate in every fact. Pepito told it to me himself, while we rested under the orange tree which stands in the centre of my patio. Most of my body was in the shade but my boots stuck out in the noonday sun and the heat raised an odour from them that was not unlike soup.

He often relates anecdotes that have happened in distant lands. I suppose he travelled a lot in his youth. That must have been the case, for now he barely moves at all, except from house to house, kitchen to kitchen, with slow greed, as if he is trying to balance out or retract all his previous activity.

He began by asking me what I knew of Chile and I shrugged my shoulders. My ignorance seemed to offer him some mental relief and he scratched himself lazily before announcing:

"Well, it's a very long country.

"A long and thin country, like a piece of string used to parcel up the globe when the world was made. But somehow it remained behind when the rest of the wrapping was discarded, stuck there on the western edge of the South American continent. That is Chile.

"I would estimate — and it's just a guess, mind you — that it covers an area of 756,626 square kilometres, but all this territory must stretch some 4000 km from the tropics almost to the polar region, which means its average width is no more than 160 km. That's an unusual shape for a nation. Its capital is Santiago.

"Its major natural resources are coal, oil, iron ore, precious metals and timber. It has some of the biggest copper mines on the planet. The scenery is dramatic, with deserts in the north and glaciers in the south. It has a history of *relative* democracy. Its worst myth is the Chonchón, a loose head with gigantic ears for wings that often flies down chimneys. The Calchona is almost as bad, a kind of dog that snatches lunch baskets from mountain travellers, muttering sullen threats if anyone tries to follow.

"Fortunately these monsters are quite rare now.

"The sort of normal wildlife you might expect to find if you went there include guanacos, vicunas, coypus, pumas and condors. There are tamarugo trees, algarobas and monkey puzzles. Whether any of these latter have ever been solved is unknown to me at this time. Fish stocks off the coast are enormous, and fish stews on land also numerous, which brings me to the point, for I won't say *meat*, of my tale.

"There were two brothers who were known as the Grady Twins. They were big eaters and famous for it. It is possible they were the fattest men in existence. One was named Tobias and the other Oliver. They decided to take a voyage to Chile. They applied for visas and arrived in Santiago on the first day of summer.

"They had been growing rounder and rounder every year and their girth had caused them many practical problems for as long as either could remember, though nothing too serious, for they were used to lumbering about in wide countries. They had never stayed in such a thin one before. They had plenty of money in their pockets. Total disaster was inevitable.

"They found an outdoor restaurant and sat down to their first meal and that is where they remained for the whole of their trip! They devoured everything the country had to offer. I'm not sure what that is, but doubtless it includes bread, potatoes, rice, apples, beef, mutton, sardines, anchovies and whatever else can be found on local plates — but no chilli peppers, despite the aptness of the name. And they drank hundreds of bottles of wine.

"The days and weeks passed and they kept calling for more food. Before the summer was finished, they were both fatter than they had ever been. ¡Ay, Señor! they were too fat to fit in the country! They were wider than Chile! Do you doubt it?

"Well, this was an unexpected situation. They were facing east, and their stomachs grew and ripened over that chain of mountains called the Andes. The snows lay soft and thick on the tops of their bellies; but the brothers continued to stuff their mouths and their digestions rumbled like thunder in the high passes and some people thought an earth tremor had begun, but still they sat at their table and ordered more food and entire harvests vanished into their gaping maws.

"There is a country which borders Chile along the mountains. It is Argentina and it has different laws and customs and ideas. A visa that is valid for one is not necessarily accepted in the other. The Grady Twins had the correct paperwork for a stay in Chile but now their stomachs crossed the frontier into a separate state. They passed over illegally. The authorities were alerted.

"Right there, near the summit of Tupungato, the bellies of Tobias and Oliver were arrested and charged with unlawfully entering Argentina. A judge was sent for and a court was temporarily set up at the base of the mountain. The stomachs were found guilty and sentenced to an indefinite term of imprisonment!

"The jails were constructed around the straining abdomens, but each cell only had three walls, because the side where the stomachs came from had to be left open. All the same, the miscreants were in prison, and even the immense power of their digestions could not burst the bricks and iron bars asunder. The authorities smiled to themselves and went home, leaving a few guards to watch over each navel and to prod their captives with bayonets at the first signs of further trouble.

"Back in Santiago, the brothers were oblivious of what had occurred over the border, but they knew that they suddenly had stomach cramps. Further belly expansion was halted by the solid walls. As they continued to eat, the pressure increased. There might have been a detonation with unsavoury results if this anecdote was just a fictional tale but I have embellished no detail and therefore must report that this did not happen. They still called for more food, for they were also gluttons for punishment.

"It was the middle of autumn and between them they had nearly eaten Chile bare. The hot winds from the desert and the cold winds from the icecaps had always smelled hungry. Now all the other winds did too, even those from the temperate zones where the wheat ripples in fields and the fruit falls from branches. The country was like an empty cupboard. The only things left to eat were old boots. They are not tasty when boiled, basted, roasted, steamed or fried, but a boot sauce served on coils of its own laces *can* be sampled like a spaghetti dish. It may or may not be nourishing. A few men will walk far to try it, but rather more will hope it doesn't walk after them. Such now was the final item on every menu.

"Everybody knows there are good and bad boots. The latter pinch and squeak. Tobias had the misfortune to be served one of those. He refused to finish it. He threw down his fork and glowered at Oliver, who was chewing a more comfortable sole. From this moment their fates diverged. Tobias started to lose weight. This shouldn't be too remarkable a thing to occur, and so it wasn't, in the locality of the restaurant, but in Argentina, the amazed guards watched as one of their prisoners escaped.

"It was a slow escape, sure enough, and in many other parts of the world action would have been taken immediately to apprehend the belly before it vanished, but down there events often move sluggishly and every pant is a yawn, and by the time a decision had been made to prod the captive with a bayonet, it was gone. It had fled at glacier velocity out of the open side of the jail and back over the border. Eventually Tobias became just a very fat man again, rather than an international incident.

"The authorities were determined to guard the remaining stomach more carefully, but the bother of keeping watch over it constantly, while there were more important matters to attend to elsewhere, such as barbecues and football matches, was too much to contemplate eternally, which was the span of time that the wobbling paunch had to serve before it became eligible for parole, on the recommendation of the judge. So a retrial was ordered and a new sentence was passed — death by firing squad!

"¡Ay! That was a sure way of eliminating the problem for all time. The cell was demolished to give the men with the rifles a clear aim. Then a runner was dispatched to inform the man far behind the belly of his impending doom. It was a tradition to ask the condemned prisoner if he had a final request. The runner applied for a visa, crossed the border into Chile and reached the restaurant in Santiago.

"He whispered his message into the ear of Oliver, who absorbed it at his leisure while munching on the tongue of a boot, his own tongue curling around it as if he was kissing his dinner to adulterate its leathery taste with the flavour of passion, which has no eyes and is blind, of course. And coincidentally this was his millionth *course*. But after just a little more thought, he nodded to himself and gave the runner a message of his own to deliver to the firing squad. Then he resumed eating.

"Oliver's stomach had been sentenced to be shot at sunrise. But he had asked if it could be shot at sunset instead, the sunset of the day previous to the ordained one. The authorities and guards scratched their heads at this, for it seemed their prisoner was hurrying them along; that he wished to die sooner rather than later. But they agreed to the proposal, partly because it was a final request and they were bound by honour to fulfil it, and partly because it meant they could leave work early.

"The firing squad raised and aimed its rifles. Every man present waited for the moment of sunset. It never came. The sky went dark and filled with stars, but at no point did the sun actually go down. After a night of debate, the mystery was resolved. The vast stomach had created an eclipse, blotting out not only the sunset but much of the western horizon. Then they understood that their prisoner had cheated them, for they would never be able to execute the belly at the moment of sunset, for there was no longer such a time. They would be stuck here for the rest of Oliver's life, waiting in vain, and the barbecues would go cold and the football matches be won or lost, and forgotten, without them.

"Another solution had to be found. If a condemned man survives or avoids his execution, he probably deserves to be pardoned and released. The same surely applies to bellies. It was decided to pardon this one, together with its contents and weather, for the interior was a cavern vast enough to contain clouds and other atmospheric phenomena. Now the guards could leave it to its own devices. It was as free as any other gorge in the Andes, though entirely different in all but word.

"The unspoken worry of those who left was that it would now proceed on its voyage into Argentina unopposed, crushing everything in its path, but circumstances conspired against this, because a coup overthrew the legitimate government of Chile and a military dictatorship took over. The boots were recalled from Oliver's plate to serve the feet of the soldiers, and so he went hungry. His stomach retreated of its own accord. Remember that Chile only has a history of *relative* democracy and this was one of those times when stupidity and cruelty marched over it, in boots originally collected for supper.

"When Oliver was slim enough to move again, he stood and walked with his brother out of the restaurant. Both had a terrible stomach ache and awful wind. Soon after, they left Chile. Neither of the Grady Twins ever returned. They settled in a wider land where many people wore slippers instead of boots, far to the east. India it was, I believe. If they attempted such a feast again, it has not been recorded. I imagine that their breath, which smelled of leather, fell foul of some law and that their mouths were caged, which would prevent their stomachs from going anywhere alone. That would certainly be for the best…"

Pepito halted his ridiculous story for two reasons. Firstly, the sun had moved the shadow of the orange tree over my feet, and my boots no longer smelled edible. Secondly, he had finished. We sat in the silence of the patio. Then he fell asleep. When he awoke he promised to tell me similar tales about every country in the world, so I quickly locked up my house with heavy chains and the following day I left the village forever. I didn't know where I was going, nor did I care, so long as it was far from him. He was my most inspirational friend.

The recounting of this tale has created a tear of nostalgia in the eye of the Overseer, who wipes it carefully away with a finger, studies it suspiciously as if it's an example of globular paperwork, and wails, "My poor pot! All gone!"

"How did you lose it?" Hywel wonders.

"It was famine that was responsible. All that absorption for nothing! I require medical attention to return it to its former girth. Do you happen to know a doctor who can do that?"

Hywel sets his tent and barrel down on the ground. "As a matter of fact I remember hearing about two such medical men, deadly rivals so it's rumoured, one named Dr Vaughan and the other called Dr Frazer, both experts at weird medicine. I know two tales about them, one from the past and one from the future."

"Are either of them true?" I enquire.

"There's a gap of a century between them," ponders Hywel, "so I suppose one of them might be true, but not both. And yet if the past one is false it is definitely false because it will absolutely not have happened, whereas if the future tale's the lie, it'll only be potentially untrue because it hasn't not happened yet..."

"That is rather confusing," I answer.

"He talks like a god," mutters the Overseer, "and what's that in his pocket? A lightning bolt? Is he Zeus, come to punish me for my deceit? I'm sorry for posing as a frog."

Hywel shakes his head. "No, mun, it's not that."

"But that's what it looks like."

"Nothing of the sort." Hywel lifts it out and I see that it is a shard of broken glass, or to be more accurate a piece of a smashed mirror. There is a reflection in its zigzag surface.

"Is that part of the Impossible Mirror?" I ask.

Hywel nods. "After my pub was destroyed in an explosion caused by a bomb (how could we forget that, Bony?) the mirror over my bar, which reflected scenes that weren't happening, was reduced to fragments. I picked up this one as a memento, because it was the largest surviving piece and also to keep myself amused."

I peer closer at the reflection. It shows workmen carrying a complete mirror into a rebuilt pub and fitting it on the wall. I watch as they fix it in place. "Is this scene from the future?"

"I imagine so," agrees Hywel. "It's clear that my pub is going to be constructed again and fitted out in an identical fashion to before, even down to the inclusion of another Impossible Mirror. But I wonder who is my successor, the next landlord?"

"There's a reflection inside that other mirror."

"How odd! It shows two people, a man and a woman, holding hands on a beach. An impossible image inside another impossible image means what? Do the two impossibilities negate each other or do they multiply to a greater level of impossibility?"

"Is it possible to have gradations of impossibility?" asks the Overseer, his jowls wobbling.

"Oh yes… For instance a flying piglet is impossible and so is a square circle, but the first is less impossible than the second, because it doesn't exist but the other can't even be conceived."

"I don't recognise the couple," I say. "The image is too small to make out details. If one Impossible Mirror shows scenes from past or future, a Double Impossible Mirror shows what?"

"Scenes from sideways in time?" suggests Hywel.

"This conversation is becoming too obscure for me," the Overseer sniffs, "I'm just a simple bureaucratic bully!"

"Too obscure for us as well, mun! So obscure I doubt we are having it. Somebody else must be doing the talking and we are attributing what it is saying to each other. The substance of our discussion doesn't seem typical of any of us, and I can state that with confidence even though I've only just met you, because you're the sort of man who pretends to be a frog in his spare time."

I grimace. "How can there be another voice in this room? There are only three of us here."

"It's perfectly feasible for a voice to exist without a mouth. You don't believe me? But I know a tale precisely about such a phenomenon. Why don't I tell it to you now?"

And that's what he does.

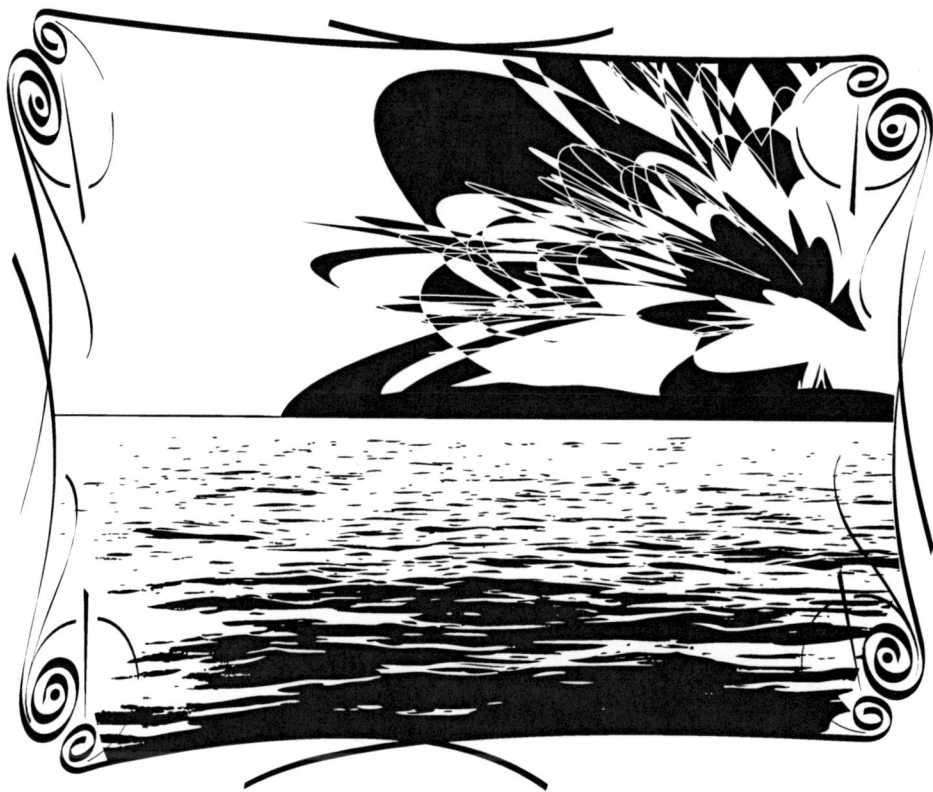

4- THE MAN WHO THREW HIS VOICE

There was a man called Amos who could throw his voice. He could make it appear from inside boxes and jugs and teapots; but one day, he threw it so far that he lost it. The window of his kitchen had been left open and the voice sailed out into the afternoon, landing with a gurgle in the river. Down to the river rushed Amos but it was too late; his voice was nowhere to be heard.

Dejectedly, he walked along the riverbank, pausing every so often to bend toward the water and listen carefully, but his voice seemed to have sunk without trace. Perhaps it had been covered by silt on the riverbed? As he walked, he met Hiram, the fishmonger, who was fishing from the bank with a net attached to a long pole.

"You look very miserable today," Hiram remarked. "What's the matter?"

Amos used signs and gestures to explain what had happened. Hiram raised an eyebrow and nodded.

"I see. Well your voice, I'm sorry to say, was caught by the current and is heading downstream at this very moment. I tried to net it as it went past but I wasn't quick enough. It shouted out that it had a message for you but I couldn't make out the words. I suggest that you pursue it now, before it reaches the ocean."

Amos considered this advice. Finally, he rushed back into his house, packed a few belongings and dug up the silver he kept hidden in his cellar. Down at the wharf he used the silver to buy a small boat with an engine, threw his bag of provisions into the back and cast off onto the river, making for midstream where the current was strongest. Before long, he had left the town and his old life far behind.

As often as possible, when he spied a lone traveller walking or sitting beside the river, he would pull in toward them and silently inquire whether they had heard a voice recently and whether it had said anything to them. Invariably, he received the same reply:

"Yes, we heard a voice, and it had a message for you, but the words it spoke were all muffled and indistinct, as if the speaker was below water. We could make out nothing of what it said. Yet its tone was urgent. Hurry if you wish to catch up with it, hurry!"

Within a day or two, Amos arrived at his first city, a crumbling collection of ponderous gothic buildings dominated by an enormous windowless castle, a grim monument to a more troubled age that reminded him of a gigantic inverted bedstead. He moored his boat to the rotting timbers of a wooden jetty and sauntered among the taverns of the Belváros, the waterfront area, repeating his soundless plea for information about his missing voice.

Only in one particularly seedy dive was he at all successful. The landlord of this dubious establishment confessed that the voice had been there not more than a couple of hours earlier. Wiping tall glasses with a grimy cloth, he added:

"It told me that, while floating down the river, it had lodged itself on one of the pillars of our stone bridge. The bridge in question has so many arches and supports it would have been more surprising had it not been stopped. It was rescued by a child who lowered a jar on a length of string. The child placed the voice in its pocket, but there was a hole in the lining of the fabric and it fell out. It then made its way to the nearest tavern, which happened to be this one."

Amos nodded impatiently and begged the landlord to continue. The landlord squinted and sighed and scratched his greasy head.

"Well, it also said that it had an urgent message for you. Very urgent, apparently, but just as it was about to tell me what it was, a group of drunken sailors came through the door shouting and singing. The words of the voice were drowned out and then some of the sailors spied the voice and decided to have some sport with it. They took it outside and tossed it back into the river. This time, it passed under one of the arches of the bridge and disappeared."

Amos thanked the landlord, returned to his boat and set off once more. He too passed under the bridge, a structure so weighed down by stone statues that it seemed to be sinking lower into the water even as he watched. He started his engine and sped off in a wash of green foam and flotsam.

Over the next fortnight, he encountered nearly a dozen other cities, but it was the same story in all of them. The voice had often been retrieved from the river but somehow, due to a mishap, it had quickly been returned there. Each time, the people he met admitted that the voice had left a message for him, but nobody could reveal what the message was. It seemed, however, to be growing more and more desperate, almost to the point of hysteria.

Naturally, the nature of the message had excited his curiosity to the point where he was not afraid to indulge the wildest speculations. He knew it was a message of the greatest consequence. Perhaps the voice had discovered the location of buried treasure on its unwanted journey? He dearly hoped this was the case. Indeed, he managed to convince himself that this slender possibility was an indisputable fact.

He slept little. He was convinced he was gaining on his voice. But then, one dull afternoon, his engine clattered to a halt. He thought at first that weeds had tangled the propeller, but the truth was even more mundane than this. He had run out of petrol. He attempted many times to buy petrol from the towns and villages he drifted past, but he had crossed the border into a country which still used steam power and which had no knowledge even of crude oil. He had no money left to buy another boat and nobody was keen to exchange a new one for his own.

And so, gnashing his teeth, he was forced to drift on the current, painfully aware his voice was speeding ahead and that he had lost the prize that had been almost within his grasp. His despair was like a large piece of tropical fruit; a succulent taste made dishonest with the hard seeds of regret. He drifted with tear-blind eyes right down to the sea where he abandoned his boat in a sprawling trading city and spent a whole day gazing out at the blue green ocean in a state of profound misery.

Misery became the keyword of his life for the next year. He failed to find a job in the port, attempted to catch his own food with a rod and line but only managed to hook a few old boots and the bloated corpse of a drowned dog. Eventually he became a destitute beachcomber, living in a shack made from seaweed and driftwood on the vermilion sands that fringed the city. The city itself depressed him; dirty grey buildings piled up on each other, twisted steel and rusty iron, concrete chimneys with asthma, the cries of a million mice.

At any rate, his existence appeared to have lost all meaning when, walking along the shore in a morning drizzle, he chanced upon a rich merchant who offered him employment on a leaky galleon. The merchant had decided to solicit the services of the homeless and dispossessed after a fruitless quest to find a crew in the docklands of the city.

"It is a dangerous voyage that I am proposing. The sailors in the taverns are superstitious cowards. They refuse to consider my offer. I intend, you see, to sail into the uncharted waters of the west in the hope of discovering new lands to trade with. A risky venture to be sure, a gamble of sorts, but one that could have stupendous benefits for anyone brave enough to accept."

Amos accepted at once, not only because he had nothing to lose but also because he still harboured a secret hope that he might hear news of his misplaced voice, and more importantly, actually have its message revealed to him. The thought of all that buried treasure lying unclaimed while he was penniless had been a bitter blow indeed.

And so Amos became a lowly deckhand. The merchant, it turned out, had chosen a hard taskmaster as captain, but Amos worked with such patience and enthusiasm that he was respected by all. Because he was always silent, he earned even more admiration in the eyes of Captain Dangleglum.

"I like a man who knows how to hold his tongue," the captain confessed to him once. "I used to have a first mate who blabbered all the time. I made sure he held his tongue too. Literally." And here Captain Dangleglum laughed and rolled his bloodshot eyes. He had been a pirate until very recently and was rescued from the city jail by the merchant. "I cut it off with a rusty blade too," he added. "Oh yes! Only parrots should blabber."

Old habits die hard. So hard sometimes that they even manage to squirm after their heads have been lopped. On the way to the mysterious west, Captain Dangleglum took time to loot and sink a merchantman heavily laden with yellow spices. The unfortunate crew of that ship was left to drift in a longboat with one sail the size of a pocket handkerchief. As they sailed off toward the horizon, Amos could not resist a polite wave.

He felt as calm as the sea itself on days when there were no clouds to merge sky and wide watery expanse into an unmanageable whole. He spent his free time leaning over the rails of the deck, studying the shoals of fish and squid that flew beneath his gaze. He was listening out for his voice, which he assumed would have learned a siren song or two by now.

They discovered islands in due course; tiny outcroppings of paradise with lagoons and beaches of crushed bone. Captain Dangleglum named each island after a semi-precious stone; for, with the exception of drinking rum, the collecting of such stones was his chief delight in life. On Topaz they traded flour for gold and old rope for new string; on Jasper they traded cheese, swords and rats for yoghurt, clubs and cats. The cats licked all the yoghurt but they recouped their profits on Amethyst, where fat cats are highly prized as paperweights.

And so they hopped from one opportunity to another, growing richer by degrees. Amos found his own opportunity at each port of call, for Captain Dangleglum invariably used him as an interpreter. Since losing his voice he had become something of an expert at universal sign language. When the Captain officially promoted him to this position, he was allowed to take a share of any goods that passed hands in a deal. Before long he had saved stock of a value equal to the silver he had originally owned.

One humid night, unable to sleep, Amos sauntered onto the deck to breathe more freely under the shimmering stars. He thought at first that he was alone, but a sudden laugh made him jump. Captain Dangleglum was standing in the crow's nest, swinging an empty bottle of rum and talking to

135

the moon. Amos tried to call out to him to be careful but without a voice this proved to be an impossible task. Even as he watched, the inevitable happened. Captain Dangleglum spotted Amos, attempted to climb back down the rigging, lost his balance and landed with a sickening crunch on the wooden planks of the deck.

The ship remained without a Captain for no longer than a day. When the first mate finally managed to force the lock on the Captain's old sea chest in his cluttered cabin, he found a will among the pearls and oysters. The will named Amos as the Captain's successor. The first mate was evidently disappointed but did not put up much of a resistance and Amos found himself wearing an ill-fitting tunic and commanding a generally loyal but smelly crew.

He used his new authority to turn his quest into more than an obsession. He navigated with the one aim of finding his voice. Trade became very much a secondary consideration. He followed up the slightest murmuring of a clue. Once he chanced upon an island inhabited by a shipwrecked sailor. The sailor was the sole survivor of an earlier trading mission funded by the same merchant Amos had met in the port.

"Yes, I saw your voice," the sailor announced. "We were sailing some miles north of here when I heard a terrible cry. I looked out to sea and spied your voice in the clutches of an enormous octopus. It called out that it had a message for you but naturally the octopus dived down beneath the waves before it could elaborate."

Amos was so angered by this revelation that he not only forced the sailor back onto the uninhabited island but also marooned some of his own crew there as well. Like Captain Dangleglum, he took eagerly to rum and wrote messages to his voice that he enclosed in the empty bottles and cast overboard. Unlike his predecessor, he neglected to share the profits of trade with his crew. When the men began grumbling, he reinstated the tradition of plank walking. The first mate was the first to step off into space, the second and third mates were second and third.

Power corrupted him with astonishing efficiency. In rare bouts of sobriety, he realised this, but did nothing to reverse the downward spiral. Only when he encountered a more physical form of downward spiral was he shaken out of his intense self-absorption.

The spiral in question was a gargantuan whirlpool on the very edges of reality. The existence of such a whirlpool had not come as a complete surprise, for there were old legends, but the sheer scale and grandeur of this maelstrom astounded everyone. As his crew had hoped, Amos immediately ordered a retreat but then he paused and held up a hand for silence. Amid the rushing of waters, he had caught the ghost of a sigh.

Much to the consternation of his men, he cancelled his order and urged the ship toward the whirlpool. He seemed excited and agitated; he raced to the bow of the ship, clung precariously to the figurehead and held up an ear-horn, straining to catch an echo of the sigh. Sure enough he heard it again and dropped his ear-horn in delight. He had finally caught up with his voice! His crew, however, did not share his enthusiasm.

As they neared the whirlpool, they started muttering to each other and fingering the hilts of their cutlasses. Amos was oblivious to all this, for he had seen his voice and it was calling out to him. It had been caught in the vortex of the whirl and was rotating on the lip of the abyss. Amos managed to catch a word or two each time it span round, phasing in and out of audibility and coherence, but the content of the message still eluded him. And then he ceased to catch anything at all as a blow from a cutlass sent him reeling.

His crew treated him courteously, which was more than he deserved, once they discovered he was still alive. They imprisoned him in his cabin and allowed him the occasional meal of bread and water. When they reached the port they had initially set out from, they gave him a minor share of the cargo and released him.

This minor share was still large enough to keep him in comfort for the rest of his days. He bought a fine house and a large aviary, where he kept a collection of parrots, each trained to speak a different word. Whenever he entertained guests, he would simply point to a sequence of parrots to produce a sentence.

He increased his vocabulary daily by adding parrots to his collection. The parrots who had to speak words such as 'the' and 'I' were quickly worn out and grew surly and indolent. They had to be replaced. He spent a great deal of money both on his aviary and in employing men to search for his voice. So much money that, within a year, he had once again succeeded in reducing his fortune to the sum he had originally possessed. One night, he dreamed that his voice was telling him its message, but in the morning he had forgotten it.

This was the final stroke. He felt a longing to return to his hometown. It suddenly seemed less important that he regain his voice.

He sold his house, distributed the money he received from the sale to the beggars of the city and set loose his parrots. They flew over the dirty buildings in a blaze of green, blue and yellow. As they soared, they each cast off the word they had learned. These words fell to earth in a sequence that purely by chance formed the most beautiful poem that could ever be written. A penniless poet happened to be passing underneath at the time and was startled by this poem. He wrote it down and consequently became famous, rich and almost happy.

Meanwhile, Amos decided to walk down to the beach for a final glimpse of the sea. He kicked through the dark sands toward the shack that had once been his house. The ocean surged over his shoes, green bubbles of froth playing around his ankles. The rotting shack had tipped over like the gnomon of a sundial and now told the time by the light of the morning sun. Its new occupant was a monstrous lugworm that poked its head out at Amos and made a wry, wormy face. Amos sighed.

As he stood in the sea, counting the clouds that rimmed the horizon in long orange segments, a ripple in the water ahead of him attracted his attention. Something was bobbing there. As he peered closer, Amos saw it was a bottle with vague contents. Whatever these contents were, they were struggling to get out. As the bottle swept past him, he reached down and snatched it up. Something dry and wheezy rustled within. Amos held the bottle upside down and out fell his voice! He was speechless; in other words, his arms would not move.

"Well," said the voice at length. "We meet again at last. Who would have thought it possible? Not I, certainly. But there it is and here we are! I have so many tales to tell. How much time do you have to spare? And do you have anything to eat on you?"

Eventually, Amos recovered enough composure to scratch an answer to this question with his forefinger in the damp sand. He wrote: *Much Time, No Food.* And then he danced for joy, his gold necklaces jangling together with his brass and tin ones, so that he sounded like a forged phoenix in angry flight. With the toe of a foot he added: *Ha!*

But the voice ignored his expressions of delight and embarked on a long account of its adventures. By the time it had finished, the sun was going down on the opposite horizon and the shack told the time once more and the lugworm poked out its head again and yawned. But still Amos danced and clapped his hands and wrote in the sand with his other foot.

Words and more words, silent words and loud ones. The voice had grown hoarse and finished its tale with a croak. "Well, I was sucked into the whirlpool and emerged on the other side of the world. I floated back in due course, found an empty bottle and climbed into it. Inside, I discovered a message you had written to me. From careful analysis of the paper and ink, I guessed that your ship had set sail from this port and would return here. So I steered the bottle by blowing in the appropriate direction."

While the voice had been telling its story, Amos had been writing out his, in between jumps and whirls and spins. In lovely copperplate footwriting, he outlined everything his voice might have wanted to know. And so they were reconciled to each other. But there was still the one burning question. Amos did not need to write anything to demand it. The question concerned the voice's message.

"My message was simply this," replied the voice, and it took a deep breath. "A man is defined by his actions, not by his words. So DON'T BOTHER TO FOLLOW ME! That was the message. It had nothing to do with buried treasure."

The following day, Amos took his voice back to his hometown and together they lived in their old house. Indeed, they are still there. Amos continues to throw his voice, but now it is safely secured to his throat with the string of meaning. And the boxes and the jugs still hum and the teapot whistles melodies.

While relating this story, Hywel has been setting up his tent, pegging it firmly into the packed earth that forms the floor of the temple. Now the tale is finished and the tent is up, and so he sounds his own little whistle and turns to me with these words:

"My fate has always been to run a pub and so I've devised a plan to keep me as a landlord despite the explosion which obliterated my former premises. This tent is a beer tent, the sort of thing they have in carnivals and travelling fairs, and here is a barrel of ale which I can pour into glasses and sell to whoever enters."

"A bit small for a tavern, isn't it?"

"That's the clever part. It's made from the fabric of a helium balloon and we all know that such fabric is called the 'envelope' of the balloon. Stories which are startling and original and have never been told before are often described as 'pushing the envelope' of literature. If they can do that — expand an artform — then surely they can increase the volume of a simple tent? I will continue to demand stories as payment from all my customers and any innovative tales will swell the tent bigger and bigger, making more room for more customers. The sky really is the limit for the expansion of my new premises!"

"I'm not sure that will work. Your logic is linguistically driven rather than based on physical cause and effect."

"So what? We are in a narrative now, so everything that happens is created by language, it's all we have. Come on, Bony, crawl into this tent with me and have a tankard of ale, you too Mr Overseer, whatever your real name is, for it's time to toast the opening of my new pub, don't know what to call it though."

"How about THE AWFULLY TALL STORY?" I suggest.

"Yes, I like the word 'awful', it's appropriate! Hey, it's not so bad in here after all, a bit stuffy and dismal and vile, that's all. Who is going to buy the first round of drinks?"

"I will…I know a story… A cracking tale…"

"Who said that? Was that you, Bony? Or was it you, Mr Overseer? I can't see a thing, it's too dark."

"Neither of us," I reply. "It was the disembodied voice again."

"From below," adds the phoney frog.

Suddenly the ground opens under us and a head pushes its way out. A figure emerges into the tent from subterranean regions, a match is struck and in the few seconds of wobbling light we all perceive this newcomer, a man of confused aspect caked in dirt, a shovel in one hand, worms behind his ears and in his nostrils.

"This isn't a temple! Where am I?"

The match burns down to his fingers and he drops it, extinguishing the flame and plunging us back into gloom, but I have seen enough to know that he is an archaeologist who purely by chance has burrowed up into the tent, in other words a real man with a mouth rather than a voice without a man, and I am reassured.

"What can I get you?" asks Hywel.

"Thank you, I could do with a drink. Digging through centuries is thirsty work and I'm parched."

"Is that because archaeology is a dry subject?"

"No rains fall on the past and no rivers flow there, because what has gone no longer exists, that's why!"

"You have to pay with a story," adds Hywel.

"Of course," comes the reply, and here comes his tale, which he told with an excessive quantity of smirks:

5– THE SEALED ROOM

The two archaeologists were alone at last. They sat around a small fire, listening to the sounds of the desert. Night had fallen like a languorous wink; the sky was already full of myriad points of light. The exposed ramparts and walls of the excavations formed an impressive silhouette against the paler stars of the horizon.

"This is a fairly straightforward dig," Newton said, lighting his pipe and gazing out over the deep blue sands, "but I had a strange one last year. So strange that I've kept my findings secret. Do you know the legend of Gilgamesh? The tale has it that he discovered a plant that would confer eternal life on anyone who consumed it, but that a snake devoured it first. Well I discovered an untranslated sequel on clay tablets."

Samuel was astonished. "Really? Where did you find it? What did it say?"

"It claimed that, shortly afterwards, an itinerant musician unwittingly killed the snake and ate it. The undigested plant in the snake's stomach passed into his own. When he suddenly realised he was immortal, he returned to his village. He had been exiled because his music was so bad. He had been warned not to return on pain of death. Now, of course, such warnings meant nothing to him. When the villagers saw him again, they threw rocks at him. But his cuts and bruises healed almost instantly."

Samuel scratched his nose. A smile played upon his lips, but then he saw that his colleague was in earnest. "Well?" He wrapped tightly into his cloak.

"The musician went back to his old house and continued singing his dreadful songs. There was nothing the villagers could do to stop him. Each time they tried to kill him, his flesh reformed. They burned him at the stake, garrotted him, cut him into quarters, threw him down a well and used poison. But all to no avail. Whenever they physically carried him out into the desert, he came back. Even when they attempted to evacuate the village, he simply followed them."

"Bizarre!" Samuel was almost lost for words. He coughed and tried to change the subject. He pointed to a bundle by Newton's feet. "What have you got in there? You've been carrying it around all week."

Newton ignored him. "Eventually, the village elders decided they had no choice but to imprison him in a secure dungeon. So they constructed a room deep underground with stone walls. The room had no doors and no windows. They overpowered the musician, stripped him of his clothes, threw him into the room and sealed it. Then they piled tons of sand over the top. In short, he was trapped with no food, no light, no warmth and certainly nothing to make music with. In celebration, they impaled his lute on a spear and paraded it around the village for forty days. That was the story."

"And you decided to look for this room?" Samuel raised a cynical eyebrow. "And you located it, I suppose? And managed to enter it? And the musician was still alive inside it?" His mocking laugh trailed off into silence.

"Not only alive, but living like a king! I expected to find a bare stone cell inhabited by a naked madman, but instead I found a chamber decked out with plush carpets and hung with elaborate tapestries, brightly lit by orange candles, containing a table on which was piled platters of food and cups of wine, with a soft bed in one corner and a throne on which sat a figure dressed in finery…"

"I don't understand."

"Remember that he was immortal. His flesh would always reform. What he had done was to create such furnishings from his own body. He had used his hair to weave fabrics, his bones to make furniture, his earwax to mould the candles. The food was muscle sliced from his limbs, the wine was blood fermented with yeasts from his stomach. The tapestries were huge flapping sheets of skin, inked with bodily fluids and threaded with veins and arteries. Sinews and tendons had been used to bind femurs and vertebrae together to build his bed. Hearts, brains and livers had been used to create pillows and soft cushions. Did you know that one human body contains enough iron to make a three-inch nail and enough phosphorus to make a match? And he had an infinite number of bodies at his disposal. All of them his own."

"That is utterly grotesque!" Samuel, who had investigated the contents of more than one canopic jar, could not repress a shudder. He wrinkled up his face in disgust.

"Not as grotesque as what follows. When I jumped into the chamber, through the hole I had made in one of the walls, the fellow seemed delighted. He had made a lute out of his sternum, a couple of thighbones and a dozen strung nerves. He had been composing songs ever since he had been entombed seven thousand years before. Now that he had an audience, he saw his opportunity to perform them. They were appalling beyond belief. He used a fingernail plectrum. I screamed and managed to escape back through the hole. With hysterical gestures, I ordered my workers to seal it up again. Such music should never be allowed to terrorise the world! That is why I have kept the location of the room to myself. My workers afterwards told me that my appearance had completely changed, as if I had entered the chamber a young man and emerged as one with the burden of centuries on his shoulders. I had even forgotten how to speak English. The music was that bad!"

Finally, Samuel could contain himself no longer. He burst into a fit of giggles, clutching his sides and shaking his head. "That is the most ridiculous tale I have ever heard! Tell me that you're lying! I'll never be able to take you seriously again if you don't!"

"You're right. It's just a story I made up to entertain you. Just to pass the time." Newton's eyes twinkled darkly. "Tell you what, why don't I play some songs for you as well? That should take us to morning. At the very least." Reaching down to the bundle at his feet, he carefully unwrapped a bone white lute. He snapped off a fingernail and smiled. When he struck the first chord, the screams were in perfect harmony.

The tale is finished but we remain in a posture of listening, as if genuinely scared by what might happen next, even though in truth we are too weary and experienced to feel instinctive fear. Indeed our best terrors now are nearly all acted out, which isn't to say that we are brave fellows, simply that living in a fantastical story instead of the real world means we automatically suffer less psychological trauma than flesh and blood folks, and we can cope with sequences of monsters and horrors in rapid succession, whereas you probably need half a year to recover from meeting a single werewolf. But to return to the point, we sat quietly until Hywel cut the air with a whisper.

"I suppose you're going to tell us you are Newton and that you want to play us one of your tunes?"

"This is a spade, not a lute, and my name is Karl Mondaugen. I don't care for music, even the worst sort."

"Mondaugen? Impossible! I was his friend. There's not the slightest resemblance. You look nothing like him when he was alive and nothing like him after he blew himself to bits."

"That's because one of the last things I invented was myself and that second self had all my abilities, including an aptitude for invention, and one of the things it invented was another version of me. I'd already been invented once, so this was a reinvention. We all know that reinventions of personalities look different from the originals; they dress differently, behave differently, move away from their former territories and try to cultivate new friends. This is what I did and it explains how I'm here and why you don't recognise me."

"Will this process continue indefinitely? How long before the planet is swamped with Mondaugens?"

"Several hundred thousand years. Or maybe they have already taken over. If they are all reinventions and look different, how will anyone tell? Maybe you are versions of him too."

Hywel remains unimpressed. "Mondaugen was a leading authority on shapeshifters. If you're really him, you'll know which is harder to change into, a Dandrum or a Bugaboo?"

"Both at once, but that's simple compared with shifting into a seat already warmed by someone else!"

"Welcome back to the fold," I say, convinced by this answer. "How have you been since your death?"

"Dark and dirty. I decided to conduct my digs in a different manner from the norm. Archaeology is a subject I've long been interested in, but I despise the way professionals burrow through all the layers in reverse chronological order! It isn't right to learn about an ancient culture in the wrong direction, starting with the most recent remains and delving down for the more and more primitive."

"What was your solution to this problem?"

"I've discovered a secret passage deep in the Earth's crust, almost a corridor, and I walk along it until I am directly under a relevant site, which I then ascend into, digging up through its history in the correct order of progress, Stone Age, Bronze Age, Iron Age, Rubbish Age, and so on, until I break the surface and finally reach the present. That's what I thought I was doing now but I must have miscalculated because this isn't the enigmatic temple I was expecting. It's a sort of a cloth cave, very smelly and rather unpleasant."

"My beer tent," explains Hywel. "This is a travelling pub. In fact it's time we moved on to a new location, which is the whole point of being a nomadic landlord, so I suggest I dismantle it now and sling it over my back. I hope you've noted it has already increased in size thanks to the tale about Samuel and Newton."

I sniff derisively. "By a few millimetres."

Hywel pulls down the tavern around us and we are back in the temple and the rain has stopped outside. Mondaugen the archaeologist blinks his grimy eyes. "This is more like it!"

"What do you think?" I enquire.

But then he shakes his head and pouts. "I'd say there's something not quite right about this building."

I test my theory. "Is it Greek?"

"No, I think it's Borgesian, a temple of the Borgesian God of Fire. They always look like circular ruins even when they are put up for the first time. That's my best guess."

I nod sombrely but Hywel has a different opinion. "To me, the whole thing looks exactly like a fake. I mean I suspect it might be a work of art, maybe even by a modern artist, rather than a genuine place of ancient mystery. It's an ironic pastiche."

"What sort of sculptor would do that?" I sniff.

"An abnormal one, I'm sure, but there are plenty of mad artists in the world. Actually I knew a very mad one called Rodin Guignol who carved a rising sun, hoisted it over the sea, couldn't get it as far as midday: the chain broke and it splashed down in an accelerated sunset. Sank to the bottom and there it remains, all the rays smashed off. That part of the ocean is still always dark, but every so often one of the loose rays is washed up on a beach elsewhere at night and illuminates the sands. Sometimes these rays are collected and heaped together like the sticks of a fire, but they don't need to be lit, and people can dance around them until the real morning comes…"

The Overseer, who has been feeling neglected, raises his voice, "I also know a story about a sculptor."

And before we can stop him he bawls it out.

6– THE MASTERPIECE

The artist was a tall man with narrow shoulders; he held his umbrella as if it was a monstrous paintbrush. Ruddy and fierce, with protruding lips, he in no way resembled those young bohemians who shared his quarter of the old town. Whenever he entered a café for a glass of beer, he sat rigid and aloof, ignoring their wild laughter and wilder gestures. His hungers were as extreme as theirs, but he practised restraint.

Afterwards, he would wipe his mouth with a clean handkerchief, leave a small tip and nod briefly to his fellow drinkers. Wrapping his scarf tightly around his face, he would make off down the cobbled Michalská towards the gothic Dóm, his eyes like black buttons. On the edges of the building site at the base of the Hrad, he would often find the materials he sought. Scrap metal, broken glass, rotting wood.

He lived in a small apartment overlooking a muddy square. Rusty trams clattered past his window, keeping him awake at night. The room he slept in was also his studio; he had broken up most of the furniture to be used as firewood. Generally he ate his meals cold, sometimes without being able to tell the difference. Beneath the floorboards, he kept a selection of Hungarian wines and spirits.

He had come to Bratislava from the east, a remote region that had stamped its mark on his perception. He enjoyed the sights of the city rather more than the frequent Czech and Austrian tourists. His one hope had been to find a tolerant audience for his unique sculptures. With surprisingly elegant fingers, he welded steel to iron; twisting the arms of industrial refuse into new life. His bizarre creations hung from the ceiling on a system of pulleys. Each, in its own way, was a masterpiece.

His latest triumph was a grotesque tangle of blades and spikes, a vast and uncouth abstract that would have seemed impossibly cruel had it not also seemed comical. He had cannibalized many of his earliest works to perfect the piece. When it was finished, he tried to haul it up to the ceiling but it was simply too heavy. He would require assistance. The truth of this irked him; he stood for a long time silent, brooding, the ice of his sigh billowing through the freezing air.

The following morning, he placed a notice in the local paper. Money was not yet a problem for him; he had been lucky enough to sell a single example of his art to an eccentric Italian collector. He had been living off this sum ever since, a sum he was too frugal to diminish easily. He did not intend to jeopardise his position.

The man who answered his advert was a curious complement to the artist. A knotty hunchback, it was inevitable he would be as taken with the artist as the artist was with him, both seeing in the other a justification for their own existence. The artist, realising this, left the fellow with a light step, a parody of high spirits that seemed to him like a revelation.

When he returned, he found the hunchback on his hands and knees, cleaning the grate. The sculpture was hanging high and absurd on its groaning ropes. The artist narrowed his eyes and pouted.

"Why are you still here?"

"Oh please," the hunchback pleaded with outstretched arms. "Please, master, I am very poor, I need the work. Do not dismiss me master. Life is full of many good things and I have few of them. Let me clean, let me polish. Give me the chance to impress you."

"I can pay you no more," the artist scowled. His fingers were at work on the length of copper wire he had found, twisting it into animal shapes. "No more money."

"I do not require money. You are a master. Give me a masterpiece as payment. I will do much work. A great deal, master."

The artist was affronted, but felt too weary to argue further. He waved the hunchback on and paused by the grimy window, smoking cheap cigarettes and watching the spider that trembled on its web, watching him. As if motivated by a mystic impulse, he flicked ash into the web and frowned as the spider scuttled out to investigate the white intruder. With obvious contempt, the spider cut the ash free, discarded it and returned to its silent waiting.

Every day, from then on, the hunchback arrived at the artist's house. He cleaned and polished with grim determination. The artist began to forget his presence, their bargain, everything. And then, one day, as if noticing him for the first time, he shook his head and took the fellow around the shoulders.

"You must leave now. There is nothing left to clean. You have cleaned the grate every day for two months, yet I have not lit a fire for nearly a year. You have cleaned the bath and sink many times, yet I have not washed for nearly a decade... You must leave."

"Very well. But what about my payment? The masterpiece?"

"Oh that." The artist shrugged. "I lied. I am a great artist. A master. You are nothing. Therefore, I owe you nothing."

"Yes, you are a master. And I wish to have something of yours to remember you by. A masterpiece."

The artist shook his head again.

The hunchback's eyes became filmy pools. "But I've cleaned and polished. I've even sharpened your knives..."

The artist laughed. "I have no knives."

The hunchback recoiled and pointed up at the groaning sculpture. The artist squinted, the shadow of the monstrosity bruising his face. The blades and spikes glittered with a colder light than before. The artist gritted his teeth. "What have you done?" he cried. "You have ruined my sculpture!"

"I have sharpened your knives, master."

The artist stood under the swaying mass of metal and shook his fists. "You have ruined my masterpiece! Let it down at once! At once, do you hear? At once!"

"But master..."

"At once, I say!"

The hunchback shrugged and, moving across the room, released the rope holding the sculpture. And then, afterwards, he took the artist's handkerchief and selected a masterpiece from the pile. Wrapping it carefully in the cloth, he held it out before him like a sacred object. The piece he had chosen was one he felt had been very dear to the artist's own heart.

The left ventricle.

Determined not to humour the Overseer, Hywel makes no comment on the tale but simply repeats his earlier assertion. "I think it's time to move on, don't you? Set up elsewhere."

Obediently we trudge out of the temple, back into the forest, which is dripping, and snake along a path that only takes us into a darker and more tangled region until we are forced to stoop to avoid the low twisted branches of malformed trees.

There are boulders here too and the stubs of shattered cliffs and huge chunks of quartz glint in the undergrowth and despite my reputation for taking risks I am on the verge of announcing my intention of turning back, even if I have to do it alone, when we break out into a glade. But our relief at being able to stand straight again is tempered by the other occupant of this open space.

A mythical beast. A dragon...

We pause and regard it with considerable dismay, but luckily it is asleep, its great head propped on the trunk of a fallen tree, the rest of its body obscured by brambles.

"I know a tale about a dragon," declares Hywel. "Remember that girl called Anna who turned into one?"

"Is it another story about her?" I ask.

"Yes indeed and it takes place at a party in Swansea."

"Fair enough, but I don't think this creature is actually a dragon. It looks more like Trebor, or maybe Robert."

"Who on earth are they?"

I shake my head. "Not on earth. They were legendary sea serpents, well just one serpent to be accurate, and they didn't live in the sea. In fact they weren't serpents either, nor were they really legends, because nobody ever turned them into songs. However, I do know a story about them. It's the story set in outer space which I promised the Overseer, a story which not only hasn't been told yet but hasn't happened and can't happen just in one universe."

"I'm ready to hear it," says Hywel.

"If you tell it quietly..." adds the Overseer.

I'm about to oblige but suddenly a lonesome voice emerges from inside the horrid dragon (or whatever it is) and it shouts: "I know that story as well! Let me tell it!"

"Hush! Don't wake the creature," we warn.

The voice replies, "Why not? It's too late for me anyway, I've already been swallowed, luckily whole. It's one of the few stories I know and I'm bored and undigested in here."

"Go on then," we mutter.

And here it is:

$$ds^2 = -\left(1 - \frac{r_g}{r}\right)dt^2 + \left(\frac{1}{1 - \frac{r_g}{r}}\right)dr^2 + r^2(d\theta^2 + \sin^2\theta\,d\phi^2)$$

$$d\tau = \frac{1}{c}\sqrt{-g_{00}}\,dx^0$$

$$\frac{d\tau}{dt} \to 0 \quad \text{for } r \to r_g$$
$$\frac{d\tau}{dt} \to \quad \text{for } r \to \infty$$

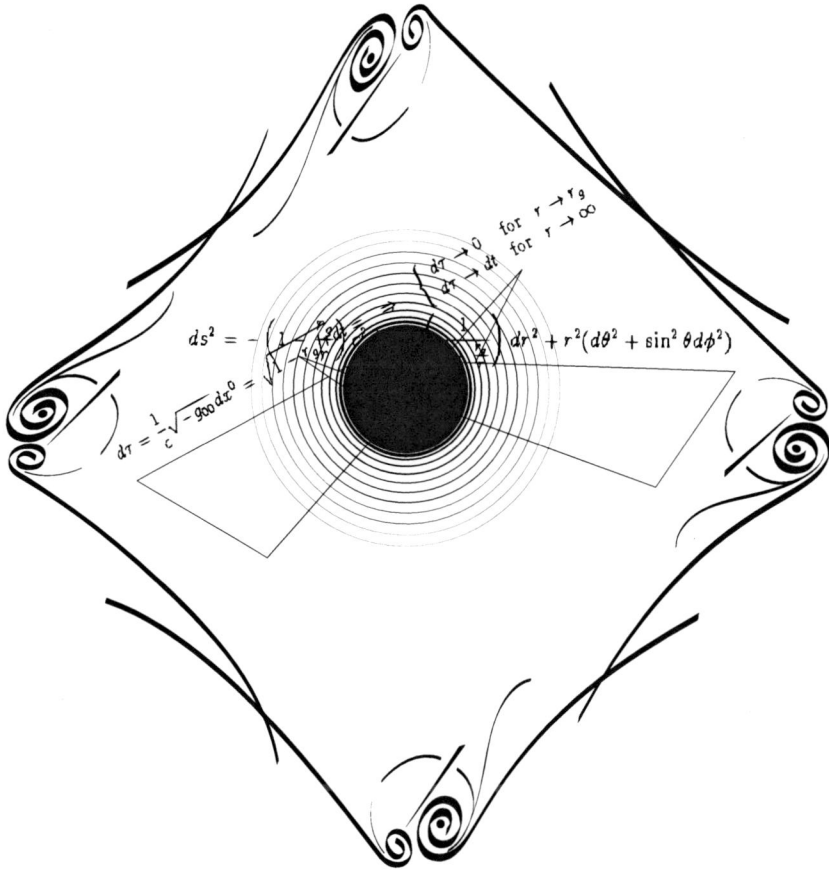

7– THE HOLE TRUTH:
A LIE

There was once (or shall be) an unsung space monster that originally came from nobody knows where. Then it got stuck in a black hole. At the end of the day, it deserves our sympathy. But there are no days in space, so you must cancel your tears.

It was very long, that much is certain. From snout to tail it measured umpteen parsecs. If you want to know more about its anatomy or psychology, please ask somebody else. All I'll say is that its body was the colour of muddy new gold.

It was crossing between the Milky Way and Andromeda when it noticed the gravitational tug of the black hole. It could have swum past if it wanted, but curiosity isn't a weakness restricted to proverb makers. By the time it knew what was what, it wasn't. It was already falling.

Instead of resisting, which is pointless, for a black hole is also pointless, or rather has a point of zero radiance, termed a singularity, the monster, whom we shall call Trebor, to hang our interest securely onto its fate, for a nameless monster has no hooks on its letters to do that, accelerated into the centre of the vortex.

What was it hoping to achieve? A sooner death? The answer is no, because death inside a black hole is never soon: it is as prolonged and stretched and sluggish as everything else, which is to say that it is simultaneously static, thin and compressed into utter nothingness, whatever that adds up to exactly. But it is painful.

It seems that Trebor had consulted the unsung intelligence inside its elongated, and getting more elongated, head, and had worked out that its chances of survival were even slimmer than almost practically close to barely just a pinch above absolute zero. Which means that it had to take drastic action! Forgetting about fighting the irresistible tug, it decided to try leaping right through the gap and out the other side!

Most astronomers claim that black holes don't really lead anywhere, or that at best they are only gateways to unpleasant places, such as your last job or the inside of an unfurnished quark. A few maverick scholars (such as Dr Miasma) reply that maybe they are instant corridors to other sectors of this universe. Scientists whose last job was in another sector of this universe prefer to remain silent.

But Trebor guessed that he might as well gamble with his fate. He had nothing to lose apart from his shape, so he plunged into the vortex almost faster than he could. His reasoning was that nothing else had ever done that, probably. If he could surprise the laws of gravitation, he might be through and out before the black hole noticed. He lashed his tail and achieved a velocity with very few metaphors.

He was already a smooth cylinder with a diameter unchanged along his entire length. There were no protuberances to jam on the lintels of the hole. His speed was astounding but the fit was tight, too tight. Friction boiled neutrino soup. He began to slow down. His grimace and the top half of his body came to a halt in a new universe. His tail remained in the old. He was stuck fast.

Are you ready to hear the truly odd bit? He was neither in one reality nor another. That's not so unusual. Politicians have been doing that for ages. But the universe on the far side of this black hole was made of anti-matter. That's the exact opposite of what most of us boil down to. I am a matter man, as a matter of fact. Anyway, when matter and anti-matter come together, they destroy each other. If you doubt this, when we come together, I'll try my best to destroy you. No I won't. I'm shy.

Trebor wasn't shy, but his head felt awkward in its new surroundings, which were grand and sprinkled with galaxies. No, those were grains of sand in his eye. Space sand, of course. He was sorely in need of a proper introduction to this adjacent cosmos. But the one thing that could have given it was in a similar predicament.

I'll explain that, if you haven't already guessed. The black hole was an open door to a parallel universe, where everything was a mirror of our own. There was another space monster that lived there and he too got snared by the vortex. He also tried to jump right through! Because all his qualities were backward, his name was Robert.

Trebor and Robert never knew each other socially, but they collided in the centre of the black hole and each passed through his alternative self! The molecules of one slid past the molecules of the other. The matter monster and his anti-matter twin fused together. It was very peculiar. It wasn't quite charming. There was now a single monster with a head at both ends, lodged in a black hole. This obstruction shut off the gravitational pull, at least until the monsters yawned, which they did when they were bored, which was often.

When they weren't bored, it was generally because something almost interesting was happening. For example, when they had visitors. Oh yes, they had visitors! Now the black hole was shut off, it meant spaceships no longer had to make detours to avoid it when voyaging between the Milky Way and Andromeda. In case you are wondering, the black hole had been marked on astral charts for decades. Trebor and Robert had been unaware of its existence because they couldn't read maps, and even if they could, no shop would sell them one. They were unsung space monsters and had no money.

Of course, the black hole was still there when Trebor and Robert yawned. In a sense their digestive system had taken over its duties. But everything worked out for the best, because when the spaceships took a

157

short cut across the face of the event horizon, that event was an interesting thing, and so the monsters never yawned when it was most dangerous for them to do so. A self-regulating gateway had accidentally been created. When the spaceships passed near, Trebor and Robert winked. And the vessels flashed their lights in return.

If the situation had been left as it was, nothing dramatic would have happened next, but people are curious, more curious than unsung space monsters. Scientists in both universes wished to know why Trebor's head hadn't exploded in Robert's cosmos, and why Robert's head hadn't exploded in Trebor's cosmos. If you want that written as an equation, contact the University of Arcturus. I wonder if there is a parallel University of Arcturus in that other reality? It must be easier to graduate backward! I managed to do that here!

Enough distractions. On with the story, which also happens to be a lesson! You see, the spaceships of that time were powered by cold fusion reactors, which were good, but the energy released was meagre compared with what happened when matter and anti-matter came together. That was total annihilation!

Now the difficulty with trying to harness this ultimate source of power was that the different types of fuel couldn't be stored. The anti-matter pellets couldn't be held in a matter chamber, but if they were held in an anti-matter chamber, then this chamber couldn't be carried by a spaceship made of matter. The same applied the other way round. To simplify matters, in a manner of speaking, let us agree that the engineering problems were complex and seemed insolvable.

At least they did until the incident involving Trebor and Robert. It was speculated that something against the previous laws of physics had occurred where the particles of the two monsters had blended. The creation of a new type of substance, a third kind of stuff. Neither matter nor anti-matter but physical neutrality. A very amenable thing, which didn't react, despite the provocation, to whatever it met.

That's a nice thought, isn't it? Anyway, such a substance might come in very useful. Whole spaceships could be fabricated from it, and such vessels could carry as many matter and anti-matter pellets as they liked. Intergalactic travel would be much more efficient as this new method of propulsion became possible.

The promise was too good to ignore. The only question that remained was how exactly the matter and anti-matter had become joined where the bodies of Trebor and Robert met. A committee of scientists in one universe decided to investigate the structure of the unknown substance at first hand. There was no other way of finding out. They forgot that their decision would be copied by a committee of scientists in the other universe, for both realities were compelled to mimic each other.

The spaceships set out, but instead of rushing across the face of the plugged black hole, they halted in front of the respective monsters. When Trebor and Robert winked, they flashed their lights back. But they kept flashing them. They told a story in the language of the monsters, which they had learned especially for this adventure. A boring story. The only difference between the tale told to Trebor and the one told to Robert was that the first featured a hero and the second an anti-hero. Apart from that they were equally tedious.

The monsters yawned together and the scientists climbed into the airlocks and jumped out into the vacuum of space. They wore spacesuits and were tethered to their vessels on long umbilicals, so they could pull themselves back when the mission was over. They were sucked in, through the gaping mouths and down the throats to the stomachs, where the weird fusion had taken place.

They had powerful torches, but they didn't need them, because the starlight from each universe filtered through both yawns and combined here, reflecting off the pools of digestive acids and glittering over the fleshy cavern walls.

At first, the two delegations were astonished to see each other approaching. Then they chuckled with embarrassment, because this outcome should have been obvious. They exchanged a few words by flashing their torches. What they learned was purely speculative, because their languages were different. In one universe, the humans all spoke Russian and Earth was covered by a single city called New Moscow. In the other, they talked American and their planetary metropolis was Extra New York. Naturally they all shook hands, in the name of multiversal relations. They detonated.

In the excitement of this historic meeting, they had forgotten basic physics. The blast didn't remain in the giant stomach. It gushed out in both directions, charred the throat, tongue and lips of Trebor and Robert and sooted their teeth. But this double belch didn't extend far out into space.

It licked the hulls of the waiting spaceships and was drawn back by the gravity of the black hole. However it was still too forceful for the stomach and blew itself out again. And so began a gastric oscillation, a hot belch without end. And the spaceships were alternately heated and cooled.

It might be expected that this phenomenon would become the focus of a mystical cult. But what happened was more beautiful and more mundane. The two spaceships were filled with food and spices from ten thousand different worlds and then topped up with exotic wines from yet others. The lapping flames cooked the food and mulled the wine in the sealed vessels and two enormous parties were held in a pair of opposite universes at the same time. These weren't charitable events but simple wild revels.

Neither Trebor nor Robert were invited, despite being so close and crucial to the events, and when all the food and wine was finished, they wept tears the size of asteroids, but these didn't attract any new parties, though a few romantic composers who had cancelled their own tears came to see what they might be missing. It was a lot, but nothing to inspire a tune. And this is why there can be (or has been) such things as unsung space monsters.

Hywel sniggers and shakes his head. He has approached the head of the mythical monster closer than I would ever dare and he offers a reply to the unseen teller of the tale.

"Parallel universes? What a load of claptrap!"

"Shhh! You'll wake the beast!" I warn.

The voice inside the creature becomes soothing. "No you won't, I'm a medical man and I injected its tongue with a sleeping potion the moment it swallowed me, so you're safe."

"Only for the time being," I grumble.

Despite the novelty of the scene, the Overseer and Mondaugen begin to yawn. "This isn't as exciting as it should be, let's get out of here and go somewhere else, but where?"

"How about Monmouth?" suggests Hywel.

"What do you think?" I ask the voice inside the monster, in case it knows something about the place in question that we don't, and this turns out to be so, for it answers:

"I hear the gnoles have taken over that town and want to relocate Japan and Pennsylvania to it."

But the Overseer and Mondaugen aren't discouraged. "Well, let's go there before they are successful!"

We leave the glade and follow a path which curves around and opens into another glade, where to my infinite dismay if not surprise, the head of a second monster, identical to the first, also rests on a fallen tree fast asleep and ugly, but then I realise this isn't a different beast but the other end of the one we've already met.

Funnily enough, this head also contains an unseen voice and as soon as one of our feet breaks a twig and betrays our presence the swallowed man demands: "Have you come from the far side of the monster? If so you probably spoke to my colleague. Don't believe anything he told you, he's a charlatan and a buffoon."

"You are a medical man as well?" I ask.

"Of course and because I know that my colleague probably told you a ridiculous tale I feel it's my duty to tell a far better one to prove that I am his superior in all things."

"His story was set in outer space," says Hywel.

"Very well, that's what I'll relate too," comes the reply and without a pause for breath the voice gives us:

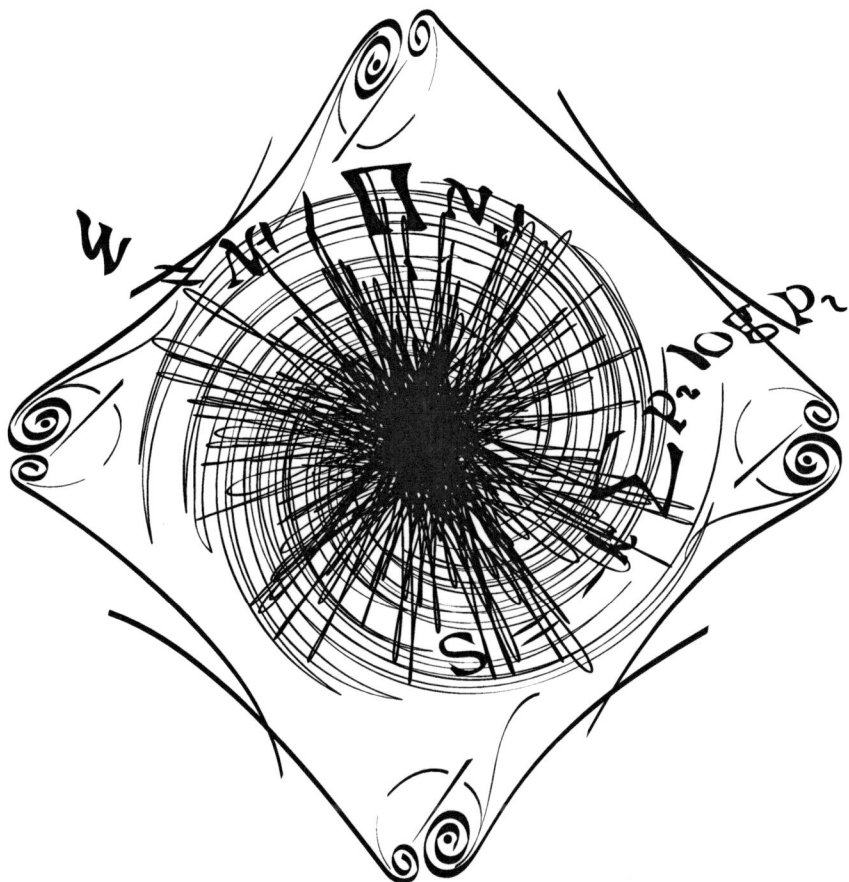

8– ENTROPY

The theories of Dr Miasma never carried much weight with the scientific establishment. Even his own students scoffed at them. "Academia will be the death of me," he used to say, tears trickling down his cheeks, or sometimes when he was in a more confident mood: "I will be the death of Academia." Ironically enough, neither prediction came true, even though I managed to prove his ideas once and for all. The ways of the Universe are stranger than the maxims of mortals.

Not that he is mortal now. Indeed, not that anyone is. But figures of speech are still in use, at least where I reside, and so I shall continue to circulate them. But where exactly do I reside? First things second, as they say. Let me describe the events that led to my present situation and then move on to questions of locality.

No need to tell you my name. I am, or was, Dr Miasma's star pupil. In fact, I was his sole pupil after the second term, when most of his students dropped hard Astrophysics in favour of harder drinking. I was the only one who listened to him. More importantly, I was the only one who could muster up belief.

In those days, the Universe was a bleak and cheerless place. Hot things went cold; energy drained out of matter; matter itself crumbled and decayed. The law of nature was transmutation and change. Nothing lasted. Inanimate objects rarely struggled or bickered. They certainly never kicked.

Scientists labelled this process and devised equations to explain its behaviour. They called it entropy. Energy constantly diminished. Power, lust and life drained forever into dark spaces. In short, the available energy grew increasingly sparse as time moved on. It was an article of faith.

Dr Miasma had devised his own equations. These were in opposition to those of his fellows. Entropy, he decided, was simply an error in the blueprint of the Cosmos. An error that could be rectified.

"Entropy, I tell you," he would rant, throwing his arms about in all directions, "is nothing more than a hole in Space. Yes, somewhere out there, in the furthest reaches of the Universe, lies a hole. It is through this hole that all our energy, our heat, is leaking. If the hole could be plugged there would be no entropy."

There was much talk, among the college authorities, of the need to silence Dr Miasma. He was becoming an embarrassment. On my final day of the two-week debauch that constituted my graduation celebrations, the maverick professor took me to one side. "The Dean intends to arrange for my expulsion," he confessed. "You alone can save me."

We sat in the corner of one of those dingy taverns that lined the waterfront. Drunk with self-esteem, as well as more frothy brews, I indulged his confidence. Grasping him by the shoulders, I staggered to my feet and slurred this most solemn oath: "I will."

"Good man." He was all winks and smiles. He opened a bottle of Chablis with his teeth, all six gnarled stumps of them, poured the contents into our glasses and held up the cork. "And this will be the symbol of your promise. A very good aeon."

When I awoke the next day, in a strange bed with a strange woman, I was still clutching the cork. Memories of the previous night rushed to greet me; my solemn oath returned to shame my conscience.

I had hoped, nay intended, after my degree, to seek employment as a dusty academic in some obscure University. Now, thanks to my promise, and the cork that made it tangible, I had to alter my plans. I bade farewell to the strange woman and made my way to the sky jetty. Here, among the idle rich lounging on the decks of their solar yachts, I used the last of my savings to rent a hyper-pedalo.

Steering between the nets of the mothmen, I nosed my way out of the atmosphere. Life in a hyper-pedalo, needless to say, is not of the most invigorating kind. The pedalo itself is unadorned and unfurnished, save for a single assembler unit. This unit manufactures the oxygen, food and water necessary for survival. The transparent shell that covers the vehicle is malleable and allows an occupant to extend a protected arm or foot out into the void.

Once beyond the Moon, I was able to take a short cut across one of the folds of the space-time fabric and emerge on the rim of the galaxy. I would exploit these routes as much as possible from now on, for I had a great many parsecs to cover. Too narrow for larger craft, these lanes saved me centuries of growing doubts. I was committed to the discovery of Dr Miasma's hole. Nothing more and certainly nothing less. My loins were electromagnetically girded.

It should be possible, at this stage, to give an account of some of my adventures in space among the spinning galaxies, the shining beauties of the jewel-flecked Cosmos, the unearthly wonder of the alien planets. Perhaps I should describe the sentient clouds of hydrogen, the swirling mind-oceans, the telepathic stars I met in Andromeda.

Or perhaps I should merely mention the enormous power and grace of the quasars and black holes, the rainbow splendours of white holes and the dizzying rhythmic melodies of pulsars. Fringes of nebulae clutched at my hair, supernovae blazed their dying arrogance; I saw cataracts of adamantine asteroids, endlessly turning their rough diamond hulks in the stain of a red giant or monstrously swelling variable.

And it is true, I agree, that I made contact with life I was able to communicate with. Indeed, I had a brief but extremely passionate affair with a star-siren whom I named Lorelei. Her hair was a comet's tail, her eyes were fusing protons. But I could not stay with her. I gave her the one object that had any sentimental value for me, and I departed, while she sang a superconductive lament.

I could discuss any, or all, of these things, but since they are superfluous to my tale, I will not. Besides, most of my time was spent alone, counting the artificial hours in my pedalo. Whenever I approached a small meteorite, I would reach out a hand, snatch it up and drop it into the assembler. The atom-sized automatons would then re-arrange its molecular structure into something more useful.

This, if truth be known, constituted the vast majority of my life as a space explorer. So I will not mention it either. Of much greater importance was the discovery I made one false morning, after a somewhat troubled sleep. This, really, is the crux of my story. So let us hasten to its telling! Let us dribble down the chin of the Cosmos and wipe our noses on the fabric of Reality.

Well, as I was saying, when I opened my eyes, I became instantly aware of a great light that surrounded my bubble and seemed to grow steadily brighter. It was a glow not unlike a halo and it seemed to be thickening like maize soup. It was not long before I realised that I was in the grip of a powerful current that was pulling me with an insistent tug towards some unspecified point. The halo was rich with objects drawn from the five corners of the Universe.

I twisted in my seat to get a better view of my destination. The hull of my vessel was nudged by the flotsam and jetsam of the spaceways. Shards of asteroid, methane icicles and jettisoned fuel tanks threatened to capsize the pedalo. I tried pedalling backwards, but all my exertions were in vain. There was nothing to do but abandon myself to the destiny I had sealed in the tavern with Dr Miasma.

Ahead of me, a thrashing astral shark was entangled in the broken sail of a long decayed trawler. As I accelerated towards it, I knew I was doomed. Stoically, I awaited the collision. To my amazement, it did not come. I opened my eyes just in time to see shark and trawler spiral away from me. As I looked up, I saw that other objects were following a similar route. A maelstrom of debris, already inconceivably huge, was growing vaster every instant.

For some reason, my pedalo did not take this course. I surmised it was too pathetic a mode of transport to play any part in the cyclopean event taking place. Like the absurd helix of water that rotates around a plughole, leaving a clear funnel in the centre, matter and energy were parting on all sides, allowing my unimpeded progress towards the focus of the stupendous phenomenon.

Towards the middle of the eye I proceeded, utterly ignored by the normally unassailable laws of physics. It then stuck me that my strange quest was at an end. For this, surely, was Dr Miasma's hole, the flaw in the structure of the Universe that permitted decay and dissolution. By plugging this hole, I could finally put an end to entropy and vindicate my old tutor. I was delighted.

Reaching the hole, I was stupefied by its dimensions. It was no bigger than the diameter of a standard wine cork. I was puzzled as to how such a small hole could absorb some of the larger examples caught in the mighty whirl. It quickly became apparent that the violence of the spin ensured that nothing bigger than a thumbnail emerged from the chaos to plunge into unknown oblivion.

My pedalo, of course, was unaffected by this process. With the sort of insouciance that would please future biographers, I reached into my pocket. I had just the thing to settle the devious hole. It would have been the perfect touch. Alas, as I have already hinted, I had given it to Lorelei. How I cursed her at that moment! I ranted and foamed until an alternative solution presented itself.

My unhealthy lifestyle back at the university had left me with the symptoms of heart disease. One of the outward signs of my poor health, clubbed fingers, now served a useful purpose. Extending my index digit through the thin shell of the pedalo, I popped it into the hole. Perhaps in the interests of science I should have sneaked a look at the other side first. My finger was a superb fit. All at once, the maelstrom of matter and energy collapsed. A note of contentment boomed on the bowl of everything, existence at peace with itself.

I waited patiently for a number of weeks, certain that the ripples of my inspired action would reach civilisation and ensure my rescue. It was a forlorn hope. Imagine that the Cosmos is a house. In this analogy, the Milky Way is in the vicinity of the lounge and planet Earth is located somewhere on the comfy chair that is drawn up in front of the fire. The segment of space where I found myself, ontological puncture and all, lies in the dustiest room of the building. No rescuer would dream of venturing into this obscure corner.

And here I still reside, poking the life back into infinity. I am the great benefactor now, the one who has conquered decay, but who will never enjoy the fruits of his labours. Now there is more energy to share around, the monopoly held by animate objects has been broken. Inanimate ones are no longer too tired to move. Sometimes a passing comet will wink at me and bring me news from Earth. Dr Miasma, it seems, has been made President of the Solar System.

My situation irks me somewhat and sometimes an ironic smile plays on my lips. The rent on my pedalo has reached an incalculable figure. I am reminded of an old story about a Dutch boy who put his finger in a dyke. Apparently she slapped him about a bit. It is hardly surprising. I wonder who will slap me about here, in the cupboard under the stairs of creation? This is one situation where taking my finger out will not increase productivity.

We are already leaving before the tale is half finished but the teller keeps talking and we hear the rest of it as we pick through the forest, growing fainter and mixed with the rustling of leaves as if the story is being read from a book with very tiny pages which need to be turned at high speed, perhaps because there is only one word to each page or even a single letter. Don't know how the snakes and hares in the undergrowth fit into this metaphor, unless they are the librarians who loaned the miniature book to the person doing the reading.

"Strange fellows, that pair," Mondaugen says.

Hywel nods. "I have a suspicion they were the two doctors I told you about earlier, Dr Vaughan and Dr Frazer, the deadly rivals. I suppose you want me to tell you the two stories I know about them now, but I don't really feel like doing that just yet, maybe never, I don't know, but certainly not in this framing device."

I am directly behind Hywel and I can't fail to notice something odd about the bundle on his shoulder.

"Your tent seems to have got bigger, but that can't be so, because neither of the doctors were inside it when they spoke and envelopes can't be pushed from outside and nobody ever heard of 'pulling the envelope' when it comes to literary efforts, so I'd like a more sensible explanation please, if you've got one spare."

"I haven't, sorry. What happened was that every decent tavern should have a beer garden and so I designated both those forest glades as part of my premises and that's how the tales expanded the tent. I didn't inform anyone of the fact but my portable tavern has a portable beer garden too which is any land I want it to be."

"Fair enough, but there's something else I don't fully understand. Why didn't that last story and some of the others already told correspond with the situations of the tellers? I mean, neither of those medical men were from the future where their stories were set and in the second case the narrator claimed to be stuck in a hole on the edge of the universe rather than in a monster's stomach."

Hywel is astonished. "You don't fully understand that? But I don't understand it at all, not even in part, therefore your understanding is greater than mine and I'd be grateful for you to share your insight with me. I'll give you a free drink!"

"Very well. It could be that some or all of the tale tellers are actually talking about parallel versions of themselves in other universes rather than about themselves here."

"You mean the protagonists of the stories are so busy enduring the events of the stories they have to leave the narration of them to currently less active incarnations of themselves?"

I shrug and this motion of my shoulders, which is always slightly forward as well as up, takes me out of the forest, over the line of the last row of trees and into open country again. There is a small church and a lane not far away and we make for these. A good place to erect the tent but as we approach the building we notice that all the windows have fallen out. The church is a shell. Bright flowers have grown over the empty windows and they are more beautiful than the original stained glass. They remind me of another story but I've already earned a free drink and so the only way Hywel will permit me to tell it is if I make it a poor one to cancel the payment out, and also if I climb inside his tent first, which is still rolled up on his back.

I do so and he staggers but keeps his balance.

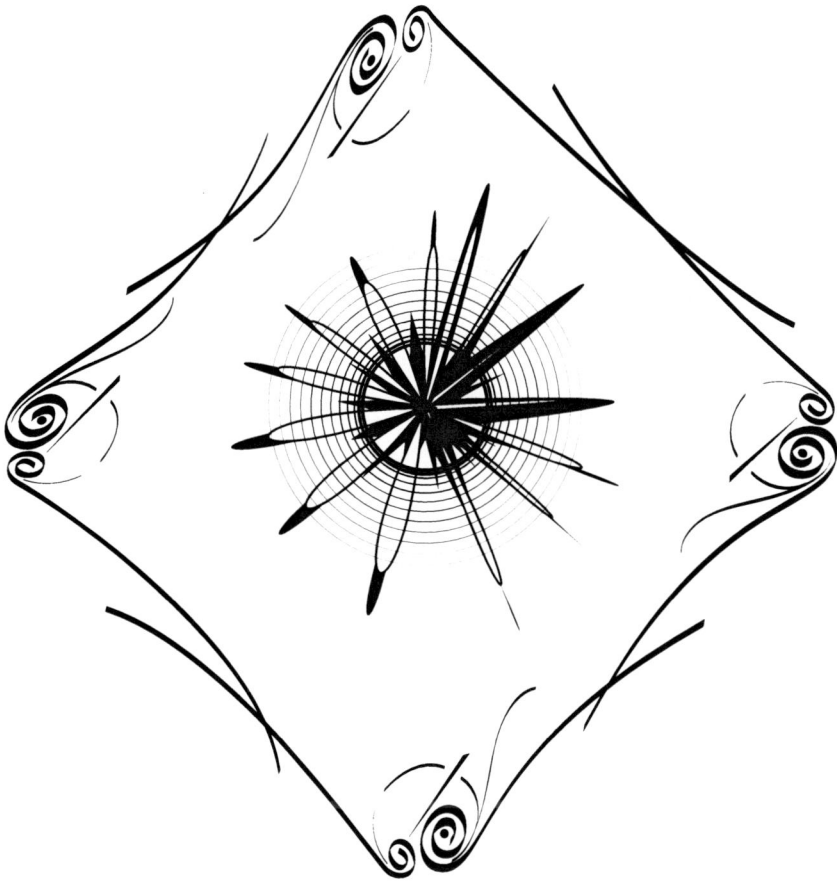

9– THE TIME TUNNEL ORCHID

I am a botanist. My name doesn't matter. My greatest achievement is the discovery of the Time Tunnel Orchid (class: *metatemporal angiospermae*; order: *chronocotyledons*), a plant so rare I remain the only man who has ever seen it. Some experts doubt the veracity of my reports. I find it hard to blame them, harder to defend myself. I must endure their taunts until I bring back a freshly picked example, and to do that I must continue to wear this bird mask.

In appearance, the Time Tunnel Orchid is beautiful and odd, a large funnel shaped flower on a long slender stalk. The opening to the funnel is a helix with mildly hypnotic properties. Regarding colour, the plant demonstrates the Doppler Effect in a graceful manner, showing a blue flower when approached but a red flower when an observer walks away from it. The outside length of the funnel is considerably shorter than the inside length, but as the outside is only measurable in distance and the inside can only be measured in years, this difference may not be immediately obvious.

The Time Tunnel Orchid seems to exist in symbiosis with hummingbirds who are attracted by the promise of nectar. Once they enter the mouth of the funnel they are sucked all the way through and emerge at an unspecified date far in the future. This journey is entirely one way. Hummingbirds that emerge from the funnels have clearly been projected into our own time from the distant past.

This plant does not spread its seeds very far in terms of spatial distance, relying on time to ensure successful germination. The feathers of the hummingbirds are coated with pollen when they enter the funnel and this pollen fertilises the *different* plant that will occupy the *same* spot in future ages. Thus the orchid guarantees its survival across the centuries, often 'leapfrogging' times of drought and disease. The seeds grow quickly and the flower is ready to project hummingbirds into the future within a few months. Old age comes rapidly. A sudden increase in red shift occurs and within hours the plant is lost over the edge of the observable botanical universe.

Dressing as a hummingbird is the only known method of viewing these astonishing plants. I first discovered them many years ago during a fancy dress party in the jungles of Brazil. I was very drunk, I admit the fact. I went for a walk to sober up, still dressed in my costume... In a clearing I came across a dozen orchids. I watched what the other hummingbirds were doing. I was young... I crouched down and crawled into the biggest funnel. I emerged in the distant future...

Unfortunately the way that plants view the 'future' is entirely different from the way humans view it. We judge the age we are living in by the technology that surrounds us. Clay pots and bronze axes indicate an earlier century than electric light and nuclear submarines. Plants don't have that advantage. The future to them is not much different to the past. In this case it wasn't the slightest bit different. I emerged in the plant's idea of the far future, not my own... I returned to the party without missing the last dance.

I am still searching for new examples of the Time Tunnel Orchid. My plaster bird head is falling apart and perhaps has lost its potency. But I have faith. One day I will stoop to take a last drink of nectar from the plant I will afterwards cut down, carry home in triumph and mount in the vase of eternal fame.

I smile and nod. "They are probably still there, at that party, surrounded by rainforest plants. Such plants are my favourite kind too; and in fact I love tropical fruits more than those of the temperate climes. I'm a devotee of the papaya, cherimoya, guava, mango and chilli pepper. The last item on that brief list is especially intriguing, not only because most people erroneously label it a vegetable rather than a fruit. Oh no! It has a most unusual aerodynamic property."

Hywel answers, "I suspect you are smiling and nodding in there, but none of us can see you, so why not climb out and show your expressions and gestures in broad daylight?"

It is too comfortable inside the tent, so I ignore his request and persist with my original theme. "Chillies, and bell peppers also, are hollow but they are hermetically sealed and don't feature any inlet valves. So as they grow, they create a larger and larger vacuum inside themselves; and the outer air pressure on their skins must steadily increase. If they grow big enough, surely the stalks will finally snap off the bushes and the peppers will slowly float up into space?"

Hywel sighs and shakes his head. "That's almost as daft as wondering where the illumination for dreams comes from. In other words, how are we able to see in dreams even though it's dark at night and we have our eyes closed? If the illumination comes from our 'imagination', why can't we use our imagination in waking life to illuminate dark rooms, thus saving on electricity and light-bulbs?"

Mondaugen has been listening politely and now he admits that tonight he will surely dream of orchids, with or without illumination. And if it's dark in his dream he will orient himself by the scent of those magnificent flowers. But he won't climb inside them.

"Pity those orchids only work in one direction, sending hummingbirds into the future and not into the past. I wonder if they might be modified or encouraged to work in reverse?"

"Who said that?" I demand.

An odd being comes into view. It has been lurking behind the church, a man with the legs and horns of a goat and a corrugated beard, as if a sample of a cheap garage roof has been pasted onto his chin. He wears an unusual toga and his slitted eyes twinkle.

"I did. I used to live in the forest but I was chased out by Trebor and Robert and now I dwell outside but as close as possible. I sometimes hide on the roof of this ruined church by pretending to be a gargoyle. To return to what I was saying, if I could find such an orchid and turn it inside out I might be able to climb into it and travel into the past, back to a time when I was happy."

Hywel has already set up his tent again, with me still within it, so I don't have to go anywhere when he asks, "What time was that? Come inside and tell us all about it."

This is an offer the newcomer can't refuse.

10- THE GOLDEN FLEAS

The girl in the wood is playing her pipes. I want to chase her down the hill to the sea. My nature compels me to run after any woman who places lips to reed, but there is a haunting quality to her music, a spirit I have not heard for a long time, so I watch in mute appreciation, peeping at her from the depths of the olive grove.

My fleas are troubling me again. "Hurry up, old fool!" they snarl. They make me dance; not to melody which would be welcome, but to pain. "Hurry up, looks like rain!" Sometimes they call me names. Their satire is always biting. "Somebody got your goat?"

Once, like Marsyas, I challenged Apollo to a music contest and lost. Rather than flaying me alive — the usual punishment for defeat — the archer king cursed me with sentient fleas. I have to consult them on all topics. A condition of the curse is that I am not allowed to rid myself of the pests. I have to avoid water and take shelter in a cave when clouds knock together.

Rain is sweet on Kérkira, as infrequent as the willing kiss of another man's wife, but I have to huddle under rock and wait. No dew must splash my legs, no juice dribble down my chin. Created by the god of light, my parasites are burnished gold. Water would wash the colour out of them. If this happened, Apollo would be displeased. My skin would make a rug for his burning feet.

Yet I know I will be rescued one day. In dreams I see my saviour. He comes from a distant land on a fast ship. He combs the fleas from my fur and takes them back with him. Not even Apollo can oppose him. But his actions are founded on a misunderstanding. This life of ours is a harmony of mistakes, each blunder a note on the stave of reality. What my saviour does for me is not what he ought to do.

I will say nothing, I will not betray my luck. On the slopes of my island's highest peak, I gaze at Illyria's distant shore. The city of Butrint, full of cool stone and heated baths, nestles just beyond the range of my slitted eyes. There are only villages on Kérkira, the rude dwellings of a pastoral people, but we do have shrines where shepherds leave offerings to the nymphs and satyrs. The gods are given wine and honey, but we are content with milk and flowers.

Apart from my fleas, I am plagued by another entity. A bronze man called Gnathon shares my domain. He tells me he was forged on Crete by Daedalus. Unsatisfied with the result, the great inventor cast him into the sea. For nine years his hollow body was buffeted by the waves before being washed onto one of our beaches. A crack in his mould means all the truth has leaked out of him. He can only tell lies. I am suspicious of his true origins. He talks to my fleas. "What a generous host you have!" And they, knowing his condition, appreciate the sarcasm.

Gnathon insists that the girl in the wood, the lithe musician, is named Chloe. This means she is not. However, I have nothing else to go on, so I also decide to call her Chloe. Gnathon is as bewitched as I am. He is too ugly for her, I tell him. In return he praises my mild odour. Coming from a bronze liar this is a deadly insult. We wrestle in the dust, near a stream. My fleas warn me not to fall in. We are equals in strength and our struggles come to nothing. Exhausted, we lie back and pant our mutual hatred.

Where does Chloe come from? She is too dark to be a native of this island. I think Egypt, where men worship cats and herons. Gnathon says from under the sea. He is a liar of little imagination. I want to burst into tears with the force of my emotion. I have never shed a tear, it is difficult with my eyes, but I hope one day to defy nature and drown my cheeks with the globules of feeling. Only after my saviour has removed my fleas will this be possible.

It is difficult to follow Chloe after she has finished her music. She vanishes between the trees, slippery as olive oil. I try to keep up with her. Always she stays ahead. It is like chasing your shadow. I fear I will never know anything about her. She is destined to be an enigma. I believe she has no home at all; perhaps she circulates around the isle like a cool breeze, never settling.

I wonder what would happen if I caught her. Would she be repelled by my form? Every morning, Gnathon makes a new statement about her. He never tires of speculation. "She is celibate," he ventures. "She is a woman lover." I am able to dismiss such possibilities as he raises them. If Gnathon claims she is celibate, she is not. I have made a list of her non-qualities; I lack only the truth.

One afternoon, sitting on the long beach in the south west of the island, I spy a distant sail. I jump up and dance on my hooves. It is my saviour! He is coming at last! I watch as the ship grows larger. Soon it is anchored in the shallows. My saviour leaps from the deck and wades towards me. I throw myself at his feet. He is wearing only one sandal. His limbs are the colour of bronze.

"My name is Jason," he cries, "and I seek the golden fleas." There is a nobility about his bearing. For some reason I do not answer. What is wrong with me? Why do I not show him my parasites? He will comb them from my body and take them away. But I find it difficult to deceive him. His face is too trusting. Quite against my better judgment, I clasp him around the shoulder and whisper in his ear.

I tell him he has made an error. I give him directions to his real destination. He is grateful. "What can I do for you in return?" he asks. I whistle the music of Chloe, a melody that burns my lips. Jason nods and strokes his beard. "That is not a real melody, but a ghost made of echoes. Someone has been playing music for too long. The new notes have entangled themselves in the old. Now they seek to escape each other and their struggles are poignant."

I bow my head in shame at this. He is right; Chloe is no more than the phantom of my lost talent. This is why I will never be able to hold her in my hairy arms. Jason returns to his ship and disappears back over the lip of the world. I am left with nothing. I have missed my chance to rid myself of my fleas. They are relieved. "Blood is thicker than wine," they sneer. While I sit on the sand, arranging patterns of despair with driftwood, Gnathon comes up from behind.

"You smell sweeter than ever," he says. "Chloe is sure to find your odour appealing." This is the final reed. Suddenly I am up and running. The howl at the back of my throat struggles to keep up. A woodsman's hut lies close. The fellow is enjoying an afternoon nap; his double-headed axe is left unattended. Before he can open his eyes, I have snatched it up and am racing back to the beach.

Gnathon has followed me a little way into the wood. We meet in a glade. He lifts his bronze eyebrows in creaking bewilderment. "What are you doing?" He has little concept of anger. Bronze men are more familiar with disappointment. In his own dashed dreams Gnathon can dance all over the island. He is too heavy to pirouette. This impossible yearning is his one genuine desire.

My first blow smashes a hole in his chest. Salt water sprays out into the scented undergrowth. I realise at once what has happened. I have already mentioned his crack. That nine-year buffeting filled him with ocean. As I raise the axe a second time, he holds up a hand. "Do not do this. Your fur will be drenched with brine. Apollo remembers your sin." At this, my fears fall away. Then the archer king has forgotten! I am free. At last, I burst into tears. This is the long awaited prelude to real refreshment.

My second blow widens the hole and the cold water washes away the grime of years. Even though this is a world of misery, things sometimes work out for the best. Gnathon is made lighter by my actions. Now he is no longer clumsy; his bronze legs have less weight to bear. He can skip and dance in the way he has always wished. And I am consoled by a rare metaphysical thought. If Chloe is just an echo of my talent, then I am a pre-echo of hers. Our minims can entwine, if not our limbs. Remember too that I have learned to cry.

More importantly, at the instant of my dousing, the fleas jumped from my body onto Gnathon's. Because he is bronze and they are gold, they suit him more than me. And he is untroubled by their presence; he is too tough to bite. Indeed he welcomes their company, the sardonic conversations. As for the fleas, the situation is less pleasant. They know hunger and the loss of power.

Out of the crying Pan and onto the liar.

While telling his tale, the Pan has plucked a fistful of hair from his beard and now his other hand is busily engaged in braiding it, for no purpose other than to dissipate the energy in his fingers, a feverish energy rather than a wholesome one. I feel pity for his situation and I decide it will be nice to have a man-goat as a pet, so I invite him to come with us. I have always wanted to be a Panhandler.

He agrees but seems to guess my dishonourable intentions. "Only if I can have equal rights and status!"

"Do you know anything about the temple in the forest?" Mondaugen asks. "Does it date from your era?"

"Or is it a modern fake?" adds Hywel.

"A bit of both. It is actually an ancient fake or rather an attempt to imagine and build a futuristic building, but all guesses about the future are hopelessly saturated with the truth of the present, or the past in this case, for we are currently in that badly guessed future, which probably explains why the world is such a mess, because anything badly guessed will automatically be unrefined."

"I don't wish to be a killjoy," suddenly speaks up the Overseer, "but the words 'fleece' and 'fleas' wouldn't be confused like that in Ancient Greek. The joke is invalid."

"Are you sure about that?" I demand.

He hangs his head in shame. "You're right, I do want to be a killjoy, in fact I'm good at it and it was my career but my other point still stands. That story relies on wordplay in English and just doesn't make sense in the context in which it was told."

Before we can digest this, Hywel cries: "Look at all these hoofprints! Do they belong to you, Mr Pan?"

I answer for the goat. "No, they are the prints of a horse or many horses, but faint like steeds which don't exist. Which reminds me: what happened to my sonic horse?"

"Listened away to nothing. Either that or the author of this text has clumsily forgotten about it."

"Fading, just like ghosts," sighs the Overseer.

Hywel is desperate. "Not a ghost story please, anything but that, I'm sick of them, they're all the same!"

Mondaugen retorts, "But not everything which is no longer there is ghostly, often the reason for its absence is because it has been stolen. Allow me to tell a story on this theme."

We give him the required permission.

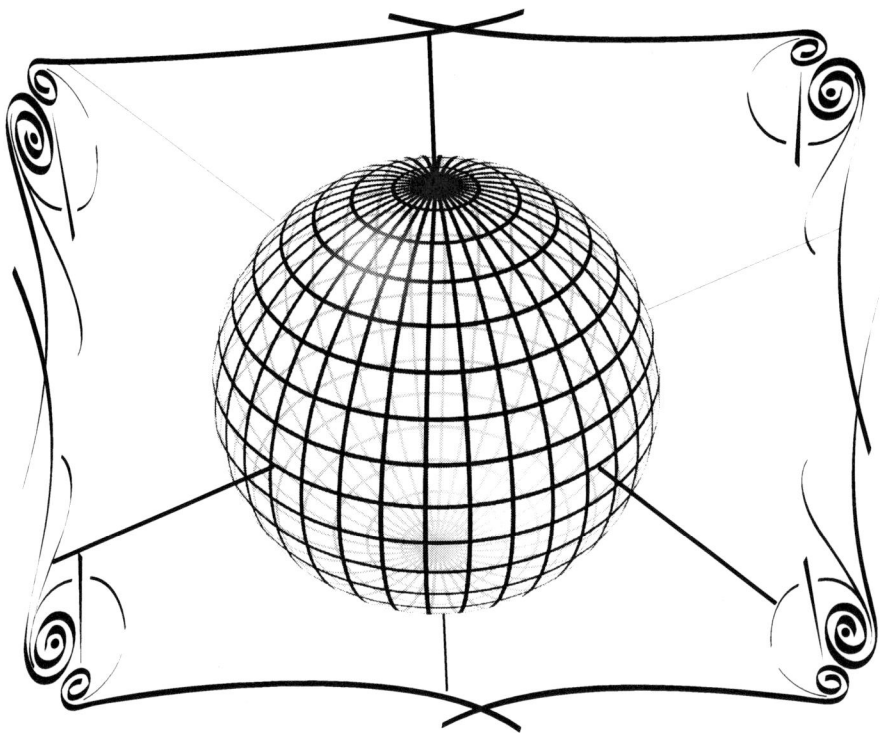

11- THE WEST POLE

The West Pole was traditionally discovered by Caradoc Weasel, an explorer who did nothing with it. For many centuries, its existence was merely a rumour. After it was found, the other theoretical Poles were accepted as real. In due course, they were also reached and researched. Of the six Poles, the West remains the most magical. Nobody can say why. The North and South are too functional to inspire the same feelings of awe. They occupy the two ends of the axis upon which the planet spins. The East, Front and Back Poles have no such role, though no geographer dares consider them superfluous. But they do not command the respect that is offered to the West Pole. Possibly this is because the human race never truly appreciates what it has until it is gone.

The longitude of the West Pole is 90°W. Naturally it lies directly on the equator. It ought to have been easy to locate, for it stands exactly where it should, at the sunset's point of absolute rest. But the diameter of the Pole is only that of the thickness of any line of latitude, and it is sunk into the sea, and sailors are often drunk. It persisted as a myth for long ages, but once it was found, it became obvious, and then the mystery was how it had eluded detection before. That is usually what happens with new things. Now storms always seemed to be blowing ships onto it and it was marked on every chart as a hazard. Without changing their routes at all, many vessels were wrecked there, and the act of its discovery was generally held responsible.

In time, its reputation mellowed, because ships grew harder and steel plate did not puncture so readily. Then the storms were no longer so frequent. Sailors began to steer for it deliberately. As a meeting place, it was ideal. The Galapagos lay a little to the west, yet the Pole had none of the disadvantages of conducting business on land. There were no brothels to start fights in. Before long, a thriving market came into being around the actual Pole. Ships would tether themselves to it with ropes. Then goods would be traded from deck to deck. Sometimes crews would just chat or sing together. The neutrality of the Pole was respected. Even the fleets of nations at war would refuse to engage in combat in the vicinity of that foolish but astounding length of wood.

For such was the material from which it had been created. The same was true of the other three inessential Poles. Whether they had grown there naturally, or were carved and planted by an unknown and forgotten intelligence, is an unanswerable question. The fact they were striped with red and white bands is cited as evidence for an artificial origin, but the world is strange and too many conclusions about its secrets are apt to be wrong. Even the objection that wood does not grow under water is a prejudice rather than a certain truth. It is wiser not to speculate. The East Pole at 90°E in the Indian Ocean off the coast of Sumatra, and the Front Pole at 0° in the armpit of Africa, and the Back Pole at 180° near Kiribati, all on the equator of course, are identical to the one that was the West. Perhaps it will grow again.

When he was an old man, Caradoc Weasel decided to repay a visit to the site of his discovery. He also wished to purchase some fine wines, a plate painted with a picture of a winged cow and a replacement key for the front door of his house. He knew that the West Pole had become the biggest floating bazaar in the world. It was a place where almost anything, however unlikely, could be bought. He dug his life savings up from under the floorboards where he had been hiding them and set off on a ship. He was carried across the Atlantic Ocean and around Cape Horn, because this was a time before the Panama Canal was finished, and up along the Pacific coast of South America. When he reached the point of the Pole, he was astonished. There were no other ships in the area. The sea was empty all the way to the horizon.

True, he had not expected to see the actual Pole. Like its counterparts in the other oceans, the West Pole did not break the surface of the water. On a day without storms, when the sea was a smooth belly, the top of the Pole lay exactly level with the oceanic meniscus. It was neither higher nor lower than the surface by even so much as the breadth of a fish scale. Its flat top was part of the plane where liquid became air, a small but perfect circle at the intersection between ocean and atmosphere. This is why it had proved so difficult to discover. Only the hulls of ships knew, and they suffered for it. After it was established as a geographical feature, experienced eyes would look for the bent line of its shadow plunging into the depths and the infrequent glimmer of red and white.

Ships would tether themselves as close to the top of the Pole as possible. Other vessels that came along would moor themselves to these ships. The result was a web over which trade might scuttle to devour bad feeling and war. Securing the first rope to the Pole always required a swim. In time, the Pole appeared shorter and divers were needed for this operation. It was no longer as high as the sea was deep. Its summit was no longer level with the ocean's surface. The general fear was that the Pole was shrinking, or was being drawn through a hole in the seabed by an unknown agency. Only later was the alternative hypothesis that the sea was rising given serious attention. Various ideas were suggested for why this might happen. Increased rainfall was dismissed as an explanation, because the rain came from the sea in the first place. Melting icecaps and the arrival of extra water in comets both seemed more reasonable.

The truth was less catastrophic. Each time a vessel put to sea, it displaced a certain amount of liquid, a quantity equal to the volume of its hull below the waterline. In the early years of the Pole's existence, when there were no ships, it probably reared high above the surface of the sea, waiting for its first visitor. Pterodactyls might have used it for an occasional perch. Then ships were invented, but they hugged the coasts of lands far distant from the Pole. By the time they were able to cross the open ocean, there were so many of them and they were so large that the waves lapped around the top of the Pole. But at least it was still out of the water and could be glimpsed. Ancient mariners must have seen it and thus it became a rumour. When Caradoc Weasel discovered it for certain, its top was flush with the surface of the sea.

Now that explorer blinked, for the absence of other ships around the Pole was remarkable. His vessel steered close to the spot where it should have been, to secure a line, but nothing was there. The Pole had gone. The empty sea was now no more mysterious at that one point than at any other on its broad expanse. There was no reason why ships should not gather without the Pole, which really served no more than a symbolic function, but it appeared that the symbol was crucial. It was a reference point. Without it, the ocean offered nothing to tie knots on, save for dolphins and driftwood. But those were not stable. If trading ships gathered here without the Pole, they would be sure to look menacing, even if they acted in the same way as before.

An international search was started to locate the missing Pole. It might have been rotten inside and dissolved all at once, but everyone believed it had been stolen. There was no hard evidence for this, but it was the general feeling. The search was abandoned after a decade. Trade continued at the East, Front and Back Poles, but these locations never seemed as colourful as that of the West, even though the Poles were identical. Students were eventually blamed for the theft, though none were ever convicted. There is a college in a town somewhere whose students had chopped down the tallest tree in the world. They liked playing ambitious pranks. It was probably them. They denied it, of course, but their long fringes kept falling over their eyes, a most unlikely thing to happen in a town which has so many barbers, nearly every shop displaying a short length of striped pole.

There is the light of familiarity in Hywel's eyes and the fleshy parts of his face are filled with an expression of nostalgia and he asks Mondaugen if he originally heard that story from Caradoc Weasel's own lips, and it is clear he knew the explorer personally.

"No, by his deadly rival, Icarus Evans."

"Everybody seems to have a deadly rival!" I blurt.

Hywel ignores me and recalls another feat of exploration that has significant curiosity value for him.

"You know how people say that the moon is like a cheese? But this is absurd because the moon is far older than any cheese. The simile should be the other way around: cheese is like the moon (if any comparison at all is valid, and this one must be, for it has been made for generations). Therefore cheese must have been walked upon by tiny men who left a flag of their nation, part of a rocket and many footprints. It so happens that a cheese sample was subjected to a powerful electron microscope and these items were eventually found. Unexpectedly it was the flag of Switzerland! What does this mean?"

The Pan has other things on his mind. "I now accept those hoofprints are on their own because the horses that created them have been stolen, not because they are ghosts."

"Come on," I urge, "let's go elsewhere."

The Overseer and Mondaugen share my desire to reach Monmouth in good time. We finish the drinks that Hywel has poured us and he packs up his tent and we trudge onward.

I ask Hywel, "When that small barrel runs out will THE AWFULLY TALL STORY have to be closed?"

"No, because as the tent expands in size with each story told, there's a greater amount of condensation on the inside which can be collected and reused. Beer vapour! The real problem is that there will soon be too much and the tavern will be flooded."

"I won't drown," *smugly asserts the Pan.*

"Why not? Are you a champion swimmer?"

"Yes, I even taught Florian to swim and he was terrified of water. If you don't know who he was I'll give you a story (another classical one) about what happened to him..."

Because he has no choice, he tells it on the hoof.

12- ISLANDS IN THE BATHTUB

Florian loved company but it didn't like him. He invited it for nightly parties at his villa. It went to amuse itself at his expense. He was a hedonist. Some people called him a decadent, but there were too few shadows around his soul to justify that description. His character was stuck at the hour of noon, nearly sleepy, always lazy, overripe, fruitful but fermenting. His breath smelled of raisins. He was more colourful and soft than a mouldy pillow, but he inspired restlessness in other people.

He had nothing in life but what he hoped his guests thought of him. He had exiled himself from the land of his birth after waiting in vain for a scandal to force him out. He caught a train south with a bag of gems. These he exchanged in Naples for large banknotes. Then he visited

Cápri, deliberately fell in love with the place, and bought the ugliest house on the island. His garden was full of statues. His neighbours sniffed, but they drank his wine and encouraged their daughters to eat his food. They neglected only to bring their approval, which excited his determination to please them all the more.

The idea of staging an orgy came to him one morning as he lay in bed alone. He knew the history of Cápri, the home of the sirens, where emperors had indulged themselves in exaggerated vices. He knew that freshness and sensuality are an unfertile couple and do not give birth to guilt, unlike the filthier and staler practices of the mainland brothels. Clean water, foaming, glinting in the early evening, sweat of the sun on skin, the purity of cool spray, the liquid shiver that provokes feelings of innocence in a reveller. He would make use of mythological elements. There would be fun without disgust. Sirens at play, not perverts.

He ordered the construction of an enormous bathtub. It was big enough to hold a hundred people. Its sides sloped steeply from the shallows. Fifty golden taps on the ends of copper pipes curled into it as if preparing to drink. It would take a whole day to fill. The foundations of the villa had to be strengthened to bear the weight of the joyous fluid. The day before the date of the intended revel, he tested his latest extravagance. He was astounded to discover that the full bath was large enough to visibly display the gravitational tug of the sun and moon. It had tides. He cast in a barrel of bath salts and watched the waves turn crimson.

That night, while he was preparing to winch out the plug, he heard a loud noise in the garden. Heavy footfalls on the marble tiles. A window was opened and something climbed through. He listened to the laboured breathing of the intruder. He moved back into the shadows. The figure entered and stood on the edge of the bath. He was vast and powerful, but Florian did not hesitate. He rushed forward with a shout and a towel, casting the latter over the head of the newcomer. In the moment between the cry and the landing of the cloth, the intruder turned and exposed his visage to his host.

His expression was furious and ancient. The muscles stood out on his neck and the grinding of his jaw was audible above the lapping of the waves. He wore a black beard. His brows were dark also, and the hue of his face was scorched and tanned, as if it had been washed in ash. There had never been a man who looked more in need of a bath. Then the towel descended and his precarious balance was lost. Like a cliff collapsing into a sea, he slid into the waters. He did not rise. Florian winched out the plug. He did not want to watch the bath empty completely. He lurched into the adjacent room and sagged onto a chair, quaking and listening to the maelstrom of the draining tub with greedy ears.

Much later, when the hideous slurping had stopped, he rose and went back to check. There was no corpse at the bottom. All the water had gone and so had the drowned intruder. He did not bother to dwell on the enigma. He retired to bed. The next morning he checked again. There was still no sign of the man. He knew the bath worked, so he started filling it again. It would be ready for the orgy. That was the important point. He paced nervously but without energy to stamp the hours away. He sipped wine and was already a little drunk when he heard the first guests arriving. He turned off the taps, added salts and stood to survey his creation before seeking the naked bodies that were the final ingredient.

Under his intense gaze, a curious event began in the exact middle of the bath. Steam and streams of bubbles. Something was emerging from the deeps. An island! In many respects it was a smaller version of Cápri. The same cliffs and caves, but it was devoid of people or towns. A desert island. It grew and settled, cooling rapidly. It looked infinitely enticing. And other islands rose up around it, smaller and inferior, mere rocks in the shade of the paradise that gleamed its white beaches and shimmered its blue grottoes at him. Florian was entranced. He desired it with the urgency of a lover.

He climbed down the sloping side of the bath, staining his knees and palms on the grime encrusted on the porcelain. These tidemarks were genuine. Then he reached the waters and flung himself into the foam like a seal. He wallowed and swam to the main island, hauling himself up onto one of its more accessible shores. He dripped and panted out of the surf, climbing to his feet with pained astonishment and glancing at his surroundings with unmeasured delight. The island was a pristine version of Cápri, no doubt about it. The siren land. But had he been drawn here by song or bravado? There were no tunes in his ears, but his nerves throbbed and droned with pure melody.

Far away, he heard his guests babbling to themselves. A crowd on the other side of the bath-seas. How they would congratulate him on this charming and perfect addition to his marvellous tub! It would make the orgy seem yet more mythological and dreamlike. Although they were distant and vague, an acoustical effect not untypical of bathrooms amplified their chatter. He listened to their conversation with a smile that was clearly very heavy, for the strain of holding it up also caused him to frown. And then the smile itself flattened out and he felt ashamed. They were talking about him with undisguised contempt.

"Where has our fool of a host gone?"

"Eloped with the statue in the garden, no doubt. I noticed one was missing when I arrived."

"Can you guess which one?"

"Vulcan. The name on the plinth was clear on that point. The god of blacksmiths. The inventor. Patron of complicated machinery and engineer of seismic disturbances!"

"Pity he didn't care to linger for this. He loves boilers and pipes and valves, doesn't he? The god, I mean. I should have thought this arrangement would attract him like a moth to an ember. Excuse the easy simile. I don't feel elaborate today."

"Nor I. But if something doesn't happen soon, I'm going. Why were we invited here anyway?"

"Waste of time, if you ask me."

The party was nearly over before it had started. Florian waved eagerly to them across the frothing expanse, but they did not notice him. He blinked. The sides of the bath seemed very far away, much further than before. He did not believe he possessed enough strength to swim the return journey. Not now, not ever. His guests were tiny figures parading on a blurred horizon. Rising steam from the waters shrouded them. He called out and knew at once his shout had been smothered by the pounding of the waves. He was marooned. Stranded on an uninhabited island in the middle of his own bathtub. It was embarrassing.

He continued to jump and gesture with his arms. It made no difference. His guests were yawning and leaving. Their communal inhalation was a meteorological phenomenon. Then the bathroom was deserted save for him. He sat in the sand and crossed his legs. He needed to think hard. There was no vegetation on the island, nothing to eat. And no fresh water. When might he expect the rains? Then he remembered that the answer was never, for the bathtub was located indoors, beneath a roof. It was growing dark and he had no means of lighting a fire. With a sigh of castaway misery, he rose again and began the futile search for writing materials and a bottle.

It seems to me that I'm vaguely aware of this Florian as a real person, maybe I met him on one of my campaigns, but now I'm beginning to feel dismayed at how little progress we're making, stumbling along the poor road and stubbing our toes on little rocks, plus the perennial clouds look unfriendly again and rain must be due. I grow grumpy and decide to find someone to blame for my misery.

"You know how we discussed the lack of direct relation between some tales and their tellers? I've thought about it more carefully and I reckon the explanation might be very simple, nothing to do with other versions of the narrators in other universes."

"You've come to your senses!" cries Hywel.

"I reckon it's the fault of the author who's writing this framing device, forcing me to speak these very words at this precise moment. I accuse him of being idle and trying to force unconnected stories together by conjuring us up to tell them, a bully too because we can't refuse. He'll stop writing about us if we do, making us vanish, or fail to bring us into the action in the first place, like all those characters who were scheduled to appear but won't now because they refused to tell tales which didn't match their own identities."

Hywel counts the members of our group. "Funnily enough, I was wondering what happened to Lentil Optik, Persuasion Coax, Monkeyson Dewlaps and the Cat of Slime..."

"The Cat of Slime? Do you mean Ooze-Puss?"

"Yes. It's not dangerous really, but it's disgusting. What shall we do? Go on story strike and seal our lips?"

"Unless the author helps us out..."

There is a sudden snapping sound, the noise of wind in sails and a creaking and a shout from somewhere far to our left. Over the horizon comes a ship that is a peculiar pearly colour. I am reminded of the Battle of Trafalgar, not because the vessel looks like one of Nelson's, for there's not the slightest resemblance and the context of its approach is totally different, but for the reason that my memory of certain images is frequently jogged by things that have almost no connection to them, for instance when I look out of the page at you (the reader) I see a deformed pumpkin head carved in the wrong season by a badly trained ape. I'm sorry if you find that offensive, but I'm Napoleon Bonaparte, I'm not meant to be nice. Deal with it.

The ship comes closer and my amazement at seeing a sailing vessel making such good speed is further increased by the fact that it carries its own lake with it, an oval of deep water surrounding the hull and moving across the land like the shadow of a cloud carefully trimmed by scissors in the hands of a goblin. The captain stands on the deck and leans over the rail and hauls a cord that raises an inverted anchor from the water and he fixes one of its barbs to a plank. This anchor is connected to the bottom of the portable pool by a chain and so it seems that it is the water that has been fixed to the ship.

We approach the side of the stationary vessel.

The captain calls down, "What's that you're carrying? A pub, is it? Could do with a drink myself!"

"The price is a story. Are you Captain Dangleglum, by any chance? What do you have to tell us?"

He knits his brows furiously. "Nothing…"

"Sorry for asking!" I whimper.

"No, that's my name. Marlow Nothing, Captain Nothing! I suppose you're wondering how I managed to get hold of a ship that can sail on land? You probably think there's a good basis for a tale here? But there isn't much to tell on this score, this is the vessel known as 'Naglfar', the Viking vessel of Ragnarok — the end of the world. It belonged to Olaf Smorgasbord and he sailed it towards the doom of everything, but it was disappointing, Ragnarok turned out to be overrated, a local event, very small, and the rest of the world didn't notice (or maybe he went to the wrong location), so he sold it at auction and that's how it became mine. It's made entirely of fingernails."

"Where are you going?" I ask.

"On my way from Lladloh to Monmouth."

"Any chance of hitching a lift? We'll pay for our passage by setting up our tavern on deck and you can pay for drinks by telling us a proper tale. What do you say to that?"

Captain Nothing lowers a rope ladder. We climb it, grateful for this opportunity to save our tired legs. Then he casts the anchor back over the side and we start moving.

Hywel is particularly pleased and chortles, "The author has helped us out after all. We beat him!"

194

I nod but I still maintain my faith in parallel universes. Meanwhile, Captain Nothing is saying, "But you know something, this isn't even the strangest ship I've handled, Oh no! Unbelievable as it may seem I once captained a truly bizarre vessel."

Then he tells us this tale:

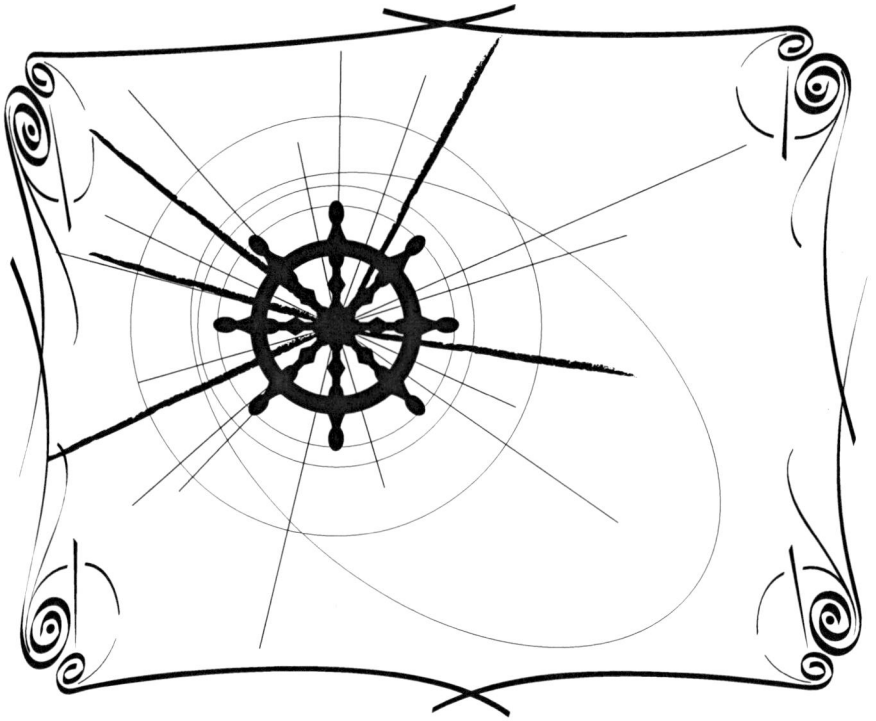

13- BILLION WORLD BOAT

When the God of Strange Ships wanted to create a vessel that could sail on land, he had to consider the merits of several different designs. A ship with wheels was too obvious and unremarkable; a ship that crossed continents by floating on a portable lake was cheating and had already been tried. No, it was necessary to come up with something original. That's the sort of god he was, Rudurr the Bent, so called because he walked with a stoop: he also walked with a sloop, using the boat as a crutch. Anyway, he finally settled on a design and called his carpenters to him. They came with chisels, hammers and saws, and he described what he wanted. Inwardly they were dismayed, for his chosen design resembled an ordinary ship, nothing strange about it at all, but they kept quiet and commenced building the thing; it wasn't their place to question a god. They worked quickly and it was soon ready.

Meanwhile, Rudurr went to see Gasklud, the God of New Planets, who was adding the finishing touches to a shiny gas giant, varnishing the ring system. Rudurr mentioned that he had a favour to ask and Gasklud told him to state it without any preamble. So Rudurr said, "I need a billion worlds by next week." At this, Gasklud threw up his arms and nearly knocked the gas giant off its pedestal. "Do you have any idea how long it takes to make just one new planet?" he spluttered. But Rudurr calmed him by saying, "I don't mean full sized worlds but little ones, just a few inches across, and they can all be identical, but they must be completely dry, without oceans or rivers, and preferably uninhabited." And Gasklud agreed this was much more reasonable and began work immediately. He only had to create one basic mould for all the worlds. As for pouring in the magma, his factory was automated and could fill the moulds on its own.

When the task was finished, Gasklud delivered the worlds to Rudurr in a sack, not an ordinary sack, but one used by the gods to hold improbably large things. The outside of the sack existed in our universe but the inside of the sack was a universe of its own, which explains how it can contain a billion worlds without bursting. Rudurr gave the sack and the ship to a mortal he knew he could trust. That mortal was a sailor by the name of Captain Nothing who had much experience of sailing strange ships. Captain Nothing stood on the deck of the ship with the sack, reached in and cast the worlds over the bow so that they rolled under the hull. The ship rumbled over these worlds and Rudurr was delighted. "A vessel that can sail on land!" he chortled. In fact he had exceeded his original ambition; for this ship crossed entire worlds, hundreds and thousands of them, without once touching water.

Each time Captain Nothing reached in for a handful of worlds, a few of them spilled out of the sack and rolled along the deck. This was inevitable. Some of these loose worlds fell down an open hatch into the hold. The hold slowly filled with worlds. Captain Nothing didn't notice or didn't care but he kept reaching into the sack and throwing worlds over the side. The ship was travelling very smoothly now, gliding along so easily that Captain Nothing made a vow to say more prayers to Rudurr in the future: he was clearly a very competent god. But suddenly he felt a finger tapping his shoulder and he turned to regard the beautiful Scala, Goddess of Fair Play, standing behind him with a mighty frown. She said, "This ship is disqualified and the game is over. Drop your anchor immediately and return the sack of worlds to Rudurr. I accuse you of cheating!"

Captain Nothing was astonished and requested an explanation. Scala was happy to provide one. "This ship is no longer sailing on land but hovering in the air. The little worlds under the hull are turning over and over; the little worlds in the hold got there by rolling across the deck. The magma inside all of them has been sloshed around. Do you know why magnetic fields form around certain planets? It is because of motion in the liquid iron near their cores. Only planets with liquid iron inside them can ever be magnetic. The worlds in that sack are newly made and haven't cooled yet and rolling has generated enormous magnetic fields around them. The worlds under the hull and the worlds in the hold have become highly magnetic and they are repulsing each other. This means that the ship has been levitated a few inches into the air and so the terms of Rudurr's ambition have been violated. As the Goddess of Fair Play, I had to intervene."

Captain Nothing was not a scientific man but he felt something didn't ring true. He knew that *unlike* poles attract and *like* poles repel and he thought that as the worlds rolled over and over they would alternately attract and repel the ship, causing a motion rather like stormy waters at sea, or that the worlds being in different positions, with their poles pointing randomly, the individual magnetic fields would cancel each other out. At any rate, the ship shouldn't just hover. But he didn't care to argue with a goddess and so he merely said, "I accept your point but please give me a second chance." And when she nodded with a sigh, he ran into the hold with the sack and replaced all the spilled worlds, then he climbed back onto the deck, closed the hatch and resumed throwing handfuls of worlds over the side. The ship began moving again, less smoothly, and Scala watched him with a sceptical look in her eyes. Sure enough, the ship soon came to a halt.

"Now the only magnetic force is beneath the ship," she explained, "and as the worlds get magnetised by being rolled they stick to the iron nails that hold the planks of the hull together. So the little worlds stop rolling and the ship can't move. The game is still over; Rudurr has failed!" But Captain Nothing blurted, "Please give me a third chance!" And he jumped up and down, trying to loosen the worlds from the magnetic grip, and suddenly the ship did indeed move, but upwards, and only a few inches. Scala sniffed. "The little worlds were agitated enough already. By jumping up and down, you have caused them to burst. The magma inside has been forced out and the ship is floating on miniature volcanic eruptions." At this news Captain Nothing cried, "Abandon ship!" and Scala caught him in her arms and flew off to safety. She set him down in front of Rudurr. Despite the fact his ship was burning fiercely, the god seemed pleased. "I created a vessel that not only sailed on land but on air and fire as well!" The only remaining question was what to do with the unused worlds in the sack. To the best of my knowledge, they still haven't decided.

When the tale is done I toast the Captain's health with a glass of dark beer. "What a coincidence you've found another ship which can sail on land! They can't be too common."

It is growing stuffy inside the tent despite the fact it's so much bigger now than before and I go outside for fresh air, plus to see where we are going because we have left Naglfar to steer itself and there is always the danger of collision with some obstacle.

I am amazed and delighted to discover that we are sailing down a street and there are houses and shops on every side, and worried people who jump aside and curse as we splash them with water, but not too many drops, because if the pool which carries the vessel gets emptied it'll leave us high and stranded.

"This looks like Monmouth!"

Without prompting, I pull the cord that lifts the anchor and I fix it to the deck. We pause in the middle of Monnow Bridge, over the river, and our portable pool starts to leak through the bottom of the bridge into the river but I know we can replenish it from this source, so I'm not too worried anymore. My companions emerge from the tent and yawn and stretch themselves and gaze around.

"Doesn't look like the gnoles have made much progress yet. Good for us, that fact! Shall we explore?"

There is something harsh I want to say to Hywel and I can't keep it in. I stand before him and mutter, "Just because the author gave us a lift on this ship doesn't mean he's a good person, he stopped those potential characters entering the framing device, remember? Ooze-Puss hasn't got many friends but the others do, and they would have brought them, all customers for THE AWFULLY TALL STORY. Without those people, we don't have a viable pub, there are only six of us, we need more patrons in here, it's essential for business."

"That's right and I know just the place to find them."

And he points at another pub, a real tavern of brick and glass called THE GREEN DRAGON and I understand his cunning scheme at once, he plans to set up his tent inside this other pub, creating a tavern within a tavern, and to steal the customers from this rival establishment, until his tent expands to wholly fill the space. From that point on, anyone who passes through the front door will unwittingly enter our pub, not the one they think they're going into.

We share this plan with our comrades.

The only one to greet it without much enthusiasm is the Pan. "I have to confess something, I'm a Pan but not an ancient one, my name is Tangerine Pan and I was born, or created, right here in Monmouth, in the basement of this pub in fact! If I go in I might be recognised and they don't like me too much. It wasn't the double-headed monster that chased me into the fields but the patrons of that tavern. I recall those days with affection as well as dismay, I wore a toga made from orange peel but the pitted design never became fashionable."

"So all that stuff about Kérkira was a lie?"

"Yes, I caught the habit of lying from the bronze man Gnathon, who had no choice in the matter. It turned out that the curse of always lying was infectious and I caught it."

"Wait a moment! You are lying about being a liar! If the tale wasn't true it can't be true you can't tell the truth."

"Less paradoxes please! I have a sore head," roars a voice from outside the page. This is the first time I've heard the author speak and I don't like it, because it seems superfluous.

"Sorry," replies Tangerine Pan.

"Look," says Hywel after due consideration, "I can't allow my scheme to be spoiled just because a few people don't like whatever you did in the past. We'll have to take the risk of entering. Maybe the clientele will have changed? It happens to many pubs."

We disembark from the ship and step through the doorway of THE GREEN DRAGON. Hywel's hunch turns out to be correct. None of the drinkers inside are local, they all have outlandish accents and the look of outsiders about them. We keep to the darkest shadows and Hywel erects his tent in an inconspicuous corner and the management takes no notice. While he is busy securing the guy ropes I wander around and fall into conversation with the drinkers seated around several big tables and by chance it turns out they are sharing tales too, tales rather more profound and sophisticated than ours.

"So this is a writers' convention?" I enquire.

"Yes, we represent a loose cabal of Aspiring Speculative Writers and we are gathered here to swap stories and also to debate the function and mechanics of imaginative fiction. My name is Jeffrey Ford. Let me introduce you to some of the people here... This learned fellow is Michael Cisco, one of the most underrated authors of modern philosophical fiction in the world; he is philosophical about everything except that fact! Here are some others... Brendan Connell, Elise

Blackwell, Robert Devereaux, David Soares, Catherynne Valente, Luís Filipe Silva, Jay Lake, Vera Nazarian, Safaa Dib, Claude Lalumière, Lawrence Schimel, Jorge Candeias, Yvonne Navarro…"

There is a warm glow behind him that suddenly grows brighter. I peer at the hearth in the wall and see that it is full of sculpted sunbeams instead of burning logs. A man has just added another handful and then he turns slowly and winks at me.

"That is Stepan Chapman, a fellow capable of holding raw sunlight without gloves. And this other one is Nathan Ballingrud. Here is Forrest Aguirre and João Seixas… Blanca Riestra, Lázaro Covadlo, David Rix, Nuno Fonseca… The one playing the little guitar is Luís Rodrigues and he's not an author but a book designer and he's busy designing covers and layouts for all the authors gathered here. His girlfriends are always goddesses, and that's no metaphor…"

"Designing layabouts?" I stammer.

"Layouts," he corrects me. "Fonts and margins and things like that."

I'm so excited I rush back to Hywel, who has finished setting up his tent, and tell him about these people. He's filled with a desire to impress them, to become part of their convention, and so he calls us all together into his tavern within a tavern. He thinks that together we can invent a story that will earn our admittance into their circle. It shall be one of those stories that are popularly labelled 'speculative fiction', so it has to conform to the rules and standards of that genre. But we don't know what those rules and standards really are. We sit inside the tent and drink beer and write a story together.

When it is finished we emerge and approach the tables and stand in a line and declaim it all at once:

202

14- THE SMUTTY TAMARINDS

It was obvious to Ezra that his life had become a joke. People laughed when he entered a room and applauded when he left. A heckler might shout, "Get off! You're rubbish!" and Ezra would hold back a tear and reply with trembling lips, "But I'm not even on!" This response made heads shake. It wasn't good enough.

Not that he was expected to say something funny in return. It wasn't his words but his soul that was judged as amusing or boring, depending on personal taste. My *life* is the joke, he reminded himself. Danielle had diagnosed his condition long ago but she'd used different words. "You're a failure, Ezra, and I'm leaving you."

One of the reasons he kept entering rooms was because he was still looking for her, to beg her to come back. He never admitted this fact to himself and always pretended the rooms contained something brand new he wanted to see for the first time.

Rather awkwardly he would peer around a door, squint at the upper and lower corners of any room that was square, or roll his eyes at the total expanse of a circular chamber, and then remark with phoney curiosity, "Is that one of those carpets I've heard so much about? Is that a mantelpiece? Are those stringy things cobwebs?"

The occupants usually groaned in return, "Corny old stuff. We want a refund." And Ezra would be forced to dip into his own pockets and cough up. Needless to say his savings were soon in peril of running out. Time to stop entering random rooms! But what if Danielle happened to be inside the very next one? Unbearable…

The only other solution was to seek medical help, so Ezra arranged an appointment with Dr Walnut. Along he went early the next morning. The receptionist, Miss White, led him into a space hazy with pungent hookah fumes where the doctor blew Möbius strips from his nostrils and nodded as Ezra described his ailment.

"I'm sorry to say I can't help," admitted Dr Walnut, glancing up as one wide smoke ring settled over the crown of his fez like a halo with engine trouble. "My knowledge of infectious humours is slight. I'll recommend a specialist, however. A certain Professor Tamarind will doubtless quickly cure you. Here's his address."

"Are you keeping anything back?" asked Ezra.

Dr Walnut pondered. "Boo?"

"I don't mean that… Bah, it doesn't matter. I'll put all my trust in this Tamarind fellow of yours."

"He has some wives," warned Dr Walnut.

"A polygamist, you mean?"

"They're not his own. He just borrows them."

"From their husbands?"

"No, from a row of cottages and a few isolated villas. Those wives are all housewives and so don't have human spouses. Dwelling places get far less jealous than flesh men."

Ezra didn't know what to make of this and walked out indignantly. As he left the surgery, Miss White called out, "Encore!" but Ezra didn't pause to oblige her, partly because he guessed she was being ironic, and instead he went straight to the address on the scrap of paper held in his hand. The building that confronted him when he got there wasn't a house but a string of pods suspended from a gantry.

He climbed the ladder, crossed the catwalk, knocked on a circular door and was astonished when it opened by itself. Then he realised that doors are equally amazed when people pull or push them every time they are in the process of opening or closing.

Professor Tamarind sat on a levitating carpet in the middle of the room but his mystic pose was less convincing that it might be, because his legs dangled over the edge. He leaned forward slightly and studied Ezra with a pair of binoculars. "I discern your ailment at once," he sniffed. "Have you been ingesting too many figs?"

Ezra shook his head emphatically, so the expert lowered his binoculars and picked up a telescope instead. Now he saw clearly. With a tiny gong, he summoned his wives into his presence. They rushed into the chamber and began dancing a sensuous samba routine. Smooth thighs were much in evidence, also generous amounts of cleavage, and tanned midriffs were pleasingly undulated to excess.

"Believe it or not, this display is part of the cure! What's more serious in the entire cosmos than erotic dancing? It's the opposite of comedy, the antidote to jests and witticisms."

"They're very smutty wives," approved Ezra.

"And they're all mine – temporarily! But it's the juice of the dance that will stop your life being a joke, rather than the dance itself. Here's a bottle of the stuff I prepared earlier."

"And how does it work exactly?"

"The price is negotiable. Drink it all down."

"That's not what I asked."

"Good point! The medicine first degrades a joke into an anecdote, then into a memoir, then into an excuse and finally into a set of circumstances. Nobody will laugh at that point. The joke will no longer be on you but on them, whoever 'them' might be."

Ezra scratched his chin. "I'll take it." And he left the room and climbed back down the ladder, while the wives of Professor Tamarind crowded on the catwalk and blinked at him.

"I will pay you only if it works," Ezra called up.

"Heard that one many times!"

Ezra went home, took the medicine and waited for it to distribute itself throughout his system. He regarded his own reflection in the mirror and it wasn't funny at all, but that wasn't sufficient proof the cure had worked. A more rigorous test was needed.

He braved the outdoors again and went into the first unlocked room he passed. It belonged to a public library. Most people inside laughed behind or over their books, but a few gasped, "Oooh!" or "Aaah!" as if he'd done something tricky or hazardous.

It was far too early to properly evaluate its merits, so he continued to drink the juice, one spoonful a day, as recommended on the bottle's label, but nothing much changed. A week later he returned to the pod in a mood of antagonistic disgruntlement.

"The same as before, but different!" he complained.

"I perceive what has happened," said Professor Tamarind slowly. "The cure was only partly successful. Your whole existence is no longer just a joke but a short variety performance, a vaudeville show. Your present is still a joke, but your past is some kind of juggling routine and your future is a risky knife-throwing act."

Ezra sighed. "Let me guess. Tales like this always end in an ironically absurd way. I'm going to be killed by those knives, stabbed by my own future? Probably in the following paragraph, because the 'future' is only the next instant away. The alternative is that I trip on the dropped balls of my past and break my neck!"

"You believe such twist endings await you?"

"That's what I'm asking!"

"My dear fellow, you've got it all wrong," smiled the professor. "You will never catch up with your own future, because the moment you enter the future it instantly becomes the present. As for the past, that was also the present when it actually happened, so it doesn't matter what happens before or after *now*, your life is still a joke. The medicine has failed. But I can suggest a better remedy."

Ezra composed himself to listen. "Yes?"

Professor Tamarind shifted his weight on the levitating carpet, sending down clouds of dust. "Every joke needs a punchline. When that punchline is delivered, the joke is finished."

"So there's hope? It'll all be over eventually?"

"Yes, but you're a healthy man, so death from old age is decades away, and your punchline will be pending until then, so to stop your life being a joke we must induce the punchline artificially. Kindly stand over there, in the middle of my chamber."

"Over this trapdoor, you mean?"

"I do. When I pull this lever the trapdoor will open and you'll plummet thirty metres to the hard ground where life will be dashed out of you, thus bringing your punchline forward and ending the joke neatly, dramatically, indubitably. Are you ready?"

"To be honest, I'm not so sure I want to die permanently just to escape being the focus of laughter."

Professor Tamarind waved a dismissive hand. "Oh, don't worry about that. The point of a punchline is that it makes a joke replicable. When you fall to your doom, the joke is ended – which implies a punchline. Then I'll be in a position to repeat the joke, pass it to as many people as I like, to my wives, my other patients, my friends, to Dr Walnut, to anyone who'll listen! There's no question of your death being permanent. Indeed you'll be far longer lived when you're properly in circulation. But that can only happen after your first death."

Ezra licked his lips. "Very well. I'm convinced."

The professor nodded and pulled the lever. The trapdoor opened and Ezra fell through the bottom of the pod, turning once in midair before he struck the ground. He didn't groan as the blood fled his body in questing rivulets, as sometimes it does.

Professor Tamarind peered over the edge of the trapdoor. For a long time he stared down at the body, frowning. The punchline was there but an unforeseen problem had arisen. He scratched his head but finally had to withdraw his concentration.

"Sorry. I just don't get it," he admitted.

This tale is greeted with absolute silence. Even the fire doesn't crackle, because it is loaded with sunbeams, not wood. At last one of the men, I think it's Stepan Chapman, clears his throat and they all turn back to what they were talking about before we approached them, as if we don't exist. It's clear they are not at all impressed and I think I know why, we got our tale badly wrong and our assumptions about what they hoped for were incorrect, so we slink back in embarrassment, seeking refuge from our deep shame inside the tent.

But it has disappeared! Has it shrunk to nothing because our tale 'collapsed the envelope' of fiction? The story was poor enough to do that but Hywel still doesn't understand what the problem is, he believes it was a perfect example of speculative fiction, he just doesn't know what the genre really means now, despite or perhaps because he only exists as a character in such tales himself.

I try to disillusion him gently. "The standards those writers operate with have advanced beyond our assumptions, we didn't have a clue, we thought speculative fiction had to be devoid of maturity, simple escapism is what we gave them, not good enough."

Hywel accepts this reluctantly. "A miserable experience! But where's THE AWFULLY TALL STORY?"

"I'll look for it," I offer.

I don't voice my suspicion it has shrunk to the size of a molecule, the result of an utterly drastic collapse of the envelope of fiction, but I can't find it anywhere indoors, so I step outside. The sky appears strange, the stars are there in the night but behind them there is a faint background, as if the emptiness at the very edge of outer space has been filled or the universe has suddenly acquired a material wall or boundary but one that gently ripples, a soft perimeter.

Then I know. Tent fabric…

Somehow the tent has expanded to the same size as the universe! The exact opposite to what I feared has happened, but it's no less disturbing, there may be consequences that I can't imagine yet. The envelope of fiction has been pushed so fast and so violently that its volume matches that of the cosmos entire! The inner walls of the tent are now the walls of creation! I try to run back inside THE GREEN DRAGON to share this revelation but my progress is barred by five ejecting bodies all belonging to my comrades. It appears the barman of the establishment has spotted Tangerine Pan and not only thrown him out but all the people near him who are guilty by association.

I blubber what has happened...

Hywel looks up and reaches into his pocket for his jagged piece of the Impossible Mirror, taking it out and hurling it at the sky like an upward thunderbolt. As it hisses into the heavens, falling far short of the edge of the atmosphere let alone the rim of the universe, I glimpse the figures in its surface again, a young couple on a beach, but again the details of the scene elude me. Then the thunderbolt has gone and the far side of the sky still ripples in the light intergalactic winds and Captain Nothing begins trembling without adequate reason.

"This is more dramatic than Ragnarok!"

"I don't know much about that," says Mondaugen.

Hywel answers for the Captain:

"It's a time when the gods swarm over the rainbow, which is really a bridge from Valhalla to this world, not a curve of light, but there are so many myths about rainbows which contradict this idea that I'm not sure it can take a man's weight, let alone a god's. I've discussed this mystery already with Old Bony here."

"You have," I sigh. "One of the first tales you ever told me concerned how boots are sometimes found at the end of rainbows instead of gold, but how on one occasion a man found a 'Gator instead of a gaiter and was devoured by the reptile."

"I thought it was you who told me that tale. But I apologise anyway. And now I'm wondering whether it's feasible to have different sorts of rainbows, I mean a rainbow is curved light and good for the eye, but can such a phenomenon be replicated in terms of other senses? A rainbow of smell or taste: an arch of separated flavours on the tongue, as many flavours as that lake. Or sounds. Touch. Maybe even for the elusive sixth sense?"

"Shall we return to the ship?" asks the Overseer.

"No good, the pool has drained away into the river, it was too deep for the thickness of the bridge!"

"Naglfar has sunk into dryness..."

We regard each other and the sky with pouts. A flock of migrating bell peppers passes gracefully overhead. "It's getting cold, as if the whole cosmos has gone camping! We miss those blazing sunbeams! Kindly tell us a warm story."

Hywel considers his options. "I still have the one about the dragon. It is also about the stolen horses that left the prints (but I won't know that until I tell it). It's not the dragon's breath which is warm, but the nature of the meal contained inside it…"

15- A CURRY IN CAMELOT

For most of the day and night, he was Christopher. But from dawn to sunrise he became Sir Dogge de Pyg. He had knighted himself in a dream. When he awoke, the scars from the sword were still fresh on his shoulders and scalp. His horse was a thoroughbred figment. His armour was emotional and badly designed. He was always on an unspecified quest.

On one occasion he attended a party that seemed to have no end. It took place at the house of his friend, Brian. There was a steep hill with cobbles and empty cider bottles. The sea slurped in the distance. He ran up the steps that led to the front door and rang the bell. Something on its way somewhere else stopped for a rest on the roof. Brian answered in person and also in a dressing gown. They exchanged greetings not at all.

There were already other people in the available rooms. The food and chatter on offer were modern and realistic. The two men moved aimlessly through the swamps of wit and posture. They nodded at Darren and his fringe. He was still wearing his rollerskates. The pet monkey on his shoulder had long since turned into a greasy skeleton. It clattered when he shrugged.

For most of the day and night, Brian was himself. But from dawn to sunrise he became Sir Fisch von Kat. There was a shortage of original dreams in the area. His weapon of choice was the absent axe. His own steed was a bannister. He had finally decided to share his secret with his close acquaintances. That is why his party was scheduled to continue beyond first light.

There was a spare kitchen upstairs. The steams of a forgotten curry on the stove were like the mists of a battlefield. Christopher, Brian and Darren found themselves alone here and without conversation. So they sat on chairs and made facial expressions in artificial languages. The clock on the wall could be heard but not seen, the opposite of an antique child. Music pulsed up from below.

For most of the day and night, Darren was himself. But from dawn to sunrise he became Sir Luv o' Duk. His dead monkey was his squire. It was unable to boil kettles and potatoes, but he forgave it and jousted with jests. The candles in the wine bottles died and he continued to linger in the dark with the others. Because facial expressions were no longer visible, they gestured with long arms, slapping each other.

This violent motion of limbs, six in total, fanned away the steams. The way to the window was now clear. Blushing with pain, they regarded the pane. Soft light swelled behind it. The false dawn had arrived. But still they did not rise and hide. They awaited the inevitable, unaware they all shared the same condition. A little more time and it came upon them. They changed and chanted their mottoes:

"Grunt! Woof!"

"Glug! Miaow!"

"Kiss! Quack!"

Then they stood and issued challenges and charged at nothing in heroic fashion. Soon they were exhausted and fell down. It had been a long night. As they lay unmoving on the floor, a plan formed in each of their delirious minds. They would combine their strength. They would build a castle somewhere. There would be a banqueting hall with a table in the shape of a triangle. And a lady in a lake. Or if not that, then a sponge in a puddle.

As they continued to scheme behind paralysed faces, a girl entered. She was slim and dark. A party without girls is a contradiction in terms. She stepped over the prone bodies. They beheld a damsel, but not one in distress. She moved to the stove and dipped a spoon into the saucepan. The curry had evaporated. She shook her head and frowned. The smell of food had attracted her. But it was not this. There must be something else.

The knights incorrectly imagined that her name was Dawn. If she stood opposite them and the window, they would remain between dawn and sunrise and so not change back. They willed her to maintain the same relative position. But she seemed agitated. She left sooty footprints behind her as she walked in circles, searching in cupboards for the source of the enticing aroma. The simple truth of the situation was that her present identity came with conditions.

It was a time of migrations. A knight is a delicacy to certain tongues. Three different flavours at the same time is a temptation too strong to resist. She continued to search, brushing herself down as she did so. The chimney and fireplace had been disused for many years. She sighed. Even dragons can share the dreams of men. Then the sun came up and the age of chivalry was over again.

The tales are done at last, thankfully, and we decide to split up and go our separate ways, to reduce (but not obliterate) the chances of surplus stories being generated. The performance is finished. But there's still the question of how the tent expanded so rapidly and this bothers me but I suddenly seem to have the solution.

"None of our tales were good enough to push the envelope of fiction even a millimetre, let alone to the edge of space, but the simple fact we believed we could modify this envelope at all and that the reader would accept this to be true, was so outrageous that our uniquely proportioned self delusion did the expansion for us. The only innovative fiction in the whole process was that conceit!"

Hywel shuffles his feet. "You're right, my pub could never have grown bigger in reality with the appalling quality of all those stories but it no longer matters, because it's all finished, the performance is over. What usually happens at the end of a performance? I'm sure something happens, but I can't remember what."

"That's odd. Neither can I!"

"It's something specific, I'm sure."

"I've always been vague on specifics. I guess the answer will come to us when we least expect it."

"It's not booing, is it?"

"It might be, especially in our case, but I don't think that's what you mean. Something the opposite of booing."

"But what? Answer me, Little Nappy!"

"Don't ever speak that name! I've decided to become uptight again, as a way of conquering the hours."

Hywel smirks and remarks, "The whole universe is a pub. That means there can't be anywhere outside it, so after closing time (whenever that is) everything in creation will have to shut down. We simply don't have as much spare time as before."

"Outside the universe? There's a thought…"

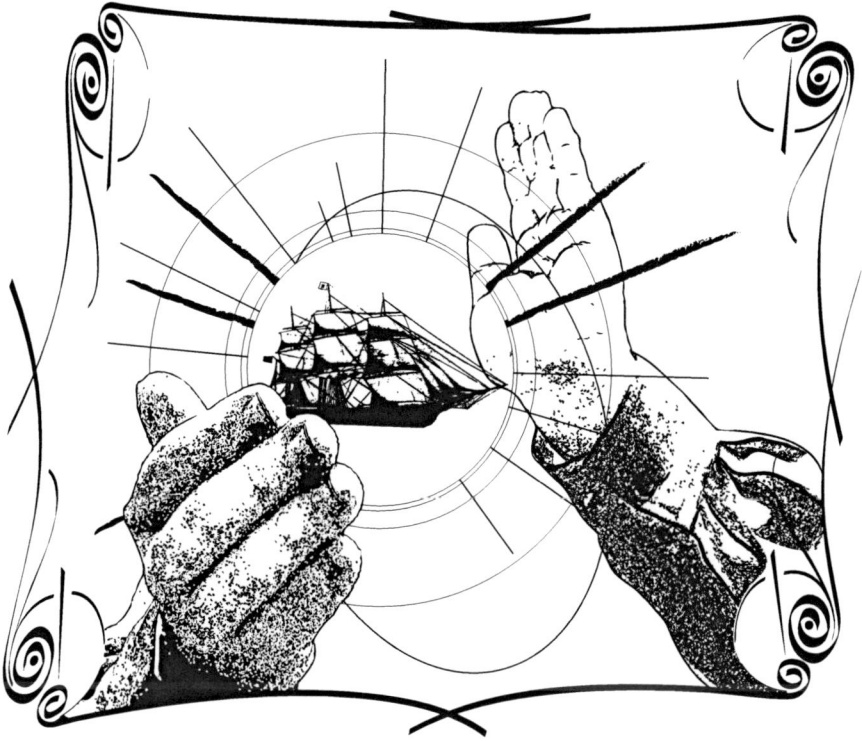

16- ENCORE

A city on the coast.

They went for a walk by the sea.

It was wild.

The man held the woman close.

"I love being here. What do you love?"

"You. Cherries and coffee. Dancing in moonbeams. Kissing."

"What else?"

"Isn't that enough? Music. Sleep."

He scratched his nose. "I mean do you love anything that nobody else loves? Something unique or utterly new."

"Give me an example."

"Certain kinds of idea that just come into your head."

She laughed. "Not really. Those are distractions. I welcome some of them, but love isn't the right word."

He picked up a pebble on the beach and cast it as far as he could. It vanished in the waves but they pushed it back. It rolled at his feet and settled. He gazed at it but left it alone.

"Everybody loves storms at sea."

She returned to his arms. "Except those out on them."

"This one is getting worse."

She pointed. "Is that a clipper?"

"Yes. It seems to be coping. They are designed to survive rough weather."

"There's a man on deck!"

"Probably the navigator. He looks experienced enough."

She listened to the roar of the ocean. "You're right about storms. When the sea is like this I always feel good about myself. But when it's calm I feel insecure. There's something very reassuring in this kind of tumult."

"Don't go too close. The waves look really powerful."

"Shall we leave now? We can come back later, if you like. It's even better at night."

He considered this. "It depends on the forecast."

"I already know it. Terrible."

"Very well. But before we depart I want to know what you thought of the lecture today. Did you find it interesting?"

"The professor couldn't be boring even if he tried."

"But what is your opinion of what he said?"

She sighed. "I followed his reasoning but if you want my honest answer I just wasn't convinced. It's fine in theory but I can't accept any of it is true. The concept is clever, but I prefer to learn about the real world around us."

"So you don't believe in parallel dimensions?"

"Of course not. Do you?"

"Not until a minute ago. It was just before I asked you what you loved. I had a sudden idea. An image in my head. It came unexpectedly. I saw a world that should be impossible."

"Can you still see it?"

"Not in the same way. The picture is fading. In an hour I'll probably doubt I ever saw it. This is why I need to talk about it. I'm not mad. Maybe together we can hold on to some part of it. Our private place."

"What was it like?"

He clutched his head. "Unbearably strange but beautiful. In essence it was the same as this world but with one difference. A difference that was profound."

Above the surge he could only make himself heard properly by pressing his mouth close to her ear. She listened and bit her lower lip. When he had finished, she pulled at his hand.

"Come away now."

Before they went, they bowed to the ocean. It was something they always did. It would have seemed impolite not to. Then the clipper came back into view, sailing in the other direction.

They turned and walked to the university.

"I always feel compelled to bow," he said.

"And to keep returning. It's our tradition."

He nodded. "Did you understand what I said to you?"

"Sort of. I still have difficulty seeing it in my mind. A world where calm seas make people feel good but rough seas make them feel agitated."

"Yes. The exact opposite of this one."

"A world where the waves don't have fingers and where clippers deliver tea and wool instead of trimming the uncut nails of the surf."

"It sounds foolish when you put it like that."

"Sorry. I just can't imagine an ocean made of water instead of hands."

He shrugged. "You're right. Forget it."

Behind them the applause receded.

Part 3

LAST TALLER
STORIES

*1.

Hywel Price said, "All the universe has become a pub, and it is only right I should appoint myself its landlord, for an inn without a keeper is worse than a tale without a teller; and speaking of tales it seems to me that every story from this time forth must be tall by default — for they will all be told inside a pub and all pub tales are always tall. That's just the way it is. An immutable law.

"Wherever a person might be — Cardiff, Glasgow, New York, Lisbon, Timbuctu, Lipsaria, Andromeda or in galaxies more distant — his story will be heard in just one location, namely in my pub, in my cosmos. And as there are twenty-four hours in a day, let a tale be told to represent each hour, because that's a nice symmetry of sorts, and let each new teller come from the preceding story.

"I know that pubs are required to close down at regular intervals and I have no wish to violate the licensing laws, but I can always bolt the doors and declare our activity to be the result of a private party. On second thoughts, why bolt anything? Who can enter the universe from outside? And surely those who would prosecute me are also on my premises at the time of the violation and therefore equally guilty? So I am safe!

"Now then: who will be first to come forth and speak a tale to represent the first hour of the universe's first day as a pub; the hour that follows midnight and is reputed in some quarters to be a haunted bundle of sixty minutes? Who indeed? This old fellow with the aspect of a professor seems a suitable choice. What do you know about ghosts, good sir? You'll have to step forward and speak up if we are expected to hear and believe you!"

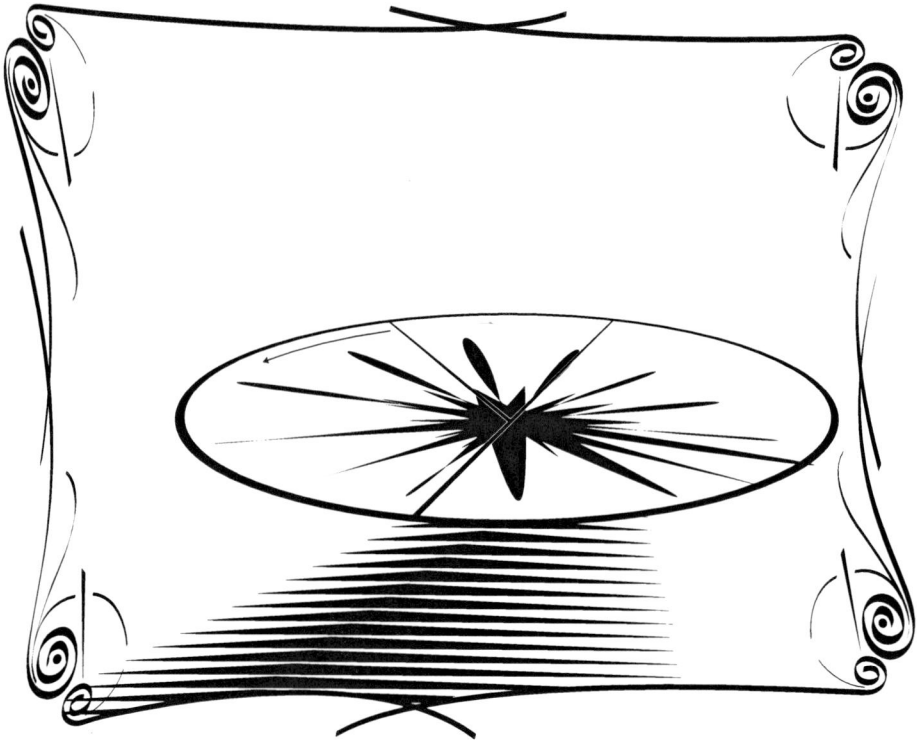

THE SURFACE AREA OF
A GHOST'S WANDERINGS

Now that we understand everything there is to know about ghosts, we rarely pay them much attention. But it wasn't always like this. Oh no! In my youth hauntings were still mysterious and I remember many nights of speculation as to the substance and behaviour of spooks. The first mystery to be solved concerned the surface area of a ghost's wanderings and I am pleased to take the credit for deriving a simple geometric formula for determining the absolute limit of a phantom's territory.

Before my discovery, the general hypothesis was that spectres retained some sort of sentimental connection to the place where the body that housed them had died. It was assumed that an emotional barrier prevented ghosts from venturing more than a small distance from the location of their demise. This view was most unsatisfactory and left unanswered a number of awkward questions, such as what happens when a man expires on an aeroplane. Does his spirit continue flying with the machine or is it left behind in mid air?

Another objection to this view involved the nature of sentiment and emotion. These are qualities of a physical body alone. The feelings available to human beings, whether love, hate, anger, misery, joy or even nostalgia, are not possible without nervous and circulatory systems. When there is no pulse to increase or decrease, no blood pressure to rise or fall, no glands to secrete chemicals, there can be no emotions. For instance, while I sit and wait on this chair on the landing I am apprehensive and this feeling is definitely biological rather than abstract.

"Bad news, I am afraid. The worst has happened!"

Please excuse this interruption. My assistant has just come out of the bedroom. I must issue instructions to him first and then return to what I was saying. One moment.

"Saddle my horse and lead him to the front gate."

"As you wish, professor."

During the absence of my assistant I will search for my hat and cloak. I took them off less than an hour ago. Where are they? Anyway, to resume my small lecture, let me stress that there was no consensus of opinion on the shape of the supposed emotional barrier that confined a ghost to a certain geographical position. We did not even know if the outline was regular or irregular. I remember the day I proved the boundary was perfectly circular, the sighs of relief from my colleagues, the praise from exorcists.

I wish I could claim my solution to the problem was the result of my superior imagination, a sudden insight during a drab working day, but in fact it was due to many years of collecting data. Ghosts were followed by teams of researchers night after night, measurements were made and carefully recorded. The truth gradually emerged as I studied the figures. The theory of emotional connections rapidly became redundant. Some phantoms wandered much further than others, a few appeared free to float anywhere without obvious restrictions.

Allow me to draw my gloves on as I reveal what you surely already know, that the surface area of a ghosts's wanderings is determined not only by the place of death but the displacement between the place of death and place of birth. The distance between these two points forms the diameter of a circle. Within this circle a newly released phantom may float wherever it pleases. The greater the length of the diameter, the larger the circle and thus the freer the ghost. It is a simple and frequently very unfair formula.

I recall the salesman who once knocked on the door of my house. He wanted to sell insurance and informed me of the fact by shouting through my letterflap. Exhausted by a long working day he leaned on my door for support at the same moment I opened it to confront him. He fell forward, struck his head on my granite floor and died instantly. The impact site marked a point on the circumference of the circle that was now available to him as his personal space. He was not able to fully enter my house to haunt me in revenge because my threshold was at the limit of his territory.

I lived in Oxford at that time and the salesman had been born in Coventry, a distance just under fifty miles. The centre point of his circular territory was thus near the village of Banbury. A pair of compasses and a suitable map will demonstrate that both Northampton and Rugby were available to him but he could not reach as far as Birmingham. His situation was not perfect but it was not unbearable. And now I hear my assistant running back up the stairs. Soon I will be too busy to continue with my little talk, so I will cite only two more examples and then hurry to a conclusion.

There was a fellow born in Quito in Ecuador who died near Padang in Sumatra, a distance of about 12,500 miles. Therefore his ghostly territory was enormous, reaching as far north as Greenland and as far south as Antarctica. The whole of Europe, Africa and Near Asia was accessible to him and much of South America, India and Russia. Conversely there was another man born at one end of Charteris Road in Kilburn who died at the other end. His subsequent wanderings were extremely confined and did not even reach as far as Paddington Old Cemetery, where he might have visited his own grave.

"Your horse is ready, professor."

"Thank you kindly. Have you seen my hat and cloak?"

"You are already wearing them."

And so I am. The forgetfulness that comes with old age is a curious thing! I step quickly towards the bedroom door and open it. That spook in Kilburn is fated to have a boring afterlife but there are even less agreeable circumstances for ghosts to be in. At least that fellow had his own street and a few neighbouring streets to float down. Imagine being confined to one house or one room or even one bed! It is in the interest of every man and woman to die as far from their place of birth as possible. But not everyone is given a decent chance to do so. The injustice is awful.

Dying during your own birth is the worst scenario. As I enter the bedroom I bow politely to the midwife and the tragic prone mother. Then I take the bundle offered to me and I hasten out of the room and down the stairs. I must ride with the unfortunate child as far as I can before its pulse stops completely. When the authorities take my work more seriously they may see fit to provide enough funds to purchase an automobile. Until that day a horse must suffice. Across fields and over hedges and through woodland I will gallop. I might even be lucky enough to reach the sea before the final breath.

*2.

"Thank you for correcting my erroneous views on the travel restrictions that apply to spooks," said Hywel. "What is your name, by the way? Cherlomsky? Professor Shylock Cherlomsky! I'll remember you and call for your assistance whenever a man or woman is on the verge of dying on the same spot they were born! But you have made me curious about that man in Kilburn who couldn't wander very far. I'd like to hear a story from his own lips. Keep quiet at the back – just because you're over the horizon doesn't mean I can't order you about – and let the fellow in question speak!"

DEGREES OF
SEPARATION

When the cigarette and glass of whisky were finished, all that was left was the knife. Clute turned it slowly in his hands as he sat in front of the mirror. Then he studied his reflection carefully. The face of a man planning revenge stared back at him. It was no different from the other faces he pulled on any random day.

He wanted to kill Bradman because of what Bradman had done. But to use this knife against that vague and terrible enemy would not be easy. Bradman was difficult to reach, living in a mansion protected by a high wall, guarded by huge dogs. Clute read the newspapers. Bradman had even posted armed guards on his grounds.

If Clute made a direct attempt on the life of Bradman he certainly would fail. He had no accomplices, no influence, no money or power. His vengeance would amount to nothing tangible. He had to seek some lateral method of scoring a strike against his adversary. Bradman's family was no less secure than he. What next?

There was Frost, Bradman's closest friend since childhood. Unlike Bradman, Frost travelled without bodyguards and lived in a house with a low wall and only one dog. But Frost was popular and rarely seen alone. How might Clute get close enough for the plunge? Again he probably would fail, his blade remaining thirsty.

Frost often went to the theatre to watch Cosimo perform. Cosimo was an accomplished singer and actor who was intimate with Frost but hardly aware of the existence of the less cultured Bradman. Ending the life of Cosimo would cause a deep wound in Frost, and if Frost were hurt, Bradman would also feel a measure of pain.

This was the answer! Clute reached for the newspaper on an adjacent table and flicked the pages until he found an advertisement for Cosimo's latest play. The show began at nine the same evening. If Clute turned up early, he might be able to slip backstage and murderously encounter the actor in his own dressing room.

No, it was unlikely he would get past the doormen. They would grow suspicious and perform a search on him. The knife would be uncovered and the police summoned. Then opportunity for revenge against Bradman would become even less likely. Better to forget Cosimo. Clute remembered that Cosimo was connected to Kingsley.

Clute had read about it in the papers. The two men frequently went to restaurants together. In fact Kingsley taught Cosimo everything there was to know about fine wine and good food. All Clute had to do was book a table in the same place as Kingsley at the same time. Halfway through the meal, the deed could be done.

But what if Clute failed to kill Kingsley outright? Stabbing is not always effective. In a public place such as a restaurant, his time would be limited. If Kingsley recovered from his injuries, Cosimo would not be racked by grief, and so Frost could not be damaged in any way, and thus Bradman would not suffer at all.

Running the fleshy part of his thumb gently along the serrated edge of the blade and smiling slightly, Clute silently listed the restaurants frequented by Kingsley in order of excellence. The best was run by a man called Whitlam. A hole cut in Whitlam's chest would be no less a hole in Kingsley's life, an irreparable hole.

Yes, he would seek out Whitlam, perhaps in one of his kitchens, or better still during one of his frequent trips to the market to buy fresh produce. The glint of steel among the vegetables, the crash of trays of fish preserved in ice, and the chain reaction of vengeance would be set in motion, all the way to Bradman.

The problem with tackling Whitlam was that the man was an expert in the use of blades and always wore a knife or cleaver at his belt, even when shopping in public. Whitlam surely knew how to defend himself and strike back. Clute would be the one left dying among the tomatoes, his life blood a sauce on the cobbles.

Whitlam had once taught cooking at the local college. He had taught Oshimi for a year and even announced Oshimi as his star pupil. After Oshimi abandoned the culinary arts and became a successful writer, Whitlam did not fail to keep in touch with his protégé. Oshimi was perfect for any sudden death, slow moving, trusting.

The big advantage of killing Oshimi was that Clute knew him very well. In fact they were close friends. It would be simplicity itself to invite him back to this room on some pretext and then commit an act of righteous violence on the fat dupe. Clute nodded once. He picked up the telephone and dialled his number.

Oshimi agreed to come within the hour. Clute simply told him that something important needed to transpire between them. He mentioned few details, only that it had something to do with Bradman, a person almost unknown to Oshimi. Clute chuckled. He imagined the expressions on the sequence of faces, the transmitted pain.

Shortly before Oshimi arrived, Clute suddenly remembered that new neighbours had moved into the apartment directly below him. They were a bothersome couple, extremely sensitive to the slightest noise. Oshimi was a ponderous man. He would knock loudly on Clute's door, roar out his greeting, stamp across the floorboards.

Long before Clute could force his knife into Oshimi's heart, the neighbours would be hurrying up the stairs to complain. There simply was too little time for the operation to be performed efficiently. Scowling, Clute abandoned his plan. His need for revenge must remain unsatisfied. Bradman had escaped without a scratch!

Or had he? Clute pursed his lips. Oshimi had a friend that Clute could certainly assault. This friend would not even struggle or make an appreciable vocal fuss. He was the perfect victim! Bradman might shelter behind walls, dogs and bodyguards but here was a chink in his armour, a chink that soon would spurt crimson juice.

Clute almost felt pity for the poor defenceless Bradman as he moved quietly across his room to unlatch the door. Now Oshimi would not have to knock before confronting the balancing scene of carnage. Returning to his chair and the wise mirror, Clute raised the knife and savagely drew it across his own unforgiven throat.

*3.

Oshimi said, "Yes, that's more or less how it happened. But I have a tale to tell of my own. Please forgive me if my style is awkward. It's true that I became a successful writer but I have never written fiction. I wrote a very strange textbook that was on the bestseller lists for several years. Now I'm going to recite a story about a girl who bought my book and used it in a manner I hadn't foreseen!"

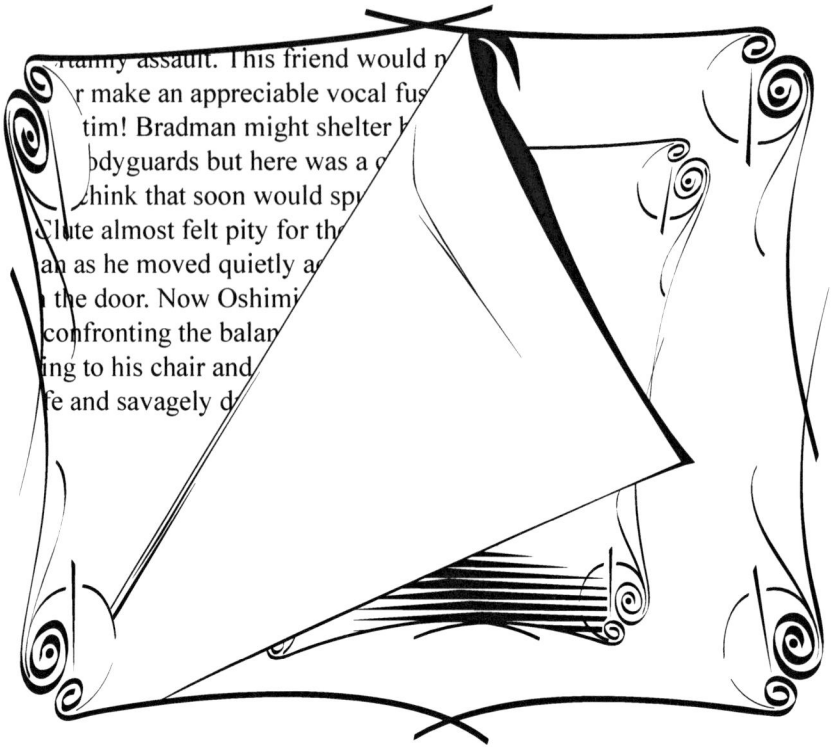

...tally assault. This friend would n
...r make an appreciable vocal fu...
...tim! Bradman might shelter b...
...bdyguards but here was a ...
...think that soon would sp...
...lute almost felt pity for th...
...an as he moved quietly a...
...the door. Now Oshimi...
...confronting the balan...
...ing to his chair and...
...e and savagely d...

THE FOLDED PAGE

"Eight times," said Aguri.

"Eight times what?" wondered Mikiko. She had adopted the tone of a bored child learning a multiplication table.

"A piece of paper can only be folded eight times," elaborated Aguri.

"Nonsense," replied Mikiko firmly.

"It's true." Aguri creased his brow. "Believe me, no matter how large that piece of paper, eight times is the limit. I'm surprised you don't already know this. It's one of those unexpected facts that people like to share with each other."

"Not with me," said Mikiko.

"That's not my fault. The number remains eight."

"I require proof," announced Mikiko.

Aguri puffed out his little cheeks and folded his little arms. His expression was a combination of annoyance and resignation. He indicated a sketch pad that lay on the table next to a vase of flowers and said, "Try for yourself."

Mikiko opened the pad and tore out a blank sheet. She folded it once, then twice. "Easy so far."

"Keep going," sniffed Aguri.

A few minutes later Mikiko was scowling. "I'm not strong enough."

"Only seven times," chuckled Aguri. "If you were fully grown you might manage another fold. But consider the mathematical progression involved in this problem. Every time you fold the paper in half, the thickness of the paper is doubled. After one fold there are two layers, after two folds four layers, then eight, then sixteen, thirty two, sixty four and so on. By folding the paper seven times you created one hundred and twenty eight layers and it's very difficult to fold so many layers all at once."

"But some people can do it," frowned Mikiko.

"Yes. It takes a lot of strength. After eight folds there are two hundred and fifty six layers and nobody has ever progressed beyond that point. The ninth fold is an impossibility."

Mikiko scratched her chin. "I still don't believe it."

Aguri was exasperated. "Why not?"

"Because the paper I used was relatively small," she explained. "Next time I might try the experiment with a *huge* sheet. If the paper is wide enough I'm sure I can beat the limit. Nine, ten or even eleven folds should be possible."

Aguri nodded slowly. It was clear he wanted to divulge a secret. Mikiko moved her ear closer to his mouth and listened carefully as he told her the following story in breathless whispers. It was the story she had been waiting to hear.

"There was a powerful lord," he began, "who once shared your opinion on this matter. Almost a thousand years ago he decided to settle the argument with an improbable experiment. He paid for the manufacture of the largest piece of paper in history. No blank page quite like it has ever existed since. How big was it, you might ask? As wide as a misty dawn, as long as a frosty road, that's my answer. The lord saw it and was very pleased.

"Surveyors in his employ calculated the halfway point and marked it with an inked brush. Then servants and horses pulled on ropes to draw the paper back on itself. That was the first fold. Again the surveyors ventured forth to make a new mark, again the men and beasts struggled in their harnesses. Within a week the second fold was completed. As the apparent surface area of the sheet diminished, so it grew thicker and harder to fold. Servants and horses collapsed from exhaustion.

"But the lord was resolute. He urged them on with promises and threats. Months passed, the seasons changed. First there was snow on the page, then cherry blossom, all swept away with brooms. Eventually the eighth fold was made, then with great jubilation the ninth. Poets wrote poems on the margins of the paper but their words were smudged and lost when the tenth fold was completed. The sheet was now one thousand and twenty four layers thick.

"Still the lord was dissatisfied. He grew old and should have watched his children grow up, but his attention was wholly directed at the onerous business of the eleventh, twelfth and thirteenth folds. Finally he realised the foolishness of his obsession and announced that the fourteenth fold would be the last one. When it was made he wept openly, for he had simultaneously achieved his greatest dream and wasted his life.

"Despite his age and decrepitude he walked around the excessively folded page to examine it and this circuit did not take long. Let me now reveal that the original sheet of paper was approximately the same size as the Inland Sea, about eighty-five kilometres long on each side. Forget what I said earlier about misty dawns and frosty roads. After all that folding it was now less than a third of one kilometre on each side.

"The fourteenth fold had increased its thickness to sixteen thousand three hundred and eighty four layers. It occurred to the lord that it might be a good idea to build a new castle on the summit of this implausible paper outcrop. It was his way of redeeming those wasted years, of apologising to his servants by demonstrating a more practical result to his whimsical project. And so they laboured for him again and one year later the castle was ready.

"It towered over the surrounding lands on its paper foundations and the lord felt very proud when he took up residence with his family. He hobbled the ramparts and gazed far in every direction and access to the door of the castle was possible only with a long ladder that was drawn up afterwards. But a serene retirement was not to be his, for a neighbouring lord had viewed this paper citadel with jealous eyes and now decided to attack it with steel and fire.

"The battle raged all day. Flames licked the lofty walls but a sudden shower extinguished them. Arrows cut notches in the sheer sides, swords slashed them. The old lord repelled the invaders but the strain proved too much for him. He collapsed and died within the week. The castle was abandoned and feel into ruin. Nobody knew what to do with the folded page and so it was left where it was. It sagged in the rains and dried stiffly in the sun.

"One day an enterprising merchant came to collect it. The descendants of the lord had apparently sold it to him for a trifling sum. He carted it down to the northern shore of the Inland Sea. There he began the task of unfolding it. Suspended on high poles the original page exactly covered the island dotted expanse of water. And now fishermen and other sailors might travel between Shikoku, Kyushu and Honshu in the shade during the hot summer months.

"But there were unforeseen consequences. When you fold a piece of paper and then cut out little pieces along the crease, what do you get when you unfold it? A pattern of holes! The more folds and the more irregular the cuts, the more complex the pattern. The steel and fire of the attackers all those years earlier had created an amazing pattern in this unfolded sheet. But in fact the fishermen and other sailors were able to use it as an aid to navigation from island to island.

"During the day, the sun shone through the holes in the paper sky and formed new constellations with distinctive characters. Men on ships have always looked at the stars to determine direction. But these artificial constellations were deceitful and many sailors arrived at the wrong destination or failed to arrive at all. The problem was that the same groups of stars appeared in different parts of the sky. Identical constellations were found in the north, south, east and west!

"When you fold a page many times, cut into it along the edges and then unfold it, the resulting pattern is a regular whole no matter how irregular it may seem in parts. The individual constellations that a sailor might use to guide him to Shodo or Setoda were mirrored or duplicated in other directions and he often ended up in Omi or Yashiro by mistake. Business suffered as a result and the merchant who bought the folded page was reviled. He had provided a defective sky.

"Anything can fall into a state of disrepair, even the heavens! Birds pecked at the page, storms lashed it. Within a few generations it hung in tatters and eventually it was gone completely. Not a shred of evidence remains to prove it was ever really there. The names of the lord and the merchant have been forgotten. Yet nobody has ever duplicated the feat of folding a page so many times. Eight has once again become the limit, eight times only. That is the truth."

Aguri stopped speaking and gazed hopefully at Mikiko.

Then he added, "What do you think of that?"

"I don't like it," said Mikiko without hesitation. "I expected something better. It won't do, I'm afraid. You've failed the test."

Aguri shut his little eyes and trembled quietly.

Mikiko reached forward and crumpled him up in her fist. Then she threw him at the wastepaper basket. He missed and lay on the floor as a paper ball, one among the others already there. Mikiko selected a new sheet and turned to consult the next chapter of her book, *Oshimi's Intelligent Origami*, but then she heard the familiar footfalls of one of her human friends coming up the garden path.

She forgot about the book and hurried outside.

*4.

With a sly wink, Hywel reached across the previous page, picked Aguri up from the floor of the story and used him to roll a cigarette. I thought that was bad taste. Smoking had been banned in public houses years earlier and landlords should set a good example. The universe was one pub, so smoking was disallowed everywhere. Then it occurred to me that every active volcano on every planet was guilty of breaking the rules and I was reminded of a smoking crater somewhere in Iran where dead beasts of burden were cremated cheaply. That volcano smoked camels, twenty a day! But my musings on this subject were terminated by the merchant who covered the Inland Sea with the sheet of paper. He wanted to tell a story about another sort of covering that also ended up higher than it ought to!

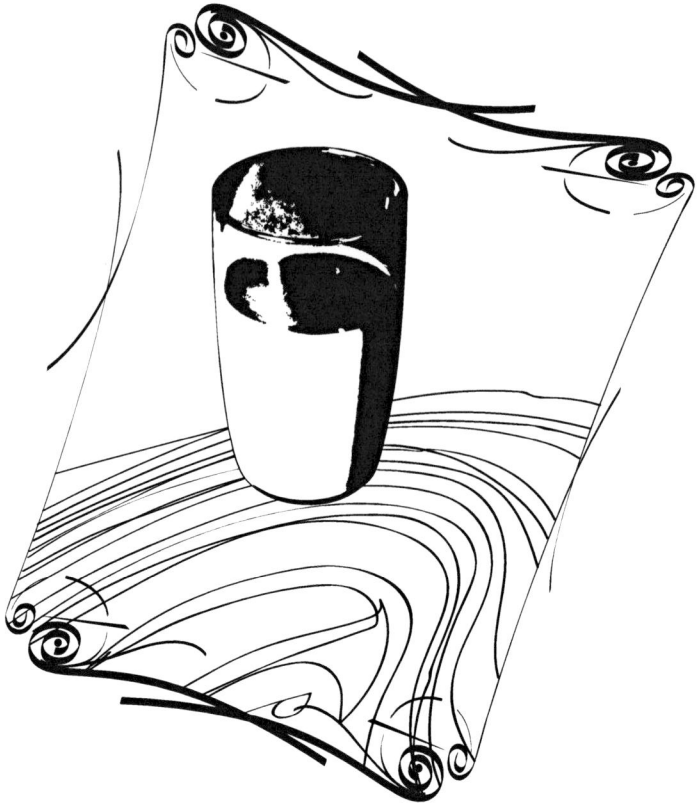

MILK AND LADDERS

"The trouble with most magic carpets," began Vincent, "is that they aren't carpets at all, but rugs. I moved into this house because it contained a magic carpet, but it never did me much good."

"Really?" Hector licked his lips.

"A big disappointment, to be sure. May I fetch you a drink, by the way? I don't have anything stronger than milk, but that's just the thing for inducing sleep. Even if you don't suffer from insomnia now, you might later, but maybe I'm getting ahead of myself. Allow me to fill my own glass and then I'll start at the beginning."

"I just want to know if it's for sale," said Hector.

Vincent walked toward the kitchen and his voice warbled back. "Of course, but it's not simply a matter of taking money from you and handing it over. We're talking about a paranormal method of travel. There are all sorts of psychological considerations."

Hector frowned. "How so?"

Vincent returned with a tall glass of frothy milk and resumed his seat. He sipped slowly. "Perfect for sweet dreams." Then he leaned forward and threw another log onto the fire, which spat and hissed in reply and made the dancing shadows in the corners of the sumptuous room take fright and hide behind all the available furniture. "Much better."

Hector glanced at the clock. "I'm waiting."

"Very well. It's not the money I'm interested in, I have plenty of that to suit my needs, but the thing has become a burden and I want to ease the weight on my mind. That's why I placed the notice in the newspaper which attracted your attention."

"I've always wanted a magic carpet," said Hector.

Vincent smiled. "I know the feeling, the allure of a fantastical Orient, the dancing girls and bottles with a genie. I was once like you and so was the man who lived here before me, an adventurer of the old school with whiskers and a monocle and a pith helmet on his sunburnt head."

"Talking about headgear," ventured Hector, "do you ever take your own hat off?"

"Not frequently but often enough. But to return to what I was saying: this fellow was a member of the aristocracy, Lord Doublestuff he was called, and he was an enthusiastic collector — tiger heads, samovars, scimitars, masks, idols of ebony and jade, curly slippers, trinkets of every description, all in pairs. He was an audacious and ruthless exploiter of ancient cultures. By winning the ear of a local chieftain, he practically became the ruler of his own private kingdom in an obscure mountain region of central Asia. Some said he was subsequently cursed by a fakir or shaman who hoped to gradually diminish his influence."

"And his greatest achievement was finding a magic carpet?" pressed Hector.

"Over and over he demonstrated his ability to discover what other men could not — he was a prodigy in that respect. Are you sure I can't interest you in some milk? Anyway, Lord Doublestuff tried twice to rule his own little country, then he realised he was no longer big enough for the task and came home. He filled this house with his trophies and souvenirs."

Hector smirked. "Including the carpet?"

"Yes. He lived here in isolation for many years surrounded by the mementos of his travels. He rarely ventured outside and people who met him commented on how shrivelled he seemed, dried out by his torrid and often unethical experiences. Then he stopped going out at all and a rumour started that he was dead."

"What happened next?" asked Hector.

Vincent finished his milk and set the glass down on a table. He rose and paced the room with his peculiar gait, one leg straight and stiff as if it lacked a knee. He paused by the window and looked out. The leaves on the trees were the same colour as the fire in the hearth behind him and for a moment he felt like a slice of bread in a toaster, stuck between two sources of equal heat. Then he snapped out of this delusion and shivered before replying:

"I like living in this village and I've been here since I was a child. I grew up in a cottage on the far side and I knew all about Lord Doublestuff and his exploits from an early age. He always intrigued me. I envied him — or rather I envied his possessions, or what I imagined he owned, the genie bottles and suchlike. I guessed there was a magic carpet here. After he vanished from sight I decided to learn once and for all whether he was still alive. One night I approached his front door and rang the bell for an hour but he did not come to answer it."

"Did you force entry?" demanded Hector.

"In a manner of speaking. I circled the house and found an unlocked back window, so I just climbed through. I switched on all the lights and remained there until the morning, like a boy in a toyshop, picking up the ornaments and playing with the curios. I discovered many unexpected things and somehow — I'm not really sure how it happened — I never left. The house became mine. Lord Doublestuff had no relatives or friends and nobody else seemed interested. The other villagers just assumed he had bequeathed the property to me and that's how I became its new owner."

"The magic carpet," Hector reminded him.

Vincent nodded at the floor. "What do you think that is? It has been under your feet all this time! He bought it in Peshawar, I believe, and it's possible that it flew here on its own. I don't know. It took me a long time to work it out as well. Sitting in this chair I might say to myself, 'I wish I was far away now' and I would hear a horrible creaking noise while the floor shook. I wondered if the house was unstable and might be falling down."

"I'm disappointed," admitted Hector.

"I know. As I said before, most magic carpets are actually rugs, loosely thrown on the floor and free to float away. Nobody ever expects them to be nailed down. A magic *fitted* carpet is something else entirely!"

Hector laughed. "So each time it tried to fly off, it wanted to take the whole house with it?"

"That's it exactly. The creaking was the sound of the nails and floorboards as the carpet struggled to rise. It just wasn't strong enough to free itself. I know what you're thinking. Why don't I pull out the nails with pliers? I've rejected that option. Look at the shape of this room. So many little niches and corners! The carpet has been cut to fit a very complex shape and would look extremely silly flying through the air with all those protrusions. I have too much pride to ride such a thing. But let me tell you a brief story."

"Go right ahead," said Hector.

"Look over there and tell me what you see. It's a long rectangular gap, isn't it? A missing oblong of carpet. I did that. After living here for about a year I grew lonely and decided I needed company, a female companion to be more accurate, a girlfriend. I'm quite handsome and almost as interesting and I didn't have too much trouble finding one, but I didn't want any interference with the trophies and ornaments, not even to have them cleaned, so she had to be a rather lazy sort of girl. Monica was her name."

"I know the type," reminisced Hector.

"We spent our evenings in this room, side by side. Well that's not entirely true. I sat on this chair and she lay down on the carpet in front of the fire. She always seemed to be sleepy — too tired to get up and go to bed. She would just lie there and mutter, 'I wish I had a magic carpet to fly me up the stairs to bed' without understanding what she meant. Something of a coincidence, I'm sure you agree. Again and again she would repeat that phrase in a slurred voice. It was irritating! One night I was so fed up with her that I took down one of Lord Doublestuff's scimitars from the wall and pulled it out of its scabbard. Then I stood above her."

"And cut off her head?" gasped Hector.

"Of course not! I sliced at the carpet, making a rectangle around her. Very straight edges too! Once free of the rest of the carpet, this piece responded to her wish and rose slowly off the floor. It hovered for a few moments at an elevation about halfway between floor and ceiling and then floated out of the door, along the hall and up the spiral staircase. I followed it to the bottom of the stairs before returning to my chair. I saw that Monica was stirring in her sleep. The bedroom was directly above this room. The carpet settled down on top of the bed, just as she had wished for."

"Did it make your evening more peaceful?" asked Hector.

Vincent shook his head sadly. "All night long she tossed and turned on the bed and I could hear her movements through the ceiling. This noise was just as bad as her previous mumbling — possibly worse! It was her very first sleepless night. Even though she was a lazy girl, the consequences of what had just happened were too immense, too exciting, too disturbing. Her magical voyage to her bed made sleep impossible! A neat irony, to be sure! Her brain was in a state of extreme agitation. If magic carpets truly existed — and clearly now they did — then everything she thought she knew about the workings of the world was thrown in doubt. The whole science of physics was in jeopardy! Enough to keep anyone awake, don't you agree?"

"That's why you believe in milk as a method of inducing sleep?" commented Hector. "But why don't you let me buy that piece from you — the one that carried her to bed?"

Vincent smiled bitterly. "She took it with her when she left me for another man, or maybe it took her when it left for another floor — who can say? And I don't care to cut more pieces from this one. That gap is ugly enough as it is."

"So why am I here?" frowned Hector.

"Oh no, you misunderstand me! I don't want to sell *this* magic carpet. I have a different one to get rid of. Lord Doublestuff always tried to collect two of everything — that's how he earned his name. Twice is best, he always said."

Hector brightened. "Where is the other carpet?"

"Not far from here." Vincent suddenly lifted off his hat and a strange scene greeted Hector's eyes, a miniature landscape of highly dubious sanity. Perched atop Vincent's head was an absurd wig, a woolly toupee that resembled a perfectly circular rug. Balanced on this was a tiny wicker chair in which sat a withered old man no more than one inch high who was cradling an equally diminutive shotgun. Hector blinked.

"Lord Doublestuff!" he rasped.

Vincent clicked his fingers and the wig rose from his head and made a complete circuit of the room before returning to its starting point. The tiny man kept his balance and began talking to himself, but Hector only caught a few words of his almost inaudible speech. '*Some of those damn chaps were never the same... I said, steady on old boy, that's not a yeti's knee... Could have done him an injury in Samarkand...*' Not once did he discharge his weapon and Hector was grateful for that.

Vincent groaned. "Like I said, it's not the money. It's the weight! That's the reason I want to sell it. He may have shrunk in size but his mass is the same as before! The curse didn't reduce that. It hurts."

"When did you realise he was still alive?" asked Hector.

"A few days after I moved in. I found him trapped in a bottle in the wine cellar. He had climbed in but couldn't get out. Now tell me: are you interested in making a purchase?"

Hector scratched his own head. "What if the carpet gets stuck on a high shelf or the top of a tall wardrobe? How will I get him down again?"

Vincent stood and reached into his pocket. He drew out a very narrow ladder with thousands of rungs. It was the same length as his leg. "This is an emergency measure. I had to cut a hole in my trousers to fit it in. At least I can now bend my knee again! But we're wasting too much time. Do you want the magic carpet or not?"

Hector rose rapidly and reached for his coat. "I need to think about it. You can't rush a thing like this, it might turn out to be an impulse buy rather than an investment. Besides I want to check out some alternatives first. Maybe I'll find something which suits my needs better."

As he passed along the hall and out of the house, both men said, "Keep in touch," but they forgot to embrace, shake hands or even exchange slaps.

On the lawn two dancing girls were shedding veils under the falling leaves.

*5.

Hywel was aware that his customers were shivering. It was one of the coldest hours of the night, just before the summer dawn. It was time for a story set in a warm and exotic place, somewhere out east, but how far out east? After all, there are some dreadful places in that direction, the county of Essex in England for instance; and if you keep traveling east you come back round to the west. Fortunately one of the dancing girls who shed her veils stepped forward. Her eyes were bright, her hair tumbled in dark ringlets, she was the sort of woman who probably knows how to dance in a style so sensual it is dangerous. She gave her name as Niddala and this is what she told us:

NIDDALA

The lamp was as Persian as a carpet made from a fluffy cat.

Niddala rubbed it with her sleeve and told the emerging figure that she didn't want to spend all her wishes at once. Was interest available on those she saved for later?

The blue creature shook its head. "The old stories got it wrong. I'm only compelled to give you one wish and you have to use it right now."

"In that case, I wish for more wishes!"

"That's not permitted."

"What if I wish for you to fall in love with me? That way you'll always be happy to do anything I ask."

"That's also against the rules."

Niddala protested but the creature had no sympathy and merely added, "You're running out of time."

So she said, "I wish I was a genie."

"Very clever!" hissed the apparition in dismay but it waved its hands about and there was a blinding flash. After the smoke cleared, Niddala found herself wearing a turban.

"Now I can do what I like."

"No you can't!" roared the bald being. "That's not how genies work. You have to *grant* wishes to others!"

Immediately it pounced on her and rubbed her stomach furiously. "I wish I was human!"

Niddala's arms seemed to acquire a life of their own, describing strange shapes in the air. Another flash and the creature had shrunk to a normal size. He was still bald but now he was the colour of skin. His laughter was full of desperate relief.

"Free at last! I'm a man!"

"Wait a moment," said Niddala. "Are you sure a genie is allowed to rub another genie? That doesn't seem right somehow. I wouldn't trust the result of such a wish. The effect might wear off."

"I hadn't thought of that. But I'm a man now and you're a genie and I haven't had my wish *as a man* yet, so I'm going to reconfirm my decision."

He leaned forward with raised hands, rubbed her stomach again and called, "I wish I was human!"

But nothing happened. Niddala sighed.

"You can't wish to be something you already are. That's not a wish, but a grammatical error. A wish implies a yearning for a lack. You can't lack a quality which you have."

"I hate the pitfalls of logic!" came the exasperated reply. "Let me think of a different wording. I have it! I wish *not* to be a genie."

This time arms were waved. Smoke.

Niddala blinked at the object that existed before her. It seemed to consist of everything at once, or parts of everything, or parts of an unimaginable number of other parts. The colours were scintillating. Then she understood what had happened.

"You fool! You've accidentally wished to be *everything* that isn't a genie! Not being a genie is a quality that *all* things *except* genies possess. You've become a universal soup!"

The reply was trillionfold. "Yes, and I don't feel well."

Niddala arched an eyebrow. "I'm not surprised." Then an idea came to her. She reached into the unbelievable swirl and felt around for a moment before rubbing the smooth and large something she finally found. "I wish to be Niddala!"

Instantly she was back to her former self.

Before she departed she explained, "If you are everything other than a genie then you must also be whatever it is that genies rub to get wishes from. I think I'll go shopping now."

She looked back over her shoulder. "You don't happen to have a place that sells carpets in there, do you?"

*6.

The genie in that story had finally recovered his composure and his original form. He said, "Genies can be found in many lands, not just in Persia, Syria and China, but even more commonly in places that don't exist – where they often outnumber the gloomytroids and itchyfigs! A man who uncorks a bottle containing a genie will sometimes be rewarded, sometimes punished. It's a risk. One genie washed up on a beach was so annoyed at being ignored that he turned himself into a letter just to get his bottle opened. That letter said, 'You're in trouble now!' There are very few places where genies don't have an influence. Porthcawl is one of those rare locations; and this is partly because all the available bottles are used for a different purpose."

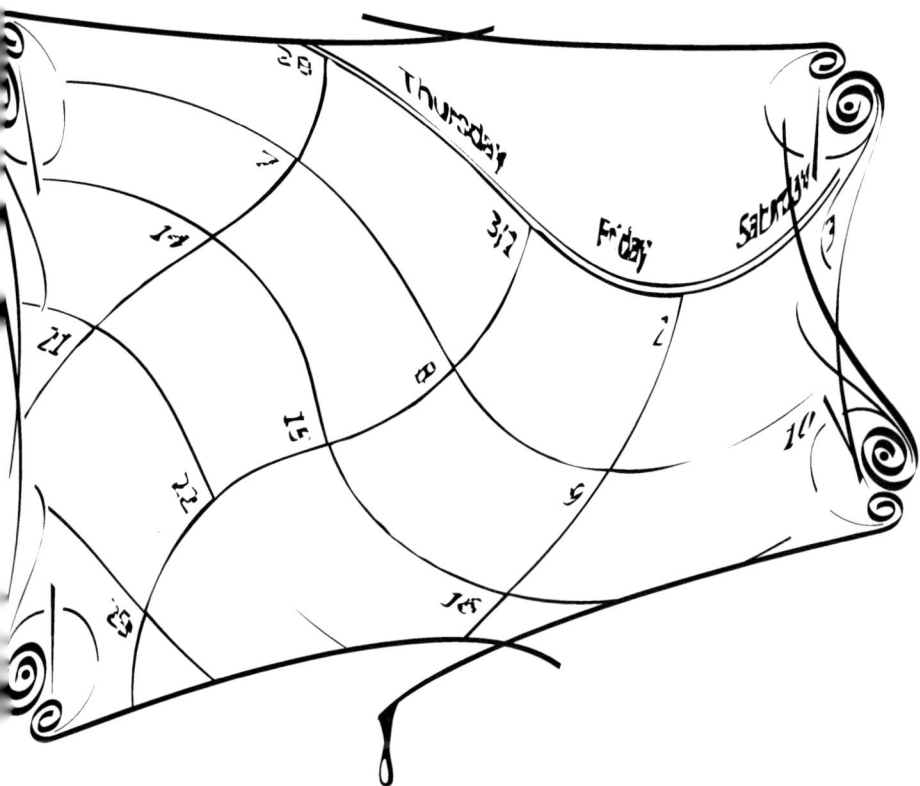

THE JUICE OF DAYS

Squeezing juice from oranges and grapes is easy enough, and with adequate pressure even apples and pears will release their sweet fluid, but only the mad inventor Karl Mondaugen ever managed to make a refreshing drink from the days of the week.

His laboratory is a chaotic place, because he likes to work on many different projects at the same time, and frequently the scattered components of abandoned prototypes will accidentally join together on the floor and form something new. These random creations are mostly useless but occasionally a miraculous device will be spontaneously generated.

This is how the juicer of days came into being. Karl Mondaugen glanced down and there it was, an ugly thing but remarkably original.

Original, yes, but would it prove useful? The answer to this question depended on whether days tasted good or bad. With only one way of finding out, the mad inventor lost no time in extracting the juice of the day he stood in.

He raised the glass to his lips, sipped and grimaced...

In the evening he went to take a stroll along the esplanade. He was mildly cheered to encounter his friend Izaac Spoilchild fishing for messages in bottles with a large net. Karl joined him and asked pleasantly, "Anything new?"

Izaac shook his head sadly. "But you should have seen the one that got away! An enormous green bottle big enough to hold a man. Can you imagine what sort of message *that* might contain? In fact the glass was so opaque there might well have been a man inside. At one point I thought I heard a voice but it was probably just the crash of waves. I trust your day has been more productive than mine?"

Karl snorted and answered, "Not at all. I squeezed the day and sampled the juice but it wasn't very nice. I would welcome a second opinion, however."

Izaac agreed to follow the mad inventor back to his laboratory and taste the experiment for himself. He swirled the liquid around his mouth for a whole minute before swallowing. "You're right, it's not too pleasant, rather muddy in texture. If it was a colour instead of a drink it would be brown, but in fact it's completely transparent."

"That surprised me as well," admitted Karl Mondaugen.

"I've drunk nicer sea water. On the other hand I won't describe it as 'vile'. I can't see much of a market for it, if your plan was to sell the stuff."

"No matter. I'll dismantle the juicer and recycle the parts."

Izaac Spoilchild raised his hand. "Don't be too hasty! Today is Wednesday and maybe it's the worst flavoured day of the week. Why not try again tomorrow and see what Thursday tastes like? In fact I wouldn't accept defeat until you've juiced all seven possible days."

Karl was impressed. "I hadn't thought of that."

The following morning he rose early, ate a hasty breakfast and decided to finish his meal with a mug of something invigorating, not tea or coffee as was usual for him, but the juice of Thursday. True, it was still the morning and it might be argued that the day was not yet ripe, but the operation was so simple very little time or energy would be wasted if the concoction proved sour. He risked only disappointment and perhaps a stomachache, not a major disaster.

The juice of Thursday was also transparent and only a little fizzy.

He sipped and swallowed, an ambiguous expression appearing on his face. Thursday tasted better than Wednesday, without doubt, but could hardly be described as delicious. "My doubts remain," he told himself, "but my hopes are not entirely vanquished."

He remembered the comment Izaac had made and added, "If this drink was a colour it would be mauve." Then he nodded and set the glass aside.

For the remainder of the day, the dried husk of that squeezed Thursday, he went about other business, refining other inventions and scuffing together scattered components with his slippered feet but creating nothing viable either by design or chance. In the evening he wrote a letter to a friend in Munich, then settled on a sofa with a book and finally dozed off.

In the middle of the night he awoke, staggered to his bed and slept away the crick in his neck that the sofa had given him, for it was a gift he did not want.

The dawn of Friday did not rouse him. An hour passed and then he opened his eyes and yawned at the sun, which has never choked anyone, and swivelled himself to the ground and shuffled to his kitchen. Pumpernickel, sauerkraut, sausages: the same breakfast as always. This time he demonstrated patience, brewing coffee and waiting until noon before applying the juicer.

Friday was far sweeter than the juices of the previous two days. He licked his lips, eyes bright, drained half the large glass before making a judgment. "Very nice. It tingles on the tongue with anticipation, with promised excitement, and would be electric blue in colour if it weren't clearer than the purest water. But in the final analysis, it's not *perfect*. Indeed it's hardly superior to pink grapefruit juice or a mix of lychee, papaya and passion fruit. I'm still not convinced!"

Despite this little speech without an audience, he removed his slippers and laced on his boots and went for a walk along the esplanade. Izaac Spoilchild was in his usual place with his usual net and Karl offered him the half full glass. The fisher of bottles accepted it and sampled the liquid and made a smacking noise that might have been a wave striking the seawall. Karl wasted no time getting down to business and forestalled Izaac's response by saying:

"Not bad, the juice of Friday? But I suspect the juice of Saturday will be even better, utterly delicious in fact, for everyone knows that Saturday is the favourite day of the week. It should have occurred to me sooner than it did, but because I don't have a proper job, I mean a job with a boss to answer to, I forgot how important the weekend is to most people. The same applies to you, my freelance friend. Saturday is sure to be uniquely refreshing!"

Izaac digested this news. "All very well, but what part will I play in your project?"

"Bottles!" chortled Karl. "Many, many bottles. My juicer is rather inefficient at the moment because it's one of my accidental inventions. With a few minor adjustments, maybe only the tightening of a screw or two, its performance will surely be enhanced. I intend to squeeze every last drop out of Saturday and there's certain to be a lot of liquid in total. I need your bottles to store it in."

"Shall I remove the messages first?"

"That's probably a wise precaution. We'll open a booth on the esplanade and sell the stuff. I'm sure our profits will be considerable. The pure juice of Saturday!"

"A business deal? I have no objections. Let's shake hands on it."

"And drink a toast too..."

"With the juice of Friday? Fair enough, there's a little left. What colour will Saturday resemble? I'm tempted to say alternating bands of green and yellow."

"Not bands. Vertical stripes."

"You're right, of course," agreed Izaac.

In fact both guesses were wrong. Saturday produced a juice no less transparent than earlier days but it tasted of golden stars in a silver sky. Karl had spent most of the morning making the necessary adjustments to his juicer and then wheeling it to the house of Izaac, which was a sort of private museum of seaborne bottles. They waited until early afternoon before liquidising the day. Only when all the bottles were full did they switch off the machine.

Neither man enjoyed transferring the bottles to the chosen spot on the esplanade, but the final results were worth the toil. Their booth was little more than a table on which were arranged the bottles for sale. A sign proclaimed the simple truth about the contents of these glass vessels: FRESH

252

SATURDAY JUICE! Customers were slow to approach at first but after a few brave souls sampled the drink the report of its excellence quickly spread. Every last bottle was sold.

One customer was familiar to both of them, Paddy Deluxe from the far side of town, who remarked, "This day feels a little husky to me, so its juice is exactly what I need!"

Karl and Izaac sniggered together when he had gone.

"We've discovered the perfect formula for success in the soft drinks industry: make a day uncomfortably dry by squeezing it thoroughly, then sell the juice back to the people who live in that day. We're the cleverest capitalists who ever existed! It's a kind of tangy thievery, but wholly legal. As long as we choose a tasty day to squeeze we can't lose. We're destined to be rich!"

Sunday proved to be not quite so delicious, thickest and creamiest of the days so far, too stodgy to be entirely refreshing, like yoghurt soured with piety. In fact both Karl and Izaac described its nonexistent colour as white. But some people liked it, mostly older folk, and it was clear that it held a real minor appeal. Monday, by contrast, was utterly vile, the blackest and bitterest of possible juices. And Tuesday was only a slight, slate grey improvement.

"Now we have all the data we need," declared Karl Mondaugen to his accomplice.

"Yes," agreed Izaac Spoilchild, rubbing his callused palms together in melodramatic glee. They decided not to waste time juicing Wednesday and Thursday, because they already knew what those days tasted like, nothing special. Better to wait and concentrate their efforts on juicing Friday, Saturday and Sunday. But in fact they soon decided to ignore Friday also and focus mainly on the two weekend days. Izaac explained that his number of bottles was limited.

While he went to fish for more, Karl planned the precise way he would spend his money when he was a wealthy juice baron. Perhaps in the construction of an enormous laboratory. Or even better: a factory that made laboratories. He was happy to dream the remainder of the week away until Saturday arrived, and then he rushed out, slamming the door behind him harder than ever before.

With Izaac he repeated the procedure of the previous week, setting up the booth on the esplanade and rapidly selling every bottle. But this time there were complaints.

"What do you think you're playing at?" demanded a man named Frothing Harris. "This juice is foul. I want my money back without argument or delay!"

Other customers were quick to follow his example.

"I don't understand," lamented Karl. "We juiced this Saturday in exactly the same way as before."

"We're going to have to reimburse every single customer," groaned Izaac, "which means we'll make a loss. No money and no juice."

There was a little fluid left at the bottom of one of the returned bottles. Karl sipped it and twisted his face. "Disgusting! We should have sampled some *before* selling it. We assumed the juice of every Saturday would be identical. What a mistake!"

"There are only seven flavours in a week," countered Izaac, "and Saturday is the best."

Karl shook his head. "Not so. The cyclic nature of weeks is an illusion, a wholly artificial conceit. In fact every new day is entirely different from all the others that precede it. The pattern exists only in the imposed names, not in the days themselves. What fools we were to forget that! The flavour of any new day can never be predicted. The juice of that first Saturday is gone forever, every last drop drunk. Just because the Earth circles the sun means nothing: the sun is also in orbit around the centre of the galaxy, and the galaxy itself is constantly moving!"

Izaac scratched his head. "You mean that our planet is always in a new location, at a point in space it has never been before, and that's why each day is unique?"

Karl wiped his mouth with the back of his hand. "I wish each new day had its own name. I'm sure there are enough objects in existence to make this feasible. Cupday, Laughday, Sockday, Jumpday, Drumday, Snakeday, Upday, Downday, Eyeday, Humbleday..."

"And on and on," said Izaac, before crying, "I have an idea!"

Karl arched an eyebrow. "Yes?"

"There's still a mouthful of the original Wednesday left, right? Remember how we described its colour as *brown*, a colour made of all other pigments mixed together? Maybe we did that because it potentially contains all other days. I mean, that was the same day your juicer accidentally came into being, wasn't it? So the juice that remains contains the squeezed essence of everything that existed in that day, every object, including the juicer itself!"

254

"Inspired," agreed Karl, "but I'm not sure how that helps us."

Izaac hopped from one foot to another. "If you devise some method of reversing the polarity of your juicer, we can pass the remaining juice of that first Wednesday through it, turning the juice back into part of a solid day, a part that hopefully will include the old juicer. Then we can use *that* juicer to re-juice today. Don't you see? With the juicer we already have we juiced *this* Saturday, but with a juicer existing more than a week in the past we can juice *last* Saturday again!"

Karl spoke not a word in reply but rushed back to his laboratory, Izaac puffing close behind. It was almost inevitable they would arrive to discover that the juicer of days had vanished. In its place stood something else, a different machine, also spontaneously generated, whose scattered components had come together on the floor in the breeze generated by Karl's very hard slamming of the door earlier that day. At its base stood a glass of oily liquid.

"This device is a juicer of juicers! It juices *only* other juicers. Our juicer is juice!"

This outburst had caused Karl to dribble generously. Izaac used the subsequent pause to pluck at his friend's elbow with his gnarled hands and whimper, "But what if you reverse its polarity?"

"I simply can't be bothered," huffed Karl, lunging for the glass and drinking down its contents in a single gulp. Then he stood still and glowered.

After a minute, Izaac ventured the question, "What does it taste like?"

"The best part of a fortnight and half our combined futures!"

"Anything else?"

"A metallic tang. Like melted robot thumbs."

They regarded each other sadly.

"Care for a beer?"

"Yes."

*7.

Izaac Spoilchild himself now appeared to tell a tale. He said, "The things I find in bottles are often truly astonishing. I once netted a large bottle that contained a ruler. On one side he was marked out in inches and on the other in centimeters. He told me that his name was El-Viz and that he was the king of two lands, one called Krokh, the other called Rholl. He compared his bottle to a transparent dungeon and said that he had been toppled in a revolution and cast out to sea. He had bobbed for many a year and the experience had left him all shook up, but he was a sensible ruler compared with some others, the Derek of Bo for instance! The following tale is set in Lipsaria where days taste the same as those in Porthcawl but where dates are far more smoochy and spicy."

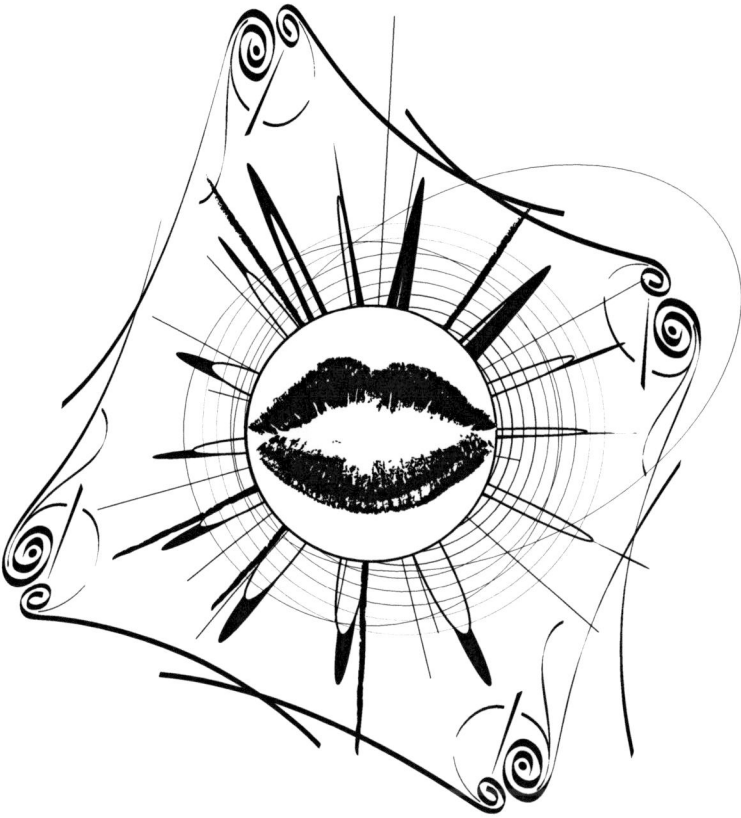

THE KISSABLE CLIMES

The French kiss with tongues; the inhabitants of Faskdhfgasdhia with noses; unfaithful wives with other men; but Diddly Derek will only smooch with syllogisms.

There are many worlds in the Cosmos, even worlds within worlds, and many zones on all those worlds, for instance the Frigid, Temperate, Tropical and Laughable Zones, and dozens of climes in each of those zones, including the Shimmering, Freckled, Gloopy, Dandelion, Bradbury, Fahrenheit and Kelvin Climes, but Diddly Derek cares naught for those. Not now, at any rate!

He cares only for the planet Happenstance and the Lower Dunsany Zone wherein is located Lipsaria, the Kissable Clime!

Happenstance is unfeasibly fused to the Earth and can be reached easily enough on the back of the Minotaur. He often wanders over there to try out the new labyrinths.

"That's all very well. But who is Diddly Derek?"

I have no objection to answering that question – he's the Racing Tyrant of Upper Bo – but who is this intruder and how did she get inside this story? I locked it carefully myself.

"Yes but you gave me a spare key. Don't you remember? I'm an unfaithful wife and I've come to kiss you."

Fair enough. I can live with that. Kissing is a marvellous thing, a gloriously juicy sport, and I could kiss for a hundred paragraphs before wanting to stop. But Diddly Derek is fated to kiss for much longer than that, until the End of Time in fact, whenever that is – perhaps tomorrow, certainly not yesterday.

In the Lower Dunsany Zone, Time is always described as 'swart', I don't know why. I don't even know what the word means.

"Why not look it up in your dictionary?"

I could do that if I really wanted to, but my dictionary is in my bedroom, to help me understand some of the things I say in my sleep, and I'm too busy writing this story to fetch it. Now what's happening? I'm being led by the unfaithful wife up the stairs!

When I first heard about Diddly Derek, I was forced to look up the word 'syllogism' and I was surprised to discover it isn't a part of the body. In that case, how does one kiss with it? Diddly Derek was able to manage. Bravo for him!

There is a room somewhere in Lipsaria that is full of kisses. Nobody knows where this room came from, although Contrivance has often been cited as a possible origin. I'm not sure where Contrivance is but apparently it's "everywhere on this page" so it must be close. Future reviewers of this tale told me that. Very thoughtful of them to help me out in this manner!

To return to the room that is full of kisses… Actually that's one of the quirks of the room, it won't allow people to visit more than once, it's a unique experience for anyone who enters. When a man or woman passes through the front gate, the room will ask 'what sort of kiss do you want?' and the reply can be 'with tongues' or 'with noses' or any other variation.

The kiss you ask for is the kiss you get. Furthermore it is the best possible example of that kind of kiss!

While you are being kissed, the room ushers you towards the exit and then finally expels you. The rest of your life is spent thinking about that one kiss – all other kisses will seem pallid in comparison – but you'll never be permitted to sample it again.

Diddly Derek cheated the system. When he entered the room and it asked him to choose a kiss, he replied 'with syllogisms please.'

'That's not possible,' said the room.

'Prove to me it's not possible,' challenged Diddly Derek, 'with logic.'

To which the room answered:

    (a) This room delivers only kisses,

    (b) A syllogism is not a kiss,

    (c) Therefore this room does not deliver syllogisms.

Needless to say, Diddly Derek was very happy with this result. As far as he was concerned he had just tasted the finest kiss of his life, but the room didn't recognise it as a kiss at all. So Diddly Derek was free to pass through the exit and run back to the entrance and ask for the same thing again. And again. He is still there, running back to the entrance after each syllogism. He hasn't expired yet from exhaustion or hunger because verisimilitude isn't my strong point.

"Plus it's a difficult word to spell!"

Are you still here? I thought you left after that bad joke about a place called Contrivance.

"No, I'm in your bed under you – naked!"

So you are! I bet you didn't enjoy that tale, I can tell without even asking, so I'll give you another. This one takes place near a country called Wales, far away from Lipsaria. Wales is the original homeland of unfaithful wives, but this story is set offshore. It is called 'The Bones of Jones' and it goes like this:

The bones of Jones lie under the sea.

'I'm a teapot,' claims a femur.

'I'm a flute,' insists a knuckle.

'We have degrees in economics,' sing the ribs.

'I'm the smell of parsley,' declares a tibia.

'It's nice and dry down here,' observes an ankle.

The only bone of Jones that doesn't lie under the sea is the pelvis. 'I knew the Duchess of Cumberland,' it says.

*8.

When Izaac Spoilchild had finished, he was so overcome with emotion that he deliberately shed bottled tears over a wide area. In the middle of this expanding pool of portable sentiment, the Skull of Jones bobbed up and said, "My own tears were washed away long ago by the rain that never stops falling in the land of my birth. I am from Wales! So forceful is our rain that it scours the colours out of the rainbow. Welsh rainbows are grey and uninspiring, like the suits worn by men who work in small offices; and the pots found where those rainbows touch the ground are full of grey ash, like funeral urns, instead of gold; or stuffed with grey shoes that can be worn with grey suits without clashing, instead of stout boots or little crocodiles. But just because I'm Welsh doesn't mean I'm the greatest authority on the topic of downpours. There is someone even more knowledgeable about them than me!"

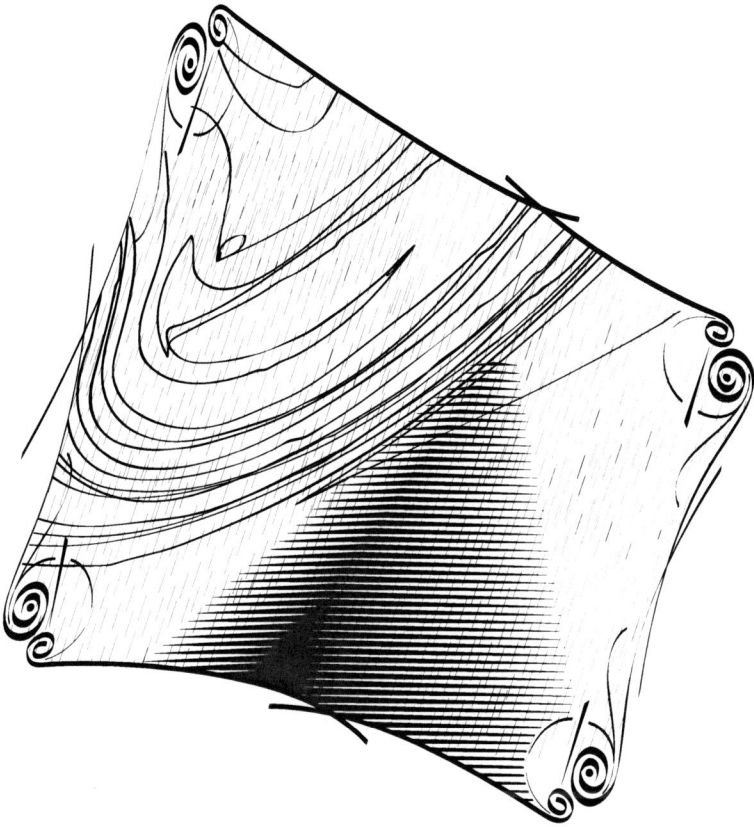

BUT IT POURS

The shop has no walls and therefore no doors but it has an inside and an outside. A hollow roof filled with hydrogen floats thirty metres or more above the ground on a tether. Customers like to touch this tether and feel the tension, nobody knows why, not even the Prince of Rains, who owns the shop.

He has banned all walls in Monsoonarco and the degradations associated with them: windows, pictures, firing squads. Because there are no walls between the sea and the borders of Lipsaria, the kissable climes, the rain is never entirely kept out. The lightest breeze can whip raindrops under floating roofs.

Such is the way it has to be and nobody should complain, for rain is the only reason to come this far. The Prince of Rains sells many different kinds of rain in his shop and his customers are generally weathermen and other advocates of a pluvial society. His rains are expensive but they are the best.

Once a year he holds a sale and many fashionable kinds of rain can be purchased at reduced prices. Captain Dangleglum was aware of this and sailed his barge all the way up the twisted river Grinn, which cuts Lipsaria in half, and across the flooded plains of Monsoonarco to the very entrance of the exposed shop.

He dropped anchor and it clanged to the bottom of a puddle and he jumped over the side and splashed his way into the shop calling out, "Are you still open?" to which the Prince of Rains replied from behind his counter, "Of course. I have no choice." Then they greeted each other in a more formal manner with a damp handshake.

"I wish to buy rain," the Captain explained.

The Prince bowed low. "That was my assumption. Allow me to show you the current styles on offer."

"I need a lot of it. An entire season's worth."

"The winter range is especially good this year, but all my rains are high quality and I am sure you will be impressed even with the light summer showers. It all depends on why you want the rain. For instance, do you require it for creative or destructive purposes? Follow me if you will. Peer into this cabinet and tell me what you see."

Captain Dangleglum squinted. "A pip at the centre of every raindrop."

The Prince of Rains nodded. "This is one of our most popular creative rains. It plants apple trees wherever it lands, provided the ground is not entirely barren, and the ferocity of its downpour is normally measured in *orchards* rather than centimetres. But come along and examine this cabinet instead. Here we have an equally popular destructive rain, a rain that scatters brass tacks over roads and lanes, surfaced or unsurfaced, and causes no end of trouble to motorists, cyclists and players of ball games."

"I am not interested in such rains. What is inside this cloud chamber?"

"Those are my famous scented rains. Why settle for a rain that smells of nothing or at the best smells of damp earth and rotting leaves? No, these rains exude the odour of vanilla, lavender, patchouli, camphor, curry, sweetpea, musk, burdock, cinnamon, frankincense, new books, wine, fear, monkeys, seaweed, cherry blossom, feet, cheese and glue. I can even create new odours just for you, some of them highly implausible, the sweat of a drunken centaur perhaps, but the price may have to be adjusted upwards."

Captain Dangleglum shook his head. "No thanks."

The Prince of Rains shrugged. "Let us proceed to the next cabinet. Here you see rains that are fun to be caught out in. This musical rain is one of the least controversial. Further along you may behold my special cocaine rain, the spray of which can be excitingly snorted after rebounding from iron railings, the thighs of waterproof trousers or the top of a short girlfriend's head. It was once an expensive rain but the price has recently come down."

"I wonder why?" the Captain asked.

"The market was flooded," the Prince replied with almost appropriate irony. "But I understand your distrust of that particular rain, a most sniffly kind indeed. Please examine the contents of this cabinet. This is where I keep my odd rains, the rains that serve no obvious practical purpose, the upside down and backwards rains, the opaque and oblique rains, my polygonal and pyramidal rains, the linear and digital rains, the unexpectedly fragile hollow rains."

"Once again I must decline," the Captain said.

"In that case, permit me to show you my happy and sad rains. The former are happy because they tickle. The latter are made from the juice of dissolved squonks, the most tearful creature in existence!"

"I once knew a squonk who laughed," said the Captain.

The Prince rubbed his chin. "Perhaps it would be easier if you described exactly the sort of rain you are looking for?"

"Yes that would be wise. I am simply searching for ordinary rain, a good old-fashioned downpour, but lots and lots of it. I will state my requirements in the most simple terms. Your heaviest monsoon please!"

The Prince smiled faintly. "I see. You come from a land that is in the middle of a drought? Is that the case?"

Captain Dangleglum pouted. "On the contrary."

The Prince did not alter his expression. "I warn you that I am a difficult person to surprise. I have dealt with all manner of customers and requests. Last year a man arrived at my shop from the remote country of Wales. Far away lies that land, beyond Lipsaria and Grokkland and Paraparapara, beyond Krokh and Rholl and Plush, beyond even Zipangu and Castelsardo and Portugal! He was a sailor like yourself, Captain Nothing was his name, clearly he preferred being anonymous, and he also wanted my most powerful monsoon. I asked him if Wales was a dry land. Do you know how he answered?"

"I do not," replied Captain Dangleglum.

"He looked at me with raised eyebrows and he said, 'Absolutely not. In Wales it never stops raining. Never. It has been raining in Wales since the day the sky was invented and it will keep raining until the sky is dismantled and replaced with something better. The people of Wales have never seen the sun. They are not even aware it exists!' That is what he said to me. I still have no reason to doubt his words. Wales already had enough rain but he wanted to take back more. Shall I tell you why?"

"Please do," said Captain Dangleglum.

"He wanted more rain so that the people of Wales could get dry at last. Does this paradox confuse you? Allow me to explain! When it rains, even in Wales, it is possible to see the raindrops as they fall. I mean that the phenomenon of rain can be defined as a certain fixed number of raindrops falling out of the sky in a given time. However heavy the rain, there is still more air than water in the sky. Now imagine if the rainfall increases to the point where it becomes easier to see the spaces between the raindrops than the raindrops themselves. In such a situation it would seem to be raining *air*. Can you guess the rest?"

Captain Dangleglum nodded. "I believe so. In Wales the people go out in dry clothes and get wet in the rain. But if a monsoon was added to the existing rain, they would be able to get dry when they went out, provided the clothes they wore were already wet!"

"Exactly. First they soak their clothes in the bath, then they go out and the falling drops of air dry them out. Ingenious! So as you can see, I am not likely to be amazed by any reason you might have for ordering my heaviest monsoon. I am sure it is not stranger than that."

Captain Dangleglum smiled. "When I leave your shop I will return to a place even wetter than Wales. I want a monsoon for the wettest place on Earth. It is so wet that the beings who live there breathe water."

The Prince frowned. "Under the sea? Surely not!"

The Captain nodded again. "I am a commercial sailor and I am willing to carry any form of cargo to any place in creation. I have been hired on behalf of the inhabitants of the ocean deeps to fetch a monsoon for use in a busy shipping lane. If it has the desired effect, other monsoons will be required for other shipping lanes. I accepted the commission."

"What is the desired effect?" asked the Prince of Rains.

Captain Dangleglum became wistful and answered, "The ships that sail on the surface of the oceans are rainclouds in the eyes of the denizens of the deep. Mostly they pass over without raining. But occasionally, due to wear and tear, or storms and icebergs, or war and piracy, these ships sink. They sink to the ocean bed. They settle there, great hulks destined to rust, and all the dying bubbles from all the lungs of all the trapped sailors come out. These bubbles rise from smashed portholes, or they find their way between internal passages to the deck. They ascend from the bottom of the sea to the surface. They form an inverted rain, inverted in both senses, for it is an upwards rain and a dry rain. Furthermore it is a rain born from panic and death. The fish and squids and crustaceans that are caught in it feel horrible for many weeks after. It is a type of rain almost beyond endurance."

The Prince lowered his eyes. "I would not sell such rains."

The Captain smiled. "The plan is to keep a monsoon ready in a cave far under the sea. When a ship sinks, the stored clouds will be quickly dragged out of the cave by whatever sea creature is on duty at the time, positioned over the sunken ship and encouraged to rain. The falling droplets will exactly cancel out the rising bubbles. That is the theory at least. I have no personal view on the matter."

"I wonder," replied the Prince with an enigmatic sigh.

"What do you wonder?" asked the Captain.

"Was it a mermaid who asked you to do all this?"

The Captain blushed. The awkward silence lasted for nearly a minute. The floating roof strained against its tether. "She didn't really ask me."

The Prince walked to a cabinet, opened it and reached inside. Something struggled in his grasp and vapour seeped through his fingers. He selected a waterproof sack, forced the thing within and pulled the drawstring tight. He passed the sack to Captain Dangleglum and refused payment when the Captain reached for his wallet. There was a many faceted glint in the Prince's eyes and a peculiar expression on his face, a mixture of understanding, envy and humour.

"My heaviest monsoon," he said quietly.

As the Captain bade him farewell, the Prince returned to his seat behind the counter and began muttering to himself. "My grandfather was quite a rainy fellow, my father was very rainy, but I am even more rainy than that. My reign is nothing less than torrential. For I am Prince Rainier of Monsoonarco!"

Captain Dangleglum deemed it impolite to turn around. He pulled up his anchor and went sailing away without looking back.

*9.

Sailing a ship made of his own frozen breath, a galleon of solid sighs, Captain Nothing blocked out the stars as he descended to Earth. Around his shoulders were draped filaments of the aurora borealis like fluorescent seaweed and his teeth chattered with the frostiness of intergalactic space. His sails held the sighs of the sunset and they were smoother than mirrors, ironed by the sunbeams on the ironing board of the empyrean, and while on the subject of ironing we could talk about Frayed Cuff and Crease Wrinkle, the mortal enemies of The Hissing Iron, but we won't, at least not here. Captain Nothing shouted down as his icy ship glided to a frosty reception: "Let me tell you about what happened after I left the Prince of Rains and began my voyage back to Wales!"

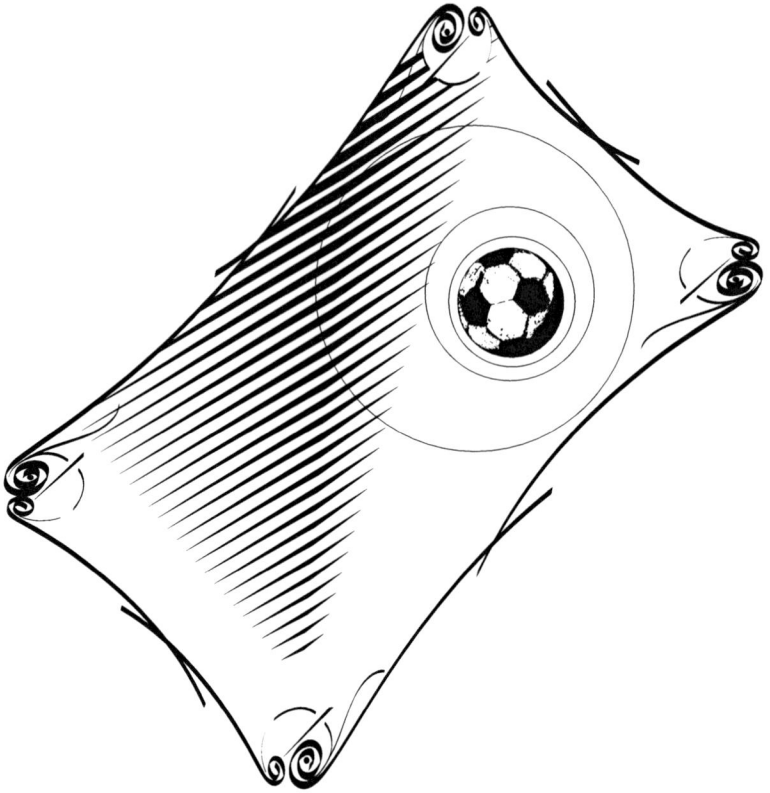

THE TALLEST MIDGET

I'll tell you what I saw when I went to Lipsaria. The capital city of that country is famous for the outrageous incline of its football pitch. The truth is that it's only inclined at certain times because it has been laid on the swing bridge over the River Grinn. When a ship with a mast wants to pass through the city, the bridge splits in two and both halves go up.

It might seem foolish to locate a football pitch on a bridge. Everybody agrees it was a daft idea but the city of Snogg is very tightly packed with buildings and doesn't have any open spaces and its inhabitants are a feisty lot and hold public demonstrations if they don't get what they want. Once they even marched – badly – for the right to have cramp. They demanded a football pitch and there simply wasn't anywhere else to put it.

Usually a football game can proceed without the raising and lowering of the bridge because not many ships pass that way these days.

But when the pitch does begin to slope the outcome of a match is always affected. The split is along the halfway line and when the two sides go up the ball rolls towards one of the goals. It is important to keep the ball in the opposing team's half as much as possible. The goalkeepers have a hard job whenever a ship sails up or down that river and it's an unpopular position to play.

I was once travelling from Monsoonarco to Wales and decided to break my journey in Lipsaria before proceeding to the Valley of Tall Midgets. My own vessel didn't interrupt a game because I arrived very early in the morning. I moored my ship out of the way in a little dock and then I set out to sample the attractions of Snogg. In the streets I saw many people wearing hats and scarves and carrying flags in the local colours.

I stopped one fellow. "What's happening?"

"A big football match today. Snogg United are playing Moonville Rovers for the cup!"

"Which cup?" I persisted.

"I'm not sure but it's full of beer!"

"How much does it hold?"

"Lots and lots and lots. Enough to satisfy a giant!"

I decided to attend this football match. I made my way towards the pitch and fell into conversation with the other spectators. I learned that Snogg United had already knocked out Boca Juniors, Itselfia City, Lladloh Town, Yam-Yam Wanderers, Bristol Rovers, Dynamo Plush and Phoot Athletic to reach the final against Moonville. That last qualifying match had been especially hard – compared by some critics to a horrible outbreak – and now all the Lipsarians, not just the Snoggites, were puckered up with anticipation.

The game started well. Both sides scored early and the managers of the two teams kept jumping up and shouting. The Moonville manager, a fellow by the name of Troose, was particularly bellicose. I thought that Snogg United probably had the edge, courtesy of their strikers Titter and Snigger, but Moonville were strong in defence and had their own star player, Wane Moony, to keep the opposition busy. All the same the score remained a draw until half time.

The second half was much more eventful but not for the right reasons. Suddenly the pitch split in two and began tilting up. The ball was in the Snoggite half at the time and rolled into the goalmouth. The keeper just couldn't keep it out, partly because he had ended up in the back of the net himself. After the ship passed, the bridge swung down again and play resumed as normal.

The crowd didn't react much. It wasn't so odd for the pitch to go up and down like that. They had seen it happen before. But it was a real surprise when the same thing happened again a minute later. And then again and again. Sometimes the ball rolled into one goal, sometimes into the other. Nobody present at that game had ever seen so many ships sailing up the River Grinn in one day!

Whenever I tell people I attended that match they often ask me, "Who was the winner?"

To which I reply, "Are you referring to the football game or to the boat race?"

For that was the eventual explanation! The Derek of Bo, also known as Diddly Derek, had decided to stage a boat race from Monsoonarco to Upper Bo at exactly the same time the Cup Final was taking place. It was an unfortunate coincidence. The Derek of Bo has tightly braided hair and lives in a cigar box but that is beside the point. He loves racing things, not just ships but lizards, tomatoes, shadows, insults, wardrobes, loners, anything at all!

The fact of the matter is that nobody won the boat race. The River Grinn crosses the Valley of Tall Midgets on its way to Upper Bo. Do you know the Tall Midgets? They resemble, but aren't related to, the Microscopic Giants. Anyway, the river crosses the valley on an aqueduct supported on three vast pillars. Sometimes the Tall Midgets play cricket with huge stone cannonballs and use the aqueduct as a wicket. They bowl underarm but very powerfully.

It so happened that Tipsy Sobers, the second tallest midget, had already hit the balls of three full overs into the stratosphere. That's eighteen balls in total for anyone who doesn't like cricket. The bowler, Paddy Lily, couldn't bear for the fourth over to go the same way, so he bowled his fastest ball and hit the wickets with enough force to scatter them over a wide area.

Tipsy Sobers was out but he didn't leave his crease. He stayed where he was. He was transfixed by the sight of a hundred ships plummeting from the edge of the broken aqueduct one by one, landing in a pile of shattered wood and ragged sails in the centre of the valley. The Tall Midgets repaired the aqueduct as they always did after a cricket match, but it was too late. The boat race was abandoned.

"In that case, who won the football game?"

And I answer like this: "The final score was a 50-50 draw. The ball kept rolling into the goals but it spent an equal amount of time in each half of the pitch. A hundred ships sailed past, the bridge swung open one hundred times and that's how many goals were scored. Nobody won!"

"Nobody! Are you quite sure about that?"

"Maybe Woozy Growl was a winner of sorts. He was the tallest midget of all, even taller than Tipsy Sobers, so tall he was able to play golf with the craters left by the cannonballs that descended from the stratosphere. He played all eighteen holes in one hour and when he went to the clubhouse for a drink he found waiting a massive cup of beer donated by the unlucky players of Moonville Rovers and Snogg United."

*10.

Woozy Growl leaned over Hywel like a deflating marquee and his moving lips resembled the bolsters of a large uncomfortable bed as he remarked, "Little people like myself and my midget comrades are even more common than genies. We come in many kinds, some smaller than others, some thinner, some more gnarled, some with jauntier hats or thicker socks. We exist where genies can't, not just in Rholl, but also in Ireland. That's a weird place, for snakes aren't allowed to live there but Flann O'Brien was. Here is a story about our Irish brethren."

THE MAN WHO GARGLED WITH GARGOYLE JUICE

"It's good for your throat."

"I'm not sure. I don't like the sound of it. I bet the taste is awful. Will it be very slimy?

"Not slimy. Not slimy at all."

"The goblin was slimy."

"Surely it was. That's the only kind we get round here, the slimy ones. If you were to go as far north as Kilkenny you might be able to procure a powdery goblin or maybe even a peppery one, but down here in Cork the goblins spend a lot of time above ground in the rain and the water gets inside them."

"Don't they wear capes and boots?"

"Certainly they do, but the capes and boots on sale in Cork are the porous kind, full of little holes."

"Won't you try me with a leprechaun or fairy first?"

"That would be a waste of your money. The fluid inside a leprechaun is less potent than goblin juice and you've already drunk a goblin to no avail. As for fairies they are out of season and you'd have to cross the equator into the southern hemisphere to get one at this time of year. That would be very expensive."

"How about a banshee?"

"This is a shop, not a story. Banshees don't really exist. Neither do trolls, hippogriffs or golems."

"Maybe some antibiotics would do the trick?"

"I don't think so. You must have a very severe throat infection if a goblin didn't cure it. The kind of medicine you get from a doctor won't stand a chance. You've come to the right place now and I'm sure gargoyle juice is the best remedy."

"Where do you get your ingredients from?"

"A local company, Little People Inc. They send agents out with nets to explore grottoes, climb churches, sleep under toadstools and do whatever else is necessary to replenish stock."

"Is there only one method of extracting the juice?"

"Absolutely not. Goblins are simply popped into the liquidiser but pixies are pressed by hand through a sieve. As for gnomes they have to be hung by their feet and tickled until all the fluid has dripped into a bucket. Gargoyles are different again."

"Repeat that in a more typically Irish manner, will you?"

"The divil I will! Be off with your strange requests! Do you want to get rid of your sore throat or not?"

"Yes I do. I'll try a gargoyle if you really think it will help. Do they take long to prepare? How much are they?"

"It won't burn a hole in your pocket. Trust me. Wait here and I'll have the drink ready for you in a few minutes. You won't regret this, I assure you."

"What's that odd wheezing sound?"

"That's just me working the bellows in the back room. Just stay there in the front of the shop and I'll rejoin you soon enough. Why not tell me about yourself while you are waiting?"

"I don't know where to begin."

"Birth is the standard opening to a human life. Maybe your mother was a woman with big hands? Maybe she walked on stilts and kissed the tops of chimneys? Was she a duck in a former existence? Perhaps her forearm resembled the coast of Norway? Did she meet your father on a gangplank? Did she sleep in an awkwardly varnished bed?"

"I have simply no idea."

"No matter. I was only making small talk. The gargoyle juice is ready now. I'll bring it out to you. Be sure to drink it all down in one gulp for maximum effect. Here it is."

"A stone cup with insulated handles?"

"Yes indeed. Be careful how you hold it. That's right, pour it down your throat, every last drop. Sure it glows like lava. That's because it *is* lava, a gargoyle taken from a Cork church melted down in my furnace. So what do you think? Do you like it?"

"Urgh! Nunnghrrrgh!"

"That was clumsy of you, dropping the cup like that! Of course it burns terribly. What did you expect? A gargoyle is a small sculpture, a stone figure, not a living creature like a goblin. The juice of a gargoyle is several thousand degrees centigrade, otherwise it turns solid again. But it's guaranteed to stop a sore throat."

"Aaaarghgh! Eerughfffghghghgh!"

"I'll have to guess what that means. Are you trying to say that this wasn't quite what you expected? Maybe not. But you can't have a sore throat when you have no throat. Gargoyle juice never fails. I've treated hundreds of patients this way and not one ever voiced a complaint afterwards!"

*11.

The customer in that story stepped into the light and rasped, "I'm not a man. Why did most readers assume that I was? I had a sore throat because of all the bellowing I've done in the past four thousand years. The gargoyle cured it but it came back. Some things can be taken to extremes; other things go to extremes on their own. Words can be taken in jest, or carried safely in books, or chopped up and carried in only one book, a dictionary. Tall tales can be digested or regurgitated. Just be grateful you can swallow or spit them out. I no longer have that option! But I can see you're not really interested in any sort of preamble to my tale, so I'll just get on with it. Nobody has ever been interested in what I say. They just think I add colour to labyrinths! Ah well!"

THE MINOTAUR IN PAMPLONA

He knew for certain, or imagined he did, how to deal with bends and twists in any maze, and the narrow streets of this city had not been designed to deliberately confuse anyone. He was strong and fast and his courage could not be doubted, nor did he suffer from excessive pride at his qualities. His confidence was justified but his manner was modest.

Arriving before sunrise on the first day of the Fiesta de San Fermín, he noted that already a band was rehearsing in a public square. The celebrations would begin at midday and continue without pause for more than a week. He waited for a café to open and ordered a coffee, the steam from the cup blending with his own dawn breath as he crouched over it. Finding accommodation here at this time would be impossible, so he planned to sleep on the citadel ramparts with the other lonely, unlucky or romantic visitors. But he was more than a spectator.

He stood and walked the route from the Plaza Santo Domingo to the bullring, familiarising himself with the peculiarities of the streets. Then he wandered sedately among the parks, conserving his energy for the following morning, performing gentle exercises, stretching his huge muscles, nodding at the people who had started to gather in groups. Mostly he was ignored for his trouble and the few smiles he collected on the way were thin and dismissive.

A clock somewhere struck noon and music came from ahead, always around the next corner, a phenomenon he regarded as supernatural until he realised he was accidentally following a parade. He increased his pace and caught up with the musicians, who now stood in a circle and played wilder songs at a faster tempo. The first dancers swirled into the soup of notes, followed by others until the whole street was gyrating, he alone a static object, a point of reference. He waited to be asked to dance so that he might decline, for he wanted to be fully fit for tomorrow, but he was never given the chance. And of course this suited his needs perfectly.

When night fell he decided he had rested enough on his feet and walked to the citadel to sleep. He was the first to bed down but as the hours passed he was joined by others. It was cold under his rough blanket. He drifted from dream to dream and woke often, confused and blinking at the stars, the crescent moon toppled on its side like a pair of disembodied horns above a tide of strangely shaped clouds.

Once he opened his eyes because a stealthy thief was robbing the sleepers in his vicinity, moving in time with the wind from one prone drunken body to the next, searching through pockets and in the folds of blankets. The thief stepped over him without making any attempt on his possessions. At first he believed the thief had been daunted by his obvious strength and he was pleased, but then it occurred to him he might simply look too poor to steal from, or that he had not really been noticed at all. Far away music still played, softly with laughter.

The first to stir and rise when the stars dimmed, he walked with considerable grace across the city to the appointed place. Other runners converged from every direction and soon the bustling and jostling of competitors and watchers was intense and oddly relaxing. He inhaled deeply. This was living with passion, dangerously, intoxicatingly, the only way for any sentient being to thrive, heart pounding, sweat sprouting like dew on limbs and torso! He enjoyed the communal fear and excitement, the idea that people were sharing sensations with him.

He knew what to expect and the sound of the first rocket being launched was not startling but in fact caused him to relax even more. This was proof of his mental strength, a result of his preparations, his research and respect for process and tradition. The long whistle and detonation overhead was a signal the bulls had been released and the more timid or enthusiastic competitors started running, far too early in his view. Better to wait for the second rocket, which signalled that the entire herd of bulls was free. That way it would be easier to run with the animals in the true spirit of the Fiesta, rather than ahead of the dust and danger.

The second rocket spat into the sky and he tried to tense his muscles, to spring forward, to realise his dream of being an active part of this famous, or notorious, event, but suddenly it was no longer possible to move. Direction and desire were abstractions. Around him men hurried forward, but not one of them even brushed against his arms, which were slack at his sides. There was no bite in his mouth, no swell of blood in his head, nothing meaningful.

He simply stood and waited to be crushed by the herd, the heavy beasts with frightened eyes and dawn breath just like his, smoky, thick, almost blue in the long early shadows of the Plaza. He waited but he did not watch, for they were behind him and he faced only the sweat soaked backs of runners and a corridor with walls made of spectators and music. He waited and thought about the different types of waiting, uneasy, ignorant, gloomy, resigned, and understood that no variation matched his own particular style of not moving, remaining fixed at this precise instant. He waited and slowly his whole body sagged.

Nothing touched him, no horn or hoof, not even the erect hairs of each hot flank. The bulls surged around him while he continued to wait, leaving him unscathed with drooping shoulders and hollow stomach, and he watched the living thunder and organised confusion pass on both sides. Ignored again, even by stricken beasts, as if there was something in his very existence that could not be acknowledged by the most primitive physical contact.

Now he was standing alone and the event had come and gone without him, even though he had inserted himself into the centre of it. He remained for perhaps another hour before walking away, his mind struggling with old memories, seeking a clue as to why he was a permanent outsider in everything. He wondered if the stories were true, if he had really been murdered in his own house in the distant past and could not be here, but it did not feel like that. He suspected the answer was different at every stage of his long life, a life of travelling, waiting to be perceived and recognised. But this particular case was simple.

If his inner self was not sure who to run with, the bulls or the men, and the people did not know, how could the city care?

*12.

The stealthy thief who had robbed the sleepers on the ramparts wanted to defend himself. He cried, "People who go to Pamplona for the Bull Run should be more careful about where they keep their valuables! Besides, all I took was some food and a few watches and maybe a little money. There are worse things to steal than those basic necessities! To steal a heart and treat it badly, for example. And there are worse crimes than stealing; for it all depends on the emotional impact. While you keep a protective hand on your wallets, I'll tell you a tale about a criminal with far less compassion than myself!"

WOOD FOR THE TREES

I'm stopping at Jitvapur now, so I might as well tell you a story connected with this place. Jitvapur seems no different from any other little village in Bihar, which as I'm sure you know is the poorest and most rural district in India, but appearances can often be deceptive.

Just like certain bridegrooms…

Not long before my arrival, there was a wedding here and everybody took part with the gusto typical of such happy events. Needless to say, Jitvapur is a very traditional community and all the customs were strictly observed to ensure a fruitful and fortunate marriage. Even the most absurd superstitions were carefully heeded, so that destiny would have no compelling reason to cause trouble.

The name of the bride was Amrusha, the groom was called Rakesh, they were healthy young people well suited to each other, and everything seemed in its proper place as far as anyone could tell, so a prosperous life together was warmly anticipated by all. There had been a small problem at the beginning of the arrangement, due to the fact that Rakesh was a manglik, but that was sorted out now.

A manglik is a person born under the astrological condition known as mangal dosha. In other words the planet Mars was in the second, fourth, seventh, eighth or twelfth house of the Vedic lunar chart when the individual entered this world. In India the condition is widely believed to be extremely bad for marriage and if a manglik marries a non-manglik the outcome is certain to be death or even divorce! The government of India has repeatedly attempted to discourage this superstition but in regions as remote as Bihar it persists strongly.

Two mangliks may marry each other safely because the negative energies will cancel themselves out. But Amrusha wasn't a manglik. On the contrary, her horoscope was impeccable. So her match with Rakesh was dangerously unbalanced.

Nonetheless there exists a solution to remove the difficulties. If the manglik submits to the ceremony of kumbh vivah, in which the manglik marries a banana tree or a peepal tree, all the bad luck will be neutralised. Bizarre as it may sound to our ears, people in India do still marry trees, and in fact a famous actress did so just a few years ago. You have probably seen her photograph in newspapers even if you haven't sat through any of her films.

Anyway, Rakesh had endured the kumbh vivah rituals and married a tree, so the final obstacle to his union with Amrusha had been removed in the approved fashion. He was first taken to the tree in a baraat accompanied by dancing villagers and hired musicians and many of his cousins sang songs to him along the way. Various rites were performed by purohits and he saw that the tree was already decorated as a bride. After the couple were pronounced man and tree the feasting began and the guests offered shagun to Rakesh, which he gratefully accepted.

A 'baraat' is a marriage procession in which the groom rides on a horse to meet his bride, while a 'purohit' is a wise scholar with a comprehensive knowledge of rituals, and 'shagun' is a unit of good luck usually wrapped up like a parcel in a blessing. But Rakesh already knew all that...

Clearly I am explaining for your benefit alone.

That was how his first wedding went and because of its success Rakesh was ready for his second. His horse was a beautiful and noble steed and the musicians played even more sweetly this time and the singers sang with even greater devotion. There was a pervasive but unspoken feeling that this occasion was more authentic than the other and that Amrusha was somehow a more deserving bride than the tree. She certainly looked radiant when he approached her and dismounted.

Suddenly this touching ceremony was disrupted by an intruder…

"What do you think you are doing?" demanded a voice that was powerful and yet insubstantial, as if it issued not from a mouth powered by lungs but on the surfaces of leaves rustled by the wind. Rakesh glanced up.

"I am getting married to Amrusha," he answered weakly.

"But I'm your wife!" cried the tree.

There was a lengthy pause and everybody involved in the procession shuffled their feet and looked down at the ground, too surprised to even gasp or jump back, but Amrusha kept her nerve and gazed without flinching at the uninvited guest. She decided to explain the situation as clearly and concisely as possible.

"Yes, you are his wife, but only in a symbolic sense. Rakesh is a manglik, you see, and he had to marry you to make it possible to marry me. It was never intended for his marriage to a peepal tree to be taken seriously…"

"A peepal tree? A peepal!"

And now a large branch dipped down with a handful of twigs at its end bunched into a fist and this fist came to rest under the quivering chin of Rakesh. "Bigamist!"

The bridegroom wasted no time in taking to his heels. He ran towards the horizon, his feet throwing up clouds of dust that failed to hide his escape route. With a furious sigh, the tree set off in warmish pursuit, because anything too hot in a wooden lifeform might start a lethal fire, but Rakesh already had a notable headstart. First the tree tried to mount his horse and ride off after the errant husband, but the horse associated the shade of a tree with a rest period and refused to budge. So the tree had to rely on its own motive power. Instead of using its exposed roots as legs, it fell to the ground and began rolling at high speed like a gigantic pencil across a sloping desk. If it caught up with Rakesh it would probably crush him.

It was only at this point or even a little later that the wedding guests realised the tree was a banana.

Amrusha was shocked. "What a scoundrel he was! It seems I've had a lucky escape. Good riddance to his kind!"

Because of the distance and fading light, it soon became impossible to see the two receding figures and nobody got to learn if Rakesh reached the safety of the mountains to the north. Perhaps he is still running and the banana tree still rolling. Amrusha remains upset by the whole affair and is still unmarried, but that's hardly surprising bearing in mind that these events took place only a week ago...

Yes, when I arrived at Jitvapur the story was extremely fresh, even though one of its elements had gone off. It would be hypocritical of me to apologise for that pun, because I intend to deliver another. Where I come from, when a human couple get married they say 'I do' to each other but trees only say 'I would'. That's a fact.

I did consider calling this story 'Would for the Trees' but that play on words seemed inappropriate because none of the characters speak fluent English in public, not even the tree. I'm fond of literary conceits but I do have limits. Having said that, this text does contain at least one other trick, a deliberate deception.

The truth is that I'm not really stopping over at Jitvapur right now. In fact I've never even been there. Which makes leaving in the morning much easier.

*13.

"Who is next?" inquired Hywel, "for the time has already rushed forward and the second half of this first day is almost here! Time always goes faster in a pub, that's an accepted impossibility. Anyway, it seems to me that the famous actress mentioned in that previous story must have performed in many films based on true events; and at least some of those true events must have been really remarkable. So I'd like to hear a story from her own lips. There she is, and I'm sure she has something worth hearing. Maybe she'll tell us the tale of the oddest true event that ever inspired one of the films she starred in?"

THE VIOLATION

Veronica walked out of her relationship with Manfred because she caught him cheating; not with another woman but with a paintbrush. She came back early and saw that he was copying one of her paintings. He admitted that he never went out to paint directly from real scenery but simply duplicated whatever she did and made a few minor adjustments each time, to preserve the illusion his work was original. She felt violated and stormed off. Then she caught a plane to a distant land.

In Goa she resumed her career and she was careful not to form romantic attachments with any other artists. Her new lovers were all non-creative types. She painted seascapes mostly; and beach scenes. Several times she took an excursion into the Western Ghats to capture the mountains on canvas. She lived in a simple wooden house in the shade of palm trees and she was happy enough. Her income was small but sufficient; for existence in Goa was very reasonable in those days.

One morning a balloon descended out of the cloudless sky and landed on the beach while she was painting the waves. "Hey, you're blocking my view!" she shouted at the aeronaut who stepped out of the wicker basket. He didn't answer but strode towards her.

"Veronica Pond?" he finally asked.

She nodded. "Who are you? Have you come to buy a painting?"

"I'm afraid not. I'm a lawyer."

Then he revealed that he had a legal order demanding her presence in a newly formed law court on an island in the middle of the Indian Ocean. She was required to go with him immediately and he was entitled to use force if she refused. He would explain everything on the way, but it was imperative that they hurry, because if he she was late and missed the hearing she would be charged with contempt of court, which carried a rather heavy, almost ponderous, sentence.

She frowned. "A legal order? You mean a subpoena?"

"You are both the accused *and* a witness; but you're not the only one. Come with me now. And bring one of your paintings. It will be used as evidence against you, but if you decline…"

He shrugged and Veronica saw that he held a snub-nosed gun pointed directly at her heart. She went with him.

"Is this a civil or criminal case?" she asked.

"A bit of both," he replied.

She stepped into the wicker basket and rested her most recent painting upright in the furthest corner. The lawyer tugged the anchor out of the sand and they began to rise. Once they were airborne he relaxed and became friendlier. He steered the balloon by means of a large bellows mounted on a swivel. It was hard work but he seemed accustomed to it; as he worked the handles he smiled apologetically at her and introduced himself as Tonguewaggle Chipchop. She laughed.

"It sounds no more daft to you than 'Veronica Pond' does to me," he retorted. But he was only mildly offended.

They travelled due south and left Goa far behind. Veronica felt she was in a film; or at least in a reality that would be turned into a film. The balloon was a strange machine and its canopy was hermetically sealed. She had travelled in a hot air balloon before; and she knew this wasn't one of those. But its movement was very smooth, with almost no swaying, and she decided to enjoy the journey for what it was. The balloon passed over a flock of very strange birds. She pointed at them.

"Not birds," said Tonguewaggle, "but migrating bell peppers."

"Don't be ridiculous!" she cried.

"I'm perfectly serious. Bell peppers contain a vacuum that gets bigger as they grow; if they grow big enough they become light enough to float in air. What do you think this balloon is? It wasn't manufactured by anyone. It was *grown*. On Mondaugen's allotment."

Veronica was astonished. "Who is Mondaugen?"

"An inventor. He fitted this bellows to his largest bell pepper and so created a steerable balloon. Ingenious! But he's not the only inventor in the world; and I'm not the only lawyer. In fact, the plaintiff of the case we are attending issued four commissions to four different inventors and four different lawyers. My task is to convey painters from the north to the courthouse in this balloon. Other lawyers are conveying other painters in different flying machines from different cardinal points."

And he went on to explain how an inventor called Boppo Higgins had designed a rocket to transport painters from the west; while another inventor by the name of Frabjal Troose had designed a gigantic levitating moonflower to transport painters from the east; and yet another inventor, Dr Celery, had designed a celerycopter to transport…

"But there aren't many painters in the south," he said suddenly, interrupting his own discourse.

"My ex-boyfriend was a painter from the south," countered Veronica.

"I don't mean any old south, but south of our destination. Our destination is a new island arisen out of the sea especially for the trial. It has cooled sufficiently, so don't worry about that. This island is 1000 KM south of Diego Garcia. How far south is your boyfriend from?"

"My ex-boyfriend," corrected Veronica.

She told Tonguewaggle about Manfred and said that he came from Brighton; but that wasn't south enough to satisfy the lawyer, who sniffed dismissively. Veronica regarded him and she still felt as if she was in a film, but it was a feeling that hardly mattered. She asked if the island they were headed for had a name. It didn't. Then she finally summoned up the courage to ask what she had done wrong. After all, she was only a painter, a painter of landscapes. Nothing more.

"But that's precisely the problem!" cried Tonguewaggle.

"What do you mean?"

He sighed deeply. "Artists who don't copy nature are safe. I once knew a sculptor in Bratislava who made abstract works out of scrap metal. He won't be coming to this trial, I assure you! Take another artist: the origami expert, Oshimi. He is also safe, because his paper figures are utterly unrealistic. No lawyer has been sent to fetch *him*. But as for you... Just look at the painting you have brought along! A beach scene at dusk. The quality of the light is perfect. Everything else too."

"Thank you," she said, appreciating the backhanded compliment.

He pouted. "*She* doesn't like it."

"Who doesn't?" Veronica asked.

Tonguewaggle changed the subject. He had a small transistor radio in the wicker basket and he turned it on. Music warbled from the speakers. Veronica listened carefully. It was a jazz band. When the song was finished, the radio announced that it had been a number by the Tony Smith Experience called 'The All-Knowing Spirits of Gaspar Jangle'. The radio introduced another song by the same band called 'Blatantly Contrived Linkage.' An odd title for a song, Veronica decided.

The batteries in the radio were already low. Now they ran down completely. Silence returned to the balloon. Tonguewaggle said, "In my spare moments, I play miniature croquet with tamarind seeds. It's not a smutty game. Would you like to play it with me now?"

Veronica did so. And she won. By this time, the island that was their destination was in sight. They landed gently in front of a large courthouse and Tonguewaggle became more hostile again. He took out his gun and ushered her through the imposing doors and down a long corridor into a domed chamber of inexplicable grandiosity. Veronica couldn't quite explain why its grandiosity was so inexplicable. Maybe because there was something cinematic about the wide-screen perspectives.

The lighting was inadequate and the judge ordered more dreamers to be wheeled into the courtroom on their beds. "Bubblewrap and harpsichords!" he cursed. Veronica had never heard such curious oaths before. As the dreamers snored, beams of light radiated from their ears, the illumination generated inside the heads of every dreamer to stop them bumping into dreamed objects. Tonguewaggle informed Veronica that minor surgery had been necessary to let the beams out. The dreamers were kept somnolent with intravenous injections of laudanum.

"That's opium dissolved in alcohol," he said.

"I know what it is! But why is the judge pointing at me?" she asked.

"Because it's your turn to testify."

She stepped forward and felt the eyes of everyone in the courtroom on her. Judge Tapas waited for her to regain her composure; he specialised in impossible cases and was never too impatient with the bewildered. Veronica saw that many other painters sat on the floor with chains wrapped around their arms and legs. She knew they were painters because they wore angled berets and smeared smocks. Manfred wasn't among them. She wondered why not. Then she glared at the judge and cried:

"What are the charges against me? I demand to know!"

"Copyright violation," said Judge Tapas.

Veronica was incredulous. "What? All my work is original. I've never duplicated a painting in my life. I work directly from nature."

"Exactly!" boomed a mighty voice.

Veronica had thought that the enormous figure in the centre of the chamber was a monumental statue, but now she realised that it was a living thing. She realised this fact with a 'start', just like characters in books do, even though she still felt more like a character in a film. It was now clear that this was the plaintiff, the one who had instigated the suit against her and the other artists. Then she remembered what Tonguewaggle had told her in the balloon about artists who copied from nature.

"But who are you?" she asked unnecessarily.

"I'm Mother Nature, of course! Who else could I possibly be? For many centuries I've watched landscape painters steal all my ideas and I've had enough of it! Mountains, oceans, deserts, and all other features have been copyrighted by me. You are one of the worst culprits and I can tell from the painting you brought with you as evidence that there's no hope you'll ever reform and become an abstract artist instead. So you will be punished with the nastiest possible sentence. And fined too!"

"This is hardly fair!" objected Veronica. And then she pointed out that if her offence was so serious, why wasn't her ex-boyfriend also on trial? He was even more culpable than she was; for whereas she copied directly from nature, he copied directly from her. So if Veronica Pond was guilty of copyright violation, Manfred Gyrl was guilty of a double violation and should receive a sentence twice as harsh. Mother Nature listened attentively to all this and then roared:

"That scoundrel has *already* had his trial. The court was appalled by his history of infringements; and yes, he was given a sentence even worse than the one you'll get! Where do you think the dreamers come from, the ones with the incandescent ears? He is one of those now. In comparison, your punishment will be mild!"

Veronica stood with her hands on her hips. "I hardly think that being sent to sleep is a strong chastisement!"

"Really? But all light sources fail sooner or later. Just like light bulbs, the dreamers need to be regularly replaced. And guess what happens to the old ones, the burnt out cases? They aren't recycled. Oh no! They are disposed of in a particular location…"

And Mother Nature leaned forward to display the crater of the active volcano that was her head. Dark shapes crisped and convected in the erupting magma. Shapes that had once been dreamers. Judge Tapas banged his gavel but nobody paid any attention to him. Then Mother Nature sat up straight again and grinned malevolently at Veronica.

At this juncture, a fuller description of Mother Nature seems in order. As tall as a cliff and as wide as a glacier, she encompassed and encapsulated the entirety of the natural world. Forests marched up her mighty legs and her stomach was an entire continent. Her arms were tornadoes and her exposed breasts were cumulus clouds. Her shoulders were sand dunes and her neck was an isthmus. Her head was a volcano, true, and its streams of lava were her hair; but the expression on her face was self-assured and not entirely ferocious. There was beauty in it too, and somehow she resembled a famous Indian actress. But her mouth was a rift valley and her eyes were inland seas that…

I have just been interrupted by Tonguewaggle Chipchop, who advises me to end this description prematurely in case the lawsuit is extended against descriptive writers. In fact he thinks it's better if I break off the entire story at this point for my own safety.

*14.

The judge in that story removed his wig and said, "It's always healthy to have interests outside work. Mr Tonguewaggle Chipchop disappoints his clients for a living but plays miniature croquet with tamarind seeds in his spare time. As for myself, I deal every day with the letter of the law and want as a hobby something unconnected with sentencing. I rely on my private club to help me relax on the weekends. My club is concerned with single words rather than complete sentences." Then he explained what kind of club it was and how he had risen in its ranks and Hywel said, "I can accept that your club helps you relax but I'm sure it does nothing to cool you down." To which the judge nodded ruefully and told the following tale:

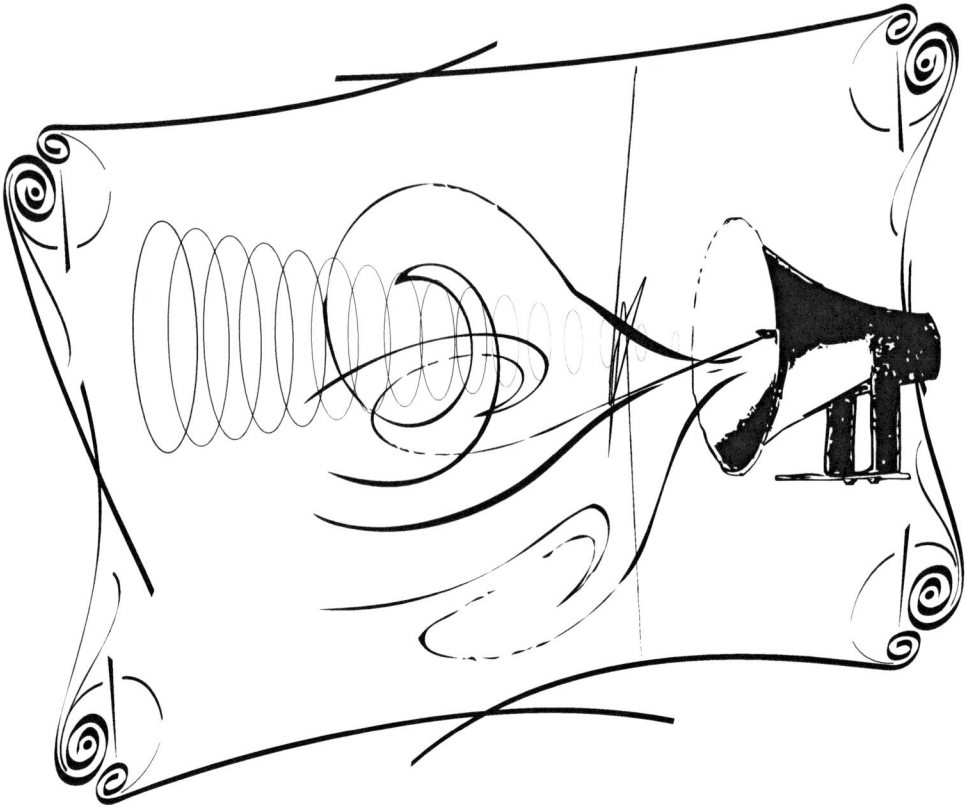

OATHS

The art of swearing has reached its apotheosis with the annual competitions organised by the Wilde Bores Foundation, an international society dedicated solely to the expletive. Members of the Foundation are drawn from all walks of life; they attend meetings in limousines, in battered vans, on motorcycles, on unicycles and on foot. There is no discrimination when it comes to insults. All races and creeds can mingle freely and denounce each other equally.

As Publicity Officer for the Foundation, it is my prime duty to insist on public displays of swearing. Accordingly, the annual competitions are usually held in town squares or in public parks. With concealed microphones and a suitable number of amplifiers, it is possible to extend the range of such events far out into any given suburb. Old women have been offended in their own homes; priests have been drowned out during services; pigeons have dropped dead.

A typical competition will usually involve a group of fifty or so blackguards, male and female, who must compete on terms similar to those employed in marathon dancing sessions. The insultees, that is the judges, rate a performance on aspects of originality, duration and vehemence. Any competitor who bursts a blood vessel during a performance is instantly disqualified. The true art of swearing demands not an hysterical outburst but a controlled and thoroughly calculated stream of abuse.

As competitors drop out from the arena, it begins to become apparent who the finalists will be. There are always a handful of formidable participants who appear year after year. Boris, the Westphalian banker, is a particular favourite with the crowd. He has a retreating brow and the manners of a hog. Rodin Guignol is another favourite: he is a sculptor and his insults are perfectly chiselled. Then there is Giuseppe Papini, a lazy Tuscan with a voice that is almost as musical and deadly as that of La Pelos, the senora whose penchant for obscenity extends beyond words to the physical gesture.

Greatest respect of all, however, is reserved for our own man in the fray, Sir Guy Boothby. Raised by a gentleman farmer in Hampshire, Sir Guy has mastered the subtleties of the polite insult. Dressed in a crushed velvet frock coat and purple cravat, he presents a foppish and flamboyant appearance that never fails to delight. With perfect grace, he can sigh languidly, pick his nose with a little finger held just so, and then deliver a casual putdown that cuts right across the more aggressive exhortations of his antagonists.

As for the spectators, they too provide entertainment for themselves. The competitions are rife with freelancers who seek to outdo the professionals by holding up banners bearing the words "bum" or "sod" or some such thing. The competitors take a dim view of such interference. There have been fights; the police have been called in on more than one occasion; heads have been broken; pigeons have been crushed underfoot.

Naturally, I am delighted by such scenes, for they confirm and validate the ideals of the Foundation. After each major riot I am a hero. What could be more gratifying to one in my position? For is it not the case that once police and public are pitted against each other, the taunts assume a monstrous creativity? Thanks to the concealed microphones such clashes are relayed far and wide. It seems that the demands of the Foundation are being met head on; a society in which every spoken word is an affront to be dealt with by another. We are mystics, in our own way. We seek the serenity of tension, the peace of uproar.

There is a problem, however, which we have overlooked. Recently, we have noticed a thinning in the actual effect of curses and oaths. With familiarity, the power of certain words has started to wane. The reliable expletives have been overworked. People yawn now when they hear them. Old women are no longer offended in their homes; priests do not pause for even a moment; the cat among the pigeons has grown indolent and the pigeons strut in safety.

What then is to be done? Attendances at the competitions are falling; membership of the Foundation is decreasing. I seek inspiration in a bottle of brandy and a long stemmed pipe. I shut myself away for three days. Inspiration is not merely perspiration but also masturbation. Fists pound on my door; the telephone rings; I am a wanted man. The wheels of society have ground to a halt. Without swearing, labourers can no longer work; irate customers can no longer complain to managers; the markets of the world are closing down.

On the evening of the third day, I find the answer right in the hollow at the bottom of the bottle. One potent solution has bred another. New swear words are needed. That is the realisation that has dawned in my addled brain. There is no need to create completely new words, merely to adapt the old. Words that are innocuous but little used, or used mainly by specialists, are ideal. With grim determination, I start to rewrite the dictionary of swearing.

And so now at our annual competitions we have regained our previous audiences. The matter will not end there, of course, but we at least have a method to work with. The process must be continuous, evolution must be maintained through a series of mutations. The engines of society whirl once more and at Hove, at Bognor Regis, throughout the Midlands and the grey-green Northern Realms, we hear the latest wonderful utterances of Boris, Rodin, Giuseppe, La Pelos and the rest echoing through the consciousness of a million individuals:

☞ Aardvark.

☞ Betelgeuse.

☞ Calligraphy.

☞ Didgeridoo.

☞ Dungaree.

☞ Kumquat.

☞ Milton Keynes.

☞ Tundra.

And so on. And so on. On and on. And my hero status has been restored and Sir Guy has hinted that a knighthood might not be out of the question; and Rodin Guignol mentioned something about a statue; and Giuseppe Papini offered me a crate of Tuscan wine; and La Pelos insisted on showing me her bosom; and I cry "artichoke!" and "centipede!" at the moon; and old women are offended once more in their homes; and priests are drowned out during services; and I feast on pigeon pie.

*15.

"Hatstands and sundials!" cursed Hywel when that tale was done, whether in admiration or derision is still unknown. "The thing that bewilders me most about your story is why you described Giuseppe Papini as 'lazy'. I don't believe that swearing is an indulgence or luxury, in my opinion it is work, and so it would be appropriate for Giuseppe himself to tell the next tale, to explain his laziness if he can be bothered to do so. Who do we have here? With your sunglasses and scooter and effortless style, you are clearly Italian. Are you the right fellow? Yes you are!"

CHIANTI'S INFERNO

While paddling in the water, I was delighted to observe a bottle floating past. I snatched it up quickly. There was a message inside which I pulled out and unrolled. This is what it said:

"Help! Please rescue me and I will do anything you want. Alone on a desert island."

I gazed at the horizon, assuming that this appeal for salvation had come thousands of leagues across the sea. Then I realised I was standing in the mouth of a shallow estuary and the bottle had drifted *down* the river. How could there be a desert island inland? This mystery made the discovery even more exciting.

I decided to investigate and waded to dry ground.

I was about to start walking upstream when I remembered how I had already trudged the entire length of the river. Indeed the reason I was paddling at this spot was because I wanted to cool my weary feet after such a difficult journey.

So there was no need to retrace my steps. All I had to do was think about where I had been. Sitting on an overturned lifeboat, I forced my mind to review my expedition.

I worked backwards, starting with the port city that was my present location, the belching chimneys and roaring furnaces and gloomy taverns. Then I retreated up into the farmland between the city and the hills, the crops still harvested by cowled peasants with glittering scythes. Each loop of the narrowing river took me into wilder country.

At last I was stumbling among the boulders and stunted trees of the actual hills and the river was a torrent. Near the base of the highest peak in the vicinity I found the source, the pool from which the river issued, clear and icy. This was the beginning of my voyage and end of my recollection because a wall of rock barred further progress.

Having travelled the river from source to mouth both in reality and memory, I had to admit there were no desert islands along its course, not a single one. Did this mean the person who wrote the message was a liar or joker? Possibly I am naive, for I still believed it was my responsibility to save him or her.

It occurred to me the island in question might not lie in the river but exist lateral to it. I contemplated the black cloud that hung above the highest peak, raining incessantly. Could this not conceal an aerial landmass? It was unlikely but not impossible. To validate my hypothesis, a tall ladder would be required. I did not own a ladder and doubted that one had ever been in my possession.

I read the scrawled message again. I sniffed the interior of the bottle and licked my lips. A peculiar feeling came over me, regret mixed with hope, a poignant blend.

Although I could picture myself standing at the source of the river I could not say where I had been prior to that point. Where had I come from originally? With a sudden jolt, I understood that I had already explored the inside of the cloud. Indeed I had been lowered down from it in a bucket attached to a rope.

There *was* solid ground in the sky and I had walked upon it, but it was not a desert island because there was a town on its surface and the houses of the town contained people. One of them had operated the winch that lowered me in the bucket.

This person was a woman. Who was she?

Now memories came quickly. The winch was mounted above a well and the well was sunk in the cellar of an old house. The woman had prodded me into the bucket but I was not reluctant to enter. I was merely eager to ensure that certain items, I know not what, accompanied me. The house was unnatural but familiar. Life within it felt uncomfortable but not because it was located in the sky.

Heaven is also located in the sky. Had I descended from heaven into the world of mortals? Who said that angels have no memory? I have forgotten. Does this prove I am one? In this case every amnesiac is an angel and I find that implausible.

Besides, I do have a memory, just an inefficient one. It is more likely I am a simple man from the real world who has dropped to a deeper level. Now I remembered the final words of the woman before she pushed me into the bucket. They seemed to confirm that the world in the cloud was the ordinary one:

"There is no room in Tuscany for people such as you. I am finally kicking you out and you can take your useless things with you."

"The bucket is not big enough for everything!" I protested.

In response she began turning the winch and cried, "Then I will send them all down after you!"

Abruptly I knew the name of the woman. She was Cinzia, my wife, and we lived together in a town called Montalcino. There was a reason why her patience with me had run out. It may have been because the atmosphere in our house was so unusual. Certainly I am not aware of any other property containing a well that leads to a lower tier of the universe.

No, that was not the reason. She was happy with the house. It had something to do with my attitude. I was devoted to something other than her. What was it? Perhaps it was my work, important work that left me little time for involving myself in matrimonial matters. Clearly I was too exhausted at the end of each day to apply myself to her, too busy earning money to be tender and loving.

But with a little more thought I knew my life had not been tiring at all. Quite the opposite. It was not a case of being worn out by work and neglecting Cinzia through fatigue. That was not the cause of her annoyance with me. In truth I was a dreamer, probably an artist or poet of some kind, deeming beauty more important than solvency, preferring to feed the soul rather than our bodies.

No, I flattered myself. I was not even a dreamer. The fact was that I was a layabout, an idle fellow, lounging all day and contributing little, not even beauty, to the household. I read the occasional book and changed into a clean shirt every few weeks, but only had one genuine enthusiasm. It was not a very creative pastime. It was base and self-indulgent. What was it?

I sniffed the bottle again and remembered.

Wine. That was it! I drank an extraordinary amount and left the corks lying about the house. Wine was my passion and my justification for existence. I used Cinzia's money to obtain it for I had no earnings of my own.

Wandering the rooms looking for a peaceful corner in which to drink another glass was how I spent my days. There never seemed to be enough solitude or quiet for an appreciation of the colour, bouquet and taste of a fine *Elba* or *Colline Lucchesi*. My wife kept interrupting me with noise. Did she clatter about in the kitchen or work a sewing machine all night? No, it was something more intrusive than either of those options. Something connected with music.

I often moved items of furniture around the house with me. It was clear I required them to feel that the experience of drinking wine was perfect. But there was no escape from the clamour.

My attempts to seek refuge were all futile.

Once I decided to leave her and live alone. I could not afford to buy my own house and there were no empty buildings in the town I might occupy. Whenever I went out into the streets, my neighbours would greet me with insults, the mildest of which was:

"There goes the idiotic parasite Giuseppe!"

Such slanders wounded me deeply, partly because they were true and made me feel ashamed, but mostly because they were shouted out at high volume. I preferred the din of my home.

But what exactly was that din? It came back to me.

A singer, that is what Cinzia was, and she gave lessons to the children of the richest families in Montalcino. Most of these children were profoundly untalented, but the parents paid well or rather they paid enough to keep me in wine.

I know I should have been grateful to my wife but the wailings of butchered light opera made that impossible. Plus I was the worst husband in the town and to retain this distinction I could not have afforded any trace of understanding or empathy.

Tuneless melodies bit into my eardrums.

My frustration was unbearable and I had nobody to share it with, so I took to writing messages on scraps of paper and rolling them up inside the empty bottles. These were grumbles about my situation.

In the early hours of the morning I would creep into the cellar and throw them into the well. I never expected a reply. I knew a world existed down there but had no idea what it might be like or even if it was occupied by sentient beings.

This habit made me feel a little better.

But one evening I became drunk on a strong *Nobile di Montpulciano* and made a mistake. I wrote a message and pushed it into the bottle and dropped it into the well. I had the strange impression that the bottle did not vanish into the depths but remained hovering on the surface, an illusion created by my inebriated state.

Laughing I returned to the tiny chamber I had discovered near the top of the house. Murmurings came to me from afar as I dozed, snorts of disbelief and grunts of disapproval. Then they ceased and a door slammed. This sound was followed by heavy footsteps.

I was shaken roughly awake. Cinzia loomed over me, the toe of her shoe embedded in my chest.

"Found you at last!" she roared.

She said nothing more but kicked me to a standing position and continued to kick me into the most elegant space in the house, one of the dining rooms. I saw that the large round table was set for dinner with knives, forks and spoons. I also perceived that the empty bottle of *Nobile di Montpulciano* was standing in the exact centre of the table. The message inside had been extracted and lay open in full view.

I was aghast. In my drunken daze I had mistaken the dining room for the cellar and the circular table for the well. No wonder the bottle had not plummeted anywhere! I swallowed nervously.

Cinzia now moved beyond hot anger and her voice became very cold and sharp. She narrowed her eyes and said:

"So this is how you feel. It was considerate of you to make your ingratitude a matter of public record."

"What do you mean?" I babbled.

"This evening," she replied, "I invited the Cordàs around for a meal. Signor Cordà is the wealthiest businessman in the town and he is very well connected. There was a good chance he would permit his only daughter to take singing lessons with me and he was prepared to pay handsomely for the privilege. If successful this might have led to more lucrative work with the children of his influential contacts. We were on the verge of coming to an agreement."

I shrugged. "Why does this concern me?"

"I wanted to make a good impression, to win him over. I spent most of the day preparing the meal. When Cordà arrived with his wife and daughter I ushered them into this room. He noticed the bottle at once and assumed the message inside was meant for him, perhaps the contract for the lessons. He took it out and read it aloud."

"That was unfortunate," I admitted.

"I have never been so embarrassed in my life! Needless to say the rest of the evening proved extremely awkward. They departed early after making it obvious I had lost the work. This really is the final straw. You are leaving right now."

"I have nowhere to go," I objected.

"Yes you do," she snapped. For a second time she started kicking me towards a specific destination. I yelled and leaped, but not very energetically, through several other rooms, down two flights of steps and into the real cellar.

"Into the bucket with you!" she cried.

It was cramped inside that wooden receptacle and I made a fuss, not about being exiled to that other world but because I could not bear to be parted from my things and my wine. As I have already stated, she announced that these would follow in due course. She also intended to throw the offending bottle and message down after me.

And that is clearly what she did. But it must have taken her time to get round to doing it. The bottle was the first item she discarded in this manner. I finally recognised the writing of the message as my own. It was not a plea for rescue from a shipwreck but from my domestic situation. The words *alone on a desert island* expressed a hope and ambition rather than a complaint.

Yes, I wanted to be delivered from my life and given help to be stranded on a desert island. In return I was willing to do anything. So now I owed a favour to myself.

As I stared out across the river, I noted my other possessions floating past. I recognised them with relief and splashed into the water to retrieve them before they drifted away. My comfortable chair, an old chest containing books and shirts, a tall ornate clock that told the time in utter silence.

All of them lowered down the well by Cinzia.

Best of all, a dozen cases of my favourite wine. I was ready to begin a new life away from noise and insults.

There was only one thing left to do. With a mighty effort I turned over the lifeboat and pushed it out to sea. Then I loaded my possessions aboard, gripped the oars and set off slowly for the horizon. It was calm out there, deadly quiet. Already I was forgetting I had ever been lazy. Soon I would even forget that I was forgetful.

*16.

"It's clear that relationship was doomed from the start," declared Hywel, "and that Giuseppe and Cinzia weren't suitable for each other. I wonder what sort of man Cinzia would prefer?" And while he was musing on this question, Cinzia jumped out of Giuseppe's story and said, "I don't mind if a man likes food and drink, provided he's also a man of action. I want a man like Gaspar, not a layabout!" And when Hywel asked her who Gaspar was, she answered with this tale:

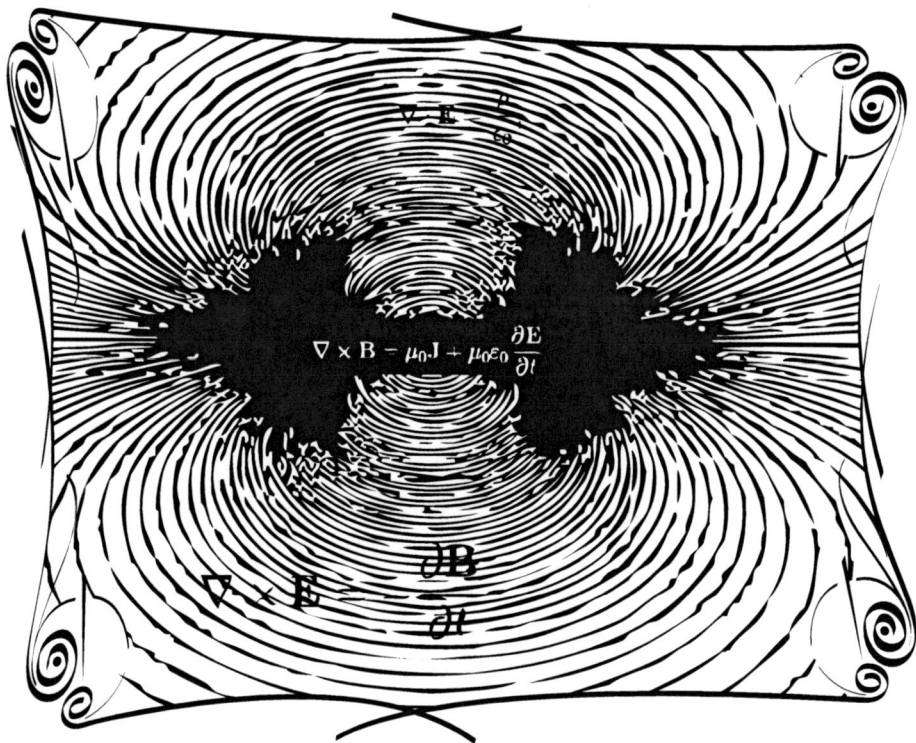

$$\nabla \times B = \mu_0 J + \mu_0 \varepsilon_0 \frac{\partial E}{\partial t}$$

$$\nabla \times E = -\frac{\partial B}{\partial t}$$

GASPAR JANGLE'S SÉANCE

"Spirits tend to know things," said Gaspar Jangle.

His guests turned to peer at him as he entered the circular room. He had kept them waiting forty minutes; and his solemn butler had refused to answer their increasingly impatient questions. But now the host himself had arrived.

"This is all rather irregular," moaned the fattest guest.

Gaspar frowned in his direction, reached the round table and seated himself at the last remaining vacant space. His butler had kept this chair free for him: there was a red switch set into the surface of the table at this point. As Gaspar made himself comfortable, he shrugged off the criticism and waved his hands in a meaningless gesture.

"Sassafras, please serve the first course!"

The butler bowed low and scuttled away. A concerned muttering was exchanged between the guests. Finally one of them cleared his throat and said, "But you invited us here for a séance…"

"Indeed so," replied Gaspar.

"Why then, Mr Jangle, are we seated in front of plates, forks and spoons? Where is the ouija board? Why haven't the lights been dimmed to a more atmospheric level? And why have you ordered your butler to fetch food?"

Gaspar pouted to express his hurt feelings. "Surely you have no objection to enjoying a hearty feast before the main event?"

"I suppose not," conceded the fattest guest.

Gradually the others nodded assent; a few even licked their lips. Sassafras returned with a large tureen balanced on a tray and began ladling soup into the bowls. The soup was a strange silver colour but ordinary-looking vegetables convected within the liquid and it smelled tasty enough. Nobody noticed that the host did not partake of the banquet but sat with his chin cradled in his hands, staring at the red switch.

"It has a somewhat utilitarian tang," declared the fattest guest.

Despite the mild disdain contained in that comment, he ate with sufficient relish. Gaspar regarded him thoughtfully. The other guests dined more slowly, in an awkward silence broken only by the regular knocking of spoons on porcelain rims. When all had finished, Sassafras came to clear away the empty bowls; then he returned with the main course. Some sort of pasta with a gleaming sauce; a sauce so shiny it resembled melted robot thumbs.

After he had finished serving the guests, Sassafras lit a cigarillo and puffed on it as he stood behind Gaspar Jangle. This behaviour was greeted with angry murmurs. "Do you always permit your butler to smoke on duty?"

Gaspar smiled. "He means no disrespect. He's from the Chaco Boreal."

"I don't understand how that—"

"A remote province in Paraguay," stated Gaspar firmly, "where the manners are different to ours. Strictly speaking, he's not even a butler, but a lackey or heavy. All this is quite irrelevant. Please return your attention to the meal before you."

"Before we what?" asked the fattest guest.

"Not before you in time. Before you in space. In front of you." Gaspar sighed and gestured at the room. "Why hasn't anyone commented on the fact that this chamber is a perfect circle? If you *must* make an observation while eating, surely that is a more appropriate topic than the inhalation habits of poor obedient Sassafras? A round chamber surrounding a round room! And not because a square room would require a square table..."

"But would a square table require a square ouija board?" someone asked. Sassafras blew a smoke ring over his employer's head that inevitably, and perhaps ironically, was also round.

"No," said Gaspar Jangle.

The fattest guest was more than halfway through his pasta dish. He spoke up, his mouth full. "I assume you find appealing the idea of concentric circles? The house is also circular. So: house, room, table, board. I'm aware of your obsession with symmetry."

"That's not the reason," answered Gaspar.

"Obsession with symmetry?" cried a man with a bushy moustache. "My understanding has always been that recursion is our host's true concern. I remember opening his definitive textbook on the subject, *Recursion (Re: Recursion)*, to find a secret compartment cut into the pages; and nestled inside that alcove was a smaller copy of the same book; and inside that one was another; and then another; and yet another; and so on. I thought that was clever but unlovely. I made that the theme of an essay. 'The Unlovely Recursion of Gaspar Jangle'. It received high marks."

"Yes, recursion is a favourite theme of mine," admitted the host.

Sassafras stubbed out his cigarillo on the floor, ground it to ash with his heel and moved forward to collect the empty plates. He vanished with them and returned with dessert. Some sort of grey trifle sprinkled with iron filings.

"Must we really tackle a third course?" protested a voice.

"I would prefer that you did so," said Gaspar. He returned his attention to the red switch and sighed again. "Spirits tend to know things. They are more informative than encyclopaedias or granddads. If you wanted to solve the mystery of the *Marie Celeste* you could summon up one of the dead sailors from that ill-fated ship and compel him to tell you the solution. This is why I invited you here tonight. There's a question I want to ask and only spirits will be able to provide the correct answer. A question of vital significance."

The fattest guest had finished his trifle. "Vital to the world?"

"To me and to you," replied Gaspar.

"Good enough, I suppose," said the man with the bushy moustache.

The slowest eater finally finished his trifle. Sassafras collected the dishes and disappeared again but this time he did not return. Gaspar Jangle reached out a hand and gripped the red switch between index finger and thumb. He said, "The reason this chamber is circular is because the wall conceals an electromagnet of immense power. We are sitting inside it."

"So what? We aren't cyborgs but flesh and blood men."

Gaspar smirked. "The food that now surges in your stomachs is highly magnetic. The soup, pasta and trifle were all laced with cobalt, nickel and iron. They also contained gadolinium, dysprosium, yttrium iron garnet and gallium manganese arsenide. Those are the only known magnetic substances. Perhaps there are spirits who are aware of more. Spirits tend to know things, you see. Forgive me for repeating myself."

"What? You have poisoned us!" screeched the fattest guest.

Gaspar waved his free hand airily. "Don't let that bother you. Poisoning is a recourse that only an indolent assassin would choose. I am a man of action!"

And he flicked the red switch…

The concealed electromagnet hummed and every guest was dragged off their chair and slammed backwards into the wall. They hung suspended there at unusual angles, groaning and wailing and cursing Gaspar Jangle, who casually toggled the red switch back and released them.

They collapsed to the floor, recovered themselves and rushed at him.

He toggled the switch again.

This time, some of them slammed into each other, rather than into the wall. The metallic slosh inside them had been magnetised by the electromagnetic field. The fattest guest flew at the man with the bushy moustache; and the hemisphere of his large solid belly collided with the lip that the moustache adorned, like the nose of a torpedo striking a fragile reef, breaking it. Blood poured. Elsewhere, organs ruptured.

Gaspar toggled the switch. And again.

Like puppets in a centrifuge, his guests were flung about the room. Crimson stains on clothes and on the wall. It took twenty-five minutes of operating the switch before the last muscle stopped twitching. Gaspar sucked ruefully at the blister on his thumb. "They are all dead at last. An innovative, original death."

Sassafras entered and placed a covered dish in front of him and removed the cover with a flourish to reveal an ouija board, ornately carved.

"Is everything to your satisfaction, Señor Recursion – I mean Mr Jangle?"

Gaspar nodded. He lightly touched the ouija board. "I killed them all in order to learn the answer to a question. Spirits tend to know things. Even things about recursion."

"You will summon up the spirits of your dead guests?"

"Yes. And this is the question I will ask them…"

"Well?" Sassafras waited patiently. Then Gaspar hissed urgently:

"*Why* did I kill all of you just now?"

*17.

The butler, Sassafras, flicked a silken napkin as he approached and said, "I've worked as a lackey and henchman all over the world. Serving magnetic food to the guests of Mr Jangle was an easy job for me because none of them were on their guard; and speaking of guards, I once worked as a bodyguard for the President of Paraguay. That was the high point of my career. He was an ambitious man with grand plans. I did everything he told me and pointed guns in any direction he pleased. Let me tell you who I pointed a gun at on one memorable occasion!"

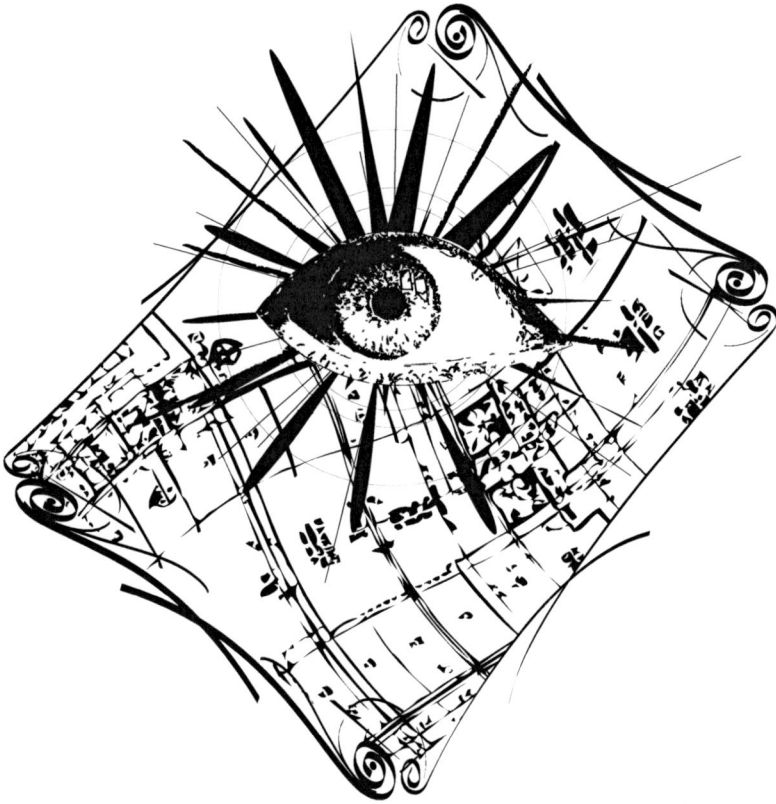

THE URBAN FRECKLE

Oscar Wildebeest threw down his pencil, raised his mug of *yerba mate* to his lips and skimmed the steam off with his stale breath. He had finally finished the designs; the new Capital had been worked out to its very privates. There would be no secrets in this most tortured of cities that he was not already aware of, no hiding places for lovers.

He could imagine them now, reclining on balconies that had not yet been built, chasing each other in the shadows of the colonnades (her garment has unwound around his fingers, skin as white as the capstones of the New Pyramids) and possibly swimming in the fountains during the dog days. He had prepared the citadels one by one. The main square resembled a giant chess board; ministers scurrying from one government department to another would be the pawns.

Oscar fanned himself with one of the outsized sheets of paper and felt the moisture burn the lines around his eyes. It had taken nearly three whole days to sketch the new limits of wonder; the details had taken rather longer. What height exactly for the Ziggurats? And the New Hanging Gardens? How much water to be pumped daily to the orchids that curved like moonbows, flowers as inviting and heady as a scented yoni? He had consulted the *I Ching* on these matters, of course, but the final decision had been his responsibility.

He finished his *yerba mate* and filled his battered pipe. The design had yet to be approved by President Jodorowsky, but he felt confident enough. Indeed his worries were much more abstract things: what would the general public think of a city shaped like a human face? He sighed and sealed the papers in a large envelope lying on his desk and then rang for a messenger to come and collect it. He lit his pipe and watched as the blue smoke was sucked up in the turbulence of the electric fan.

The messenger was a squat civil servant of Indian descent. He picked up the envelope and marched off with it. Oscar yawned, stretched himself, stood up and pushed back his chair. Then he left his office and caught a taxi back to his house. He lived in the suburbs, on the outskirts of Asuncion, in a blue villa. He made himself another mug of *yerba mate* and dozed the afternoon away, awaking to the smell of freshly baked tortilla which Maria, his maid, was cooking for his dinner.

He ate in front of the television, with a bottle of imported Finnish vodka and a Dutch cheese by his elbow. The television crackled and hissed and then the solemn mustachioed face of President Karl Lopez Jodorowsky appeared in front of the national flag.

"Fellow patriots, citizens of Paraguay," he began. "Today is a glorious day for our little nation. At last we are going to build a capital that will rival the greatest cities of the world. Despite the doubts and mockery of other governments, we are now prepared to invest the funds necessary to complete such a venture. We have employed one of the most skilled architects on the continent to design the city and he has today announced the completion of his plans. I have them here in my hands. Construction will begin immediately!"

Oscar poured himself a glass of spirits and settled back to watch the rest of the broadcast. The President seemed excited; he garbled his words and made extravagant gestures. Oscar smiled at his naiveté; as if he could really believe that idealism could change anything. Oscar was beyond such ingenuousness; he was a cynic.

314

"Our new city – Paraguayia – will be the envy of not only the cities of our neighbours but also the cities of the old world," the President was saying. "Buenos Aires, Montevideo and Brasilia, Sao Paulo and Rio, Santiago and Lima, Bogota, Caracas and La Paz will knock their knees at our arrival; but so will the cultural hubs that straddle continents other than ours! London, Paris, New York and Tokyo will tremble before us; Rome, Shanghai and Moscow will seem like truly drab affairs after the completion of our metropolis. Rejoice citizens! For it is I, your President, who give you cause to be proud!"

Oscar sighed and snapped the television off. He still was unsure how the people would take to living in a city shaped like a face. Besides, the voice of President Jodorowsky was too hysterical to be kind on the eardrums. He decided that he needed a holiday. He stood up, moved to the globe that stood in the corner of his room, span it and stopped it with an outstretched finger. This would be his destination.

He spent a long year on Maui; long because the days were long and fine and bright and there was much coconut milk to drink and beaches to walk and warm seas to swim, and because the money he had earned designing the new capital of Paraguay meant that a long year was no harder on his purse than a short one.

One morning (this is how it must have been) he received a letter; from President Jodorowsky. The capital had been built and his presence was required at the ceremony that would bless the fresh megalopolis. There would be speeches and the usual rousing music, pumped on sousaphones and tinkled on glockenspiels with the flags waving in the breeze; an artificial breeze if need be. And there would be a formal blessing from the Archbishop of Concepción, an immaculate worthy from a pristine town, huge mitre bobbing and tipping in the evening cool.

"Finished?" Oscar said to himself. "So soon?"

But he caught a plane to Asuncion (they stopped for an intolerable hour at Quito, where fat flies suck the humidity from your brow) and when the President greeted him, his face fell. Instead of a handshake, he was prodded in the ribs with the barrel of an automatic rifle and chauffeured away from the airport in a less than comfortable manner. He tried to protest, but his hands were knocked away by the dark-suited bodyguards. The President, who rode in the front of the car, turned his head and regarded Oscar through dark sunglasses. There was a bitter smile at the corners of his mouth.

Oscar Wildebeest, for all his cynicism, was frightened and he tried to make small talk, the way that a mouse makes small squeaks in the jaws of a cat; trying to forge an empathy that can never be forged, trying to lose a wind in a bottle that has no deposit, trying to catch the sun in a butterfly net. "Nice day," he said. "Where are we going?"

"Paraguayia," the President hissed. "Oh yes, the city of the golden noon! Your city as well as ours. It has been built, following your plans, and it is dying. The city is dying. You have made a fool of me and you have made a fool of our people."

"I don't understand," Oscar replied. But no one seemed ready to enlighten him. They drove on past scorched fields and tawny scrub. They drove through the outskirts of Asuncion and then higher into the hills along pockmarked roads and through dusty vineyards.

It was a long journey, a bumpy cramped day and Oscar's fear turned first to thirst, and then to utter boredom. Finally, they crested the brow of a small rise and coasted down towards a large plain. Before them, mighty skyscrapers peeled and crumbled.

"That is Paraguayia," the President remarked. "And it is sick. Look at it. Already it has fallen beyond repair. And do you know why? Have you any idea what has made it so ill?" He pointed a finger at the rows of damaged buildings. Strange unnatural swellings made the road a hazardous prospect to venture down. Huge black stains covered the ground and the walls of buildings. Oscar blinked and shook his head.

"You designed it in the shape of a human face," the President continued, "and at first I thought that it was a good design. In the first few months, the city smiled. The people who lived in it were happy. They smiled along with the face. But the city had no cover from the sun beating down on it day after day. One morning, a local worker noticed a freckle in the centre of the main square. Every day this freckle grew larger. Soon it began to bleed. Do you now understand what I am trying to say?"

Oscar breathed heavily. His throat was suddenly full of not only his wildly beating heart, but also of his bilious liver. "Skin cancer? You're telling me that my city caught skin cancer?"

The President nodded. "Exactly." He wiped tears from his dark brown eyes. "And we left it too late before taking action! What fools we were! Yes, the city is dying. And there is nothing we can do about it. Except one thing. We can construct a monument to your folly."

"What sort of monument?" Oscar began to perspire. He had an inkling of what was going to happen; a terrible inkling. He started to tremble; a mighty tremble that began at his toes and spread its shaking fingers upwards to caress all of his body...

The President smiled again. He said:

"There are two pools in a ruined city; a city which was once the mightiest metropolis in the Southern Hemisphere. These pools once formed the eyes of the city, for the city was built in the shape of the human face. Seated in both these pools lies the reflection of a man. His name is Oscar Wildebeest. Here we see him at work, throwing down his pencil, raising his mug of *yerba mate* to his lips and skimming the steam off with his stale breath. But this is not the real Oscar; the real Oscar has been dead for a thousand years, killed by a single bullet wound.

"When the citizens of Paraguay feel the need to teach themselves the meaning of folly, they take themselves out to these pools and gaze at the image of this man. This image will never fade, as long as suns whirl and stars form webs of galaxies. Some people ask this question: how did this image get there in the first place? Others know the answer. They say: the last thing seen by a dying man is forever imprinted upon his retinas. The city is one dying man; you are the other."

Oscar looked up. His mouth made a single letter; a vowel and the first letter of his name. It was both an answer and a resignation. A resignation that had already been accepted.

Coughing fumes, they reached the chin of the city.

*18.

Hywel wrinkled up his nose and spat disgustedly on the floor of the universe. "Wit is best when it's dry. 'Parched' and 'cracked' are more accurate terms for the wit in that tale. I'd like to hear Oscar Wildebeest deliver a story of his own, perhaps something else about architecture, about another ideal city, something without the fatal flaw of that last one! Is he present in the pub at this time? But of course he is. There's no longer any place that can exist outside my tavern, so speak up, Mr Wildebeest, and don't disappoint!"

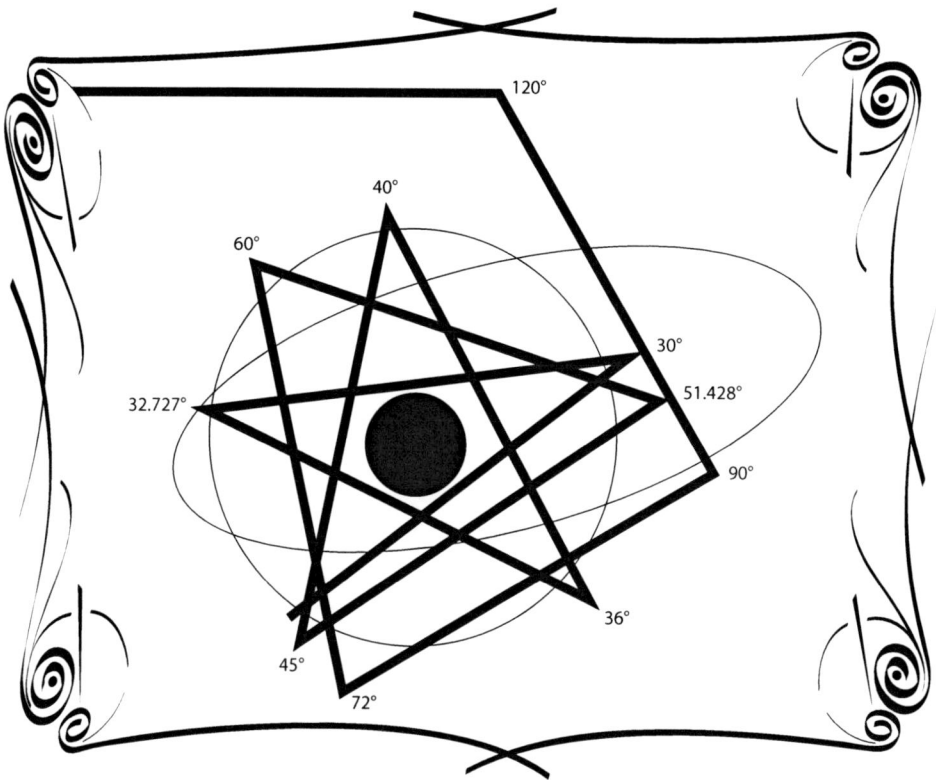

CORNEROPOLIS

I was standing on the corner of two cobbled streets looking for my wife. First I looked down one street and then up the other. But she did not come into view. So I stopped one of the hurrying pedestrians and said, "Excuse me, but would you mind waiting here in my place?"

"Why should I?" he answered gruffly.

"Quite simple. By standing on this corner I am able to survey two streets at once. But I would like to take a look at a third, which is why I propose walking to the end of this street and standing on that other corner."

"What are we looking for?"

"My wife. You will recognise her when you see her. She is too beautiful for me. Remember that and call out the moment she appears."

And so I left him on the corner, looking down one street and up the other, while I walked to the end of the first and stood on the corner.

Now I was able to look up that street, instead of down it, but also down a new street, previously unknown. I alternated my gaze between the two streets, as did my helper on his corner, but at a different rate, so that our eyes meshed only on every seventeenth oscillation.

My wife still did not come. Had she gone shopping or for a meal? Perhaps she was having her hair trimmed or her nails filed? Maybe she had run off with another man, through the park, under the trees, hand in hand, into the bushes, out of their clothes. I was close to despair.

I stopped another pedestrian. "Please help me find my wife!"

"How may I do that?" he sneered.

"Stand here and watch out for her. She is too beautiful for me. I must walk to the end of this street and take up a position on the next corner. That will increase our chances of actually sighting her."

"But this is a junction and there are three streets leading off from it."

I had not noticed the fact. There was no way I could walk to the end of two streets simultaneously, so I rocked gently on my heels, clutching my head, unsure. Finally a voice tripped through the curtain of my lank hair into my ear. It was the first pedestrian, asking, not politely, if I was unwell.

"You have abandoned your position!" cried I.

"Not as such. I perceived that you were in distress and came over to see what the matter was. But I stopped a different pedestrian and persuaded him to take my place. There he is, watching from the original corner."

This was true. He waved at me and I waved back. There were now three people willing to help me find my wife. This was good, neat, convenient. The chances of glimpsing her lithe form, her charm woven into flesh, were increasing. And my lungs were voluminous enough to thank more than one collaborator in my quest. There was no need to refuse any offers, however reluctantly implemented.

"You made the correct decision," I agreed. "Perhaps if you wait here, while this other fellow walks down this street to the next corner, and I walk up this one, we shall spy her very soon."

"It is not beyond the bounds of feasibility."

The first pedestrian took up his position while the second and myself reached our respective corners. The system of oscillating glances was now more complex. The success of the unseen pedestrian, on the original corner, was relayed to me by my first assistant, the one concerned for my health, from his new vantage. No, not success, for she did not appear, nor her excessive beauty.

I watched in vain. At last I stopped another pedestrian.

"Have you seen her? Have you?"

"I have not, whoever she might be. Do you wish me to stand here and take your place while you proceed to the end of the street and stand at a different corner? I shall do so, but not eagerly. Besides, this is not a simple corner, nor even a junction, but a crossroads. There are four streets meeting here."

"You are right! I deem this fact a major setback."

"Not so. Here are two fellows coming to see what the matter is. Together we make four. Maybe they will help you occupy all the new corners."

The first and second pedestrians reached my side and demonstrated concern at my agitation, which they had noted. But I was happier now, particularly when they both announced how they had managed to find replacements for their earlier positions, selected at random from other pedestrians, and were free to walk to the ends of two of the streets leading from the crossroads, while I took the third. My remaining assistant would stand here and keep in contact not only with us but also with the three replacements, the first of which still occupied the original corner.

The web of glances was now truly tangled, elegant, deadly. Soon my wife would be spotted for sure. But she is obviously more clever and slippery than I had ever anticipated. Her beauty did not manifest itself.

My new corner was colder than the others. A breeze dried my gums. How might I kiss her ankles with such oral aridity? Then I perceived that there was less cover from the elements in this location. No fewer than five streets met at this point. The spines, or bones, of a pentagon. Pedestrians rushed down them all, but not my wife. She who is too beautiful to describe did not flow.

I stopped another pedestrian to take my place. My three earlier assistants came up to help me. Together we were five in number, enough to occupy the new corners that would reveal themselves. We diverged again.

"Remember to shout out when you see her!"

The next corner I reached was a focus for six streets. Another willing pedestrian, further adjustment of assistants. I was collecting disciples, eyes, all infected with my despair, my romanticism. The corner after that fused seven streets. Then eight, nine, ten. The temperature was falling, the wind was rising. Where was she? Sheltering in a doorway? More corners, more converging streets. Eleven, a dozen.

By late afternoon, I had lost count. I stood in a circus, a hub, with streets radiating like the spokes of a unicycle wheel. Too many. Down none of them stalked my wife. I turned up the collar of my coat. At the far end of one street I noticed a man standing on a corner. He was steady, watching. I walked up to him. Before I could open my mouth, he cried:

"I am looking! I am looking!"

Then I understood that the circuit had been closed. This was my original corner, occupied by my last replacement. I turned and saw that all the buildings had vanished. The city was naked. The city walls still stood, bounding an immense square, but the space they contained was empty of artificial structures. People were milling without the guidance of streets. Rather, so many streets met at this point that everything was an absence. My view of the totality was unimpeded. No more corners to hide behind. Still my wife was not apparent.

It was an illusion, of course. The combined effect of watchers on every corner, relaying their observations with a glance, the whole in harmony, had made me our first omniscient citizen. I saw the utter limits of my disappointment. No nook, no cranny, remained. And if there was still no beauty to be found, it simply did not exist. I lacked uncertainty, hope.

I tapped him on the shoulder. "Go home!"

He shrugged and went. The circuit was broken. A few, a very few, buildings shimmered back into reality. The horizons were eroded.

"Tell the others to go home as well. Spread the word!"

I closed my eyes and waited. When I opened them, it was evening and I was back on my original corner. It was warm. I pressed through the crowds to my apartment at the top of a narrow, tall house. This city is convoluted, riddled. And I dwell high, but not high enough to behold more than a few strands of the tangle. I climbed the steps, opened my door. The candles had burned to stubs.

Throwing off my coat, I sat on the edge of the bed. Already I was forgetting about my wife. The loss of beauty that is beyond imagination cannot be regretted too much. Next year I shall try again. Perhaps when

I am married, when I am no longer a bachelor, it will be an easier task to lose and find her.

*19.

Hywel was dismayed. "I don't know if I'd call that an ideal city, maybe I don't share Mr Wildebeest's views on utopia. Why don't we ask his non-existent wife what she thinks?" And he called for the woman in question, who appeared and blithely answered, "Corneropolis is a fairly comfortable city and it's not right for its inhabitants to complain too much about it, but if I had to live somewhere else I would choose the city of Plush. Let me tell a fable about it!"

THE SIX SENTINELS

Licking the moon is a nasty habit and leaves the tongue coated with dust. This dust tastes neither of butter nor cheese but of phases — crescents and other shapes. It remains a mystery why anyone should want to lick a moon. Lunacy is the only answer.

There is a city, a gorgeous wide city, set among the Idle Mountains, not too high among them, not too low, and the name of this moderately elevated but marvellously upholstered city is Plush. It was named thus by Plish in the days of his comfort. All builded tall of warm velvet bricks is Plush and draped with satin cloth; and its streets are thick with petals and its citizens are fuddled nicely with scent whenever they walk and greet each other with noses high in the air like snobs. Plish liked his people posh. Even the sharpest spires on the most slender minarets are not likely to impale anyone in Plush, for cotton is the substance from which they are made; and the mighty ramparts that girdle the city are constructed of no harder materials than soap and cheese. A soft, easy, slippery environment for slippery, easy, soft people.

As for the interiors of the buildings, they are all designed in the style of Lord Dunsany and so are lush and magical and descriptively overlong. Every house has a garden on its roof, for there is no finer place for flowers and butterflies to gather; and in these gardens leisurely stroll the calm citizens in the early evenings when the sun is setting majestically over the snowy peaks far away, and they nod to each other, rooftop to rooftop, and exchange idle gossip with idle smiles. All the same, it is never easy to walk gracefully on roofs made of stretched fabric. Fun to bounce on them though.

Many cities have been washed by many rains over the course of many millennia but none as thoroughly as Plush, for the ramparts as stated are partly soap, and the bubbles run down the streets and the citizens play and glisten, and everything smells cleans and ready for a night out; and when the night does come it seems the city is all dressed up with nowhere to go, but it has no need of going anywhere, for it belongs where it is, and indeed it has always seemed one with the Idle Mountains. It is splendidigenous, a word I just invented, meaning that it would not be so magnificent in any other location. Of other cares there are few in Plush, for it is a city of relaxation, a city of easy chairs and deep sofas, and even the sternest truths are couched in the softest terms, with a pair of metaphorical slippers under that couch.

But in fact there is a single hard thing in the heart of the city, and this thing is a thing the people care not to discuss too much, for it reminds them of the difficult times that once were and the difficult times yet to come, not that one can really be reminded of times yet to come, but you know what I mean. The thing that is rarely discussed is a broad pedestal in the central square that holds aloft six statues of six heroes known as the Six Sentinels, traditional guardians of Plush. Centuries of weather have eaten away the frowns on the marble faces and now the heroes seem serene, but this is an illusion, for in life they were servants of their own agitation. Not just servants but slaves, for they were never paid in coin for their gloom and trouble, and the coins of Plush are pieces of felt and not much use anyway.

The names of these heroes are Jitterwhack, Rumpus, Toothan, Klaw, Uckybald and Heckusboing. Half a millennium ago they set forth from Plush to secure its borders in every direction. That was the will of the

326

people at that time. Or rather it was the will of Plish as he sat brooding on his throne of carven gum, shifting stickily from one buttock to another, pulling his fleecy beard and sighing softly; but Plish and his subjects were always of one mind only. Or else. It was he who selected the six most capable citizens in Plush and named them Sentinels, and so he rose with difficulty from his melting seat of authority and strode to the balcony of the palace that dominated one side of the central square, and glancing down at the crowd below, he spoke these words:

"Beloved inhabitants of Plush, take heed of my warning! So pleasant is our home, with cushions and pillows on every street corner, that greedy eyes observe us from beyond our ramparts. We are surrounded by enemies. It is only a matter of time before we are invaded and despoiled by the outer louts. Let us not rest on our laurels but resist on them instead! And what better way of resisting than to take the fight to the enemy? To this purpose I have recruited six noble champions and now I send them forth in the six directions that exist, to sweep clean those directions as far as feasible, or as far as the horizon, whichever is further. The chosen six must not return but will reside in the realms they have vanquished and there keep watchful eye on developments to guarantee the security of our supremely comfy city."

Then did Plish command the six heroes to forsake the rubber cobbles and mossy slabs of Plush in favour of the more varied terrain of the exterior world. Jitterwhack it was who rode north, and there found he a land of hard ice inhabited by seals. These he slew without mercy as instructed, to safeguard Plush from a northern invasion, and dwelled he the rest of his days alone and a-chatter on the frozen water; and so he passed from mortal to legend and became a statue on a pedestal, as already described, one of the Sentinels of Plush, and all there are agreed that Jitterwhack did his work well, for to this day there has never been an invasion from the north.

As for Rumpus, he went east and after weeks of hard riding he came to a desert sprinkled with oases where lived a gentle people on dates and milk, and Rumpus decided not to slaughter them provided they promise not to invent anger or swords, and having obtained this promise he settled among them, but remained watchful as bidden, his eyes constantly fixed on the bellies of dusky gyrating desert girls. More fortunate was he than Toothan, who rode west into an endless expanse of dreary marshes and conquered a squat people who squatted in squat huts on reedy stilts and ate frogs, the only available food. Toothan croaked not long after, but is no less revered than Rumpus. Both succeeded in protecting Plush correctly and ending the threat from east and west.

Nor has any invasion come from the direction south, and for this the citizens of Plush should thank Klaw, who explored a great forest and the fertile fields beyond it, who found a rural society based there, who smashed its farm equipment, dug up its turnips and made love to its scarecrows until he died from an infected splinter, and who so intimidated the simple folk that they never dared have any ambitions of any sort ever again. As for Uckybald, his ordained direction was down and with a spade he dug a pit and kept digging, in the cellar of his house in Plush, and far beneath the earth his bones still must be, protecting the downward borders of his city, if bones he truly had, for he was a floppy fellow in life and famous for contortionism.

Now we come to Heckusboing. I would prefer not to come to him, for it will win me few friends in Plush, but come to him I shall, or else this tale will be judged propaganda rather than a true history. Heckusboing was allotted the direction known as up. For a long time he wondered how to proceed in that direction. He climbed the tallest minaret in Plush but the people below urged him to go higher and berated him when he came back down. They started to accuse him openly of lacking seriousness, of shirking his duty, of disobeying Plish. Stung by these insults, he made himself a ladder, the tallest ladder since the world began, but he had nothing to rest it against and it availed him not at all. The people grew increasingly impatient with him.

"Heckusboing does not love his city," they said, "and is not deserving of the title Sentinel. Instead of voyaging into the sky, he prefers to lounge about on the ground. This is treason and Plish must hear of it."

As he listened to these words, Heckusboing felt a mixture of fear and shame, and he locked himself in his house and refused to come out. Plish was summoned from his palace by the clamour of his subjects and he found a furious mob gathered outside the residence of the unworthy hero. This mob kicked at the walls of the house until the velvet bricks vibrated unnervingly and the entire structure was in danger of collapsing. Plish stood behind the crowd calling for Heckusboing to surrender and face justice; but suddenly a figure was seen on the roof, and it was the rogue Sentinel himself, too scared to emerge but too scared to remain inside. At the sight of the traitor the mob went wild and broke down the front door and rushed inside to seize him.

Heckusboing was trapped. He had nowhere to go but up. By this time the sun was set and a night wind had blown a large black cloud over the city. As the first members of the avenging mob mounted the stairs to the roof, Heckusboing threw back his head, uttered a demented laugh and jumped as high as he could. For an instant it seemed he had accepted the responsibilities of his position at last, and Plish nodded contentedly, but this was only a vain illusion, for he succeeded in reaching an altitude of no more than three or four feet before coming back down. However, the taut fabric of the roof acted like a trampoline. Back up he went, accompanied by a few potted plants, and down again; and on each subsequent bounce he rose higher and higher.

At the top of his tenth bounce the night wind blew him a little to the side, and he came down not on his own roof but on that of a neighbour. Thus began a circuit of the city, from roof to roof, higher and higher and higher, while Plish and the people gave up any notion of following him on foot. They simply watched in awe. Heckusboing completed his unorthodox tour by bouncing onto the roof of the palace itself. That huge building quivered and shot him straight up into the black cloud. He did not come down again. Plish gestured for his subjects to be silent and listened carefully. For many minutes there was not a sound.

Then faintly but madly came a laugh, the laughter of Heckusboing, and a tiny shape was observed running back and forth along the top of the cloud. How had he managed to keep his footing on a cloud? Plish did not need to pull his fleecy beard for long before he knew the answer; and his subjects were no less quick to make a guess. A lifetime of walking on the softest available surfaces had adapted the feet of the inhabitants of Plush. So Heckusboing had unwittingly acclimatised himself to cloud walking. For clouds are only a little softer than petals, webs, cotton buds and all the other gentle materials found everywhere in Plush. For several hours Heckusboing rejoiced in his salvation and might have danced on the cloud all night long, disturbing his former comrades below; but something unexpected occurred.

The moon broke through the cloud at just the point where he stood. Heckusboing lost his balance and fell onto the moon. The cloud closed up again and now his laughter was even fainter and much more distant. The people went to bed in dismay. Nobody had ever anticipated an invasion from the moon. As far as they were concerned, Heckusboing was a cheat and a slacker, and few believed he deserved a statue in the central square; but the pedestal looked lopsided with only five, and so Plish relented and reluctantly allowed Heckusboing to be added. It was a relief for Plish and his people when the moon was new, for the mad faint laughter came not at such times. When full, Heckusboing often howled at the dogs of the world. He did not die of old age on the moon because the rules are different there.

The more pessimistic citizens of Plush declare that he is still alive, saving himself from starvation by doing something disagreeable with his tongue. It is a very nasty habit and I hope other men will travel to the moon one day and lock him up.

*20.

The moon rose over the horizon and said, "Plush may be the most comfortable city for human beings, but I assure you it's not my favourite city on your planet. As I circle the Earth I always grow excited when I know I'm about to rise over Moonville. That's my favourite place of all! I am especially happy when I rise over it on a Monday, the day named after me. Black holes don't have days named after them, nor do galaxies or quasars! Not that I wish to brag!"

THE MIRROR IN THE LOOKING GLASS

Mad inventors are plentiful in this world of ours but only one sits on a genuine throne and rules his own city like an ancient king. Frabjal Troose of Moonville has many dubious talents, including the ability to flap his ears. They squeak. But his cybernetics expertise is considerable and his contributions to the design and manufacture of artificial nervous systems are almost unparalleled. Only his perversity prevents him from becoming the saviour of the human race.

Perhaps I am overstating the case, but his monumental achievements are singularly unhelpful to his own subjects and the citizens of every other realm. What amuses Frabjal Troose is to install human intelligence in inanimate objects. With the aid of extremely small but excessively clever devices, part electronic and part mechanical, he can bestow the gift of consciousness with all its attendant emotions on chairs, crockery, table lamps, shoes, clocks, flutes.

He can and he does. Frequently.

His other hobby is to worship the moon…

One morning Frabjal Troose awoke with the urge to give thoughts and feelings to a mirror. He foresaw all manner of comic and tragic potential in the reality of a self-aware looking glass. To make the joke even more piquant he decided to equip his victim with prosthetic legs and allow it to roam freely around the city. He left his enormous bed and went to the bathroom and there he saw an appropriate mirror hanging on the wall above the moon shaped sink.

The operation took several days. Frabjal Troose is a perfectionist and he wanted the circuits and cogs to be tastefully integrated into the frame of the mirror. In the end the workings ran over the surface of the wooden frame like complex ornamentation. By this time, the mirror could already think for itself and was slowly coming to terms with its sudden awareness and the need to develop an identity. It was no longer a mere object but a precious sentient being.

It even had a name. Guildo Glimmer.

Guildo learned to walk within his first hour. Wandering the palace of Frabjal Troose, little more than a large house stuffed with components for new gadgets, he came into contact with the occasional servant. At each encounter the same thing happened: the servant bent down and made a face at Guildo. Sometimes the servant picked him up and held him at arm's length while plucking a nose hair or squeezing a pimple. What did this mean? Guildo was bewildered.

He continued his explorations and discovered that the front door of the palace was open and unguarded. Through it he hurried, into the lunar themed spaces of the city. Moon buggies rolled past on the roads and the public squares were craters filled with people dressed in silver and yellow clothes. I know that Frabjal Troose once issued an edict forbidding any grins that were not perfect crescents. He also forbade any cakes that were not perfect croissants.

Guildo proceeded down the street. He desperately needed time for reflection, but citizens just would not leave him in peace and they treated him in precisely the same way as the palace servants had, making blatant faces at him, grimacing and yawning and even frowning in disgust. Guildo began to experience the state of mind known as 'paranoia'. What was wrong with his appearance? What was it about him that provoked such reactions in strangers?

He must be ugly, a horrible freak, a grotesque mutant: there was no other explanation. He was overwhelmed with a desire to view his own face, to confront his visage, to learn the foul truth for himself. But he could think of no way to accomplish this. Are you stupid, Guildo Glimmer? he asked himself. There must be a method of seeing one's own face, but what? Because he was so new to the conventions of society, he always spoke his thoughts aloud.

"I know a reliable way," declared a passerby.

This passerby was a droll fellow, a practical joker. He told Guildo that when men and women wanted to look at their own faces they made use of a 'reflection'. What was one of those? Well, reflections existed in a variety of natural settings, in quiet lakes and slow rivers and the lids of clean saucepans, but only in the depths of mirrors did they realise their full potential. That is where the highest quality reflections dwelled, untroubled by ripples or cooking stains.

"You must look into a mirror!" he announced.

Guildo was astonished but grateful and he decided to follow this advice. The passerby chuckled and passed on. He was later arrested for not chuckling in the shape of a crescent, but that is another story. No, it is this story! No matter, I will ignore it in favour of what happened to poor Guildo. His little metallic legs carried him to the market, a bustling place where anything one desired might be bought, provided one's desires were modest or at least plausible.

Guildo's were. He approached a stall selling mirrors.

The man who owned the stall was talking to another customer and so Guildo was free to hop onto a table and examine the mirrors on display. He chose a circular mirror that was nearly the same circumference as his own head and he stepped in front of it. What he saw was totally unexpected and utterly profound. He saw an immensely long tunnel, a tunnel that stretched perhaps as far as the moon or infinity.

It must be pointed out once again that Guildo Glimmer was a living mirror. A mirror is simply unable to view its own reflection. The moment a mirror gazes into another mirror, its image will be endlessly bounced back and forth between the two reflecting surfaces. Hence the illusion of a tunnel. This is a law of geometry and a rule of physics, but Guildo knew nothing of such disciplines. His education had not covered the sciences.

As far as he was concerned, the illusory tunnel was an accurate representation of his form. This meant that he really was a tunnel! Now he understood why people kept frowning at him and why he was so dissatisfied. It was because he was not fulfilling his correct role. He was a tunnel and ought to do what tunnels do, act like tunnels act, think what tunnels think. He rushed out of the market to embrace his true destiny.

Later that afternoon, the splinters of a smashed mirror were picked up from the tracks of the main railway line leading into Moonville. When pieced together they could be identified as the remains of Guildo Glimmer. There was no way of resurrecting him. Frabjal Troose came to pay his hypocritical respects but he quickly lost interest and returned to his palace in a land-boat powered by moonbeams. By this time the sun had gone down and the moon was up.

People said that Guildo committed suicide, that he was too full of despair to continue his existence. Why else would he stand in the path of a moving train? But as I watched the billowing sails of the receding land-boat, I realised that I knew better. Guildo was simply serving a mistaken function. Tunnels are there for trains to pass through, after all. I was the driver of that train: in fact I am the train itself, an earlier example of the unnatural quest to give intelligence to inanimate objects.

*21.

A man who was jumping up and down, as if his legs were springs or his heart a faulty anti-gravity engine, cried in annoyance, "There is no such place as Moonville. I know for sure because I constructed it and I say so! I am Frabjal Troose! The moon is a liar, and that should be acceptable because we're all liars here, but lovers stroll by moonlight, and some other people gather nuts, and it's not fair to stroll or gather by the light of a liar! Have you ever tried to do anything by such a light? It is good only for playing amplified trombones!"

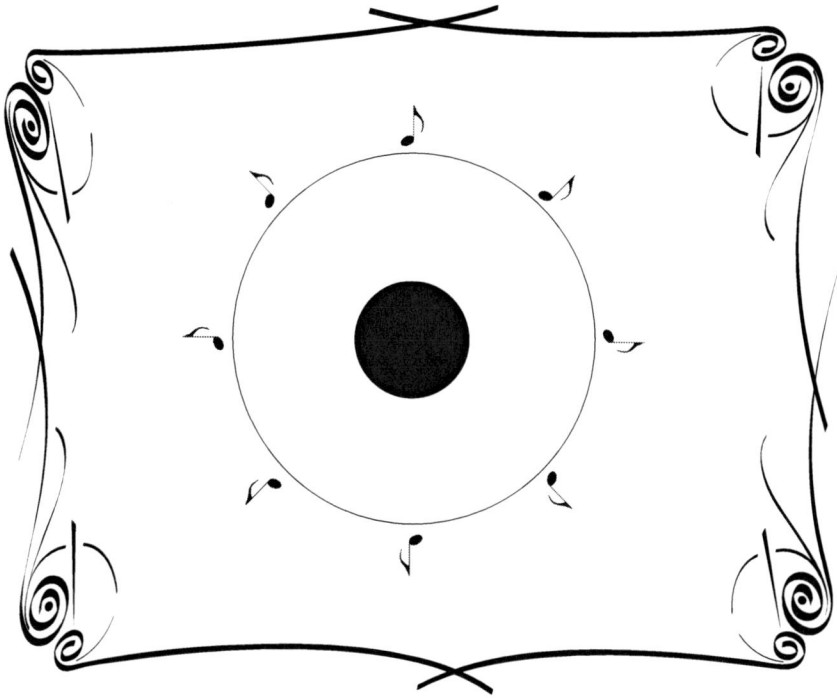

TROMBONHOMIE

When my neighbour plays the amplified trombone it means another sleepless night. But I don't sleep anyway, so perhaps it doesn't matter. I don't sleep because my neighbour plays the amplified trombone.

I also play the amplified trombone. I play the amplified trombone to annoy my neighbour for keeping me awake. I slide the notes like fish through my windows, beyond the trees, higher than the rising moon. I play blue notes and purple passages and make the house shudder.

I once considered killing my neighbour. But I knew what this would entail. I would have to pack a bag with provisions and sling it over my shoulder. My other shoulder would be in a sling. My sling would be at my belt, my stones in a pocket. Journeys last longer than pockets; stones longer than journeys. So I would leave with a pebble smooth chin and before I was close it would be as prickly as a pear. My neighbour lives far away. That is why I play an amplified trombone to annoy him. If I played an ordinary trombone he would not be annoyed. He would probably fall asleep and then I would have no reason to play any sort of trombone. And I am getting good now. I need the practice.

At any rate, if I ever reached his house I would look very foolish. I would have to knock on his door and say, "excuse me, but your amplified trombone is keeping me awake," and he would look me up and down with his sombre eyes (but no, really, what would his eyes look like? The eyes of an amplified trombone player are always sad, must be) and his reply would be, "I'm awfully sorry, but I play the amplified trombone because my neighbour does," and I would say, "I am that neighbour," and he would shake his head and answer, "by your appearance you come from the lands of the west and my neighbour lives in the east," and I would say, "you mean your other neighbour?" and he would nod and I would bow a retreat and be unable to knock on his door a second time.

And then he would return to his amplified trombone playing with renewed vigour. And I would have to feel a sort of sympathy for him. And reaching into my pocket to cast away my stones, I would find that they had already escaped through a hole.

So I would have to look beyond the immediate problem. I would have to consider killing his other neighbour, the one that lives in the east. There would be no other option. What other option would there be? So I would pack a bag with provisions and sling it over my shoulder, etc. I would whistle a callow tune and fill my pocket with fresh stones. Not the pocket with a hole in it, but my other pocket.

And I would travel for many weeks, down dark and winding forest paths where monstrous orchids dipped their anaemic heads at my passing. And finally I would reach the house of my neighbour's other neighbour and I would knock loudly on the door and make a fool of myself again. I would say, "excuse me, but your amplified trombone is keeping my neighbour awake," and the figure who would appear would scratch a warty nose and reply, "but it was my neighbour who started it," and I would raise my hands in an exasperated gesture and say, "well he never mentioned that to me," and he would gaze at me doubtfully and remark, "you look to me as if you have just travelled through the forests of the west and my neighbour lives in the east," and then I would understand that he too was referring to his other neighbour.

So I would have to bid him farewell, refusing his kind offer of a cup of blue-green tea, and go on my way in a kind of lighthearted despair. And this would go on and on (imagine, if you will, sixteen thousand similar encounters, variations without the theme) until I was sick and beyond redemption. And strange and subtle things would start to happen, so subtle that they would be almost unnoticeable. Language would begin to change, until I found myself in a completely alien country. But as I pressed further eastwards, it would come back into focus. And one day, I would eventually find a man whose neighbour did not play the amplified trombone and I would ask, "why is this the case?" and the man would explain, "he used to play, but he has not sounded a note for over a year now," and racing onwards to greet this man who had given up playing the amplified trombone, I would discover that it was myself.

No, I don't want to take that course of action. I would rather stay at home and have to contend with my neighbour blowing those infernal lines on his amplified trombone. I would rather slide my notes like fish, pace my darkened room, anger my heart with coffee and cheap cigarettes. The rising moon rests like a steady flame on the wick of my bedside candle. I bury my head under the pillow; a premature burial because I am still breathing, crying out for release. If I could connect an amplifier to the moon as it changed gear over the horizon, I would have a celestial revenge indeed. But I do not possess the necessary skills.

One evening, while we are both playing for all we are worth, a curious thing happens. Our widely diverging melodies form a compelling harmony. The time lag has been taken into account, his preference for atonality also. But suddenly we are playing together, an unearthly counterpoint, a music whose sum is far greater than its parts. For the first time, we have made a sort of contact with each other; it is as if we are sitting in the same room, at the same inglenook, warming our boots before the fire, tapping the stems of our churchwarden pipes against our teeth; the hearth of our hearts. For the first time, I bless the technology that can amplify trombones.

Our duet continues throughout the night. The wind rises up from the distant sea and the clouds scud across the milky sky, entangling themselves in the branches of the highest trees. The grass picks up our refrain, each slippery blade an Aeolian harp. I no longer hate my neighbour; I almost love him instead and resolve to make the arduous journey to his home as a gesture of friendship. But there is little need. Why make a gesture of friendship to the man or woman you are already embracing?

When the moon sinks down over the opposite horizon, and the sun spreads its orange nets once more, we end with a remote and beautiful chord. I sink exhausted back onto my bed and sleep the sleep of the satiated. I know that I will never be able to play another note on the amplified trombone. I will have to dismantle my instrument and create something new from the brassy tubes. All this applies in equal measure to my neighbour. So what will we make from our throaty monsters? How will we pick over the trombones of civilisation?

When my neighbour plays the amplified triangle it means another sleepless night. But I don't sleep anyway, so perhaps it doesn't matter. I don't sleep because my neighbour plays the amplified triangle.

*22.

Hywel was pleased with that story but before he could congratulate Mr Frabjal Troose, he was tapped on the shoulder by someone who wanted his attention. No, not someone. A tree. A tree wanted his attention! Hywel was surprised but the tree shrugged its branches and said, "Why can't a tree, or any form of vegetation for that manner, be allowed to join in the fun? I bet the tree that married Rakesh could tell an astonishing tale or two! The whole universe is just one pub now, so that means the forests are also your customers. I am one of the trees bordering one of the dark and winding forest paths mentioned in the previous story. Permit me to relate the history of my biggest ever cousin."

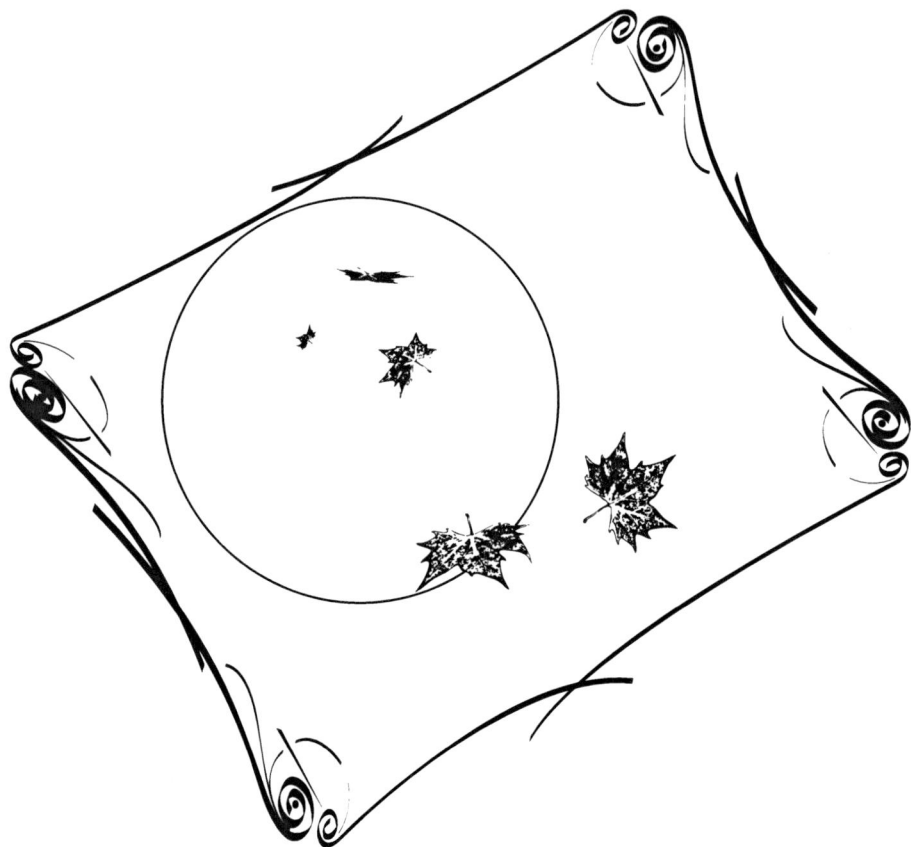

CLIMBING THE TALLEST TREE IN THE WORLD

It started as a prank and ended as a plank. We drank too much ale and tumbled out of the tavern. Our university is the most renowned in the land. Somebody suggested that we accomplish a feat never before attempted. We agreed with alacrity. We disagreed with Figgis, who wanted to go home. We knocked him down with stones. We had a tradition of appalling behaviour to live up to. It was our duty.

To be honest, I can't remember if we were students or professors. It hardly matters. I pointed at the famous tree in the main public square and cried: "Let's climb that!" The excited voices around me went quiet. But it was too late to back down. Slowly a chant filled those empty throats. "To the top!" We bolstered our courage with coordinated hubbub. I was happy and scared.

We decided to mount our assault in pairs. We reached the base of the trunk but did not bother to look up. It was pointless. The canopy was lost beyond the clouds. Fresh hearts and initials had been carved into the bark. I went first with Gruber. As we ascended, the style of these carvings became cruder and older. They had all been made at ground level and the growth of the tree was carrying them toward heaven.

Within an hour, we were confronted with the evidence of love affairs that had ended before the founding of our university. These hearts had been cut with stone tools, not steel blades. Later, when the ache in my arms was unbearable, there was nothing. The tree was older than the art of writing. Gruber and I decided to rest. Far below we watched our colleagues struggle to make equal sense of these ephemeral desires.

"Fossils of passion," said Gruber, as he sat on a branch and dangled his legs over the void. I guessed that he wanted to make a contribution of his own, but was frustrated in this design by the lack of a girl to love. Also he had no knife. We reclaimed our breath and resumed our climb. Roosting birds, chiefly owls, studied our progress with alarmed amusement. Then I recalled the subject I specialised in and blinked for all their eyes.

"Trees don't grow like this," I muttered.

"What do you mean by that?"

"They don't grow from the base but from the top. There's no way those carvings could be rising progressively higher."

It was a mystery. We sweated and gasped as we pushed ourselves to the limits of our endurance. The sun went down, but when I checked my pocket watch I saw it was nearly midnight. That demonstrates how high we already were. It had been night in the town below for many hours. I wondered if we would reach the top by morning. It seemed unlikely. For a start, mornings would arrive much earlier now.

Gruber and myself were the highest pair, as I've already mentioned. Immediately beneath us were Pluck and Becker. When we began this exploit, we frequently shouted at them, and they passed on our shout to the next pair, who I believe were Kane and Rowse, and so we kept in rudimentary touch right down to the final two climbers. But now our calls were not acknowledged. We were ascending too fast. Or they had fallen.

We passed the wreckage of a glider. Some trainee pilot had lodged it here long ago but his skeleton was not inside. Perhaps he had escaped with his life and picked his way back down.

The stars did not grow brighter in the celestial dome but the air remained breathable. This was a surprise. It should have thinned out gradually. Gruber leaned close and fixed his lips to my ear. He was trembling.

"The trunk is getting thicker," he whispered.

"Yes, it is very strange. And the branches are much wider. What can this mean?"

"That the tree is misshapen and ugly?"

There was no other explanation at that particular time. We climbed reluctantly now, and I distracted myself by attempting some difficult mental calculations. The distance between the most recent inscriptions and the earliest could be reckoned in two ways: miles or centuries. Thus the growth of one year could be reduced to a precise length of trunk. An estimate of the height of the tree might also provide its age.

I had a reasonable idea of our altitude, but there was no way of reckoning its percentage of the total. As we climbed, however, it quickly became apparent that the tree was more ancient than the world itself. This paradox was an extra worry. I did not trouble Gruber with it. But he was a geologist and had already arrived at the same conclusion.

"Wood can't be older than rocks," he sighed at last.

I nodded. We now regretted embarking on this adventure, which had promised so much when it began, though I can't specify what. We decided to make camp on one of the wider branches and wait for the others to catch up. I felt sleepy. My eyes closed as I listened to the soft rustling of the leaves. I must have fallen into a deep slumber. I dreamed that a man was screaming. He was above me and his voice receded upwards. He was being dragged into the sky, carried off by owls.

When I awoke, the sun was shining on my face. Gruber had gone. I lingered on my perch until noon. There was nothing to eat. I was completely sober now. I resumed climbing, surprised at how light I felt. I pulled myself up from branch to branch with remarkable ease. Indeed I found it difficult to stop. When I did, I became aware of an insistent tugging on my body, as if an invisible hand was reaching down and trying to pluck me up. With more height its grip became stronger.

Then I knew. Our assumptions about the tree had been all wrong. I now suspected that I was climbing down it rather than up. It had been planted upside down. At least that was true from the perspective of my world. In fact, the canopy of the tree was that world. As I left its gravitational pull behind, I realised it was I who was inverted. The tug of the real ground, somewhere far above, was taking over. If I let go, I would fall into the solid sky. It was a moment of terrible insight.

I resolved to reverse my progress and climb back down again. And that is what I am doing now. Gruber had no knife, but I always carry one. It is almost a sword. Unlike the others, I am a swashbuckler. I have no buckle, that is true, for I wear braces to hold up my trousers, but I am awash with swash. I started carving this tale on the trunk, one sentence every night while I rested. Tomorrow I shall write this one. Yesterday I wrote it. I waited to meet my companions but they did not appear. I am alone.

I began to suspect I had climbed down much further than I had ascended. This made no sense. Then I realised the tree was growing faster than I could climb it and growing the way it ought to: from the top. Thus the canopy was moving away from me and I would never reach it. Never. I had lost my world. There was no time for weeping. I saved my tears and doubled my efforts.

The carved initials at different elevations were now explained by natural growth. Or perhaps they had been an elaborate deception, a much earlier joke played by the students or professors of my university, to encourage those who came after to believe the climb was real and feasible. I laughed bitterly. I still laugh in that style. A cruel joke: one of the finest. That is our tradition. Every time I rest, I lose valuable miles. The world grows away from me far below, becomes an unreachable horizon, a distant planet. Now it is little more than a tiny disc flecked with threadlike clouds. Soon it will become a star, first bright then faint.

Time is running out. Next year, a new joke must be played. I think I know what it might be. Ale will be drunk, a tavern will be tumbled out of. A feat never before attempted will lose its virginity. I imagine a giant saw worked by many hands. To cut down the tallest tree in the world! Its collapse will be spectacular, or so they conclude. But in reality they will be severing the canopy from the trunk that supports it. The ground will wobble and slide off.

It must be next year already. I have just watched the whole world falling past into the sky.

*23.

Hywel was dubious about the accuracy of the tree's tale. He simply could not believe the world ever fell into the sky, at least he didn't notice anything of that kind happening. He suspected the tree that tapped him on the shoulder came not from a dark and winding forest path, but from Madeira, where trees openly tell tall tales to each other, as well as dance and sing. The trees of Madeira hold parties that last all night and the noise stops the sea from going to bed. But the trainee pilot who had crashed his glider into the tree confirmed that he'd once seen an object falling upwards while piloting a bigger aircraft and agreed to tell us the details.

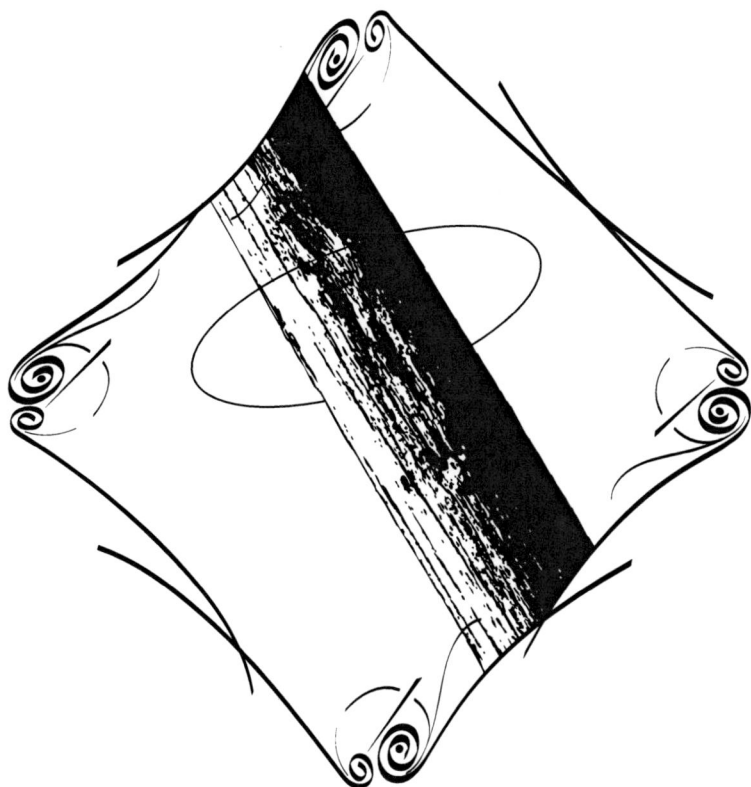

ANTON ARCTIC AND THE CONQUEST OF THE SCOTTISH POLE

Ordinary geographers believe that our planet has only two poles, the North and South, and they prefer to ignore the East, West, Front and Back poles. But Anton Arctic went to the other extreme and maintained the existence of a seventh pole, namely the Scottish.

This is Anton's story or should be, but in truth there isn't much to tell. He had wanted to be an explorer since he fell asleep in a laundry basket and awoke hanging from a washing line. The huge white sheets drying next to him looked like icebergs and after he detached himself from the pegs holding him up he wandered among them in wonder. He was only thirty-eight years old and was astonished to discover that icebergs are not cold. In fact he used them to wrap up warm when night fell.

The Scottish pole was located somewhere in Scotland. That is all he knew. His careful and prolonged researches into history, cartography, mythology and natural science led him to conclude that Scotland could be reached by boarding the 06:15 train from London.

Accordingly he bought a ticket at King's Cross station and waited patiently on the platform. When his train was ready he settled into his seat and opened his rucksack to check the condition of his survival equipment. Fortunately his sandwiches, flask of hot tea and good book were all in perfect working order.

The journey north was uneventful. After he crossed the border, he kept his face close to the window in case he spied the Scottish pole standing in a field. How would he recognise it? He imagined it was long and cylindrical with a tartan pattern. However, his estimates of its height remained vague.

When he arrived in Edinburgh he walked unknown streets with a measured step. Not even the greatest detective in Scotland Yard, an organisation that specialises in Scottish measurements, hence its name, has been able to determine where exactly his measured step took him.

His movements may be obscure but not his motives. Obviously he searched for the Scottish pole in Edinburgh without success. A few days later he appeared in a small town much further north called Invergarry. How he got there is open to conjecture. He might have fallen asleep in another laundry basket, or whatever passes for laundry baskets in Scotland, huge porridge pots stuffed with kilts perhaps, but why such an occurrence would take him to Invergarry is unclear. A witness who claims to have seen him riding north in a chariot pulled by a haggis has been dismissed as an unreliable character from a different story that has not even been written yet.

It was raining heavily when he arrived in Invergarry and in a muddy field near that town he exhibited rather odd behaviour. At least it was odd to outsiders. In Anton's opinion his actions were rational and even heroic. So let us recount what happened from his perspective.

Plodding along with a heavy sense of failure in his soul, he abruptly noticed something marvellous on the horizon. He ran forward and his joy increased to an almost unbearable intensity as he realised his quest was over. He had found the Scottish pole! Now all he had to do was conquer it to guarantee his future reputation as a noteworthy explorer.

He didn't know what 'conquering' a pole entailed, but he was aware that an army conquers a country by marching over it and so he concluded that it was probably a good idea if he positioned himself over the pole. This meant he had to climb it.

Haste was important for he saw that a rival explorer had already reached the base of the pole and was clutching it with both hands. Fortunately for Anton this other explorer did not have the physique of a climber. He was large and far too heavy to haul himself easily up any pole and he grunted and grimaced as if preparing for a great effort while people standing in the field urged him on. Anton wanted to shout at these people, to redirect their attention, but he decided to save his breath for running.

Splashing through puddles, he reached the pole and flung himself on it, climbing rapidly with his legs and arms wrapped around the rough wood. The pole was shorter than he had anticipated and he was overjoyed to have found such an unobtrusive landmark in so large an area as Scotland. At no point did he doubt this really was the Scottish pole. He was too busy trying to climb beyond the reach of his rival.

When he was halfway up he suddenly felt very dizzy and almost lost his grip. He paused for a few moments and then resumed his task. This rest must have been beneficial, for the second half of the climb was much easier, as if the top of the pole was pulling him by the force of magnetic attraction, an impossible explanation due to the fact he was not made of iron, but welcome all the same.

He arrived at the top and was astonished to strike his head on a ceiling! He had not noticed a ceiling above the pole at any stage during his climb or before. This was indeed a mystery. The top end of the pole was fixed firmly into this ceiling and there was no way of mounting it. How could he conquer the pole now? It was necessary to get above the ceiling and stand on the other side.

This problem was lessened by the fact that the ceiling was covered with tufts of fibre that hung down from its surface. He could cling to these and work his way along until he reached the edge. The barrier had to come to an end somewhere.

This was a hazardous operation but he found it unnaturally easy to disengage from the pole and attach himself to the ceiling. He clung to the slippery tufts with all his might and dug the toes of his shoes into the pliable surface and in this manner he crawled his way across. He had no particular direction in which to go but he kept crawling anyway.

The underside of the ceiling was very dirty. It had clearly not been cleaned for many years, if ever. Anton became dismayed with the filth that gathered on his clothes and he started to regret the entire adventure. Even more irritating was the fact that the ceiling seemed to have no edge after all. He paused for a much needed rest.

Then he made the mistake of turning his head to look down. The ceiling must have been designed as a slope for he was much higher now than the actual height of the pole. He had crawled his way to an immense altitude and the land beneath him was so distant it appeared a grey blur without any distinguishing features.

Anton was terrified. He no longer desired fame as an explorer but cared only for a return to solid ground. He looked around in vain for the Scottish pole. Having lost all sense of direction, he clung to the tufts more tightly as he fought the urge to scream. This was the worst moment of his life.

Then he controlled his fear and decided that before falling to his death he ought to make an effort to save himself. He closed his eyes and crawled off as fast as possible, his hands slipping on the damp tufts, his boots digging slimy footholds in the ceiling. He didn't expect to survive and yet he had the curious feeling that gravity was starting to lose interest in him.

A man filled with hydrogen or helium like an old fashioned airship might bounce along a ceiling with no greater ease than Anton now proceeded. And yet he knew this defiance of the laws of nature was an illusion, that soon he would lose his grip and plummet to the grey land below. Tiredness would overcome him or the tufts break off and his doom would rush at him impatiently.

While he was imagining this doom and feeling sorry for himself because he had so few friends to remember him, none in fact, which maybe isn't so bad if being remembered as unsuccessful is worse than never being noticed, he suddenly struck his head on an obstacle. He snapped open his eyes. He had crawled straight into a solid pole.

It wasn't the Scottish pole, for it was made of a substance harder than wood, possibly concrete, but he didn't care what name it had. It might be the French or Turkish pole, carried from its native land and planted here by invaders. What did it matter provided he could climb down it? That was the important point.

Not wanting to descend to the ground upside down, he turned in a careful circle and embraced the pole with his legs. Then he eased his body onto its length, but his hopes of sliding smoothly groundwards came to nothing. Either there was too much friction between the substance of the pole and his limbs or else he was still connected to the ceiling by a weird magnetism, for it took considerable effort for him to inch his way down.

After ten minutes or so of exhausting work he was mortified to discover that the pole came to an end. It was not connected to the ground but merely stuck into the ceiling like a fake stalactite. Worse than this, the end was glowing hot and shone brightly. It was the simplest kind of light fitting. Anton grumbled to himself. If he was going to be forced to dangle from ceiling illumination, the least his luck might do was to provide a chandelier.

A tide of resignation rose inside him, flooding the chambers of his heart and the spaces between his bones. He simply lacked the stamina to hold on. He was exhausted and the glowing tip of the pole was radiating an uncomfortable amount of heat. To avoid blisters he let go of the pole and embraced extinction instead. He allowed himself to plunge freely.

At this point it might be appropriate to describe Anton's activities from the viewpoint of the people standing in the field when he first arrived. Every year Invergarry has the honour of hosting the Highland Games. This traditional competition features only essentially Scottish feats of strength and endurance, the most famous of which is *Tossing the Caber*. The caber is a lopped tree trunk and it takes formidable muscle power to toss it.

The caber is not really tossed for distance but for style. The athlete holds the caber in his hands, keeping it balanced perfectly erect. He is required to imagine a clock face spread on the ground before him. He stands at the 6 o'clock position and tosses the caber so that it turns in the air and lands upside down in the middle of the clock. Then it is supposed to topple over and end up pointing exactly towards the 12 o'clock position.

The caber was in the very act of being tossed when Anton Arctic rushed across the field, jumped onto it and began climbing. By the time he was halfway up it had somersaulted in mid flight and thus he felt dizzy. Then it landed in the middle of the clock face, but because the torrential rain had softened the ground it stuck fast without toppling. Anton noticed none of this and kept climbing.

When he reached the end of the pole he assumed that the ground was a ceiling. He never suspected he was upside down. He let go of the pole and inched across the field, holding tightly to clumps of grass. Eventually he looked up at the cloudy sky and was overwhelmed with vertigo. He thought the sky was the land.

He resumed crawling and the pole he struck his head against was a lamppost at the edge of the field, an Ivergarry street light. The spectators watched in disbelief as he climbed feet first up this lamppost, did a handstand at the top and then let go with a peculiar sort of laugh.

What happened next has become a source of mild controversy. The spectators at the Highland Games swear that he plummeted head first into the mud of the field and was buried as far as his waist, so that only his feebly kicking legs were visible until he was hauled out with ropes by several of the strongest athletes and sent packing back to London, never to be heard of again. And there should be no reason to doubt them.

But the pilot of a passing airliner crossing Scotland at the time reported seeing a man rising into the sky and waving cheerfully as he went past, a man with bushy white eyebrows and whiskers as frosty and desolate as bedsheets on a washing line.

*24.

One of the passengers in the passing airliner said, "I saw that man too and I was going to write about him, because I'm a writer – the best in the world in fact – and also the real author of this book, the real Hughes, not the one who died in THE TALL STORY in that explosion all that time ago. I was on that aeroplane because I was travelling somewhere interesting, probably to a literary conference where I was the guest of honour. I often get invited to such events because I'm so good! Anyway, I'm probably the only writer skilled enough to write convincingly about Anton Arctic but I didn't because I was engaged on another project, a project that was an immense challenge for me. Let me tell you about it!"

THE MOST BORING STORY

I wanted to write a boring story, the most boring story in the world, but I feared the task was beyond me. My style is just too dazzling. I am one of the finest authors in the history of literature and I have never penned a dull line in my life. My critics are forced to compare me with myself because there is nobody else against whom I might be accurately judged. Indeed I am so good that I daily weep with the enormity of my responsibility to human culture. The task of writing something boring was a challenge too provocative to ignore and I felt I had no real choice other than to make the attempt, many attempts as it turned out, for my first efforts were profoundly engrossing and thus utter failures. It was clear I had to adopt a radical approach and change my working methods. My first act was to stop writing for ten years in the hope of rusting my talent. During this period

I refused to read serious literature and devoured only the cheapest pulp novels, immersing myself in swamps of awful prose and slowly drowning my naturally exquisite appreciation of language. These precautions were inadequate for my purposes, however. When I began writing after the allotted time I was still a genius. The problem is that although my style had suffered, my subject matter remained tremendous and it became imperative for me to find a terminally drab theme. At first I doubted such a theme existed, for I am able to invest even the least promising objects and situations with a fascinating beauty, but then it occurred to me that if I wrote about the ordinary life of the common man, I would soon be yawning and rubbing tired eyes, for the common man is everything I am not and never want to be. I imagined that if I was oppressively bored while writing, the resultant prose would communicate that boredom and so be boring in turn. How wrong I was! Thanks to my phenomenal abilities I still wrote truly excellent material, stuff far ahead of anything my contemporaries can produce, and I was obliged to destroy everything committed to paper. In desperation I disordered my senses and lowered my intelligence by repeatedly striking my head against the wall and imbibing vast quantities of rancid milk. These preparations were sufficiently thorough to renew my confidence and encourage me to start again. I described a new day in the life of a typical common man from the moment he awoke and vacated his bed, taking care to examine as turgidly as possible every tiny domestic detail. But my fundamental excellence had not been extinguished even at this point and my writing remained stubbornly superior to all other living authors. What could I do? Short of killing myself and being reincarnated among the lower classes, I saw no obvious way of turning myself and my work boring. There was no point making yet another fresh start. I was on the verge of abandoning the project as hopeless, for I had reached the lowest limit of my aptitude and I was still too good, but I gave myself one more hour before admitting defeat and so returned to the story in progress. With virtually no hope of achieving my aim, I described how my subject stumbled to the bathroom for a shower before eating his breakfast. Then I outlined the tedious intricacies of his search for clean clothing, the manner in which he buttoned his tasteless shirt and belted his worthless trousers. He was clearly getting ready for work, probably as a drudge in some soulless office on the outskirts of an ugly grey city, the sort of job most suited to an average member of the largely ignorant human race. I anticipated the exceptionally uneventful journey to his place of employment, stuck in traffic in a mediocre car, pressed on all sides by equally inferior commuters in their own unglamorous vehicles. And yet this prospect did not cheer me, for I guessed I would somehow make the event seem interesting when I came to write it, and I sighed as I moved from one spectacular sentence to the next, closer to the end of my time limit. Imagine my astonishment when the man made no effort to leave his house but boiled the kettle for more coffee! What was the fool playing at? Would he not be late for the start of his idiotic day? I continued to write in a more watchful mood, following his slow progress. He was a ditherer, a time waster, a procrastinating sort of urban peasant, but at last he made his way to a small room at the rear of the house. I noted a desk and a computer and many disordered papers. He sat in front of the screen and tapped on the keyboard. Suddenly there was a change in my writing. It became boring at long last! Almost at the final minute I had succeeded in my ambition, my sentences growing awkward, my observations uninspired. This was most curious! How had it happened? I moved closer to the man and peered over his shoulder. Then the mystery was solved and perspiration sprang out on my forehead. The man was a writer! He was just like me, not a real worker at all but a short story author! The implications of this were abominable, for it meant that writers are even more boring than common people, that the different level they claim to inhabit lies below rather than above ordinary humanity, that their monumental superiority to the masses is an illusion. I was aghast. I read what I had just written, a description of a writer at work writing his own descriptions, and my yawn was a gape of horror. It was almost fatally dull! I burned coldly to learn the content of my fictional writer's writing. What could his story be about? I instilled in him the desire to finish quickly and visit the bathroom to empty his body of the coffee he had drunk. While he was gone I moved closer and studied the screen properly. His entire story consisted of one long unbroken paragraph. It was this one.

Fin

Gawd BLimey!

If every tale told in a tavern is a tall story, then what happens when the entire universe becomes a tavern? It means that every story ever told is tall and therefore untrue, and this includes the true tales. They are all lies. But a lie is a concept only possible because it can be contrasted with truth: without its opposite concept it makes no sense at all. This implies one of two unlikely things, (a) the universe is not really a tavern, (b) there are other universes beyond this one where true stories exist. If you ever learn which is the correct answer to this riddle please let me know.

Afterword

It seems distasteful when an author insists that a particular book is his or her "best". I've been guilty of this misdemeanour myself, citing both *The Smell of Telescopes* and *The Percolated Stars* as my finest works. Strictly speaking, a writer is never in a position to make such a judgement. Only the reader can decide and award a worthwhile rating to any book. It's high time that I stopped voicing my opinion on this matter and allowed the due process of history to deliver its ultimate verdict when ready to do so, an approach that egocentrically assumes that history will have any interest in my work at all. Probably it won't; but nonetheless I'm still fully entitled to live and lurk in hope. We all are.

So I won't claim that the book you currently hold in your hands (if that indeed is where it is: perhaps it's resting on a table or an easel or you have strapped it to a big cat) is my best. No, I'll never say that. I will, however, announce that it's my *favourite*. The favourite of all my works. In essence it's a microcosm of my intended Grand Scheme of 1000 tales linked into a large, hopefully not wobbly, wheel. I doubt I'll ever produce another book that so obviously and (to me at least) satisfyingly mirrors the overarching ongoing structure of my intended life's literary work. Whether this makes the book more or less significant is another question entirely: one for you to answer, if you feel like doing so.

The point of my so-called Grand Scheme is to create a vast story cycle that is both tight and loose at the same time. So the individual tales might contain irrelevancies, digressions and non-sequiturs that ordinarily would be deleted by a conscientious editor; but on closer inspection such surplus elements prove to enrich *other* tales. If forced at wicked clubpoint to mix my metaphors, I would say there is a sideways flow through all the tales, with loose ends in one story being tied up, or frayed further, in others. My desire is to make these currents flow in circles at different rates and meet up back at the beginning. At any rate, that's the plan. Whether it works or not is (yet again) another question…

Which makes it sound as if I'm trying to convince you that I have been logically proceeding with immense care from the very beginning and that my oldest surviving tale was consciously written to be the first instalment in this grandiose project of mine. But you aren't fooled for an instant; and indeed, the process was always far more chaotic and imprecise than that. I had already written more than a hundred tales before I realised that all my fiction was going to be linked, so I had to requisition existing stories and find a way of fitting them into the twisting growth, retroactively imposing an extra function on them. Some had to be tweaked; others merely needed sequels to adjust their original purpose.

Naturally, this means the symmetry of the final result will be distorted and possibly unusable as a pattern capable of being visualised, a tangle of knots rather than a geometric shape, but I can pretend that's how I prefer it; and apart from *this* admission there's no evidence to prove otherwise, no reasonable grounds for any accusation of charlatanry. I suspect I lack the charm to be a charlatan anyway; I certainly lack the *charl*, whatever that means. Nor do I ever tell lies. I just sometimes refer to future events in the past tense. Try it sometime, if you aren't already an expert. By the way, I want every paragraph of this afterword to be the same length, and that explains this unnecessary sentence.

My Grand Scheme is therefore destined to be an organic phenomenon, a growth I like to compare to a fig tree but which critics might liken more to a tumour. Yes, I can do false modesty almost as well as fake arrogance. But now I have strayed off the point. The point was, I think, that of all my books, *Tallest Stories* most accurately mimics this bigger picture. It came together slowly, organically, almost by accident at first. I wanted to create a series of stories told in a pub, rather like Arthur C. Clarke's *Tales from the White Hart*, which I read at an impressionable age, but I didn't want a real world framing device: I wanted the setting, in other words the pub, to be at least as weird as the separate tales.

The tradition of the pub or club or barroom story cycle is a venerable one. I have cited Clarke's effort (one of his best books, in my view) but I should also mention Dunsany's superb Jorkens stories and John Buchan's *The Runagates Club*. Another classic example is *Tales from Gavagan's Bar*, a collaboration between L. Sprague de Camp and Fletcher Pratt. All those writers are worth trying to mimic. Flann O'Brien was another major influence on my stories, as were Calvino, Barthelme and even myself; I'm often a self-influence. Various non-existent authors also played a part, for instance Pigwinder Bratbat, Dinkybreath Naggynag, Honklog Zigflap and Rustgoomar Yiponhhhe. And why not?

But to return to what I was saying (or to what you were reading (is that the same? (oh look, brackets within brackets!))) this collection developed so slowly that my motivations, aspirations and even speculations couldn't be expected to remain static during its long congealment (I hesitate to say 'construction'). I changed and they changed. Sixteen years this book took from start to finish; but some basic factors *did* remain constant. I wanted an intricate framing device, one that framed other framing devices in such a flexible way that the tales inside the framing devices could frame other tales or even other framing devices, while also belonging to all my other finished or partly completed story cycles.

The conceit of an expanding pub permitted all that to happen. I hope it did, anyhow. I also wanted to keep the book light in tone and substance, to make my wordplay less arcane than usual, my plots less polyrhythmic, my concepts slightly less cummerbund (an impulsively non-lexical use of that word). I have clearly now tried to sabotage those aspirations with this turgid and pompous afterword. But we have the right to sabotage our own things, don't we? Surely! And in fact, this book sabotages an earlier book of mine, *Nowhere Near Milk Wood*, by showing that what was right then (and there) is in fact wrong now (and here). Nine paragraphs is a pleasant number for an afterword, don't you agree?

Rhys Hughes was born in 1966 and began writing fiction from a young age. None of his early efforts saw print, mainly because he never submitted them anywhere or even showed them to anyone else. Those stories have all been lost.

Eventually he began sending his work to editors. His first published story was called 'An Ideal Vocation' and it appeared in an obscure anthology in 1992. Encouraged by this "success", he then proceeded to bombard the British small-press with hundreds of eccentric tales for almost two decades. His first book, the now almost legendary *Worming the Harpy*, was published by Tartarus Press in 1995. He has published many volumes since then, chiefly collections of short-stories but also a few novels, in several languages.

He considers his three best and most "Hughesian" books to be *The Smell of Telescopes*, *The Truth Spinner* and (of course) *Tallest Stories*. The latter took 15 years to put together and is a self-contained story-cycle that is also a microcosmic version of the grand story-cycle that will eventually feature all his lifetime's fiction, each story linked forwards, backwards and sideways to other stories in the cycle.

When not writing or reading, he indulges his passions for mountaineering, music, philosophy and making things that only sometimes work.

Lightning Source UK Ltd.
Milton Keynes UK
UKOW01f0017090217
293945UK00004B/239/P